PATRIOT FUTU

PATRIOT FUTURE

A Novel by

Milton Johns

LYFORD
Books

This book is dedicated to my parents, Milton E. and Ann L. Johns, who have always believed in me.

• • •

I want to thank all my friends and family, who read draft after draft of this book, and everyone at Presidio Press who helped make my first novel a reality.

I also want to thank Mark Boll, Quino Diaz, and Peter Hammond, who, respectively, took me through Ranger school, put me in the cockpit of a jet during a modern-day dogfight, and gave me some well-needed grammar lessons.

Finally, special thanks go out to Jim Kerr, who has been my biggest fan and harshest critic from day one.

Copyright © 1997 by Milton C. Johns

LYFORD Books
Published by Presidio Press
505 B San Marin Drive, Suite 300
Novato, CA 94945-1340

Library of Congress Cataloging-in-Publication Data

Johns, Milton.
    Patriot future : a novel / by Milton Johns.
        p. cm.
    ISBN 0-89141-581-5 (hardcover)
    I. Title
PS3560.036P38   1997
813'.54—dc21   97-7054
                                                    CIP

Printed in the United States of America

Introduction

November 19, 2004, Stanford, California

Jesse Davies cursed again, slamming his hand onto the desktop. "Damn. I cannot believe it!" he shouted.

He looked over his shoulder at his roommate. The other Stanford University freshman lay on his bed, writhing and sighing. His face was partially covered by a wraparound visor, from which wires ran to a pair of gloves and a torso harness, which he also wore.

"Arthur, you wanna keep it down, please?" Jesse implored.

The tall, spindly, fair-haired Arthur James turned his head toward Jesse.

"Sorry, man. I'm working on Ms. Virtual November. I love redheads."

Jesse frowned. "That's sick. With all the problems in this world, we've used the microchip to perfect computer porn."

Arthur shrugged. "Different strokes . . ."

After a momentary silence, Arthur sat up and removed the visor. He stared across the room at Jesse, his face reflected in the soft blue glow of his CRT. Arthur glanced at his watch.

"Well, you've been in there six hours. Find anything?"

Jesse pushed his chair back from the desk and rubbed his eyes. "Nothing. Nothing. I still just can't believe it."

Arthur rolled his eyes. "How much more time are you gonna waste anyway? Give it up. It's over. Accept it. Life goes on."

Jesse shook his head. "No, man. It's bad enough we lost the election, but I promised we'd carry this district."

"Bad luck," said Arthur.

"Bad luck? We've voted Democrats into virtually every elected office in this district, including the presidency, for, like, thirty years!" exclaimed Jesse.

"At least it wasn't the Republicans," Arthur offered.

Jesse sagged in his chair, leaning his elbows on his knees. "I can't tell which is worse. I mean, Karl Jensen is a mean-spirited son of a bitch, that's for sure. . . ."

"Republican tradition," said Arthur, unfastening the torso harness.

"Yeah, but, come on. New Liberty party? These guys just came out of the woodwork. Bart Benet decides the only thing he hasn't bought yet is the presidency, and then this New Liberty bunch just . . . appears. Old Bart Benet may be rich, and they're probably the best-organized political machine I've ever seen, but . . ."

"But Benet is as crazy as a shithouse rat," said Arthur.

"Exactly. I just don't see how people bought all that 'social justice through industry' bullshit," said Jesse.

"Well, if you think about it, he took the far left away from the Democrats, with all his 'universal guarantees,' and he split a lot of big business money away from the Republicans," said Arthur.

Jesse shook his head. "Yeah, I know. But I just . . . there's something bugging me. I can't put my finger on it."

"What?" asked Arthur. He rose from his bed and stowed his equipment in a desk directly across the cramped dorm room from Jesse.

"I've been going through these returns. I'm trying to work my way east from here. In some districts, New Liberty got ten percent of the vote or less. In the districts they carried, they had, like, thirty-five percent or so. But the districts aren't . . . contiguous. The districts seem isolated from one another."

"Look," said Arthur, slipping into a pair of sweat pants and a T-shirt. "Four years from now, everyone will have wised up, and we'll boot 'em out. People were just looking for a change. Mix things up. Besides, how much damage could they really do in four years anyway?"

Jesse's eyes widened. "Plenty. First of all, Henry Kersey as vice president? Gimme a break. And their programs . . . if they ever pull any of them off, they could ruin the country."

Arthur climbed under the covers of his bed. "You're overreacting. I bet not even half that crap will get through Congress. And if it does, it sounds unconstitutional anyway. You know the gun nuts won't have any part of it."

"Yeah, but there's a possibility . . . a slim possibility. . . . You know four of the Supreme Court justices are in their late seventies and early eighties?" said Jesse.

"I still say you're overreacting. Besides, you should have realized no one would vote for a Democrat named Wally," said Arthur, rolling over onto his side.

"Walter. Walter Purvis. First African American presidential candidate," said Jesse.

"First *Democrat* African American presidential nominee," corrected Arthur.

"Whatever," said Jesse. He turned back to his CRT and tapped the screen to review a new data set. "I just got a bad feeling about this New Liberty. Henry Kersey may be only their vice president, but I think he's a dangerous man. He is a dangerous man."

1

June 20, 2021, San Diego, California

The San Diego Emergency Zone, or E.Z., was relatively small, and the decrepit, two-bedroom Cape Cod was at dead center of the Red Sector, on Fifth between F and G streets. Red Sectors were generally considered unsafe even for police. Three blocks away, in the parking lot of an abandoned convenience store, members of the Federal Police Force, West Region, Southwest Division, 20th Branch Narcotics Detectives, operating out of Charlie Substation headquarters, were gathering. They were about to exercise their automatic "probable cause" search, as allowed in an E.Z.

The emergency zones were exempt from the requirements of the Social Sufficiency Amendment (SSA). Therefore, law enforcement in the emergency zones was similarly exempt from the requirements. Created by the National Urban Emergency Act of 2007, emergency zones were the legacy of the failed economic and social programs prior to the New Liberty administration. Crime, violence, drug addiction, and poverty had taken complete hold of American inner cities. And the prison system could not physically accommodate the crush of prisoners. More and more convicts were released from prison to the "regional arrest" program, being confined to designated areas of inner cities. The programs mandated by the SSA had shown positive results in the beginning. With the legalization of all narcotics in 2005, drug-related crimes decreased by over fifty percent. The Universal Employment Act, also enacted in 2007, guaranteed jobs for all American citizens. American inner cities be-

4

gan to experience a renaissance at the end of the first decade of the twenty-first century.

But the drug jazz brought an end to the rebirth and rekindled, even more dramatically, the drug problems of the late 1990s. Jazz was created in China, where the Communist government succeeded in developing a dramatically powerful mind-control drug. While the goal of the original program, started in 2002, was to control the actions of persons injected with the drug, now called *xin ji* (pronounced "seen-jee"), the scientists found that the drug allowed some individuals to manipulate objects by thought, thereby creating a telekinetic enabling effect. *Xin ji* superstimulated the brain's signal-sending capability, actually allowing the electrical impulses to leave a subject's body. Most subjects in the early days of the drug's development were killed instantly, their brains literally fried by the overpowering electrical impulses created. The researchers learned more with every experiment and became more sophisticated in the design of the drug's chemical architecture and the dosages meted out. They shortly discovered that some subjects responded differently than others, and that only one subject out of the first five hundred showed any manipulative ability. Over the course of several years, *xin ji* was honed until finally, the researchers had developed a drug that would not kill its users, but also that would allow, in varying degrees, the manipulation of objects by thought.

These breakthroughs allowed profiles to be drawn of individuals who could exploit the drug, and testing developed to confirm telekinetic abilities. The drug itself was further refined so that any person could receive doses of the drug and not expire. Those persons who were not telekinetically enabled (called "tekes" by popular parlance) would experience wild hallucinations, intense euphoria, and heightened adrenal stimulation. Those who were telekinetically enabled did not suffer the hallucinations or addiction problems, but, rather, through controlled doses could use their abilities on a day-to-day basis. Once the prototypes were stabilized, experimentation for military purposes began. By the year 2011, the Chinese had developed numerous military uses for telekinetically enabled personnel. The drug was first introduced to the battlefield at Karachi in April 2011, when telekinetically enabled troops were able to shroud Chinese positions by manipulating the appearance of a smoke screen. This tactic delayed the enemy identification of their positions and, counterattacking, Chinese troops were able temporarily to throw back the invaders.

The Battle of Karachi also served as the introduction of the drug to the United States. Interrogation of Chinese prisoners after the battle, and of those Chinese prisoners of war who sought asylum in the U.S. at the conclusion of the war, revealed the existence and nature of the drug. It was reproduced in experimental form at the United States Army Nuclear and Biochemical Research Labs in Aberdeen, Maryland. Shortly thereafter, the formula, along with sample batches, was stolen from the lab. Word on the street traveled quickly, and the drug, nicknamed jazz by its earliest abusers, began its scourge of the country.

With less than one-tenth of one percent of the world's population able to exploit fully the telekinetic enabling effects of the drug known on the streets as jazz, most junkies were weak or harmless. While the highs of jazz for any user were higher than any previous narcotic to hit the streets of America, the lows were correspondingly low. A user could expect hours of nausea, migraines, tremors, and muscle spasms once the drug's incredible sense of well-being had passed. With the only remedy for the "hangover" being another jazz hit, the drug was, in most cases, instantly addictive. Most jazzers had suicide, insanity, or murder to look forward to in the short run. But the addiction was so strong, this need for the next fix so consuming, jazz was the most dangerous drug ever to hit the streets of America. Not to mention the danger posed by the one in a thousand individuals who could exploit the drug. Any person who was telekinetically enabled was required by law to register with the federal government. Unregistered telekinesis was a federal felony. While legalizing narcotics had removed most of the street trade a few years back, jazz was a drug, due to these secondary effects, that would never be legalized.

Detective Sergeant Carl Grafton stood in the side doorway of the unmarked police van, preparing the final orders for the search. Grafton was a twenty-year veteran of the force. He was of average height, with graying brown hair. He wore a drooping brown mustache and had sleepy brown eyes. But behind the eyes there would sometimes be a spark, like the one that was glimmering now. Though his overweight, middle-fifties body would not betray it, as a young man Carl Grafton fought one hundred miles behind Iraqi lines with the 101st Airborne during the land offensive of the First Gulf War. Carl Grafton had seen his share.

He spoke to the four black-clad and helmeted detectives inside the van. "All right, we're about ready to go. Remember, we're expecting two European males on the premises, certainly armed and dangerous. These two have been effectively doubling their distribution operations by cutting pure liquid jazz into roughly one-fifth portions with window cleaner. We're gonna take 'em out of circulation for a few days, destroy whatever supply and apparatus they have, then hope not to see them again."

"We've got a marked cruiser for backup in the rear alley, an' we've also got cruisers closing off either end of the street. Okay, Bentley, you're trained up on the hydraulic ram?"

Thirty-year-old Detective James Bentley, his brown hair and black eyes hidden behind a black balaclava, lifted the door-breaking device from the van floor between his feet to show his affirmation.

"Well then," said Grafton. "I need a volunteer for . . ."

"I'll take the door," said the detective in the rear seat.

Grafton shook his head. "I figured as much, since you always volunteer for the door."

The detective shrugged.

"You know when you take a door, you get first pick of assignment on the next operation," Grafton reminded the detective.

"Then I pick the door," said the detective. He reached under his left arm and withdrew an old Colt .45 from its holster. For emphasis, he worked the slide back, then let it slam home.

Grafton pointed at the man. "Suit yourself, Sheridan, but keep it up and you ain't gonna make retirement."

Federal Police Detective Matthew X. Sheridan shrugged again. "I'll take my chances."

Rookie Federal Police Officer Mark Johnson sat in the patrol car at the east end of Fifth at G Street. His partner, Officer Joey Gast, had been rambling on for ten minutes about the narcotics detectives. Whenever Gast spoke about Carl Grafton, Johnson listened. Otherwise, Johnson tuned out the veteran cop.

The whole Grafton investigation was a bust, Johnson thought. Three months of work not worth a pile of shit. But there was one beneficial outcome; he had gained a passing interest in one of Grafton's detectives, a loner named Sheridan.

The van screeched to a halt in front of the Cape Cod, and the detectives sprang from the sliding door. Sheridan ran side by side with Detective Bentley. The other two detectives trailed them by five yards, and Grafton, puffing after four hard paces, brought up the rear.

As they neared the porch, all four men began screaming. "Federal Police! Open up!"

They barely broke stride ascending the three creaking porch steps. Sheridan stood to Bentley's left, holding his Colt in a two-handed grip. The two men nodded simultaneously. Bentley held the hydraulic ram in both hands. He swung the device backward, then leaned into the door as he slammed the ram forward. As the ram made initial contact with the door, just above the dead bolt, two opposing servocylinders sprung forward, driving the internal cylinder into the door with an extra five hundred pounds of force per square inch. The door and door frame were shattered into splinters.

A split second after that, Sheridan was through the door. Standing in a short hallway that ran north to a filthy kitchen, Matt swept his pistol left and right to cover the two other doorways in the hall. Out of the doorway to the left, a huge, hairy bear of a man leapt into the hall, leveling a twelve-gauge pump shotgun at Matt. He screamed an unintelligible oath and fired.

As he pulled the trigger, Matt slammed himself flat against the wall opposite the direction of the shotgun muzzle. A dozen buckshot pellets ripped through the drywall where Matt had stood an instant before. Matt now squeezed the trigger of the Colt twice as he tracked the barrel on a diagonal across the man's body. The first slug slammed into the man's right elbow, shattering bone and shotgun stock alike. An instant later, the second shot drilled into the shaggy man's left knee. The shotgun slipped out of his useless right arm, and the man followed it to the dirty carpet.

Matt moved quickly now in the direction from which the man came, Bentley close behind. The hairy man, clad only in a greasy pair of cut-off jeans, was wailing like a baby. Bentley dropped the ram in the hall and produced a pair of handcuffs to secure the hairy man.

Matt stopped at the left doorway, then spun into it, dropping to his right knee. A Fuego machine pistol chattered from within, and a half dozen 9mm slugs ripped into the door frame where Matt's head might have been had he not ducked.

Matt found his target instantly, a tall, stringy young man with a sharp goatee and a dozen tattoos on his bare chest and arms. Before the tattooed man could change targets on the auto weapon, Matt tracked a diagonal again, firing twice, once at the right elbow and once at the left kneecap. The big .45 roared and the tattooed man went down in a heap, the Fuego dangling from his index finger.

The rest of the team was in the house now, racing down the main hallway. Matt sprang to his feet and crossed the room in two steps. The tattooed man still had the machine pistol dangling from his fingers. He screamed and clasped his knee with his left hand.

Pistol pointed downward, Matt commanded, "Drop the weapon."

The skinny man did not immediately respond. Matt stomped his wounded right arm to the floor with his booted left foot and kicked away the gun with his right. The man screamed.

"You're under arrest," said Matt in a perturbed voice. He bent over and picked up the Fuego.

Shortly, he heard the other three detectives yelling out, "Clear," from the rest of the house. Grafton peered around the doorjamb.

"Detective, the orthopedic surgeons downtown are gonna pass a petition around to make you start killing some of these sons of bitches. Your little right-and-left maneuver is keeping them awful busy."

Sheridan dropped the clip out of the machine pistol and cleared the unfired round in the chamber. Then he holstered his own weapon.

"Two more pukes that won't shoot back or run away from me," growled Sheridan.

Sheridan turned and walked down the hallway and out of the house. He turned sideways to accommodate the second wave of people into the house: medics. Outside, Matt walked to the sparse lawn and dropped to one knee, his back to the house. He removed his helmet and rolled up his balaclava, a late spring breeze refreshing him. He rubbed his eyes, his gloved right hand brushing back a few stray strands of his short blond hair peeking out from the head covering.

Another one down, he thought. *How many more to go?* Every time he went into a jazz house or broke up a street buy, he saw his brother Tommy. *The kid had potential until he got mixed up in this shit. Lots of potential. Gonna be a lawyer, he always said. Well, can't hold that against him. Bright kid. Bright enough not to follow me into the Marines,* Matt thought. Matt had been out of the service for only a few months, after his shoulder rehabilitation, when Tommy turned up missing from classes at Pepperdine. Matt had tracked him down to a cardboard box in an alley in San Francisco's Chinatown. Jazz had torn up his brother's body. His brother's mind was yet to be seen. Matt got him into a program associated with the V.A., and in a month was in good enough condition to be sent home to his parents in Pennsylvania. But the look in his eyes when Matt found him, the vacant, soulless stare that greeted Matt, was burned into his memory. The look haunted Matt, a look Matt saw hundreds of times a day. Each time he saw it, it burned a little hotter in his stomach.

Matt stood, stretched, and rolled his shoulders. He headed back to the police van. *How many more to go?*

Two hours later, Matt Sheridan walked to his car in the substation parking lot. The late afternoon was quite warm and humid, and he felt his short-sleeved tunic beginning to stick to him. He thrust his hands deep into the pockets of his jeans.

Twenty yards behind Matt, the door to the substation swung open and Carl Grafton emerged.

"Hey, Matt, wait up a second," Grafton called out. Matt turned toward him slowly, taking advantage of the pause to retrieve his sunglasses from his front pocket and put them on.

"What's up, Carl?" Matt asked. Matt would call him by his first name only out of uniform. *Protocol,* he thought.

Grafton puffed as he approached Sheridan. "Hey, Matt, you got something going on tonight?"

Matt shook his head and dragged the toe of his boot across the parking lot. "Uh, Carl, I don't know if . . ."

"Just, you know, Diane and I would love to have you come over, spend some time with us if you want. We can put some steaks on the grill . . ."

Matt looked at the older man. "I appreciate it, Carl, but . . . maybe tonight's not good."

"Hey, Matt, come on, we'd really like to have you come by tonight. I'll break out my good Scotch, watch some of those old Rambo movies. Spend the night if you get too boozed up . . ."

Matt grinned. "I really appreciate the offer, Carl, but . . ."

Grafton grabbed Matt's thick upper arm in a meaty hand. "Come on, Sheridan. I know what today is. You shouldn't oughta spend it alone. . . ."

Matt removed Grafton's hand firmly but gently. "Carl, really, I appreciate the offer. But I'm not great company on a good day, let alone today. Another night, I promise. Tell Diane I was asking for her."

Grafton nodded and sighed. "Your call, Matt. If you change your mind, just come on by the house."

Matt backed away toward his car. He made a gun out of his index finger, then dropped his thumb trigger. "I appreciate it, Carl. Next time, I promise."

Matt had taken only a few steps, when he saw a prisoner transport wagon pull into the station lot. It coasted to the secure door on the side of the building, where prisoners were received and processed. Matt waited to see who was bringing people in. A uniformed officer, who Matt recognized by face but not name, hopped out from the driver's side. From the passenger side, Deke Scully emerged. He saw Sheridan instantly, and raised a hand in greeting.

Everyone's friend, Deke Scully, Matt thought. *I wonder how many scouts he busted today.* Sheridan gave a brief wave in return.

Scully turned quickly to the wagon, headed for the rear compartment. Matt put one leg into his car, then decided to see who Scully was bringing in. In a moment, Scully led six handcuffed prisoners from the van. Five of the six looked like average John Q. Publics to Matt, but, curiously, one wore what Matt remembered to be the garb of a Catholic priest. As Scully led the prisoners to the station, he turned toward Sheridan, his back to the people. He smiled and jerked his thumb over his shoulder toward the prisoners. He pressed his hands together, fingers skyward, then rolled his eyes and silently mouthed some words in a mocking fashion.

Matt sighed as he sank into the car. Prayer in a public place was Scully's favorite bust. *Fortunately, Social Sufficiency enforcement is not in my job description*, Matt thought.

Matt Sheridan stared vacantly at his drink. Water from the melting ice swirled into the bourbon, seeming to leave a film. He poked at the remains of his ice cube, then dragged his wet index finger across his drink napkin. *Damn National Beverage Bourbon always looks funny*, he thought. He could still remember, and not that long ago, swilling Old Grand-Dad at the O Club in Iran. *Not that long ago.*

The bar roared tonight, rock and roll and strained voices competing with each other for dominance. Matt raised the glass to his lips and emptied it. He pressed his lips together tightly as the harsh liquor scorched his throat. He swallowed hard and exhaled. He pushed the glass away from him, toward the waitress who had reappeared almost on cue.

"Hurt me again, please," he said, almost whispering.

As his glass disappeared, he placed his palms over his eyes, rubbing. He could still see Jenny's face. Davey's face. Five years. Tonight.

"Shit," he mumbled. He felt the tears well up inside, but he knew they could never fall. His throat tightened. Palms still over his eyes, he placed his elbows on the table and held his head. Every year for the past five years this night had been the same. *It wasn't much different from most nights*, he thought. Sitting by himself, drinking, blaming himself for events without blame, feeling guilty for actions without culpability. Mostly feeling sorry for himself. That was a particular despair that felt even better when one massaged it.

Matt was oblivious to the music and activity in the bar tonight. Credo's, in the fashionable but aging Seaport Village area, was popular with San Diego's young adult crowd. Matt didn't really like the place, but he could see the lights from the naval air station out of the bar's picture window (he'd arrived early and managed to snag a booth next to it). The dance floor was already packed.

The waitress soon returned with Matt's drink, and he stared into it, poking again at the ice.

"Hi!" said a nearby female voice.

Matt looked up from his drink, interrupted, but still not completely attentive to the situation.

"Up here. Hi!" a woman in her early twenties waved her hand to draw Matt's attention.

Matt half shook his head, then looked up. The tall blonde flashed him a video-star smile. He afforded himself a quick glance up and down. The young woman was poured into a pair of old nineties-style jeans. They complimented her figure well. "I'm sorry?" he said, looking into her deep blue eyes.

"Wanna dance?" she asked.

Matt could feel his face begin to flush. He was thankful that the lights from the harbor spilling through the picture window were not bright enough to permeate the darkness and betray him.

He smiled at her sadly, and shook his head ever so slightly. "No, no thanks."

Unused to rejection, the woman's smile fell. She shrugged her shoulders and returned to the dance floor. As she walked away, the tight jeans confirmed Matt's assessment that she was in excellent physical condition. Matt sighed again as she left.

As he watched her leave, movement two tables away caught his eye. Examining the occupants of the table, Matt felt a tingling run up his spine. Four young men sat at the table, two with distinctive J-shaped scars on their foreheads. Jazzers. Among the various street gangs that peddled the drug, this self-mutilation was a defiant symbol of jazz use and unregistered telekinesis. Matt's heart skipped a beat, then began to pound.

While three of the young men were shabbily dressed, the fourth was fairly well appointed. *Classic setup for a narcotics buy,* Matt thought. He watched as the tallest man, with a J-shaped scar, furrowed his brow. A drink on the table hopped once, then toppled over. *Untrained, very weak,* Matt thought. *Decision time coming. I don't need to get involved here. Besides, nothing has happened. We're outside the E.Z. If I do anything, the place will be swarming with lawyers and cops. They haven't done anything anyway; nothing has changed hands. Maybe . . .*

Matt's mind was made up for him as one of the shabbily dressed men, the smallest one, shifted in his seat during the animated conversation. His trench coat fell open—he was wearing one despite the fact it was late June—and even in the darkness of the bar clearly revealed the stainless steel finish of a Fuego machine pistol holstered under his left arm was visible.

Matt stood slowly with a quick, reassuring pat to the small of his back. He moved toward the other table cautiously and realized that despite the fact that his heart was racing, he had stopped breathing. *Easy now, easy.*

"Can I speak to you guys outside, please?" Matt asked in a firm but quiet voice, just loud enough to be heard.

All four men looked at him incredulously. The well-dressed man looked confused and frightened. *Looks like he wants to get out of here anyway,* Matt thought.

The taller man, who was no doubt in charge of the group, spoke. "Who the fuck do you think you are?"

"Concerned citizen," Matt said, adding a half beat later, "asshole."

The small man, seated closest to where Matt stood, rose from his seat, putting his hand inside his coat. The "leader" stood along with the third of their party. The third man walked around the table. He stood to Matt's right, and the small man with the Fuego stood to Matt's left. The terrified fourth man sat absolutely still. An oldie, "Don't Cry," began to pour from the bar's audio system speakers. Matt reached carefully into his tunic and withdrew a metallic oval object that hung from a nylon cord around his neck.

The leader turned to the small man, who was not decorated with a scar, and gave him an almost imperceptible nod. "Roach," he said.

Bar patrons began to scramble for safety. Conversation stopped, but the music blared on. The proprietor appeared behind Matt with a baseball bat in his hands.

"I'm callin' the cops," the bartender warned.

"Stand back, sir," said Matt. His right arm shot out, pinning Roach's hand, which gripped the Fuego, to his side. With his left hand Matt caught the collar of Roach's haggard fatigue jacket. As he pulled Roach toward him, Matt drove his forehead into the man's face. The head butt smashed the cartilage of Roach's nose. With the help of his heavy boot, Matt drove his heel into Roach's right instep, breaking the bone. Roach's hands flew to his face, then he doubled over as his right leg gave out. As he fell to one knee, Matt drove a cocked elbow into Roach's spine between his shoulder blades. Roach dropped to the floor, unconscious. The Fuego clattered to the floor as well, and Matt used half a second to kick the gun away from him.

The third man leapt forward, his hands around Matt's throat. Matt dropped his arms to his sides, then jerked them violently upward. He pressed his hands together, forming a wedge. Matt drove the wedge between the man's forearms and knocked them apart, breaking the hold on his throat. Matt hopped slightly on his right leg, raising his left foot. He then stomped down on the floor with his left foot and, kicking, drove his right foot upward between the man's legs. Matt's boot impacted on his groin, crushing his testicles. The third man dropped to the floor, retching.

Matt turned his attention to the leader.

"Turner, what's goin' on here?" shouted the frightened "client," who remained seated.

Turner glared at his erstwhile patron, then eyed the door nervously. He drew a switchblade. Matt walked toward him.

"I'll kill you, asshole!" Turner screamed.

"Put it down. Let's not get anyone else hurt here," Sheridan said evenly.

Turner rushed Matt and slashed at him with the switchblade. While Matt was able to dodge the brunt of the blow, the knife tore through the short left sleeve of his tunic, opening a four-inch gouge in Matt's exposed biceps. The young client looked at the cut on Matt's arm and saw that the blood from the wound was flowing freely onto a laser tattoo just beneath it.

"Shock Marines," said the young man, recognizing the tattoo, loud enough for Turner to hear. Turner looked at Matt again, wavered for a moment, then lunged forward with the switchblade. Matt sidestepped the knife and caught Turner's right wrist with his right hand. With Turner's right arm extended, Matt slammed the palm of his left hand into Turner's elbow. Turner's arm bent backward at the joint, his radius and ulna snapping like twigs. He screamed and dropped to his knees, clutching his shattered arm. Matt drove his right fist into Turner's temple, sending him to the floor.

Matt stepped back and surveyed the situation. He turned to the proprietor and showed him the metallic oval object he wore around his neck. The Federal Police detective's badge flashed in the man's eyes. Matt turned in a full circle, displaying it to the anxious crowd of people who were now coming out from under tables and behind the bar.

"I'm with the government. I'm here to help," muttered Sheridan.

2

August 28, 2021, San Diego, California

Federal Police Detective Matt Sheridan turned the patrol cruiser onto the ramp for G Street off Interstate 94. The cruiser's big internal combustion engine—or intercom, as they were affectionately known—growled incongruously among the humming civilian traffic. He was stuck in the big bomb for at least three more weeks; the off-duty altercation with the jazzers had blown his cover. The Fed-standard minimum for uniform duty assignment length following compromise of cover was ninety days. He had twenty-one more days until he could request a new undercover assignment.

Not that he minded driving the National Motors '20 Defender Intercom all that much. This beast could cruise at 120 miles per hour, and generated over 300 horsepower. No apologetic electric car could touch it for acceleration. But it gobbled up fossil fuel and belched out deadly carbon monoxide like the dinosaurs of the eighties and nineties. *With the damage internal combustion engines did to the environment, as well as to the human beings who happened to be living in that environment, it made sense,* Matt thought, *that the government controlled them. Well, controlled all fossil-fuel-burning vehicles and propulsion systems, but especially cars.* With the unlimited cheap electricity provided by the national network of nuclear reactors, intercoms were unnecessary for the general public.

Detective Sheridan was eager to return to the streets of the emergency zone undercover. The nine-to-five routine was fine for some, but it bored him. Nine to five meant patrolling a beat outside the emergency zones, investigating stolen bicycles, social infractions, plastic fraud, and the like. And having to deal with the lawyers:

federal lawyers, police department lawyers, civil rights lawyers, corporate lawyers, and on and on. He hated all the lawyers, with their smug self-satisfaction at mediocre jobs well done, but Matt realized that they were necessary, crucial, for the federal legal system to meet its Social Sufficiency requirements. There were no lawyers in the emergency zones.

The Defender rocked as it crossed the speed bump blocking the entrance to the West Region, Southwest Division, 20th Branch, Charlie Substation headquarters of the Federal Police Force. Matt snaked the intercom among the marked patrol cars, the unmarked "hummers," as the detectives called their electric cars, and patrol vans until he found a spot near the entrance.

Leaving the car, he bounded up the front steps of the building, entering through the plate glass front doors. He walked past the receptionist at the information desk, giving her a polite smile, and went to the door marked POLICE PERSONNEL ONLY. He placed his right hand on the Optics 200 laser ID plate, and spoke his full name into a small microphone projecting from the doorjamb. The doorknob clicked twice; he turned it and entered.

He walked down the long, narrow corridor that was behind the door, past his own small office cubicle, and went directly to the office of Captain Luke Frazier. Frazier had been a cop for over twenty years, starting out as a uniform in Los Angeles and moving down to San Diego after the consolidation of local, state, and federal law enforcement organizations with the National Security Act of '05. The transition was quite disruptive in most parts of the law enforcement community, and still was not complete in some areas of the country. But the multiple layers of law enforcement in the country were ripe targets for the New Liberty budget cutters and social engineers. A unified law enforcement structure saved billions of dollars each year. Luke Frazier never liked the idea of the consolidation, but he was a cop's cop, and he followed the orders of his superiors.

Matt walked into Frazier's small office, rapping on the door frame as he entered. Captain Frazier looked up from his keyboard, where he was hunt-and-peck typing a weekly report to the 20th Branch commander, Chief Marvin Donnellson. Frazier was a large, burly, gray-haired man with large, sunken brown eyes.

"Sheridan, come in, grab a chair," Frazier said almost cheerfully. "Be with you in just a sec."

Frazier looked back at the keyboard, then up at the screen of the computer on his desk. "These damn 986s are slow as shit." The 986 was the first model introduced after passage of the Information Sufficiency Act. Prior to that act, criminals, terrorists, and purveyors of socially insufficient material could send data into cyberspace without restriction. The ten-year transition program mandated by the act replaced and standardized information systems so that cyberspace could be patrolled by law and sufficiency enforcement agencies. With the programming advances early in the second decade of the century, one information specialist could monitor thousands of communication access points. Not only would communications that had violent, sexual, or socially insufficient material be flagged for investigation, protocols were developed to flag material using euphemisms or codes as a cover of socially insufficient material, which in itself was an implied violation of the Social Sufficiency Amendment.

Captain Frazier finally pushed the keyboard away from him, touching the screen of the computer monitor to change the application in which he was working.

"I called you in, Matt, because I saw that you submitted a request for Tactical again," said Frazier.

"Yes sir," said Sheridan. He had volunteered for time on the Tactical Response Team for the substation because it was the only assignment that would get him back into the emergency zone sooner than his ninety-day undercover suspension required. Tactical, or TRT as it was sometimes called, served warrants, arrested fugitives, assisted in major jazz busts, and served as backup in hostage and shots-fired situations. Tactical was the most dangerous job in the Federal Police Force, and as a result, accepted only volunteers. Even after volunteering, applicants were further screened for physical and mental fitness before being assigned. Married men were seldom allowed to volunteer for Tactical. The pay was double for Tactical, but the longest assignment one could receive on Tactical was fourteen days. An officer could volunteer twice per year for Tactical without a waiver.

"This is your fourth request this year, Sheridan. This requires chief-level approval. Are you that broke?" asked Frazier.

"No sir, just bored," replied Sheridan. From the change in the look on Frazier's face, Matt knew that he had given the wrong answer. "I'm sorry if law enforcement here in the substation isn't as glamorous as all the video cop shows. I'm also sorry that regulations require a ninety-day icing for you. But volunteering for Tactical is something you don't do out of boredom. I don't need cowboys and heroes on my Tactical teams, because I usually end up burying those dumb shits. Look, Sheridan, you've done three rotations with Tactical. You've more than got your tickets punched for the year. You're a good cop, a good detective. I don't need you to live out some death wish by getting a de facto permanent assignment to Tactical," said Frazier.

"Captain, let me take back the 'bored' comment. Let me rephrase myself. I'm requesting Tactical again because it's what I do best. My father always told me, whatever you do in life, just be the best. Well, I'm a cop now, and among the things that cops do, going through doors after bad guys is what I do best. I won't argue the danger with you. But I almost feel as if I have a responsibility to volunteer if I'm good at this. Maybe some other guys would get killed in a situation that I'd scrape out of. That guy's blood is on my hands . . ."

"Sheridan, cut the friggin' melodrama." Frazier sighed, then continued. "I'm approving you at my level. It'll be a day or two before the chief's office processes the message online. I'm approving you because I realize you're probably the least likely in this substation to get killed on Tactical. And don't think it's because of any skill, Sheridan. I think you're just lucky," said Frazier.

Sheridan looked the captain in the eye and knew that Luke Frazier was lying. He stood, involuntarily patting at the pistol concealed in the small of his back, as was his habit.

"Thank you, sir," said Sheridan.

"Whatever you say, Detective," said Frazier, turning back to the screen of his monitor.

"Oh, shit!" muttered Matt, pulling up short from the side of the Tactical Response Team armored van. The six-to-six shift team was assembling in the underground motorpool area of the substation before moving out. Matt had profaned upon recognizing Lieutenant Arnold Murphy. *Of all the friggin' people to draw to lead a TRT, I got Murphy,* Matt thought. *I may very well get killed today.*

Lieutenant Arnold Murphy had been on the Federal Police Force somewhat longer than Matt. He had started in a college work-study program as an administrative assistant, mostly pushing buttons, researching files, and performing personnel administration activities. After completing his college degree, he passed the sergeant's exam and was immediately offered a spot from the list. Shortly thereafter, while still in the admin branch of the Southwest Division, he passed the lieutenant's exam and was offered an immediate spot. Realizing he needed at least two years in the field before he could make captain, Arnold had pulled a few strings with his congressman, for whom he had coincidentally campaigned in the last election, and Murphy was made detective lieutenant. Murphy's actual time in the field amounted to a two-week familiarization after the academy and the one-week crash training course for new Tactical officers and volunteers. He had excelled in his police career despite his lack of aptitude, and now had secured a Tactical assignment. Nonetheless, there could be no substitute for experience and common sense on the street. *I can see the future New Liberty politician in him,* Matt thought. Not that he thought being a member of the New Liberty party was bad, but Matt had a deep-seated distrust of politicians. He hated politics and everything for which it stood. It was artificial, phony, and contrived, he often thought. Nothing ever changes, for all their speeches and pontificating. Nothing had changed in the country in almost twenty years that Matt could remember. The same people get elected year after year anyway, he would think. What a waste of time and energy. He himself hadn't voted in years.

Watch Murphy kiss my ass, thought Matt.

"Captain Sheridan, welcome," said Murphy, obliquely offering his hand to Matt, flashing an orthodontist's dream smile.

"Detective Sheridan now, sir," said Matt, reluctantly shaking the hand offered him, which reminded him of a fresh beef cutlet. Matt hated this especially insidious trait of Murphy's, calling Matt by the rank from which he was honorably discharged from the Shock

Marines. Lieutenant Arnold Murphy was the only person on the force to do so.

"Yes, of course," said Murphy, a smug grin spreading infectiously across his pockmarked face. He was a little man with carefully styled red hair and a carefully styled "little man's complex."

Without another word, Matt brushed past Murphy to greet the other members of the team. There were seven team members, and they would be spending the next two weeks, six A.M. to six P.M., together in the cramped, heavily armored police van. Sheridan had worked with most of them in the field previously on various regular assignments. Murphy, unfortunately (in Matt's opinion), was Sheridan's second level supervisor in the detectives organization in the substation.

Matt stepped through the rear door of the van and was greeted by the coarse voice of Detective Sergeant Carl Grafton. Matt was surprised to see him on the Tactical team. Not only would that make two supervisory officers in the same team, but also, Grafton was married with two children. Grafton was regaling one of the younger cops, one whom Matt had never seen before, with his favorite traffic accident story.

". . . so anyways, I'm trying to sort this hit out, both cars completely creamed, and the medevacs are comin' in. Well, the driver of the one car, he's taken the windshield in the forehead, like a hatchet, he's dead at scene, DAS. The medics are rushin' around, trying to get as many people into the choppers as they can. Six people between the two cars. So anyways, they pick this one guy up off the ground, he's got a bad head wound too. So they put him on the stretcher, and they're takin' him up to the chopper, when one of the medics sees a brain lyin' on the street. Just a plain ole brain by itself. So he looks at the guy on the stretcher, then the brain, then the guy on the stretcher, and he bends over"—Carl had to restrain himself briefly—"and he throws the brain on the stretcher with the guy." Carl erupted with laughter.

"This friggin' guy shows up at the hospital with an extra brain! Can you believe it?" Carl finished.

Matt smiled weakly, having heard the story at least a dozen times before. He looked at the young cop, whose nameplate read "Johnson." The young man was smiling also, but looked distinctly pale. Grafton told that story to all the rookies. It was his own twisted litmus test for new cops.

Matt patted Grafton on the arm. "Good morning, Detective Sergeant. I see you're warming up young Johnson before we make our breakfast run."

Grafton turned away from the young cop, who was now swallowing hard. "Sheridan, what a surprise to see you on Tactical," he said with sarcasm.

"Likewise, sir," said Sheridan.

"Yeah, well, with Winter Holiday coming just three and a half short months away, and two grandkids to buy for this year, I'm starting to put some money away now," said Grafton.

Matt sat down next to Grafton on the bench seat lining the closed left side of the van and extended his hand to Johnson, seated on the opposite bench.

"Hi, Matt Sheridan."

"Mark Johnson. Nice to meet you. I've heard a lot about you," said the young cop.

"I hope not from Sarge here," said Sheridan.

"No, but around the force, you know, here and there," said Johnson.

"Well, welcome aboard nonetheless," said Sheridan. Sheridan reached beneath the seat and unfastened the patrol helmet secured there. The helmet was almost identical to the one he wore in the Shock Marines, complete with wireless com, oxygen generator and regulator, and telescopic visor. The differences between this model and the one he wore in the service were that the police model had internalized the com set (doing away with the backpack uplink unit), and it did not have a hookup to a chem suit. For Tactical duty, all officers were assigned special (and expensive) jumpsuits (worn usually over a sweat suit or gym shorts, depending on the weather) made of Borlon bulletproof fabric. Borlon had replaced Kevlar several years before as the standard bulletproof fabric. The metallic state properties of the recently discovered element lunium were found to produce a filament-thin thread with the flexibility of cotton and twelve times the strength of steel. Borlon suits, woven with the lunium thread, could stop virtually any projectile under one inch in diameter.

Officer Reginald Martinez, a native of the San Diego area, climbed into the driver's seat of the van. Murphy (of course, Matt thought) sat in the front passenger seat. Lastly, two African cops, one Detective James Bentley and the other Officer Mike Davis, climbed aboard and sat on the bench on either side of Officer Mark Johnson. With all aboard, Martinez pressed the door-secure button, which slid the van door closed. Martinez engaged the com system, which would both link the van as a node in the Federal Police com net and establish channels and frequencies for each of the team members who would be using the van as their remote com control station.

Arnold Murphy swiveled the passenger seat around to face the rest of the team.

"Good afternoon, gentlemen. I'm sure you all know me; I'm Detective Lieutenant Murphy, ranking officer for the next two weeks. I've made out the duty assignments for the team as follows: Officer Martinez, you will serve, obviously, as transportation and logistics officer, providing tactical backup as requested. Sergeant Grafton, you will operate the Command Center functions. You do know how to operate the com links, don't you?" Murphy asked, eyebrow raised.

Grafton projected a sardonic smile. "Yes, I can work the com. I've been working with com since they set up the network for the force . . . sir," he replied. Grafton had worked for Murphy for nearly a year now, and the lieutenant damn well knew that Grafton had worked with the com system for many years.

"Interesting. You know, funny you should mention it, but I was on the Acquisition Board with Commissioner Franklin, well, he wasn't commissioner then, when the system was first procured for the Federal Police."

Gimme a friggin' break, Matt thought. *This guy can't go more than fifteen minutes without talking about himself or dropping a name.*

"Officer Johnson, I see you were rated ninety-four with the Winchester at the academy," Murphy continued.

"Yes, sir," replied Johnson. The .300 Winchester Magnum had been adopted ten years before as the official "long range antipersonnel" weapon of the Federal Police. It wasn't quite socially aware to call them sniper rifles anymore. Most often they were just referred to as Winchesters. Winchester Arms, of course, had been bought out by the American Arms merger in late 2008, but the model was still referred to as the Winchester out of respect for the former company's firearm tradition. Matt remembered rating ninety-seven during his military transition training.

"Okay, Officer Johnson, you've got the Winchester," said Murphy.

Grafton's eyes narrowed. "Ever had Winchester duty on the street, kid?" he asked.

"Uh, well, actually, no," stammered Johnson.

"Sergeant Grafton, that's not necessary. I've made my assignment, and I have full confidence in Officer Johnson," said Murphy, a note of ire in his voice.

"Yes sir," muttered Grafton.

"The rest of you will form the Tactical field team, responding to me. Any questions?" finished Murphy.

No voices were raised. Murphy nodded to Martinez, and the van was set in motion.

"Gentlemen, by a stroke of good luck, due to the magistrates' system crashing last night, we have no warrants online so far this morning. District put out a bulletin last night with a heads-up on possible CAP activity this week," announced Murphy as the van pulled onto Broadway amid heavy traffic and headed west toward the harbor.

Matt knew the Confederation of American Patriots to be a terrorist organization sworn to the overthrow of the Federal States government. It was the first major domestic militant organization to arise in America since the private militias were outlawed in the late 1990s. The CAPs, as they were called, were the largest, best organized, and most secretive political group ever to arise in America. They began their existence with the basic political tools of propaganda, seditious literature, and agitation of public demonstrations. Matt remembered how Bryan Carruthers, lead news anchor at the CNA network, succinctly described them: The CAPs profess a doctrine of racism, chauvinism, elitism, and fascism. They oppose everything that the success of New Liberty and the SSA had brought to America. The CAPs, of late, perhaps out of desperation, had turned to acts of terrorism, attacking government and media targets across the country.

Internal Intelligence and the office of the Secretary of Security had over fifty thousand agents dedicated to stopping the CAPs, whose own numbers were estimated in the thousands. And despite the fact that many CAP operatives had been killed or captured in battles with Department of Security forces, their level of manpower and supply of illegal weapons (private possession of firearms was outlawed in '06, so virtually any gun fell into this category) seemed stable.

As the van rolled west against very light morning commuter traffic, Matt walked quickly to the equipment locker and entered his ID code. The lid swung open upward, and Matt removed one of the M16A4s contained therein. He tapped his code into the computer log affixed to the inside of the locker lid. He grabbed several magazines for the rifle, two sets of hand restraints, a collapsing police baton, and two stun grenades or "flash bangs" as they were still called.

"Uh, Detective Sheridan, we don't need our equipment just yet," said Detective Lieutenant Murphy.

"Yes, sir, I realize that, but I like to double-check everything," replied Sheridan, nonetheless returning to his seat with the equipment.

"So you're saying you don't trust the logistics folks who outfitted the van?" challenged Murphy.

Matt had to bite his tongue to stifle himself. "No, sir, I don't trust the equipment. I always check my equipment," said Matt.

Murphy did not immediately respond. Matt added, "I can usually tell how people will function, but not equipment."

Murphy glared at Sheridan. Sheridan did not return the look, but instead concentrated on working back the bolt of the rifle.

The men of the First Shift Tactical Response Team leaned against their armored van after an unusually quiet morning. The team was enjoying a lunch tradition: a chili dog from the little carry-out stand at 26th and J streets, across from Grant Hill Park. The day was unusually hot and humid for early September, and Sheridan felt a slightly uncomfortable trickle of sweat roll down his back. Sergeant Grafton sat dejectedly in the van, eating an instameal. The vendor had actually checked his health ID today and found that Sergeant Grafton's last semiannual had disqualified him from chili dogs and the like for six months. The vendors, and most food service establishments, rarely ran a health ID scan, but if an inspection was imminent, or an undercover health inspector was suspected, they scrupulously ran the checks. Grafton was equally dejected by the fact that Murphy also bought an instameal and decided to keep Grafton company in the van.

Detective Sheridan licked the last greasy gob of chili off his fingers, wiped his hands and mouth carefully with a napkin, and disposed of it properly. He had opened his jump uit to the waist to cool down (Borlon fabric was nonbreathing and subsequently served as a portable personal sauna for the wearer), and now was shrugging his six-foot, one-hundred-ninety-pound frame back into it. As he placed his right arm into its sleeve, the fabric of his T-shirt pulled, drawing up the left arm's short sleeve.

"Nasty cut," remarked Officer Johnson.

"It's pretty much healed," replied Sheridan.

"Shock Marines, huh?" asked Johnson, staring at Matt's laser tattoo.

"Afraid so," said Matt, slipping on the left arm of the jumpsuit and securing the Velcro from the waist to the collar.

"D'you see action?" asked Johnson, who realized, even as the words came out of his mouth, that was a stupid question, even for a rookie.

Matt stared at him for a moment. "Yeah. That's why they called us Shock Marines, as opposed to Mild Surprise Marines," he said sarcastically. He turned abruptly and hopped into the van. Officer Martinez grabbed Johnson's arm.

"That was stupid, Johnson."

"I realize that," said Johnson.

"Sheridan was at Karachi," said Martinez.

"Shit, I didn't know. They took eighty percent casualties at Karachi on the first day," said Johnson.

"Yeah, Sheridan was one of them. He got the Purple Heart, Silver Star, and the Navy Cross for that action. But he don't like to talk about it. So don't ask him anymore," said Martinez.

Rebuked, Johnson silently shook his head.

"And in case it comes up, don't ask him if he's married either. His wife and kid got killed in a car accident five years ago. He definitely don't want to talk about that," continued Martinez.

"Thanks. I'll keep my mouth shut," said Johnson.

The men turned to enter the van, when Grafton shouted out to them.

"Move it, girls! Just got an 11-99 come in on the com. Gotta move!"

Martinez ran to the driver's door while Johnson ran to the rear. Bentley and Davis were close behind him as the door slid shut.

"What do you have, Sergeant?" asked Murphy as Martinez brought the van to life.

"Officer down, officer needs assist. Shots fired. Convention Center," said Grafton. He punched a code into the van's onboard computer on the wireless keyboard on his lap. On the windshield in front of Martinez, the van's heads-up display projected a green holographic image of the instrument panel and Grafton's computer screen.

"Twenty-sixth to Island to Fifth. Thanks, Sarge," said Martinez as he swung the van onto 26th Street.

The ride was surprisingly quick, and the TRT (Tactical Response Team) van was apparently the first backup at the scene. At the east end of the alley that ran between the towering glass-and-steel San Diego Convention Center and the North American Trade Center, a Federal Police patrol car sat with lights on and doors flung wide open. An officer's legs were hanging out of the driver's side.

"Com one, everybody," shouted Grafton. In unison, the men tapped "com one" on their helmets. Face shields were pulled down, and oxygen regulators snapped backward onto the helmet in the open position.

Murphy's voice came over com one quickly. "Gentlemen, I don't need to remind you that this call is outside the emergency zone, and applicable standards of conduct and rules of engagement are in effect," he said.

Martinez pulled the van directly behind the patrol car, which was perpendicular to the alley, blocking the entrance. Officers Bentley and Davis deployed first, left and right, from the rear of the van. They quickly took covered positions at the front and rear fenders of the patrol car. Sheridan was next, moving to the stricken officer. Johnson and Martinez followed Sheridan, similarly setting up behind the patrol car. Murphy was last out of the van.

Matt gently turned the wounded man over. He was conscious, but apparently in shock. His right index finger was still depressing the emergency button on the unit's dashboard com. As he moved, he groaned through clenched teeth.

"Vallario," Matt said, reading the officer's nameplate, "it's okay, we're TRT. Where are you hit?"

The officer did not answer, but looked downward. Matt followed his eyes and saw that the officer had been shot once in each leg. Matt folded down his throat mike and spoke.

"Sarge, what's the twenty on Medical?"

"I've got ambulances one and thirty away," replied Grafton from the van.

"Ninety seconds, Officer Vallario," said Matt.

Matt turned to see Murphy hovering behind him. Color was draining from his face.

Matt scanned the alley to size up the situation. Some thirty yards away, a small pickup truck was parked sideways across the alley, next to a service entrance to the Convention Center. Between the pickup and the building stood a man, obviously injured, holding a pistol to the head of an unconscious police officer, slumped in his arms. An unmarked police cruiser blocked the far end of the alley, one officer behind the car with her pistol drawn. Another officer lay in the alley in front of the car.

"Nobody move! This cop is meat if anybody moves!" shouted the injured assailant.

Murphy spoke over com one. "Sheridan, Davis, get to the far end of the alley, take up positions with the other officer. Bentley, Martinez, you're here with me. Officer Johnson, set up at the patrol car for a go shot."

"Sir, that's not a great setup for a go shot with the Winchester," Sergeant Grafton interrupted, breaking over the Com.

"Thank you for the input, Sergeant," said Murphy sarcastically, emphasizing the word *Sergeant*. "Everybody move!"

Sheridan and Davis slowly backed away from the patrol car, rifles at the ready on their hips. A safe distance away, they turned and peeled left. The North American Trade Center building stood to the left of the Convention Center, also a monster of steel and glass, less

than three years old. Sheridan and Davis ran to another alley beyond
the Trade Center, making their way to the rear of the building. Behind the trade center, rifles at their shoulders, they crept carefully
toward the unmarked patrol car, which they could now see blocking
the west end of the alley.

Officer Davis and Detective Sheridan had finally reached the unmarked patrol car. Detective Nancy Edelman, also of Substation
Charlie, looked at Sheridan and Davis.

"Shit, about time the cavalry got here," she said.

Sheridan and Davis took positions on either side of her, resting
their rifles on the trunk and hood of her unmarked car, respectively.

"What've you got, Edelman?" asked Officer Davis.

"Hank and I were in the neighborhood doing a check on a plastic fraud. The patrol unit called for backup. Looks like we had two
perps trying to get into the locked service door there; alarm company got a false reading on a key card entry and blew the whistle. The
patrol unit responded to the silent alarm. That's when the backup
call came. When we got here, one of the uniforms and one of the
perps were down, lying beside the truck. The other perp was on one
knee next to the truck, wounded. The other uniform had crawled
back to the patrol car. Hank jumped out and headed toward the
truck. That's as far as he got," she said, motioning in the direction
of her partner, who lay groaning in the street.

She continued. "That's when the perp grabbed the uniform who
was down. I started to go get Hank, and the perp fired at me. Hank
waved me off. He's shot in the knee."

Matt knew Detective Hank Bethany.

"Hank, it's Sheridan. What's your status?" he shouted.

As Sheridan spoke, the perpetrator in the alley fired a shot that
sailed over the car.

"Don't fuckin' move, I said! Get me out of here or this cop is
dead!" shouted the gunman.

Matt spoke on com one. "Lieutenant Murphy, Sheridan. Davis and
I are in position. We've got one more casualty, uh, injury, down here.
Any more info?"

"Sit tight Sheridan. Medevacs are touching down just behind us.
The Civil Liberties Deputy and Hostage Team are about five out.

Looks like it could be CAPs. Officer Vallario tells us that the pickup is full of weapons. Your orders are to secure the west end of the alley and sit tight. Stand by for further orders."

Matt looked into the sky above the east end of the alley and saw two medevac choppers beginning their precarious descent to the street between the downtown skyscrapers. The use of medevac choppers in such emergencies had increased the survival rate of shooting victims by eighty-five percent.

The gunman, still holding the slumped form of Officer Carlton, Vallario's partner, became suddenly agitated. "What are those choppers?" he screamed. "Get them outta here!"

Lieutenant Murphy's voice emerged from a speaker on the van, routed through the com system.

"This is Detective Lieutenant Murphy of the Federal Police. The sounds you hear are medical helicopters. Just relax and we can resolve this situation without anyone else getting hurt."

The gunman shifted suddenly, wrenching his victim around.

"You gotta get me outta here! I want a chopper now!" he screamed.

Sergeant Grafton watched breathlessly in the van through the van monitors. "Lieutenant . . ." he said over com one.

"Sergeant, I don't need your input here. We're waiting for Hostage and the CLDs (Civil Liberties Deputies). That's procedure."

"Lieutenant, we're gonna have at least one dead cop on our hands here in a second. This guy is ready to perk. We gotta take him out!" shouted Grafton.

"Sergeant, you're out of line. We've got three and thirty till our relief arrives, and we will hand over the situation—"

"Fuck you, Murphy, that cop'll be dead in three and thirty. Officer Johnson, this is Sergeant Grafton. Take the go shot."

"Officer Johnson, do not fire your weapon, that is an order!" shouted Murphy.

Officer Johnson looked at Murphy, standing some fifteen feet from him. Bentley and Martinez looked as well, hearing the entire conversation on com one.

"Johnson, take the goddamn shot!" screamed Grafton.

"What's goin' on here?" shouted the gunman, pressing his pistol to Carlton's temple. "I'm gonna kill him, you bastards!"

Spittle flew from Grafton's mouth. "Shoot, Johnson, you lousy fuck, shoot!"

"Johnson, you hold your fire! Grafton, you are dismissed!" shouted Murphy.

Grafton screamed, "Take the shot. Take the goddamned shot!"

Johnson looked at Murphy again. Murphy yelled out, "Johnson!"

A sharp crack echoed through the alley as a single bullet tore through the gunman's head, the top of his skull exploding upward like a freed champagne cork. The gunman's body dropped to the alley as if a switch had been thrown, turning it off. The gunman's pistol clattered uselessly to the street. Officer Carlton, his head having rested just below the gunman's chin, fell to the street as well, covered with humanity.

At the west end of the alley, Detective Matt Sheridan rose from his crouched position, his nostrils tickled by the whiff of cordite curling skyward from the smoking barrel of his rifle.

3

Parker Hudson stared quietly at the lights of Georgetown, across the Potomac River from his Rosslyn, Virginia, apartment. The sun would be rising in about thirty minutes, but the city was still dark. Already, the headlights of the desperate early commuters were piercing tiny holes in the darkness; the vast, faceless minions headed to their vast, faceless offices to perform their obscure bureaucratia. For most of the rest of the country, it was only a short trip from bed to desk for a light speed trip on a fiber-optic cable to their office in cyberspace. Looking to the south, the warning lights of the Washington Monument strobed their sentry to the government VTOL (Vertical Take-off and Landing) commuters that were already swarming in and out of National Airport. The State of New Columbia was coming to life.

Parker sighed, knowing that just a few miles in any direction of the compass from where he stood, another eight hours of violence was coming to a close. The Comarva (New Columbia, Maryland, and Virginia) Emergency Zone was now the largest and most violent in the nation, outpacing the New York City E.Z. in violent crime rates just weeks before. After the promising strides of the late nineties and early units, the New Columbia metropolitan area had slipped back into the patterns of violence and addiction with the emergence of jazz as the street drug of choice, one dose costing about an average week's wage for most users. In the eighties and nineties, drugs and crime had often been associated with the poor, African sections of the city. Jazz was a much more socially sufficient narcotic, in that its slaves were drawn from across every socioeconomic and ethnic category. The Comarva E.Z. had been created in recognition that the New Columbia metro area problems could not be isolated in the individual police districts defined by state boundaries. The Comarva E.Z. allowed Federal Police to work across district jurisdictions, thereby giving law enforcement officials the greatest latitude. Despite the working arrangements, the Comarva E.Z. statute, and the SSA Urban Relief programs, four or five people were undoubtedly killed while Hudson slept. Maybe some cops too. His cops. Hudson hated being East Region, Comarva Division Chief. *Sure, it had been an honor and an accomplishment to make division chief last year at age forty-five. But Comarva!* He could barely stand it anymore.

"I see the moon is still out," said a female voice from behind him, chuckling softly.

He turned back toward his bed and realized that standing naked at the window, his bare butt was facing his guest.

"Very funny," he said, turning back to the lights. He ran his fingers through his wiry hair, formerly black, now gray. He liked the thought that she was looking at his butt.

"Looking for something in particular out there?" the woman asked.

He snorted. "Yeah, a new narcotics lieutenant."

"You're not gonna find one standing there," said the woman. "Unless you're attempting to attract a pervert with binoculars."

"I need to attract someone who's never heard of Comarva."

Hudson walked back to the bed and sat on the edge, his back to the woman. She propped herself up on one elbow, pulling the covers modestly up over her bare breasts. With her free hand she pushed her silver-streaked blond hair backward off her face. Playfully, she dragged her index finger lightly down the center of his back, causing him to arch it and shudder. He glared at her over his shoulder, and as he did, she pulled him to her.

"How long have you been standing there?"

"A couple hours, I guess."

"Look, why don't you let this go and worry about it at the office. You can still get an hour of sleep. You need it."

"If I wasn't under so much pressure from my anal-retentive boss, I wouldn't worry about it."

"Just tell your boss you haven't found the right person yet," said the woman. She laid her head back on the pillow, pulling him closer to her. As the light from the city trickled in through the parted bedroom curtains, a beam played across her blue eyes, and they sparkled like prisms. She was forty-five years old with a body twenty years younger. *Those eyes melt me,* Parker thought. He slid beneath the covers next to her.

"My boss has heard that before. Besides," he said, running his hand down the length of her long leg, drawing it over his hip. "If I weren't sleeping with my boss, she'd have fired me by now."

Karen Russell, presidential appointee, Department of Security, Office of the Assistant Secretary for Internal Security, East Region Director, smirked as she reached beneath the covers and grabbed Parker.

"When you say the boss has you by the balls, you mean it, huh?" she said with a mischievous grin. Hudson was trim, sharp, handsome; neither tall nor short. The only features distinguishing him as a cop from a maturing male model were three turns in his nose with which he had not been born. Karen liked the broken nose. It had character.

Hudson's eyes widened. "I've got a meeting with the old battle-ax at eight o'clock."

Karen pressed her lips to his and pulled him on top of her. "You better think of a good excuse for being late."

Matt Sheridan sighed as he slumped into the single chair in his understated apartment. He was twenty-four hours into seventy-two hours of "administrative leave with pay" following the incident at the Convention Center. He had expected to be fired; actually, he might still be fired if Murphy had his way. Grafton was already gone, transferred to Mountain Region, Idaho Division. Six more years and then retirement, at least they gave him that. *I would be working a SLOW/STOP tool on a road crew by today,* Matt thought, *if the public response to the incident hadn't made me a local hero.* Within the first hour of the shooting, the news broadcasts along the West Coast portrayed him as a villain, shooting a man convicted of no crime well outside the emergency zone. As the day progressed, however, it was learned that the innocent suspect was a wanted CAP operative. Plans were found on him and his partner detailing the placement of a large explosive device in the Convention Center. The Association of Electronic, Online, and Print News Media just happened to be convening there that day. Upon that revelation, overnight Matt Sheridan had become slightly famous. He was now portrayed as a gutsy cop. Editorials among the local media focused on the spreading problem of CAP terrorism and the shared duty of government and citizens to help bring that scourge to an end.

Matt picked up his entertainment remote from the floor and was pointing it at his console when Pasha, his Siamese cat, leapt into his lap. Pasha had turned up at his apartment door one evening, just over five years ago, and moved in. Matt posted notes in the building and talked to a number of people about the cat, but no one, including Matt, had seen the animal before. So "that friggin' cat," as Matt first called him, became Pasha and stayed. Matt had not been a cat person, but grew to love Pasha. The animal was very social, and Sheridan could scarcely keep the thing off him when he was home. Pasha never left the apartment, never cried at night, never marked his territory, never clawed furniture, and would respond to virtually any command. Pasha seemed to know Matt's good days and bad days. Today Pasha curled into Matt's lap, resting his head on Matt's flat stomach, and looked upward sympathetically at his roommate.

"Yeah, it's been another bad day, Pasha, my man," Sheridan sighed. He stroked the animal's head with his right hand and clicked his entertainment console on with the remote in his left. He couldn't decide if he was more angry than brooding, so he selected Dvorak's Ninth, the New World symphony. He then selected the channel for closed-captioned transmission of the Central News Agency, a twenty-four-hour news and specialty programming network. Finally, for a change of pace, he changed the aromatic from sea spray to pine forest. He reclined in the chair, gently cursed himself for not fixing a drink in advance of getting comfortable, and settled in an attempt to unwind. Pasha snuggled his head in Sheridan's lap.

The international news flashed past rapidly. Famine widened in Europe as the economic collapse continued to spread. American troops restored order in Tehran after three days of rioting in protest of the expansion of the American-Arabian Protectorate.

He'd heard enough. He skipped past the Sports Network, the

Hollywood Channel, the Video Network, and the Cooking Channel. Matt had just switched to the History Network when the onscreen "incoming" icon began flashing. He engaged the audio but disabled the outgoing video. Captain Frazier's face appeared onscreen, in a picture-in-picture box.

"Sheridan speaking."

"Matt," said Frazier, using a first name as he rarely did, "I need you in my office first thing tomorrow morning."

"I thought I was on administrative leave," said Sheridan sarcastically.

"You are. But I demand your person here at 0700 tomorrow with bells on."

"What's up?"

"I can't discuss it over the com. But it behooves you to be here on time."

"Yes, sir!" snarled Sheridan.

Frazier, perhaps thinking that Sheridan had also disabled the incoming video, shook his head ruefully, then disconnected. Sheridan smiled at himself and followed suit.

He pushed Pasha off his lap gently and rose, headed toward the one-bedroom-apartment's small, immaculate kitchen. He had always admitted to being something of a neat freak, and his apartment was the strongest testament to that observation. From the living room, the tight hospital corners of his bed could be seen. There were no typical single-male-living-alone clothes strewn about, no trash on the floor, no illegal posters of scantily clad women advertising alcohol or marijuana. In fact, his apartment bordered on bareness, with its main distinguishing feature being three walls of floor-to-ceiling bookcases, filled with an eclectic collection of books: French and Russian literature, strategic doctrine, music history, philosophy, twenty-first-century history, cooking, and martial arts. The shelves also held his various magazine publications. He had published a few items before the war, mainly dry, procedural type articles on infantry tactics and strategy. After being wounded at the Battle of Karachi, Matt spent months in and out of service hospitals while his shoulder healed. Often restricted as to activities, Matt wrote often. He wrote to keep his mind focused, to expand his thoughts beyond the sterile confines of his hospital surroundings. He hadn't written a single word of text since Jenny died and he'd joined the police force. The spirit just didn't move him anymore.

Often Matt wondered why he kept all the books, when he could store every single word on one CD Write-Read. But he derived too much comfort from the books, perhaps as a throwback to his childhood. Whatever the case, the books dominated his apartment. He had no other adornments in the house save one framed print of Picasso's "Guernica," which hung in the short hallway from the living room to the bedroom. One chair, the entertainment center, a dining set, and a litter box. That was it.

Matt pulled an instameal from a mostly empty refrigerator and popped it in the microwave. He neatly set a place for himself at his small dining table, napkin folded. He sat, counting the remaining ticks until his "gourmet" beef Stroganoff (including real beef!) would be ready, and his eyes wandered to the white pine shelf above his sink. Three-quarters of a liter of National Beverage Gold Select Bourbon taunted him. Movement in the corner of his eye caught his attention, and he noticed Pasha had dutifully taken up station at his feet.

"As a matter of fact, I think I will join you for a drink, Pasha," said Sheridan, rising from the table. *Twenty-four hours ago I killed a man,* thought Matt. *Fuck Frazier.*

Sheridan sat in Captain Frazier's office, on time, his supposed interlocutor twenty minutes late. He wore a crisply pressed white tunic with a units-style thin, straight cravat. His body still emitted a vague odor of stale bourbon, and his fiery red eyes betrayed his activity of the previous night. *Fortunately they can't see inside my head,* Matt thought, *where a little man with a pickax is working on my cerebellum.* He ran his hand through his short blond hair. *I need to go back home and continue being on administrative leave for about six more hours,* he thought. *Damn National Beverage Bourbon!*

A female uniformed sergeant entered Frazier's office with three cases of computer disks, smiling politely at Sheridan as she walked over to the captain's desk. As she set them down, one of the cases, set not quite precisely flat on the desk, according to natural law, slid from the desk to the floor, spilling its contents. The sergeant muttered something under her breath, and Matt lifted his head.

"Izvinitye, pozhalsta, ya vas slushal govorit' pa ruskie?" Excuse me, did I hear you speak Russian?

The woman looked up quickly, startled, and responded.

"Da, ya nemnogo govoriu pa ruskie. Vee tozhe?" Yes, I speak a little Russian. You too?

"Da, nemnogo, yesli, vee govoritye pa ruskie luchye chem ya." Yes, a little, but you speak it better than me.

The woman laughed. "I actually majored in Russian at UCLA, another lifetime ago."

"Me too. Penn State. And I see we're both putting our Russian to good use as cops, huh?"

"My choices in San Diego were cop or salesclerk," said the sergeant.

Matt stood and went over to Frazier's desk and assisted the sergeant in collecting the final stray disks from the floor. "My choices were cop or road crew. Road crew is pretty dangerous though."

"Sheridan!"

The conversation was interrupted as Captain Frazier squeezed his six-foot-four, two-hundred-thirty-pound body through the doorway. He was followed by a smaller, older man in a civilian-looking suit with a badge clipped to his belt.

Sheridan whirled and stood, almost saluting from instinct.

"Good morning, Captain," said Sheridan.

"Whatever you say, Sheridan," said Frazier as he eyed the female officer leaving his office. "Sheridan, have you ever met Chief Donnellson?" asked Frazier.

"No, sir," Matt responded. He extended his hand to the civilian-clad man.

Donnellson took the hand, shaking it perfunctorily. "Detective Sheridan, we need to talk to you about a few things. Do you have some time?" asked Donnellson.

He was asking only to be polite. The chief doesn't ask for your time.

"Sure, got all day," said Sheridan.

Frazier assumed the seat behind his desk. Sheridan sat back down in front of the desk, and Chief Donnellson sat in the other visitor's chair next to Sheridan. He turned to face the younger man.

"First off, we need to talk about the shooting at the Convention Center. Ballistics, autopsy reports, and the feed from the com are all in and have been analyzed. We've found that you didn't actually fire the shot that killed the CAP."

Matt's jaw dropped. "What the hell are you talking about?"

Donnellson glowered at Sheridan. "It turns out that you and Officer Davis fired simultaneously. That's why only one shot was heard. Ballistics matches the slug that killed the CAP with Davis's rifle, not yours. The slug you fired was not recovered."

"Respectfully, Chief, this is pure bullshit. What's going on? Davis was right next to me. I fired one shot. Davis never fired. He never even said he fired. I'm not proud of the fact that I had to kill a guy, but what's the deal with the story changing?" Sheridan demanded. He looked at Frazier, and Frazier looked away at his monitor, pretending to be involved in something else.

Donnellson shifted in his seat. In a new position, the overhead lighting reflected off the shiny pink stretch of scalp between his ears that his hair had years before abandoned. *At least he didn't grow his side hairs long to comb them back across the top,* Matt thought.

"The story hasn't been changed, Detective, we've just straightened it out. You needed to know that you didn't kill that man."

"Okay, if you say I didn't kill anybody, I didn't kill anybody. Fine. Have you informed Davis?" Sheridan asked sarcastically.

"Officer Davis is well aware of this situation."

Sheridan sat back in the chair and rubbed his eyes.

"So I'm off administrative leave?" he asked.

"Well, that leads us into our next topic of discussion," Donnellson said.

The chief is holding back a smile, Sheridan thought.

On a clear day, Hudson could see the Washington Monument eight miles in the distance from his twenty-first-floor office in the Skyline Tower. Today was gray, nondescript, dreary. Hudson hadn't really noticed the weather, as he had spent most of the morning poring over personnel files. Screen after screen of applicants, potential applicants, and rejections. He had already pissed off all his captains, especially Captain Blair of Narcotics, in deciding that he would make all selections of officers at the lieutenant level and above. They were also pissed off because he intended to pick from outside the Comarva district. His captains felt that an insider who knew the area, knew the streets, was necessary. The vacancy was created because a veteran, Maryland-native lieutenant had recently been killed in his own station house.

Hudson was pulling his hair out because the two candidates he had proposed had been rejected by Karen Russell, who had final authority on all personnel decisions. She reviewed each applicant file for several hours behind closed doors, in her office some forty feet from his, and rejected the candidates without comment. *Which was her prerogative to do,* he thought. She wouldn't explain why, at work or in bed. So Parker Hudson plodded along unsuccessfully, each day bringing new heat from down the hall.

He was calling up file thirty out of three hundred for the day, when Karen strode through the door, no knock.

"Okay, Hudson, it looks like I've saved your ass again," she said, walking in front of his desk.

He looked up at her with a very tired expression on his face, but said nothing.

"I was talking to an old friend out on the West Coast, ran a hypothetical problem I had in my office past him, and just thirty minutes later I downloaded this," she continued, tossing a CD case at Parker.

He grimaced and opened the case, looking blankly at the CD. "This is?"

"This is your new lieutenant. You'll review his application, find it suitable, and then suggest it to me for the position."

"What if . . ."

"No what-ifs. You need the slot filled, I'm doing my friend a favor, he's doing me a favor, and we can get back to business, which, by the way, is catching bad guys," she lectured.

Parker hated when she launched into her little sermons. "If you don't mind me saying, you're taking a pretty keen interest in this position, aren't you? I mean, a regional director assisting in the selection of a lieutenant?"

She smiled, taken aback. "No supervisor is beneath helping a subordinate. Besides, you've told me how important this position is to your organization. I'm just trying to help out."

He relented, smiling. "I don't remember you helping out the New England division chief when they had to replace those two captains last year."

She picked up a small scrap of paper from Hudson's desk and grabbed a pen. She scribbled a note as she spoke.

"You have the advantage over the other division chiefs by being colocated with the regional director's office. Call it good luck."

She threw the note at Hudson, turned on her heel, and strode out of the office.

Parker admired her departing aspect, smelled her subtle perfume as the scent trailed her through the doorway, and imagined what she'd look like wearing a dress to work. The slacks she wore were very flattering, but he sometimes longed for the good old days, when women were allowed to show their legs in the workplace. He realized that skirts were a symbol of subservience to men, though, and actually agreed with the Fedstandard for office attire. He shook his head and read her note.

I'm not screwing the other divisional chiefs, it read. For the first time that day, Parker Hudson laughed out loud.

He looked at the CD case on his desk and decided he would need coffee before tackling it. Grabbing his Department of Security regulation coffee cup, he left his office and strode toward the executive kitchen. He smiled good morning as he passed his administrative assistant, Christopher Dino, seated at one of six desks, separated by partitions, in an open work area just beyond his office door.

"Good morning, Mr. Hudson," said Christopher in a lilting voice.

Hudson knew that just ten, fifteen years earlier, Christopher would not have been accepted, let alone survived, in a law enforcement environment. The SSA had quashed the bigotry that would have kept Christopher out of the office. *Christopher was a damn good assistant, dedicated and professional in all his duties,* thought Hudson. *The fact that he likes guys is really none of my business.* He shook his head again as he entered the kitchen.

The kitchen featured a single brew coffee machine with twenty-two separate selections. He placed his cup under the machine's dispenser and selected Turkish coffee. He was the only one in the office who would drink it, but he exercised one of his few perks when the machine was ordered and had Turkish coffee included as option twenty-two. He drank a lot of the stuff during his three years in the MPs in Kuwait, and had taken the habit home with him. His cup still had the tarry residue of yesterday afternoon's last cup, but he hadn't rinsed it out. *Helps seal in the flavor,* he thought.

The coffee was dispensed in just about ten seconds, and he made his way back to his office. As he passed Christopher's desk, he ordered him not to send any calls through for at least one hour. He sipped the thick coffee carefully as he pulled his office door closed behind him.

He absently dragged his hand along the back of the two synthetic leather chairs in front of his desk, then returned to his position in front of the monitor. He opened up the CD case with one hand as he sipped the bitter coffee, his lips scorched from the hot liquid. He slipped the disk into the computer's CD drive. A single file icon appeared on the screen. He touched it and it opened. *What a surprise,* he thought, *a personnel file.* He read aloud to himself.

"'Sheridan, Matthew Xavier, Detective, Federal Police. West Region, Southwest Division. Date of birth, 12 December 1988.' Uh, let's see. 'Six feet, one eighty-eight, blond and blue,' blah blah blah."

Parker drew his finger down the edge of the file on the screen, skipping over vital statistics, health record, and financial status sections of the report.

"Okay, 'married in '11, Jennifer Lynn Bailey, first child born in '14, uh-oh . . .'" He read the synopsis of the car accident that had taken the lives of Jennifer and David Sheridan. Sheridan, Matthew Xavier had been uninjured. There was a peripheral report in the file, but Parker chose not to read it. *I don't need any more pathos right now.*

"'Professional history.' Interesting. 'Navy ROTC, Penn State University, commissioned Second Lieutenant USMC, '11. Active duty with First Shock Marine Group, Interrogation Specialist.' Shit, he speaks, let's see . . . Chinese, Russian, French, Spanish. 'Saw action in the Mexican Crisis, Battle of Tijuana, citation for bravery, Purple Heart.' Hmm, skipping ahead, 'led platoon in Operation Lightning Strike, Battle of Karachi' . . . shit . . . 'Purple Heart, Silver Star, Navy Cross. Battlefield promotion to captain.'"

Hudson pushed his chair back from the desk, rubbing his eyes. *This guy's a friggin' war hero,* he thought. *Why the hell is he a cop?*

Hudson pulled himself back to the desk and sipped his coffee, now slightly less scalding than before. He flipped through Sheridan, Matthew Xavier's current employment file.

"Okay, 'worked San Diego, passed the detective's exam after only one year on patrol, military experience substituted for time in grade, veterans points, made undercover Narcotics. Multiple Tac Team assignments, numerous citations, blah blah blah.' Hmm, Mr. Wonderful has never even taken the sergeant's exam," noticed Hudson. He flipped through the file, dragging his finger along the screen. "Says here he's turned down promotions to corporal. This guy is supposed to be my lieutenant?"

Hudson closed the file onscreen and ejected the disk. He took a last sip of his coffee and left his desk, headed for Karen Russell's office. He turned left out of his own office and went down the hallway. After a short walk he reached the secretarial area for the regional director's staff, and he smiled politely at Betsy Holleran, Karen's seventy-three-year-old secretary. As usual, Betsy scowled at Parker but let him pass through the doorway into the director's corridor. The carpet color changed, moving from the Comarva spaces to the regional director's hallway, as if to remind any still unsure of the relationship between organizations that one was in a different league at that point. *Power carpet,* he thought.

Parker rounded the corner of her doorway, which, as usual, was open, and walked unannounced into a video conference in progress. Karen sat sideways at her desk, facing the telescreen and transceiver monitor. On the screen was a red-faced, white-haired, corpulent man who Parker recognized immediately. He stopped in his tracks, then turned quietly to leave.

"Mr. Hudson, please," said Russell.

"Sorry to interrupt, Ms. Russell, Mr. Secretary," Parker stammered.

"No, Mr. Hudson, the secretary and I were just discussing your situation," smiled Karen as she swiveled in her chair to face Parker.

Parker smiled wanly. "If you're sure I'm not interrupting."

"Not at all, Hudson. Please, sit down at the monitor," said Louis Hathaway, Assistant Secretary of Security, Internal.

Parker grabbed one of Karen's synthetic leather guest chairs in front of her desk and dragged it beside the high-backed executive chair in which Karen sat. He tried inconspicuously to place the disk case in his tunic pocket.

"Ms. Russell and I were discussing the difficulties you've been having in the Comarva, and your program to personally select officers at the lieutenant level and above. I like that personal commitment to the effort, Hudson. I know you've got your hands full with Comarva, but if anyone can turn Comarva around, it's you. And Ms. Russell," Hathaway added. Hudson noticed a slight slurring of his words, and wondered if the redness in Hathaway's nose was from Irish heritage or Scotch whiskey.

"Thank you, sir. We're trying very hard. I've got a lot of dedicated, brave men who risk their lives every day to try to get this area under control, but it's not easy," offered Hudson.

"Yes, well, I think Detective Sheridan will have a positive impact on your operations," said Hathaway.

"Sir?" asked Parker, startled.

"Karen, uh, Ms. Russell just explained that you were having a little difficulty bringing him on as a lieutenant, since he hasn't taken the qualifying exams and his short time in grade. As you know, that requirement can be waived in the form of a direct appointment at the assistant secretary level. If this man is as important to you as Ms. Russell described, I have full faith in your, and Ms. Russell's, judgment. The forms will be online in just a few hours," said Hathaway.

Parker Hudson looked vacantly at Russell. She smiled. "Thank you, sir. This is going to be great for Comarva. Isn't it, Hudson?"

Parker could only nod his head weakly.

"Very well. If you'll excuse me, I have another incoming video online. Ms. Russell, Mr. Hudson," said Hathaway. The screen went dark.

Hudson looked at Karen Russell. "Respectfully, Ms. Regional Director, can you explain to me just what the fuck went on here?"

"You were having a problem. I solved it for you."

"Without telling me? Without a hint? You've done all this behind my back!"

"Take it easy, Mr. Hudson," Karen said, formalizing the exchange. "You still work for me. Supervisor's prerogative."

"Supervisor or not, I refuse to get railroaded into this decision. Maybe this guy is right for the spot . . . I don't know. He doesn't cut it on his record alone. The guy's a war hero, he's been a good cop, but he's got no supervisory experience, he hasn't taken any of the qual exams, and he's coming in over people with years of seniority on him. This isn't just a snap decision you can make for me," said Parker.

"Shall I call the assistant secretary back and tell him I lied, and ask him if he'd please forget everything I just told him? Do you realize the political clout I have to expend to get a secretarial-level approval?"

"No, look . . . I just don't understand why you're so hot for Sheridan. Nothing remarkable about him, in my opinion. Good, but not spectacular."

"Well, I got a personal recommendation from the regional director out in San Diego. And I got a hunch about this guy. Gut feeling, you know. I think you need a young outsider to shake up some of the complacent old farts you've got running Comarva right now."

Hudson glared at her.

"Present company excluded, of course," she added.

Parker stood and sighed. "All right, I'll reconsider. But I need to talk to him first, myself."

"You can talk to him in person tomorrow," said Karen.

Hudson wrinkled his brow as he dragged the guest chair back into its place of intimidation. "Say again?"

"You can talk to him in person tomorrow. That's when he's reporting for duty. Good day, Mr. Hudson."

Matt Sheridan sighed quietly as the Arizona desert flashed past him. He held his head in his right hand, resting his elbow on the window ledge of the MagLev train streaking eastward. *Ten lousy hours to New Columbia,* he thought. *Plus a stop in St. Louis. This is taking forever!*

He was jostled ever so slightly as the train began a minor adjustment. It was turning south to avoid a ten-mile chasm cut in the desert by a stubborn river that refused to dry up. He looked out through the train's tinted windows and watched a vulture circle high in the desert over some unfortunate lower member of the food chain. And just as quickly as the bird had come into view, it was gone, another memory Matt was rapidly escaping.

Matt stood and excused himself as he climbed over the dozing Asian lady who sat next to him. In the aisle of the passenger car he was able to stretch his legs, and he cracked his spine by twisting left and right.

A lighted arrow pointing to the club car caught his eye, and judging by the saliva that suddenly poured into his mouth, he guessed a drink wouldn't be a bad idea. He walked effortlessly toward the front of the train, where the club car was located. He remembered riding an old diesel train as a kid, being tossed back and forth along the aisle as he struggled to the lavatory to throw up. Riding the Mag-Lev was much like flying, except that air travel was now exclusively reserved for the military and federal government. His last flight was on a double-decker hospital plane out of Oman to Germany, several lives ago.

He pushed quickly through two intervening passenger cars and arrived in the club car. Several other people apparently had the same idea and arrived just shortly before he did. He stood at the back of the line against the right wall of the car. The bar was ahead and took up the right half of the car. The left half of the car had several courtesy seats, arranged front to front so that riders could talk face-to-face.

As he waited, Matt glanced about the car, looking for nothing in particular. He did a double take on the second row of courtesy seats, and his heart began to pound. *Jenny?* He looked closely at the petite brunette in the second row. He stared now, fixed on the piercing green eyes just above the cover of the paperback novel she was reading, set off dramatically by her shoulder-length dark hair.

"Sir? Sir?" the bartender interrupted Matt's vision.

"Oh, sorry, uh, bourbon and ginger," he ordered.

Matt rested both elbows on the bar and closed his eyes briefly. *I wonder how Pasha's making out back in the baggage section.* The animal had never been in a carrying cage before, actually never in any cage before, and had protested loudly to Matt.

Matt's drink was shoved under his nose, and Matt handed over his plastic.

"Cash or credit?" asked the bartender.

"Cash account," replied Matt. Actually there was little hard currency left in circulation, but one's liquid assets account was always referred to as the cash account, mostly out of tradition.

The bartender placed the card on the laser reader, which, being an old clunker, took nearly fifteen seconds to read, record, and debit the transaction. The newer ones took under five seconds.

Matt took his drink and turned away from the bar, his eyes drawn automatically to the second row of courtesy seats. She was staring back.

"Want to sit here?" the young woman asked. She had taken up the last courtesy seat directly opposite her with a carry-on bag and removed it now so that Matt could sit down. *Or anyone could sit down,* he thought. *That's a legitimate offer.*

Matt's heart leapt. "I, uh, I, well, uh, yeah, okay, sure. Thanks."

He sat, his knees a respectable few inches from her. He smiled weakly, heart racing. *This woman is stunning,* he thought. Her nose wasn't quite the same as Jenny's, her mouth was slightly different, but otherwise she was his wife's picture. She smiled at Matt, then went back to her paperback. Matt's expression collapsed. *She was just being polite.*

"Long ride to New Columbia," he said feebly.

The woman lowered the book. "I bet. Fortunately I'm getting off in St. Louis." She raised the book.

Matt felt his stomach churn and his face flush. He took a sip from his drink and stared vacantly out the window at the vast and empty desert. He counted one hundred and twenty seconds to himself.

"Have a nice trip," he said, rising from the seat and stepping into the aisle.

The young woman raised her eyes and nodded pleasantly.

Matt stepped away, angry at himself. *I'm still not ready for any of this shit,* he thought. *I'm not setting myself up to get embarrassed like that. No more.*

Matt slumped back into his ticketed seat, crawling across the sleeping Asian lady so as not to baptize her with bourbon. He pressed the button on the seat back in front of him for the tray table, and it slid up and out from its housing. He set his drink down and dug into the carry-on bag he'd stowed beneath the seat. He pulled out a Department of Security briefing package on the Comarva Emergency Zone, which Frazier had given him. As he opened the front cover, he noticed Frazier's handwriting on the title page.

"Have fun in hell, kid" was all it said.

Karen Russell squirmed slightly in the uncomfortable chair. The glare from the setting sun, streaming through the window in front of her, made her squint, and no doubt the office was configured to maximize that effect. She stared across the desk at Dan Reilly, executive director of the National Association of High School Athletics Coaches, his back to the window. She hated coming up to his office.

"Next time we'll meet in public," Reilly announced. He opened a wooden box on his desk and withdrew a cigarette.

"That's illegal, you know," remarked Karen.

"No shit. I'm not a cop, so who cares? Are you going to arrest me?" asked Reilly.

"I forgot that Internal Intelligence was immune from the law."

"I think you forget that you work first for Internal Intelligence."

"How can I forget? I just like to get into the policewoman role, that's all."

"Well, turn policewoman off for a few minutes. And don't forget you still work for me." Reilly paused for effect. "So you've got Sheridan coming east?"

"He'll be in Comarva tonight. He reports for duty, to Parker, at 0800 tomorrow."

"We need to give him some time before our first meet. You're sure about this guy?"

"You've seen his record. I've talked with Mickey Briggs out in San Diego. He knows Sheridan's captain and the branch chief, Donnellson. They say the guy is straight as an arrow. Quiet, unassuming, apolitical, loyal. Doesn't like to get involved. Best of all for our purposes, the guy's a natural killer but won't admit it. Fearless. We'll have a bit of a problem getting him used to the lieutenant's job. He's turned down all promotion offers since he joined the force, but I think we can swing him around. A few psych quirks, but nothing dangerous," said Karen.

"I hope he's got some personality. Not just everyone can do infiltration work," said Reilly.

"Sheridan did some interrogation in the Corps. He's had a taste of the business. We're not starting from scratch."

"Refresh my memory. How'd we find this guy?" Reilly asked.

Karen Russell frowned, repeating the story for at least the third time in twenty-four hours. "We were investigating Sheridan's sergeant, Grafton, for possible ties with the CAPs. Turns out he's not a terrorist, just an asshole. We had an agent on him, Johnson, actually, the young guy outta Phoenix?"

"Name's familiar. Continue."

"Well, Johnson had just started the investigation of Grafton. It's funny, because Johnson had just finished at the Castle," she explained. The Castle was the nickname for the Jacobson Academy, a reproduction of a seventeeth-century French château outside Denver, where all Internal Intelligence agents received formalized training in their craft.

"So on his first draw he has to go to Federal Police Academy as part of his cover. Anyway, Johnson was doing background checks on all the cops in the substation, when he came across Sheridan's file. We've had it for a while. I wish we could recruit him directly into I.I.," she continued, "but he'd never work out. He's got no strong political leanings one way or the other, that we can tell. He loves his country, though, and that's what we need right now. That's what I'm banking on."

"Yeah, like our two captain friends in New England Division," Reilly interjected.

Russell frowned again. "Johnson gave me the whole story on the CAP shooting as soon as it happened, and so, given the circumstances, we rushed him out here."

Reilly stood and lit the cigarette. He turned his back to Russell and looked west toward the Blue Ridge Mountains, shading his eyes with his left hand. From his desk high in the Clinton Building in Tysons Corner, he could see the few remaining farms in northern Virginia beyond the urban sprawl. He dragged deeply on the cigarette, held the smoke in his lungs for a moment, then exhaled through his nose.

"I'm still not comfortable that we couldn't use party members instead. I gotta get someone inside the CAPs, but if he gets turned . . ."

"You know the party guys can't pull off the act. These bastards are sharp, Dan. If they don't have data on I.I. and party members, then they see right through them as soon as they approach. That's why our ops go down all the time. That's why we lose agents. And that's why Sheridan is perfect. He's an outsider—no close family, no political activity, no previous I.I. links. So he fits the profile of the CAP's recruiting targets. He's a cop; he's got access to weapons. They'll want him," said Karen.

"But can we trust him?" Reilly asked.

"Sheridan is a soldier. He follows orders. If he knows this is for the good of his country, he'll do it," she answered.

"And if he doesn't . . ."

"At this point, that's a chance we have to take," Karen interrupted.

Reilly took another long drag on his cigarette, then nodded. "Okay. I'll get back to you in a couple weeks and we'll see how he's doing. Make sure you run into him from time to time so he remembers who you are. So when you do approach him—"

"It's not unexpected, I know," Karen interrupted. "I graduated from the Castle too, remember?"

Reilly turned to her, smiling. He stared down his crooked nose at her, cigarette dangling from his lips. Though not very tall, the muscular fiftysomething-year-old emanated a powerful presence. His appearance lent credibility to his cover as a former high school wrestling coach.

"You know that this effort is receiving attention at the highest levels," he said, removing the cigarette.

"So you've told me. A dozen times."

"If we lose this guy, or he's compromised, there's a lot more to be lost than just our jobs. Our government is in great peril."

"I know exactly what's at stake," said Russell.

"Does Hudson have any clue as to what's going on?"

"He's pissed at me for hiring someone behind his back, but he'll get over it. I think I've sold him on the idea that I'm helping him out because of our relationship."

Reilly grinned and stubbed out the cigarette. He took a mint from the candy dish on his desk and popped it into his mouth. He tugged at the sleeves of his tunic to even them at the wrists. He cocked his head as he looked at Karen.

"And how is your little 'relationship'?"

Karen grinned. "At least he's good in bed."

"Think he's better than me?" asked Reilly.

Karen stood, brushing some imaginary lint off her suit. She did not look at Reilly, but turned for the office door.

"We'll never know that, will we, Dan?"

The River View Towers stood just outside Interstate 495, the Capital Beltway, in Virginia, just inside the recently expanded Alexandria city limits. River View Towers comprised seven relatively new, majestic, glass-paneled high-rise apartment buildings. They were located, conveniently, at the River Tower Metro Station. Matt struggled out of the station and across the street with a suitcase, a garment bag, his carry-on, and the screaming cat in the carrier. He made it into the lobby, where he claimed the key card he'd been instructed to pick up, filled out a few forms, and finally was bade good night.

He fumbled to the elevator, activated it with the key card, and took the opportunity to glance around the lobby. The building was late units-style in design and decor. There were a few chairs and a sofa in the lobby, obviously placed there out of aesthetics rather than comfort. He was impressed with the entry security system on the building (himself having to beg the night manager to let him in), which was of some comfort, since he was well within the Comarva E.Z. The district director required all of his men, as well as himself, to live in the E.Z. Matt could respect that.

The elevator arrived shortly, and Matt slung his belongings into the car. The rest of his sparse apartment furnishings would be delivered in a few weeks. No one else was waiting in the lobby, and when the elevator arrived, Matt boarded alone. He directed the voice-activated automated elevator to the eighth floor. Moments later, the ascending car slowed, then halted. The control computer announced the floor, the time, and the temperature. Matt stepped out into the hallway, headed toward apartment 801.

The lighting in the hallway was dim, but the light aqua-colored carpeting provided some brightness. The building had a sterile quality to it, not quite hospital-like, but at a minimum, it seemed controlled, secured. The air in the building was the typical "mock fresh" generated oxygen, with the same air being constantly recirculated through the "fresh-simulating" generator.

Apartment 801 was at the end of the long east-to-west corridor, into the middle of which the elevators opened. *At least I'll have a corner apartment,* he thought, *if never a corner office.* He set his various bags down in the hall, causing Pasha to meow even louder, and fumbled with the key card in the lock. The lock clicked open, and holding the door with one hand, Matt attempted to sling his bags in with the other. Pasha did not appreciate being tossed into the room.

Matt did not hear the door to apartment 805 open. He also did not hear the door close silently, nor did he hear the figure who strode up behind him. As Matt was wrestling the last suitcase into the apartment, a hand appeared on the apartment door just in front of his face. He dropped the suitcase and whirled around in a half-crouch.

"Oh, you scared the shit outta me," he said, breathing a sigh of relief.

"I'm sorry. I heard the cat out here, and when I saw you fighting with those bags, I thought I'd try to give you a hand," said a young woman.

"Huh. Thanks though. Fortunately that was the last one," said Matt. Unconsciously, he looked the woman over from head to toe. *About thirty-three, thirty-four, five seven, light brown hair, shoulder-length, brown eyes, round face, not beautiful, but . . . attractive. Standard curve-concealing athletic jumpsuit. Socks, no shoes. Long fingernails, haven't seen those in years.* As he returned his gaze to her eyes, he noticed she was grinning. *I'm busted,* he thought, realizing his quick glance up and down was as noticeable as a solar eclipse. *Nice smile.* Blood rushed to his face.

"I'm Courtney Powell," she said, grinning at his embarrassment. She extended a slender hand to him.

Awkwardly, Matt thrust his hand at her. "Matt Sheridan. Nice to meet you."

"Nice to meet you. I'm down in 805, let me know if I can help you with anything. I'm the semiofficial welcome wagon for the floor."

"Okay, uh, thanks. Courtney."

She turned lithely and walked back toward her apartment. Matt watched her walk away, again disappointed at the obfuscating nature of the jumpsuit. Halfway down the hall, Courtney turned, giving him a half wave, and caught him staring again.

"Good night, Matt."

Matt went into his apartment. "Good night, Courtney."

He stumbled as he entered, turning on the lights for the first time. The apartment was partially furnished. *Even when my things get here, it will still be only partially furnished,* he thought as he bent to release the frantic feline.

Pasha bolted from the cage and ran directly to the living room from the doorway, which was furnished with a single couch and a small entertainment console. The cat continued to the left of the living room into a small dining area, which contained a small table and two chairs. Pasha turned left again, skidding across a vinyl tile floor in the kitchen, and found himself back at Matt's feet at the doorway.

Matt reached down and picked up the animal. "You missed the bedroom, I think." He held the cat close to him and felt Pasha's heart racing. The cat was definitely agitated.

Matt walked down the hall from the doorway, past the living room into a longer hallway leading to the bedroom. The bedroom was a modest size and included a master bath.

Not bad for subsidized housing, Matt thought. In reality, all housing that was not privately held was subsidized by the federal government. One's rent payment was based on a proportion of one's salary, and any balance was guaranteed by the government. The federal government, as a means of controlling the prices of housing that skyrocketed after the blanket subsidies went into effect, owned most apartment buildings in the major metropolitan areas. This complex, too, was federal property.

Of course, I guess I am still paying for it one way or another, Matt thought. Nonsocial indemnity recipients such as Matt had seventy-five percent of their salary withheld for federal investment. It was steep and had been a sacrifice for many in the early years, but the New Liberty economic program had paid off the federal debt in eight years. New Liberty had instituted the social programs of the SSA, as well as the emergency defense force-structure rebuild program of 2004 to 2010, with no public debt.

In the bedroom Matt found a regent-sized bed (Matt still called them queen-sized, even though some found the term offensive), a small nightstand, a radio/alarm clock with a remote com handset, and a small dresser. Suitable.

Matt sat down on the edge of the bed, and the collective fatigue of his trip hit him like a MagLev. He managed to set the alarm, kick off his boots, and take his pistol from its holster at the small of his back. He realized he hadn't fed Pasha, nor put out a makeshift litter box, when sleep reached out to him with gentle but forceful hands and pulled him to her bosom.

4

Matt shielded his eyes from the bright morning sun as he looked upward in admiration at the Skyline Tower. Built in the late eighties, the angular glass building still gleamed, exuding confidence and power. The metro and electric bus rides had been uneventful, and Matt was silently thankful for the transportation "rebellion" that had taken place in northern Virginia in the late nineties. Disgusted commuters voted out of office, or forced to resign, every major planning official in the area, demanding common sense and vision in transportation planning. As a result, just over twenty years later, one could get from any point in northern Virginia to any other point in the Comarva area quickly and for a reasonable fee.

Matt entered the tower and went to the elevator lobby, noticing that the federal police offices weren't listed on the building directory. An elevator arrived and several people stepped out. He boarded alone. He asked for the twenty-first floor, and the elevator politely told him to have a nice day. With no other stops, Matt was on the twenty-first floor in fifteen seconds.

He stepped out of the elevator directly into a reception area. Hanging behind a large synthetic oak reception desk, he recognized the wall-sized emblem of the Department of Security. He approached the desk, and a young Asian woman smiled warmly at him. She was in uniform, which surprised Matt, since most other facilities had civilian or automated reception areas.

He returned her smile and handed her his plastic and orders disk. "Hi, I'm Matt Sheridan. Reporting for duty to, uh, Mr. Hudson."

The woman placed the plastic over a laser scanner, and Matt tried to read the reflection from her monitor on her soft brown eyes. The woman then popped the CD Read-Write into her computer and read Matt's transfer orders.

"Can I get a print please?" she asked, pointing to a handprint reader at the edge of the reception desk.

Matt did as he was requested, and after a few seconds the woman nodded. She handed the plastic and the disk back to Matt. A buzzer sounded and a paneled door, almost indistinguishable from the rest of the paneling in the reception area, opened to his left.

"Follow the hall all the way around to the Administrative Section. Someone there will escort you to Mr. Hudson's office."

Matt followed the hallway past numerous small offices and partitioned areas where the bureaucracy of law enforcement was obviously being handled. He marveled at the view from the window offices, the architecture of the building making nearly every office a corner office. He soon arrived at a large area divided by many partitions. As he approached, he noticed a man in his late thirties standing, apparently waiting for him. Matt extended his hand.

"Good morning, Lieutenant Sheridan. I'm Christopher Dino, Mr. Hudson's administrative assistant. He's waiting for you this way."

The man turned and walked down the hall. Matt followed him a short distance, and they turned, walking into an open office. An average-sized man with graying hair winced as he sipped scalding coffee, reading his monitor intently. He stood almost immediately.

"Ah, Lieutenant Sheridan. Welcome to Comarva. Parker Hudson," he said, extending his hand. "Please, have a seat."

Hudson directed Matt to a chair in front of his desk and nodded to Christopher. Christopher backed quietly out of the office, closing the door. Hudson sat on the front edge of the desk.

"Lieutenant, I'm glad you could make it here on such short notice."

"No problem, sir. Just following orders."

"Orders or not, I'm sure it's a major disruption in anyone's life to pick up and move like this."

"We'll see. I don't have a lot of baggage to carry around," said Matt. Parker nodded somberly.

"Detective, I want you to know that you are coming to us with recommendations at the highest levels. I was reviewing your file again this morning to familiarize myself some more. I thought we'd chat for a few minutes, then I'll have Captain Flavius Blair come by. He's the captain of narcotics detectives in the Comarva, and you'll be reporting to him."

Sheridan nodded.

"First of all, I want to say that I am very impressed with your military record. Actually, I'm honored to meet a real war hero. . . ."

"I'm not a war hero, sir. I did my job and survived, that's all."

"Well, looking at your record, if you're not a hero, I can't imagine who would be."

Matt looked down at his boots. "Sir, all the heroes are in ditches in Pakistan. I'm just a survivor."

Hudson looked away and cleared his throat. "Just so you know, I spent ten years in the army, MPs. I did three years in Kuwait City."

Matt grinned. "Lovely town, isn't it?"

Hudson shook his head and moved back to his seat behind the desk. He spoke in a slightly sharper tone of voice.

"You realize, Sheridan, that this is a major promotion."

"Not my idea, sir, but, yes, I do."

"I know it's not your idea, Sheridan, but you've got to live with it. And me. And the people you'll be working for. And the people who'll be working for you. I have just one question I want to ask you. You did a solid tour as a patrol officer, very quickly jumped to detective, and then you stopped. You've never taken the sergeant's exam, and you've turned down previous promotion offers. So why have you turned down the promotions?"

Matt sighed, then looked Parker Hudson in the eye. "I don't like ordering men to die. And I don't like ordering men to kill."

"Well, Lieutenant, I've got news for you. I don't like it either. Hell, I've had three officers killed this month. Another five were shot. And I can't count how many perps we've had to shoot. But sometimes we have to grow up and accept responsibilities. You've been selected for this job for your abilities and potential. The responsibility goes with the turf."

"And I don't have any choice."

"Correct. And I don't have any choice either, if I can be so frank. It wasn't my idea to bring you into this position," said Hudson.

Sheridan did not respond, but shrugged his shoulders.

Hudson rubbed the bridge of his nose, as he could feel a stress headache starting to grow behind his eyes. He touched the speakercom on his desk.

"Christopher, will you send in Captain Blair, please?"

A moment later a tall, lithe African entered the room. His eyes were hidden behind opaque black sunglasses, and the office light reflected off his clean-shaven head. He wore an impeccable police-issue jumpsuit, all the creases sharply starched. He turned to Parker and nodded. Parker directed him to the chair next to Matt. He sat quickly, crossing his legs.

"Lieutenant Sheridan, this is Captain Flavius Blair. Captain Blair owns all four hundred narcotics detectives in Comarva, and he will be your immediate supervisor. Captain Blair reports to Chief Sam Goldberg, who owns Narcotics, Vice, and Sufficiency Detectives. Chief Goldberg reports to Mr. Jimmy Franklin, who is director of detectives, who reports to me," explained Hudson.

Sheridan stood and turned to Blair. Blair looked Matt up and down once, but did not stand. Matt returned to his seat slowly.

"Flavius, I'm not going to go into too much about what Sheridan's duties will be, since that's your rice bowl, and I'll stay out of that. Most of the transfer circuitwork is complete, so there'll be only the routine stuff to finish when you get to the substation. I know Matt here was not necessarily your first choice, but I made the decision, and I'm sticking by it. I know you don't like a lot of things I do, so I'm not asking you to like this decision. Just make sure that Sheridan has the resources he needs to do his job."

"Matt, Captain Blair will take you over to Substation Alpha, in Alexandria. That's your duty station. I trust he'll fill you in some more. I apologize for the briefness of this meeting, but I've got eight thousand cops and a million bad guys to look after today."

Hudson stood, signaling that the meeting was ending.

"Lieutenant Sheridan, I'm sure you will excel in your new position, and I'm glad to have you on the team," Hudson said, more for Blair's benefit than Sheridan's.

They shook hands, Parker clutching Matt's left elbow in a traditional "feel good" squeeze. Blair folded his arms, making sure that both Europeans knew he would not shake today. Blair turned abruptly and, without word, strode out of the office. Matt nodded at Hudson and followed. Blair was two steps out the door ahead of Sheridan when Matt walked into Karen Russell, entering the room simultaneously. They bumped with moderate impact, and Matt could feel her breasts brush against his chest.

"I'm sorry. Excuse me," he said.

She grasped his upper right arm. "No, excuse me, I'm not watching where I'm going."

"Karen," Hudson called out from behind Matt. "Good timing. This is our new narcotics lieutenant, Matt Sheridan."

Karen made eye contact with Matt. "Lieutenant Sheridan, what a pleasure. I'm glad we were able to bring you out east. You've got quite an impressive record."

"Thank you, Ms. . . ."

"Russell. Karen Russell."

"As in East Region Director of Internal Security Karen Russell," Hudson interjected.

Matt was duly impressed. "Ms. Russell, it's a privilege to meet you."

Karen snorted. "Tell me that after you've been here a few months."

Matt opened his mouth to respond, but was cut short by Blair, standing at the end of the hallway.

"With all due respect, Ms. Russell, we have a lot of work ahead of us, and I need to get my new lieutenant"—he spoke the word *lieutenant* with the most scorn one could inject—"down to the substation and get him to work."

"Indeed. Carry on then, gentlemen."

Matt had already hoofed down the hall to catch up to Blair.

"Captain, I detect some animosity . . ."

Sheridan took his cue from Blair and rode in silence in the unmarked hummer to the Alexandria Substation. He noticed a change in environment as they moved through the Green Sector of the E.Z. to a Yellow Sector. Green Sectors were generally safe, where most commercial and public business was conducted. Green Sectors also contained most of the reimbursable housing, such as the Riverview Towers. Green Sectors were still dangerous as spillover areas, though, and therefore were the regions most recently incorporated into the E.Z.

Past the Masonic Museum, near the King Street Metro Station, Blair turned left onto West Street, continuing to Princess. The buildings in this area, the Yellow Sector of the E.Z., were noticeably more run-down than in the Green Sector. Many appeared vacant, or, at best, uninhabitable. Matt saw no more than a handful of people out on the streets. The area had a grayness to it that Matt had never quite seen before.

At Princess, Blair turned right and continued for two blocks toward the Potomac, approaching the Alexandria Substation. The Alexandria Substation had been built on the site of a former Alexandria Adult Detention Center, which was burned to the ground during riots in '01. Built with money appropriated under the Urban Emergency legislation, the substation served as headquarters of the Northern Virginia Division Narcotics Detectives, Comarva E.Z., Nova Narco, in the vernacular. The building itself housed numerous other Federal Police functions, but Nova Narco was its primary tenant.

Looks like a friggin' fortress, Matt thought as they approached the automated guard station at the vehicle entrance. Blair maneuvered the hummer in between what looked like two old-fashioned state turnpike ticket stations. Blair slid his plastic into a slot in the driver's side machine. Matt glanced idly at the station to his side. Behind a slightly less than opaque Plexiglas plate, Matt saw the distinctive six barrels of an Eraser. He cursed to himself.

Blair grunted something at Sheridan.

"Sir?"

"I said , 'We need to get an access code written onto your plastic.'"

"Yes, sir."

Matt returned his attention to the building as Blair proceeded slowly down the concrete ramp to the parking garage. Several metal barriers retracted into the ramp as he progressed. The building itself was windowless, blockish, and the color of sandstone. It seemed about five stories high and occupied most of a city block. It reminded Matt of the old CENTCOM headquarters in Riyadh.

Inside the parking garage, Captain Blair pulled into a spot bearing his name and rank stenciled in white, near the elevators. After another automated security check at the elevator, they rode to the third floor. The elevator opened directly into a hallway of offices. Most were empty. The hallway was the quietest law enforcement establishment Matt had ever been in.

"Welcome to Nova Narco," said Blair as they passed the modest offices. They were small, but, based on the single nameplate above each door, apparently accommodated only one officer. The walls, and doors to the hallway, were all glass. Matt could tell, as some of the office walls were smoky in color, that the glass was Multi-Shade, which darkened and lightened by user selection.

"Awful quiet," said Sheridan.

Flavius Blair's head snapped around.

"Funeral this morning, Lieutenant. We bury an officer a month out of this substation."

Matt stopped in his tracks, stunned. "Parker Hudson didn't attend?"

Blair scowled at Sheridan. "If Parker Hudson went to every cop's funeral in Comarva, he'd never work mornings."

"I had no idea . . ."

"Have. You have no idea. You don't have a clue what you've bought into."

"Respectfully, sir, I didn't buy into this. I was transferred. I didn't ask for this position. I was assigned."

Blair's brow furrowed. The volume of Sheridan's voice rose a notch.

"And respectfully, sir, I do have a clue. I may not have seen it in this magnitude, but I have seen the problem. I've gone through plenty of doors, and I've buried plenty of friends. I've been jumped by junkies, and I've knocked on nice suburban front doors at midnight to tell Mr. and Mrs. Whitebread that Junior was dead. Now, I didn't ask for this friggin' job, but that doesn't mean I can't hack it. Don't confuse my lack of titles with a lack of ability. You don't have to like me, Captain, and you don't even have to respect me if you don't want to. But you damned sure better not underestimate me," Matt said, his right index finger pointed in Blair's face.

Blair's first instinct was to snap the finger over backward, but he managed to restrain himself.

"That'll be the last time you point a finger at me, Lieutenant," said Blair quietly. He continued walking.

They walked without further comment to the end of the hallway to the door of a larger office, decorated with the name placard "Lieutenant." Beneath it was an empty placard slot. Two men sat in the office. They stood as Captain Blair entered the office.

"Lieutenant Sheridan, I'd like you to meet your two sergeants. Detectives Noah Benning and Oscar Vo." The European and the Asian each in order extended his hand to Matt. Benning was a fortyish European, rumpled, with dark brown hair and sleepy eyes, a thick mustache, and a thick middle. His grip was strong, but his hands were soft. Vo was a thirtysomething Asian, wearing an impeccable fall suit, slender, serious, severe. He wore his dark hair close-cropped, and he smelled of expensive cologne. His thin lips turned up ever so slightly in a very official smile.

"Detective Benning handled most of Lieutenant Solinsky's operational matters, and Detective Vo handled most of the scheduling and admin. Would you gentlemen agree to those statements?" Blair looked to the two men. Both shook their heads in the affirmative.

"And Lieutenant Solinsky?" asked Sheridan.

"Killed in the line of duty," said Vo quietly.

"A couple months ago, they brought a guy in here for questioning that we'd busted for possession with intent. Turns out he was a teke. We didn't have any of our teke officers present, so we didn't know he was working. They had him in one of the interrogation rooms, and they cuffed only one hand to the chair. He pulled Solinsky's pistol out of his holster from across the room and got one shot off with the free hand. Officer Sloane was in there with 'em, and he fired at the same time, but the teke drilled the lieutenant right here," Benning said, pointing a meaty index finger below his left ear. "Sloane shot the punk dead on the spot. Took Jake three days to die."

"Strange to find a teke like that," offered Sheridan, which elicited chuckles from Benning and Vo, but only a shaken head from Blair.

"You believe that one-in-a-thousand bullshit? Here in Comarva, we're closer to one in twenty. Something they don't tell you about in the Welcome to Comarva read file, Detective Lieutenant Sheridan. Oh, sure, the national average may be one in a thousand, but every goddamned one of them is out here. Comarva is the Federal States capital of jazz and tekes. We are the central distribution hub for the whole friggin' continent. This ain't San Diego, with its five-square-mile E.Z. We aren't busting high school Europeans who go into the wrong part of town for a quick jazz hit. We've got the pushers, the users, the addicts, the tekes. They've got the guns; they've got the plastic. That's why I'm burying a cop a month. This isn't crime anymore; it's guerrilla warfare. We gotta keep the Green E.Z. from going Yellow, the Yellow from going Red, and the Red from exploding. When we arrest these punks, where do you think they go? The prisons are full, my friend, and they send 'em right back to us. We're zookeepers, and the animals have guns!" lectured Blair.

Matt sagged into one of the mismatched synthetic leather visitor's chairs in front of the desk. "Great."

Benning looked down at his shoes, and Vo stared up at a ceiling tile he suddenly suspected was out of place.

"Well, Lieutenant, I'd love to stay and chat, but I've got important things to do. Sergeants Vo and Benning have actually pulled together a transition program for you, which I have already approved, so they can bring you up to speed on what's specifically going on right now. I don't have regular staff meetings; you'll come when I call. Don't come to me with problems unless you're going to prison yourself, or you're dead, in which case, I will call you. Your administrative assistant, Clark Rosecroft, should be along any minute. He's always late anyway. Any questions?"

"No sir," was all Matt could say.

Blair nodded to the two sergeants, then strode away down the hall. Composing himself, Matt walked to the chair behind his new desk.

When Blair finally disappeared in the elevator, Matt turned to the two men.

"Okay, first things first. You don't have to answer this question, but I'd appreciate an answer. Did either or both of you apply for this position?" he asked.

Benning and Vo looked at each other briefly.

"Both of us did, sir, I won't shit you. We made the lieutenant's list last summer, and we're about to expire. Have to take that damned test again," said Benning. Vo nodded his agreement.

"Well, gentlemen, I want you to know that if you feel like you need to transfer, or there's another lieutenant slot open, I'll understand. But I need you guys here desperately. I want to do what I can to keep you guys onboard."

Benning elicited no reaction. Sergeant Vo shrugged his shoulders.

"As of right now, I'm appointing two deputies. Sergeant Benning, you're my Deputy for Operations. Sergeant Vo, you're my Deputy for Administration. Official titles."

Oscar Vo looked quizzically at Sheridan. "Deputy Lieutenant?"

"Call it whatever you want. Everything goes through you guys before it gets to me. You make the decision and recommend it to me. I'll approve all your decisions. I want you guys doing exactly what you've done before, but now I want you in charge of your own areas. I'll be busy enough just trying to figure out what's going on for the next month. I'll put out an online this afternoon. Fair?"

Benning smiled. Vo frowned. They both nodded yes.

"Good. It's a done deal," said Matt. He rose to shake their hands when he noticed, beyond Benning's thick frame, a young African man bounding down the hallway toward them. He was short and stocky and his clothing was disheveled, one corner of his striped casual tunic hanging out of his sagging pants. He had his nose buried in some sort of colorful magazine, a hardcopy, and seemed to have another one rolled up in his back pocket.

"Can I help you?" Matt called down the hallway.

Benning and Vo both chuckled as the young man finally looked up from his hardcopy.

"That's your admin assistant, Rosecroft. He's somewhat infamous in the substation," said Detective Vo.

The African smiled broadly at the mention of his name as he neared the office.

"Clark H. Rosecroft, at your service," he said with an overdone flourish.

"Mr. Rosecroft . . ."

"Just Clark, please."

"Okay, Clark, nice to meet you," said Matt. As he looked Rosecroft up and down, he couldn't help staring at the bottom of a transdermal patch on his arm, partially covered by his short-sleeved tunic.

"Oh, you've noticed this already," said Clark, rolling up the sleeve. "I guess they didn't tell you, but I'm on temporary duty from Special Services. I'm your court-appointed teke."

The words were out of Matt's mouth before he could stop them. "I hate tekes."

Matt's head was swimming when he finally made it to the parking garage. It was almost ten o'clock when he finally sent Vo, Benning, and Rosecroft home. They'd covered quite a bit of background material, until finally exhaustion was appearing on each man's face. He counted off the numbered parking spaces softly to himself, until he reached the hummer that would be his while stationed in Comarva. It was a typical government-issue light beige hummer. As expected, the keys were in the ignition. He got in, turned the motor over, and headed out of the lot.

As he neared the exit, he noticed someone under the hood of a car. It was Benning. Sheridan pulled up next to him.

"Problem, Sergeant?" he asked.

Benning looked up at Sheridan. "Piece of shit's crapped out on me again. Third time this month."

"Tango Uniform?" Matt asked, then quickly looked around the garage. Even the abbreviation for the old navy slang "tits up" was a sufficiency violation.

Benning's frown fell, and he chuckled. "Tango Uniform," he said, nodding.

Matt gestured to the passenger seat with his head. "Come on," he said. "I'll give you a ride home."

Benning shoved his hands into his pants pockets. "Do you mind?"

"No, come on," said Sheridan, gesturing again. "It's late."

Benning closed the hood of the car and strode to the passenger side door. He sat down heavily, and Matt exited the garage.

Benning gave Matt the brief directions to his apartment, a mid-rise just a few miles away in a Green Sector. The ride was short, but uncomfortably silent. Pulling into the parking lot, Benning cleared his throat, then spoke.

"You wanna come up for a minute? Grab a beer? I really appreciate the ride," said Benning.

"It was no trouble," said Matt. "It's late though. You probably want to—"

"Naw, come on up. One beer," said Benning.

Matt shrugged his shoulders. "Okay, one beer. Thanks."

The two men emerged from the car and headed for the sidewalk to the apartment building.

As they approached the redbrick structure, three small faces appeared in a well-lit second-story window. Benning pointed.

"My kids are still awake," he said.

Matt smiled and nodded.

"You have kids?" Benning asked.

Matt's smile faded very slowly. He shook his head. "No, no kids."

"Oh," said Benning. "Married?"

"No. All I have is a cat," said Matt softly.

Benning shrugged. He didn't speak again until they had walked to the second floor of the building, and he opened the four locks on the door.

"It's just me," he shouted as the door opened. Benning and Sheridan stepped briskly into the apartment, and Benning closed the door.

The three small faces now appeared in the hallway as young boys. They ran to Benning, and he hugged each one in turn. They then turned and ran back through the doorway from whence they came. "Seth, Benjamin, and the little one is Noah, Junior," Benning said, pointing out the departing boys.

Seeing the young boys, so vibrant and full of life, Matt's chest began to ache.

"Great-looking kids," said Matt.

Almost on cue, a woman appeared from the adjacent dining room area. The woman was about as overweight as Benning was, dressed in a blue turtleneck and oversized jeans. Her light brown hair was streaked with gray, and she wore it big in the latest eighties retro style. She looked disjointed, perhaps even frumpy, but her sad green eyes and rounded face offered a fleeting glimpse of the beautiful young woman who had married the rock-hard athlete-turned-cop some twelve years before. She greeted Benning with a peck on the lips.

"Dear, this is Lieutenant Matt Sheridan. He's my new boss. My car crapped out, and he was nice enough to give me a ride home," Benning explained.

"Kathy Benning," said the woman. "Nice to meet you, Lieutenant."

Matt extended a hand, and they shook. Her hands were small but swollen. Matt looked into her eyes, and then at Benning. He could feel his chest tightening again.

"I offered the lieutenant a beer for his generosity," said Benning with exaggerated politeness.

Kathy winced. "Can I offer you a lemonade instead? We're out of beer." She turned to Noah. "Remember, you were supposed to—"

Benning grunted, then frowned. "Stop and get some on the way home tonight," he said, finishing her sentence. "I forgot."

Matt held up his hand. "That's okay. Uh, look, it's"—he glanced at his watch—"almost ten-thirty. I don't want to keep you away from your family anymore. Can I take a rain check on the beer?"

"You sure? It's no trouble if you want to stay," said Benning.

"I can make some coffee or iced tea," said Kathy. Matt felt a hot spear piercing his chest.

Matt smiled. "No, thank you. Another time. Thank you though, very much."

Noah and Kathy simultaneously looked a bit crestfallen, "You sure?" Benning asked.

Matt nodded. "I'm sure. Thanks for the offer though," he said, reaching behind him to grasp the front doorknob.

"Okay," said Benning. "Another time."

"See you bright and early tomorrow," said Sheridan, opening the door. "Nice to meet you, Kathy."

"You too, Lieutenant," she said, giving him a short wave.

Without another word, Sheridan was bounding down the steps, headed for his car. He gasped for air, overcome by a feeling of suffocation. As he walked rapidly for his car, he didn't notice the three faces in the window waving good-bye to him.

Matt looked across his desk at Noah Benning and Oscar Vo. Both men were visibly tired, their eyes growing redder and puffier by the minute. Matt was tired too, this being the third fifteen-hour day in a row since his arrival. He smiled as he looked over at Rosecroft in the corner of the office, his head resting on the back of his chair, snoring loudly, but still holding the department file they discussed some twenty minutes prior.

"So, from the looks of things, the Gutters are definitely the most dangerous of the jazz gangs," Matt said.

Oscar Vo rubbed his eyes. "Definitely. And they also hold the distinction of having the most dangerous leader." He slid a hardcopy picture to Sheridan, at which Sheridan stared. "Anthony Liu. His street name is Cha. Cha was a bad actor before he got into jazz gangs. Over two dozen juvenile arrests, followed by a career in crime. He's been recycled through this E.Z. six or seven times."

Matt nodded. Benning added, "Cha is a dangerous man. But the gang is extremely loyal to him. Just as much out of fear of his retaliation for disloyalty as anything else."

Matt rubbed his eyes and rolled his head around, his neck cracking. He lifted his left arm and rolled his shoulder, loosening the stiff joint.

"All right, enough. Forty-five hours in three days is enough."

Vo stood almost instantly, smoothing the wrinkles out of his suit. Benning turned in his chair and swatted Rosecroft across the shins with a backhand slap. Rosecroft woke with a start.

"Time to go home, sleeping beauty," grunted Benning.

Rosecroft stood, disoriented. "I was . . . uh . . . I was just reviewing the file on the . . ." He turned to the front of the folder to read its label, "The Duke Street Boys."

"Rosecroft, we did the Duke Street Boys, like, yesterday," said Benning. Sheridan and Vo laughed.

"Uh, Lieutenant Sheridan, it seems that I may have—"

Sheridan raised a hand to Rosecroft. "Forget about it. Good night, Clark."

"I was just—" continued Rosecroft.

"Good night, Clark," Sheridan repeated with a little more insistence.

Rosecroft gathered his files and staggered out the office door. "Good night, sir," he said, and disappeared down the main corridor.

Vo and Benning shared a laugh. "See you tomorrow, gentlemen," said Matt as they left his office.

Matt was collecting some CDs to review at home, when Benning reappeared in the office moments later. He was carrying a covered plastic serving dish. He knocked on the doorjamb, and Matt looked up.

"Sergeant?" Matt asked.

"Sorry to bother you, sir," said Benning, approaching the desk. "My, uh, wife, Kathy, sent this along for you."

Benning handed the dish to Sheridan. Matt extended his hands awkwardly to receive it. "Sergeant—"

"Noah, please. Look, when you said you couldn't stay the other night, my wife—"

"I'm sorry about that, Noah, but you see how much work I have. And I'm . . . generally not good company," said Sheridan.

"Well, anyway, I told her you were . . . single and living alone, so she thought . . . Well, she sent this so maybe you won't have to worry about cooking for a day or two."

Matt looked at the dish, then Benning.

"It's chicken something," said Benning, shifting his weight from foot to foot.

"Thank you very much, Noah. I really appreciate this. This is very nice of you," said Matt. "Please thank your wife for me. Tell her we'll get together another time."

Benning nodded. He began to retrace his steps to the door.

"You best go home and get some rest, Lieutenant. Leave that stuff for tomorrow," said Benning.

"We'll see," said Sheridan.

5

Jimmy White Horse was naked with the exception of his night vision lenses, lycra athletic supporter, and the Sykes-Fairbairn combat knife strapped to his right shoulder blade. He moved purposefully, neither slow nor fast, half-crouched to avoid low branches and to see the ground better. His head still swam a bit from the vapors of the black antiradiation camouflage paint that covered his body, but the twenty minutes he'd spent in the cold stream water had made him alert. He clenched his teeth to keep them from chattering in the forty-degree chill of the northeastern Pennsylvania forest. *I hope I live to catch pneumonia,* he thought.

Through the dense overgrowth, in the distance, Jimmy could see the first of the automatic rotating spotlights around the complex. He slowed to a stop and breathed deeply. Squatting, Jimmy could see the first set of heat sensors in the trees some twenty yards from his position, and just behind those, the motion sensors. He touched the marble-sized lump below his right eustachian tube for reassurance, then walked calmly toward them.

The body temperature of most forest animals was well above 98.6, and originally the mission planners thought that he should go into the sector overheated, maybe wearing a Borlon suit. However, for the sensors to register thermal presence without kinetic indications would most likely trigger an anomaly alert. And, judging by the number of bullet-riddled deer corpses the morning patrols carried out of the sector each day, they could pretty well figure which thermal and kinetic indications would trigger. The planners concluded that athermal and motionless was the way to penetrate the area.

The athermal part was easy enough. Combined with the antiradiation paint, lying naked in a mountain stream on a forty-degree night was certain to lower the body temperature just enough, temporarily, to get past the heat sensors. Motionlessness was tough to fake. Unless one was telekinetically enabled. *When in doubt, call in a teke,* Jimmy thought.

The effect had been especially difficult to create, and, so far as he knew, had never been officially recorded. While tekes had performed many remarkable feats in recent years, there was no record of a moving person simulating lack of motion. Not that it couldn't be done, just that it never had been done. Because absolute lack of physical motion was not possible, Jimmy would do the next best thing: Make the sensors believe that nothing was moving. While he could disperse or confuse the infrared emissions from the motion sensors, the sensors still would not receive a constant signal. The sensors did not necessarily detect positive motion, but, rather, detected deviations from lack of motion. After two months of daily experimentation and practice, Jimmy had honed a technique whereby he located the source of a motion sensor's infrared emissions, concentrated on the transmission sent out, then replicated the transmission in return. When he moved in front of a motion detector, it was as if his shadow was passing. And now, as a shadow, Jimmy began to cross through the sector.

The technique was especially exhausting, because it required absolute concentration on the infrared sensor and its emissions. He located the motion sensor covering the sector he was entering, then nestled high on a pine tree, its branches pared to allow clearance for the unit. Several yards away, he noticed the machine gun emplacement, probably with a three-hundred-sixty-degree field of fire, linked to the sensor. The sensor was working at five pulses per second. Jimmy concentrated on the return infrared pattern. Beads of sweat broke out on his forehead despite the aching chill that still gripped his body. He walked into the sector steadily, matching his steps with his breathing. There could be no interruption in his concentration as he matched the five pulses per second.

He could feel his strength being sapped as he neared the far edge of the sector. Lights were getting closer, and he could make out the shadowy outlines of the nearest building in the complex. The marble under his ear tingled as his body drew more of the toxin *xin ji* that enabled his actions. Sweat rolled into his eyes and stung him, and he bit the insides of his mouth to keep from wiping them. After seven agonizing minutes, he stepped into a clear-cut band of forest that skirted the complex, in front of the electric fences. He fell to the forest floor, gasping for air. He'd made it through.

He allowed himself only one minute to recuperate. Lying on his back, he looked up at the stars in the cloudless, moonless night sky. As a boy, he'd spent many nights in the Arizona desert, avoiding his alcoholic father, watching the stars gleam like the headlights on the highway that ran through the San Carlos Tribal Compensation Territory. He dreamed of getting off San Carlos, going away, far away, being free. The army was a good way to stay out of prison, in the beginning. Then airborne school, Rangers, the war in Iran, the mission. . . . He'd spent a fair amount of time in military prisons since then. And now he was risking his life to get back into a prison. But he had no intention of staying.

The Chase Federal Maximum Security Detention Facility had been a landmark in the Back Mountain region of Pennsylvania's Wyoming Valley. The most serious offenders from the Northeast were sent to Chase, mainly because of its reputation for security. No one escaped from Chase. As Chase became overcrowded like all the prisons in the Federal States of America, more and more candidates for incarceration in Chase were released in the emergency zones of Philadelphia and Pittsburgh. But there was one offender deemed dangerous enough to the government for an exceptional admission to Chase, who was at the time resident in the building closest to Jimmy, past the thermal sensors and beyond the electric fence. Roy Horace was one of the last men that New Liberty wanted out of prison. He was one of the first the CAPs wanted out. Horace could destroy New Liberty. For that reason, when he planned the operation, White Horse decided he would go in himself. This was the CAP's most important and dangerous mission to date. Jimmy White Horse was going to bring him out. With a little help.

Jimmy rose to a crouch and approached the fence. A huge spotlight swept the perimeter automatically, and he was careful to shield his vision from the light, lest his lenses blind him. The engineers calculated the maximum depression of the spotlight, and he knew that if he stayed close to the fence, the light would shine beyond him. He peered across the empty gravel yard, beyond the fence to a heavy emergency exit door. Behind a small window in the door he could see the outline of a face with his light-amplified lenses. By now the face was looking down at the handheld tracking device it had been provided. The americium capsule that Jimmy swallowed two hours before would be lighting up the small green bulb in the tracker. The bulb would be held up to the window in acknowledgment. The electric fence would go offline for fifteen seconds. No more, no less. After that, the alarm on the emergency door would go down for one minute. No more, no less. Then Jimmy would only have to defeat seventy armed guards inside. . . .

Jimmy picked the light in the window out of the night with his night vision lenses. He ran for the fence without hesitation. The fence was ten feet high, topped with two strands of barbed wire. He scrambled to the top of the fence, thankful that the links were copper-coated to conduct electricity and did not cut into his bare hands and feet. At the top, he laid his chest carefully across the barbed wire, grasped the far side of the fence, and propelled himself up and over.

The impact on landing jarred his body, the gravel crunching below his heavily callused feet. Jimmy shivered when the fence went back online, the hair on the back of his neck standing on end as the powerful current surged again. In an instant, he crossed fifty yards of the complex to the emergency door. It was open. He was in. Just under one minute left.

Inside the building, he discarded the lenses. *Not gonna worry about fingerprints,* he thought. *They'll know it was me anyway.* He was at the end of a dimly lighted corridor that turned to his right, to the south, at the opposite end. Just beyond the turn was the guard station, he knew, and beyond that station, his target.

He padded toward the turn in the corridor, drawing his knife from the scabbard on his back. The corridor was apparently an afterthought in the design of the building, some fire emergency requirement that everyone had forgotten; it was not lined with video monitors as most of the other corridors in the complex were. It was selected by the planning team specifically for that reason. Jimmy approached the corner and dropped to his stomach. He poked his head around the corner like one of the many snakes he'd hunted as a boy.

At the guard station, some fifteen yards from his position, sat two uniformed correctional officers. They were oblivious of his presence. As he surveyed them, he noticed that one, a tall, hard-looking man, wore on his lapel the crest of the Special Services division of the Department of Security, Internal. The other, a round, overweight man with an unruly gray mustache, did not. *Garden-variety guard. This complicates things,* Jimmy thought. He placed the knife between his teeth and rose to a crouch.

He focused his eyes on the overweight guard. The nameplate on his uniform read "Clancy." The other guard's nameplate read "Starr." They sat sideways to Jimmy, facing another corridor running from their station to the west. Behind them, to the east, was a security door. Clancy stared at a video monitor, and Starr keyed data into a computer terminal.

Jimmy began to move toward them, and the lighting in the corridor improved with every step. The guards would not expect someone to approach from this direction, however, and their minds would be slow to respond to the input from their peripheral vision.

Jimmy could soon see completely over the console, behind which the guards were seated, and he focused on the chair holding Clancy's wide girth. He concentrated. *Shit, this guy is heavy,* Jimmy thought.

Clancy's eyes widened as suddenly, unexpectedly, he and his potbelly were going over backward in the chair.

"Whoa!" he shouted.

"What the fuck!" shouted Starr, turning toward Clancy, showing his broad, muscular back to Jimmy White Horse.

The Native American closed the distance between himself and the console in four loping paces, knife now in hand. He struck like a phantasm turned loose from someone's nightmare, driving the knife in his left hand downward from behind, slicing through and crushing Starr's larynx. Starr clutched at his throat, forgetting about the American Arms Standard 9, 9mm pistol holstered on his hip. For good measure, Jimmy flipped the knife deftly to his right hand and slashed Starr from his right collarbone to his right shoulder blade. Nerves severed, Starr's right arm fell useless to his side.

Clancy was still struggling on the floor, unable to extricate himself from his chair. Jimmy concentrated on his lower jaw, and Clancy's mouth was pinned closed. He stepped on Clancy's right hand with his left foot, preventing him from reaching his sidearm.

Starr finally fell out of his chair, gurgling, paralyzed. Jimmy reached down and pulled Clancy's Standard 9 from its holster, clicked off the safety, and pointed it downward.

"If you want to live, you keep your mouth shut," instructed Jimmy White Horse. He unfurrowed his brow and Clancy was able to speak.

"Yes, sir," said Clancy, trembling.

"Open cell two. You fuck up, you die," growled White Horse.

"Yes, sir."

As Jimmy drew a bead on him, Clancy moved to the terminal in front of Starr's corpse. He punched in some codes, and a small red light went on above the cell two section of the control panel.

"You can open it right at the cell," said Clancy.

"Wrong. You're gonna open the cell . . ." said Jimmy.

Without further instruction, Clancy jumped to his feet and moved to the security door. Jimmy pushed it open and held it cautiously as Clancy moved through.

Behind the door was a row of six cells. Numbers two, five, and six held occupants. Jimmy went immediately to cell two, gripping Clancy's left arm.

The young man in cell two looked up, over the tops of thick glasses. His brow wrinkled all the way up to his curly blond hairline. He sat at a small desk, the cell around him crammed full of books. He set down the thick tome he had been reading, thoroughly confused.

Clancy pushed a release toggle on the cell door, and it recessed into the wall. The young man, of medium build and slightly tall, stood, tugging at the pockets of his bright blue jump suit. Jimmy motioned Clancy into the cell with the pistol.

"Mr. Roy Horace?" asked White Horse.

"Uh, yes," said the prisoner reluctantly.

"My name is James White Horse. I'm with the Confederation of American Patriots. I'm here to get you out."

"Uh, okay."

Jimmy White Horse flipped the toggle on the cell door as Roy Horace stepped out. Clancy sat feebly at the desk as the cell door closed.

"Mr. Horace, we've got to run like hell."

"Okay Mr., uh, Horse."

The two ran out to the guard station, turned right, and headed down the dimly lit corridor. At the end they turned left and sprinted for the emergency door. Only a few seconds left, thought Jimmy. They crashed through the door, and he held his breath. The alarm didn't trigger. It made little difference, because they were about to make noise anyway.

Out of the building on the gravel, Jimmy told Roy to cover his ears. He did as instructed, and Jimmy fired the pistol into the air, waited for a count of three, then fired again.

"Keep your fingers crossed," he said.

Exterior lights came on at several points on the building, and just seconds later the first alarm began to sound. The two men pressed their backs against the building, waiting. Jimmy concentrated on the emergency door, pinning it shut. Jimmy could hear voices from inside the building, some thirty seconds after he fired the shots, when he heard the humming in the distance. He couldn't help but smile, and he elbowed Roy Horace in the ribs playfully. Roy was still confused.

Over the treetops came the small black VTOL, its muffled turboprop engines purring. It crunched down on the gravel, rolling to a stop just feet from the two men. Jimmy could hear shots from a rooftop nearby.

A side door opened and the two men ran to it. A woman with close-cropped blond hair sat in the pilot's seat. There was an empty copilot's seat up front, and two bench seats in back large enough for four more passengers. The pilot smiled at Jimmy as he hopped into the copilot's seat. Roy climbed onto the passenger's bench.

"Let's roll!" he shouted over the whine of the turbines.

"No shit. Rock and roll!" shouted the pilot.

The first rounds began to carom off the aircraft's hull as the VTOL rolled a few feet and began to lift upward. After a cautious ascent of about fifty feet, the pilot opened the throttle, and the small craft disappeared into the night.

* * *

Another week of this crap will kill me, Sheridan thought. He was struggling with four ecobags of groceries, attempting to put his key card in the door without having to set down the bags. He had spent the past week almost exclusively in the company of Rosecroft, Benning, and Vo. They were drilling him on local procedures, ongoing investigations, and notable miscreants in the E.Z., and giving him guided tours of some of the most dangerous neighborhoods in North America. Their unmarked hummer had been shot at twice, hit once. Every time Matt got to a point in his tutelage where he thought he could make a break for the field by himself, another call from the good Captain Flavius would come in, "suggesting" the "transition team" review another case, tour another neighborhood, read through another manual. *This shit is wearin' me out,* he thought.

Matt had almost maneuvered the card into the slot, when the weight in one of his bags shifted and slid off his hand. The bag landed in the hall with a crash, as two of the four bottles of Spanish red wine therein smashed against each other. Matt's door swung open easily. Somewhere inside Pasha meowed at him.

"Shit!" Matt shouted louder than he had expected. He bent to retrieve the soaked and dripping green mesh bag.

The door to 805 opened, and the young woman he'd met in the hallway *(Courtney, wasn't it?)* emerged, laden with a laundry basket. Matt spun his head in her direction.

"Hi! Sorry I made so much noise."

"Oh, hi. I really didn't hear anything. These doors are pretty thick. Just headed down to the sonics to get some laundry done." Courtney noticed the dripping bag.

"Oh, no, was that wine?" she asked.

"*Was* wine, yeah," said Matt, standing with the bag at arm's length. "Fortunately, it looks like two of them lived." He shoved two grocery bags into the apartment with his foot. He set the third down and reached into the fourth, withdrawing a dark, one-liter glass bottle.

"Yep, two bottles. Good Mediterranean red too."

"Sounds goods," said Courtney.

The words were out of Matt's mouth just as he was trying to stop them. "Care to join me for a glass?" *Shit, no!*

Courtney smiled. "Sorry. I've worn my last article of clean clothing today." She lifted the overloaded laundry basket for emphasis.

Matt could feel his face burning. *I wonder if I look just red, or beet red. Try not to look completely foolish,* he thought.

"It won't take long though. The new sonic can run a load in about ten minutes. Maybe I'll stop by later," she said.

Matt weakly returned her smile, knowing a polite excuse when he heard one. "Anytime. I'm not going anywhere." *How true!*

Without further word, Matt grabbed the two bags in the hall, entered his apartment, and closed the door. Pasha was waiting inside, twitching his tail in a doglike fashion.

"Pasha, my man, I will never learn to keep my mouth shut. Talking before thinking is really becoming a problem."

Putting away the groceries and cleaning up the residual mess from two bottles of spilled red wine, took several minutes. He finally got everything into its proper place, neatly aligned in the cabinets. He stocked his food in roughly alphabetical order in the cabinets, to keep it neat. Jenny always hated that and used to drive him nuts by secretly swapping the places of the macaroni and cheese with the cereal (*Jenny, there are Ms in the Cs again!*).

After checking the automatic dispenser on Pasha's food and water bowls, he poured himself a full glass of wine and settled into his easy chair, which had recently arrived from San Diego. As usual, he turned on CNA (Central News Agency) with the sound off and selected Berlioz's Symphonie Fantastique. Another good brooding piece. He forced his boots off and extended the chair's footrest.

Feet up and eyes closed, he finally began to unwind. He had a sudden craving for a Havana cigar, but quickly pushed the thought out of his mind. *Cigarettes will get you a citation, but a cigar will get you jail time.* He was drifting off to sleep, near the end of the second movement, when there was a light tapping on the door. He was slightly startled, a bit disoriented, but he shook his head to clear it, then headed to the door. It was Courtney.

The distinguished, muscular man with the twisted nose stood next to the tall, long-legged blonde in the history section of the CD store. They were alone.

"Thanks for meeting me on short notice," said the man.

Dan Reilly never says thank you, thought Karen Russell. "It's my job, Dan. You're the boss."

Reilly grunted. "You've heard that Horace is out."

"A little while ago, yeah."

"No one realizes how dangerous Roy Horace is. People will die. People are going to get killed."

"People are already dying, Dan."

Reilly scowled. "No shit, Karen."

They stood without speaking for almost a minute as some other customers passed the history section, headed for the pop culture section.

"What's Sheridan's status?"

"He's been on only a week. They're keeping him busy with admin stuff, from what Parker tells me. They figure if they can keep him in the office doing circuitwork, he'll be out of their way on the street. I haven't seen him."

"We need to get him in as soon as possible. When can you approach him?"

"Dan, this will take a couple of weeks. I'm not gonna just walk up to him and say "Hi, Matt, remember me? Wanna be an undercover intelligence agent?"

Reilly scowled. "As quickly as possible. Just make it happen."

The casual discussion had roamed freely, starting with cats, ranging to apartments, living spaces, and the dread of moving.

". . . so with my entire life's possessions of basically what you see in this room, I moved back east," said Matt. He sat facing backward in one of his two dining chairs. Courtney sat politely in his easy chair across the room, not too close, not too far. He drained the last of his third glass of Spanish red.

"So you're from around here originally?" Courtney asked. She was still working on her first glass of wine.

"Well, Pennsylvania actually. Can I freshen up your beverage?" He pointed to her glass.

She looked at the glass and nodded. "Sure, this is excellent."

He walked to her to take the glass, careful not to accidentally touch her fingers in the exchange. *Our little chat has gone quite nicely so far,* he thought. The wine had loosened him up enough to talk without his usual paranoia of embarrassment or impropriety. He was in the critical transition phase of the alcoholic effect, where he was still charming. *One more glass of Spanish red certainly wouldn't hurt.*

Taking her glass, he turned and headed toward the kitchen.

"Do you always wear your gun?" Courtney asked in a quiet voice.

Matt patted the small of his back in his habitual manner.

"Oh, sorry. I always forget to take it off. I guess I take it off only to sleep."

"No reason to be sorry, I was just . . . you know, startled for a second," Courtney said with a nervous laugh.

Matt reached around and unsnapped the holster from his belt loop. He set the gun, in its holster, on the dining table. He went to the kitchen and began opening the second bottle of wine.

"Well, I can understand being wary of guns, considering where you live. If it's not too presumptuous of me, can I ask why you're living in a Green Sector Emergency Zone?" Matt called from the kitchen.

Courtney sat up straight in her chair.

"I teach at an on-site school in Arlington."

"On-site? I thought all the schools had gone to remote instruction. Jeez, they taught on-site back when I was in grade school."

"Well, I teach early elementary to physically challenged children. They need the special attention they can't get from a computer."

Matt returned to the living room with the wine. "I thought only cops and crooks lived in E.Z.s."

She mock-scowled at him. "Well, I'm neither one of those, so you thought wrong. Actually, a lot of hardworking, honest people live in Green, and a few in Yellow Sectors here. People have to live somewhere, and we can't all afford to live in unsubsidized suburbs."

"You just don't seem like the emergency zone type, that's all."

"Why, because I'm European?" she asked, frowning.

"No, because you didn't try to steal my groceries tonight," Matt said. He sighed to himself as she smiled again.

"So you must not be from around here originally either," he said.

"No, I'm from upstate New York, near Syracuse."

"Not too far from where I grew up. Wilkes-Barre."

"Wilkes-Barre, really? I've driven through there on the interstate a hundred times."

"One of our main resources, the interstate."

The conversation lulled for a moment. *Think of a topic, think of a topic*, Matt's mind raced. *Just don't say anything stupid.* Courtney broke the silence. Weighing at least seventy pounds less than Matt, the red wine was starting to work on her system too.

"So, do you like being a cop?"

Matt stared into his wine. "Well, yes and no. I mean, this job is better than any of the others that were available to me when I got out of the service, but . . . I'm not a cop. It's weird, but I just don't fit into their society. I've had a couple of friends who are cops, but I didn't really socialize with them. These cops, my men, detectives, especially, are different. They socialize together, live near one another; their wives talk to one another. It's a little society within society. And they're good people too, despite all the hate they deal with everyday. I'm . . . just not one of them."

"Then what would you rather be doing? You said you were in the Army?"

"Shock Marines, actually. My service days are over. I was sort of a linguist."

"Linguist doesn't sound bad."

"Yeah, that's what the recruiter told me. But when they're short on infantry specialists, guess what the linguists do." The tone of Matt's voice had hardened somewhat.

"Oh, no," she said softly. "I'm sorry I mentioned it."

"No, don't be sorry. I'm the sorry one," Matt said. *Here's another golden opportunity beginning to spin out of control toward the ground,* he thought.

Courtney stood and smiled, walking toward Matt. She took one more sip of her wine and set the half-empty glass on the table behind him.

"You're not sorry. I've enjoyed our little visit. I'd love to stay longer, but I've got clothes to fold. Next time it's my treat."

Matt stood and walked her toward the door.

"I'll take you up on that," he said, holding the door open for her.

"I hope so. Good night, Matt," she said. She took his right hand with hers and warmly pressed her left hand to it.

"Good night," Matt said, closing the door. *Hey, look, I'm smiling.*

Owen Thomas limped through the scattered underbrush, stepping heavily on his left foot and leaning on a cane to assist his right leg. His long hair, formerly gray, now silver, nearly white, was pulled back into a tight ponytail. He breathed in the fall morning air, just on the cusp between warm and cool, and let the scent of the towering pines clear his head. He was approaching the line of ten men lying on their stomachs in the dirt. He transferred the cane to his left hand, as the arthritis in his bullet-shattered right ulna was beginning to spread fire through all the nerves in his arm. He approached the men, propped up on their elbows, firing Winchester .300 Magnums slowly, carefully, at targets some two hundred yards in the distance. These were the ten best marksmen in the CAP organization, sent from local cells as far away as California and Florida to train at the current national headquarters. Wherever Owen Thomas happened to be at any given time was really the headquarters, and right now that just happened to be the Pocono Mountains.

The weapons roared one after another, but Thomas did not cover his ears or jump at any report. He stood with arms folded, behind the first man. He observed with his right eye, the left long since lost. The empty socket was covered by an eye patch.

The first rifleman squeezed off a round, and Thomas tapped the sole of his foot with his cane. The rifleman looked over his shoulder at the middle-aged man and smiled. Thomas returned the gesture and grunted.

"Let's have a look."

Dutifully, the rifleman worked the bolt on the Winchester, clearing the rifle, and handed the weapon to Thomas. He took the rifle and put his right eye to the telescopic sight. He quickly acquired the target in the scope. All the shots were within the center bull's-eye ring.

"Don't waste any more ammo, son, you're shooting fine," said the former general.

"Thank you, sir," replied the rifleman. Thomas had already moved on.

He followed a trail down a small hill that led to the rear entrance of a gymnasium. The building looked abandoned from the outside.

As he reached the building, he pulled open a creaking, rusted door, hanging on to time-rotted hinges. He stepped into a pitch-black vestibule, across which was another, more substantial door. This, too, he pulled open. He was then in a brightly lit room, with a double-reinforced steel door. He punched a code into the practically antique electric cipher lock, and the door clicked. He pushed it open.

He entered the playing area of the gymnasium, converted now to the national operations and command center. He waved weakly with his right hand at the three men behind the .50-caliber machine gun just opposite the door through which he entered. They nodded to him.

He limped on toward a cluster of cubicles created with six-foot portable partition walls. Numerous men and women typed feverishly at computer stations, some simultaneously talking on the com. With her long, dark hair piled on top of her head, Judy Duba hurried up to him.

"Judy, I want only good news," said Owen Thomas. She was his unofficial deputy in the organization, one of the group from New Liberty's Progressive Caucus who had originally supported Owen's presidential candidacy.

She grinned. "Follow me, then, old man."

She walked past him and around the closest portable partition and peeked around the corner. Judy knew he hated frivolity like this, but her own excitement was betraying her.

"Our latest import model from Canada has just arrived," she said.

Thomas rounded the corner and saw a muscular young man with long, dark hair seated at a desk, scanning computer files. He stood when he saw Owen approach.

"White Horse. Took you long enough," said Thomas.

"A month was quick," said the young man.

"Did you bring your friend with you?" asked Thomas.

"No, I left him in Canada," said the young man sarcastically. Few people could afford that kind of sarcasm with Thomas. Owen smiled, then extended his aching right hand.

6

The President of the Federal States, Henry Kersey, looked through tired gray eyes at the men and women assembled around the conference table in the large classified meeting room in the West Wing of the White House. Approaching seventy, and though he moved more slowly than when he first became president, intensity still burned in his eyes. Kersey was in the first year of his fourth full term as president.

His last challenge for the office had been during the campaign of 2016—2015, actually—when one of his own party members, a retired general, made a run for the nomination. The general was gunned down in Las Vegas by a mentally challenged man who believed himself to be Sirhan Sirhan. But New Liberty persevered and fought on for social justice.

The past twelve years had been successful beyond his, and the founders of the New Liberty party's, wildest dreams. New Liberty had accomplished much for the American people in the past fourteen years, and for the world. The Mexican Insurrection was put down. The Chinese were stopped in their gambit for the Middle East. And American business had come to the aid of a crushed and humbled Europe in the worst times of their own Depression.

And still there were those who threatened his government. Ruthless terrorists who would kill man, woman, or child without compunction.

He'd called the National Industrial Council to reassure them that, despite the recent spike in incidents of the Confederation of American Patriots's terrorist activity, his administration was working quickly to stamp out the problem. He would meet later in the day

with the National Media Council as well. The members of these coun-
cils, and the estates of American government they represented, were
close partners in this new America.

Kersey lifted his head, the signal that the meeting would begin.
Unconsciously, he ran his hand along the right side of his full head
of gray hair. *Always, image.*

"Ladies and gentlemen, I want to thank you for assembling on
such short notice. I will try to make today's meeting very brief," he
pronounced. He glanced around at the attenders: Mary Dunleavy,
Entertainment and Leisure; Brian Kimble, Manufacturing; Jancy
Kramer, Health; James Covey, Transportation; Wilber Gross, Agri-
culture, Food, and Beverage; Cynthia D'Aluiso, Information Systems
and Technology; and council chairman, Frank Bremer, Energy. A few
were absent, but the president couldn't remember who they were.
Normally, he'd have one of his snot-nosed private-school minions to
prompt him, but this morning's meeting was closed-door. He had no
other White House staff present. *Besides, this was as much a New Liberty party meeting as it was an executive to industrial branch meeting.*

He continued. "We've all read the latest unclassified precis from
Internal Security on the rise of terrorist incidents in the country,
specifically concerning the Confederation of American Patriots. I
have no need to explain to all of you the threat that they pose to
America and her citizens, and the threat they pose to American government and industry. Let me reassure you, though, that I have read
some of the restricted planning data that has resulted from the precis. Our Internal Security personnel are the best in the world and
are making important progress against this terrorist group. I ask for
your continued cooperation in the industrial branch, as you have always so graciously given, and in a very short time, I assure you, we
will have this threat under control."

The president turned to walk out of the room, no further dialogue
or questions necessary. *This was how I like to end these meetings,* Kersey
thought. *No haggling, trick questions, petty bickering. I'm the goddamn President of the Federal States.*

"No, Kersey!" shouted Frank Bremer, slamming a meaty fist into
the table, loud enough to startle several council members. "'Under
control' is not good enough. 'A short time' is not good enough."

President Kersey turned toward Bremer slowly, disdain on his face but anxiety in his heart. Bremer, a two-hundred-plus-pound six-foot-three Texan, stood. A huge longhorn-steer belt buckle appeared incongruously from beneath the table as he stood, set off from his mega-buck Italian suit. As he pointed a thick index finger at Kersey, plainclothes Secret Service agents emerged from behind doors at either end of the room. Kersey signaled them with both hands, and they paused.

"Goddammit Kersey! People are getting killed. Americans. These are terrorists on American soil!"

"You're right, Frank," said the president, evenly. "You're absolutely right."

Matt stared at his watch as eight o'clock neared. This was the third Wednesday in a row that Courtney was coming over for a glass of wine. Though they'd talked at length, Matt realized he'd said little, keeping to topics like the weather, sports, and current events. He'd revealed very little about his personal life, in fact almost nothing. But then, neither had she. Nonetheless, he was enthralled. He kept thinking about her, hoping to pass her in the hallway, looking forward to the next Wednesday. *This is almost like some Pushkin romance of chaperoned meetings and sterile discussions,* he thought. *With wine instead of kvass, of course.* He'd struggled with himself to open up, but . . . he just couldn't. He was afraid if he opened up a little, he wouldn't be able to close up.

The knock at the door startled him despite his anticipation. He trotted to the door and opened it.

As expected, there stood Courtney, smiling. She was in a sweatshirt and jeans, casual but premeditated. Matt returned her smile. "Come on in," he said, making a sweeping gesture to the apartment with his right hand.

"Thanks," she said, breezing past him. *She smells good,* Matt thought.

She walked toward the dining room table, where their previous conversations had taken place. He had in advance prepared two wineglasses and opened a bottle of red wine. He pulled back her chair a bit for her to sit down, then he seated himself.

"Red wine?" he asked.

"Of course," she said, grinning. He poured two glasses.

"Cheers," he said, raising his glass to her. She did the same.

"Exciting day today?" she asked.

He shrugged. "The usual. I still haven't had much time on the streets yet. I'm bogged down with these damned administrative projects. I want to try to get a little closer working relationship with my men, but they still seem a little cool to me so far. Oh, well," he said. He noticed that she was staring at her glass.

"You?" he asked.

"Nothing exciting for me. The usually teacher business," she said. Suddenly her eyes widened. "Did you see the news about that CAP attack in Pennsylvania?"

Matt nodded. "I caught something a little while ago. They broke into a prison or something up in Pennsylvania, right? Actually near where I grew up."

Courtney nodded vigorously. "They said there were a dozen of them, killed some guards and freed some murderers."

Matt shook his head in disgust. "Nice bunch of guys, huh?"

"It's frightening," said Courtney. "My father is a New Liberty ward captain up in Syracuse. There's a bunch of them out in the woods up there. He's scared to death of them."

"Has he ever been threatened by them?" Matt asked.

Courtney wrinkled her brow and pondered for a moment. "No, not personally. Not that I can think of. Why?"

"Just curious. Police guy stuff kicking in," said Matt, shrugging.

"Have you ever had a run-in with them?" Courtney asked.

The image of the shooting in San Diego flashed in Matt's mind. "A couple of times."

"Are they as bad as they say? President Kersey says they're the number one threat to the country right now," she said.

Matt shrugged. "I guess I know only about as much as anyone else. They seem like a real bunch of bastards. They've taken up arms against the government."

Courtney nodded. "Well, I'm glad I'm not involved with New Liberty anymore."

"You used to be?" Matt asked.

"Well, I helped my dad out with some of his projects before I went to college. That was back in the early days. I never continued in college."

"That's good," said Matt, instantly regretting his phrasing.

"Why do you say that? You don't like New Liberty?"

Matt shifted in the chair, then drank. He reached the wine bottle across the table to Courtney and filled her glass. "I can take or leave New Liberty, I guess. Politics just turn me off. Too many better things to be doing with one's time."

She smiled, then said in pedantic fashion, "But you can't have a representative government without politics."

"Nothing changes. Why bother?" he said, a hint of frustration in his voice.

"Well," said Courtney, raising her eyebrows, then sipping her wine. "Then do you follow football?"

Matt smiled. "I love football."

They discussed the sport for nearly twenty minutes before the bottle of wine ran empty. Courtney excused herself when it did, kissing Matt softly on the lips before returning to her apartment.

Matt Sheridan rubbed his aching eyes as the light in his office got worse. It was eight o'clock, and he had been in the office for fourteen hours. The last twelve he spent staring at his terminal, alternately typing and dictating. Clark Rosecroft sat on the other side of the desk, staring at an auxiliary monitor they'd hooked up to Matt's machine. Matt was filling out the required information related to a shooting in which one of the Nova Narco detectives was involved earlier in the week. Mike Bromberg, an eight-year veteran of the force, had pursued a jazz dealer, who'd just sold him four liquid ounces (a month's supply for a serious addict) through Alexandria, and had run the perpetrator off the road just across the E.Z. boundary into Fairfax County. Before Bromberg's backup could arrive, the jazzer jumped from the car and began firing a pistol at the detective. Bromberg returned fire, killing the dealer. Counsel for the county, the state, the public defender, and the civil liberties agency had arrived before the dealer's body was removed from the scene. Sergeant Benning had filed his reports, and Captain Blair was prepared to file his, but could not without Lieutenant Sheridan's report. Lieutenant Sheridan's report, equal to fifty hardcopy pages, was still incomplete. Sheridan rubbed his eyes again.

"Next time anybody shoots a perp in pursuit, they damned sure better drag the bastard back into Alexandria before they call in," Matt swore, swiveling away from the monitor in his chair.

"That would make everything easier. But I'm sure you mean that in jest, and not in a serious opposition to the civil rights and civil liberties regulations imposed by the Social Sufficiency Amendment?" queried Rosecroft. The twinkle in Rosecroft's eyes told Matt his chain was being exquisitely jerked.

"Have I mentioned that I hate tekes?" he retorted.

"Numerous times."

Matt stood, hands thrust in his pockets. He was having a hard time concentrating on the report. He'd dreamed of Courtney again last night, dreamed of making love to her. He wanted to see her again soon. Yet here he was, stuck filling out paperwork attesting to the fact that Detective Bromberg had received his required sensitivity training for the past two quarters, and on and on.

Abruptly, Matt said, "Rosecroft, what do the personnel think of me?"

"Excuse me?"

"What do they think of me? For as long as I've been here, nobody besides you and Benning has really talked to me without it being official business. I mean, I hear muttering in the halls, conversations stop when I enter a room. What's the problem? Straight shit, Rosecroft."

Rosecroft squirmed a bit in his seat. He'd long since kicked off his boots, and now wiggled a big toe sticking through a hole in his sock.

"Straight shit? They don't know what to think of you. They think you're aloof. They also think that you're humorless and stiff, mainly because you've displayed no humor or loosened up around them. They also think you're useless because Blair won't let you run your own shop or get out on the street."

Matt slumped into the visitor's chair opposite Rosecroft. "Useless?"

"Perhaps my characterization was a bit strong. Ineffectual."

Matt propped his chin in his hand. "Humorless?"

"You asked for my opinion, straight shit."

"Well, then, tell me how I can start to loosen up. I want my men and women to at least respect me, if not like me. I'd hate for them to think I'm an asshole."

"*Asshole* is your word, sir."

"Thank you, Rosecroft," snarled Matt.

"To start, you could drink a beer with the day shift when they get off. That's always good for bonding. Loosen your cravat. Tell an illegal joke or two. They like that. When you live with pressure, with your ass in danger for eight, nine, ten hours a day, you need a release. I think you're capable of that."

"You're absolutely right. Let's forget this friggin' Bromberg report for tonight and get the hell out of here. Blair is gonna be mad at me anyway. I'm buying if you know a good spot."

A smirk appeared on Rosecroft's face, which quickly grew into a beaming smile.

"I know just the place."

The ride north on Old Confederate Highway had been uneventful despite the fact that Sheridan's unmarked hummer passed through a few dangerous Yellow Sectors. He grew concerned as Rosecroft directed him to continue north, and they neared the area of Arlington, Virginia, formerly known as Crystal City. The '04 recession left the tall, gleaming office towers vacant and neglected. The area had lately become a haven for jazz dealers and housing-impaired E.Z. denizens. The net result was that the area was declared a Red Sector, and no regular police protection was extended into it. Jazz dealers and their muscle flunkies walked the streets openly porting automatic weapons. The area reeked from the accumulation of unburied dead bodies: suicides, overdoses, double-crossed dealers, warring gangsters, and desperate buyers. National Guard units performed weekend service by escorting Health Department vehicles that attempted to clear the bodies once a month.

They exited the highway at 12th Street and turned right onto Eads. They then turned left on Army-Navy Drive. Rosecroft directed Matt to pull into a dimly lit parking lot on Fern Street, just across the line from the "Coffin City" Red Sector, as it was known.

"Nice part of town," Matt muttered, exiting the car and patting the small of his back.

"Hey, we're cops. Relax," said Clark as he led Matt across the lot to a run-down twelve-story office building. Over the entrance to the bottom floor there was a neon sign that flashed SHANKY'S.

They passed through the door into the darkened bar. A machine was blasting randomly generated techno-rock, running the currently popular protocols. In the center of the establishment, on a raised, lighted stage, a naked young blond woman with preposterously large, augmented breasts gyrated at least one-half beat out of sync with the music. A huge bald European with a scraggly goatee rose from the stool he was warming by the door. Clark reached into his tunic pocket and produced plastic, which he flashed to the European.

"My guest," said Rosecroft, pointing to Sheridan. The bouncer nodded and waved them past.

Clark shouted into Sheridan's ear above the blaring music. "The owners are geniuses. Just before the Sexual Exploitation Statute went into effect a couple of years back, they bought this place for next to nothing, due to its charming location, and the fact that its main attraction was about to become illegal. Then they applied for, and received, a grant from the National Arts Foundation to study the relations between human kinetics and sexuality in the arts. Thus, when the statute went into effect, they were exempt from prosecution, since they were conducting government-funded research. Now, it just so happens that private contributors to the research effort, like myself," he said, flashing his plastic, "often like to stop by and view the research. And of course, you have to be able to feed and water your benefactors . . ."

Matt laughed out loud, shaking his head. They moved toward the bar, located at the rear of the establishment, beyond the center stage and numerous surrounding rickety tables. As they approached the bar, Matt smelled a vaguely familiar odor, then saw nearly a dozen small orange-red lights trace arcs in the darkness.

"Cigarettes?"

"Yeah, the patrons can usually tell who the cops are," explained Clark.

"And they're ditching their cigarettes?"

"Yeah. Funny thing is, the unspoken rule in here is that when cops come in, as some of us do with some frequency, we leave our badges outside. I mean, if we started enforcing the infractions in here, everyone in the whole place would be incarcerated. Exploitation, social insufficiency, alcohol consumption by unhealthy persons, building code violations, and on and on. But if we busted the place, we'd have no place to go; this is the only establishment of its kind within a hundred miles. But two things don't float: smoking and doping. They made me, so they're ditching their cancer sticks," explained Rosecroft.

Sheridan continued laughing. They finally reached the bar, and two patrons were eager to offer up their seats. Matt and Clark obliged them and plunked themselves down. As one of the bartenders approached, Matt slid his plastic across the grimy bartop toward her. She was a heavyset woman in her forties, with a beautiful smile but ponderous jowls betraying her sedentary lifestyle. Behind her stood a huge man of six and a half feet, who seemed to be supervising the bar.

"Two National Lights, *por favor,*" said Matt. He could actually feel himself relaxing in this most unlikely of places. The bottles of beer arrived momentarily, and he turned on the stool to face the stage.

The young blonde continued her gyrations, looking distracted, almost bored, by the whole thing. Clark put two fingers to his lips and whistled.

"I love you!" he shouted.

The blonde turned toward him and waved.

"I'm in love already," said Clark. He turned to the bartender and handed her his plastic.

"Ten, paper, please."

The bartender placed his plastic on a laser reader atop a register and pulled out ten stiff scrip bills.

"Don't see those much anymore," remarked Matt.

"That's another reason why I come here," responded Rosecroft.

He hopped off his stool and went to the edge of the stage. The blonde walked over to him immediately, moving the fore and aft of her lower body within centimeters of Rosecroft's face. He danced in place, swiveling his hips to the music. Matt laughed out loud at the bar.

"I'm gonna need a few more of these if I gotta watch him dance all night," he said to the big woman behind the bar. She laughed with him and produced two more National Lights.

The song ended and the blonde walked down the steps off the stage, yielding to the long-legged redhead who appeared from the "Staff" area in the hallway behind the bar. Clark followed the blonde and she, holding all ten of his bills, appreciatively kissed him on the forehead. He pretended to swoon, and followed her as far as the bar. He returned to his stool, and the blonde disappeared down the hallway.

"You are almost as entertaining as the women," Matt said.

"Yeah, but I don't have tits like they do," laughed Rosecroft.

Matt pointed a finger at Clark. "That comment was not socially sufficient, and I will speak with Sergeant Fisher in Sufficiency tomorrow about an investigation."

For a second, Clark Rosecroft thought he was busted. Matt then curled his finger into a fist and launched a stiff jab into Rosecroft's right shoulder. He laughed. Rosecroft exhaled, also laughing, followed shortly by "Ow, that hurt!"

The camaraderie was interrupted as the blonde who had previously performed ran up to the bar from the rear hallway, in tears.

"Brian, you gotta come upstairs quick," she shouted at the huge man behind the bar. "We're gettin' robbed!"

She turned and ran back to the hallway, the huge man two steps behind her. A pistol-gripped semiautomatic shotgun had appeared in his hands.

Matt stood, patting the small of his back. "I don't like the looks of this." He grabbed Rosecroft by the arm who still stared fixedly at the redhead, but Matt dragged him off the stool.

As they rounded the corner of the bar, the heavy woman shouted, "Hey, you can't go back there!"

Matt reached inside his tunic and withdrew his badge, hanging from its nylon cord. He continued down the hall as Rosecroft fumbled in his wallet to find his badge. He was unsuccessful.

The hallway was dark, and just beyond a set of double doors that led to an alley running behind the building a set of stairs led up to the second floor. A small sign on the wall, barely legible in the dark, read RESEARCH STAFF ONLY. Matt checked the double doors. They were unlocked from the outside. He then walked slowly to the bottom of the stairs. Rosecroft's hand clamped down on his shoulder. "Someone's working up there," said Rosecroft very seriously.

Matt turned to him and nodded. "Awful quiet though," he said. And then, almost as if to contradict him, a shotgun roared upstairs, almost lost in the din of the bar. The venerable Colt Model 1911A1 .45 was in Matt's hand, and he clicked off the safety. He bounded up the stairs two at a time. Rosecroft matched him step for step.

Nearing the top of the steps, Matt saw that the second floor doubled back over the main seating area of the first floor. He carried the pistol over his head as he rotated to make the turn at the top of the steps. At the far end of the hallway, toward the street front of the building, a single light broke the pitch darkness of the upper floor. Some fifty feet away he could see a scraggly, lanky young European in a torn fatigue jacket, holding the shotgun the huge man had carried upstairs. Matt slammed up against the wall to his left. Rosecroft followed suit.

Matt walked along the wall, the Colt shifted to his left hand to lead. The scraggly man was screaming at someone, and saliva flew from his mouth in his agitation. He had not turned toward the hallway, and the music from the first floor provided Matt audio camouflage as he moved. Rosecroft squinted occasionally, gauging the power of the opposing teke.

At about thirty feet away, Matt realized they would soon catch the eye of the scraggly man. He turned and looked at Rosecroft. Clark nodded. Matt broke into a run down the hallway, Rosecroft sliding along the wall.

When Matt was about twenty feet away, the scraggly man turned, leveling the shotgun on his hip. As he jerked on the trigger, Matt dove to the floor. Eight .38-caliber shot pellets roared over Matt's head, about where his intestines had been just a split second before. His elbows propped on the floor, Matt squeezed his trigger once. The

Colt bellowed, and a single slug ripped into the scraggly man's face just below his nose, blowing his brains out through a gaping hole in the back of his head. The scraggly man dropped to the floor, his body jerking spasmodically. From down the hallway, Clark yelped in pain.

"Rosecroft!" Matt yelled as he leapt to his feet. He ran to the door and dropped to one knee, using the door frame for cover. From inside the room a pistol fired, sending bullets into the opposite door frame.

Sheridan sized up the situation in an instant. Just inside the room to his left lay the huge man, a huge hole torn in his huge chest from the huge shotgun. The blonde stood next to him, screaming, her face streaked with running mascara. On the floor, next to an impromptu dressing table, lay a second blonde, bleached type, naked save for a set of six-inch heels. Her nose was obviously broken, and numerous fresh welts, vaguely 9mm pistol-shaped, were raised on her face. An African in a long black coat knelt next to her, clutching a wad of scrip bills in his left hand and firing a 9mm-pistol in Matt's direction with his right. Behind him, in front of two grimy windows overlooking the street, stood a third man, a European, small, slight, and even more scraggly than his recently deceased companion. He had waist-length greasy black hair pulled back from his forehead to reveal a bright pink scar in the shape of a J. His eyes were wide and wild, but he focused them now on Matt.

Matt turned his aim on the African, whose shots were coming closer to hitting him. In an instant, Matt could feel himself being lifted by the throat and thrown across the doorway into the room like a rag doll. He crashed against a closet door in the wall opposite the dressing table, his legs landing across the body of the first scraggly man. The scarred man's wild eyes followed the arc Matt's body traced in the air and kept his focus on him. Matt felt an enormous pressure on his chest. The African cursed as he changed his aim and fired a bullet into the chest of his dead partner.

Rosecroft then burst into the room, dragging his left leg. He and the scarred man locked eyes, and Matt could feel the pressure let up from his chest. The African fired again, this shot creasing Matt's chin. The crying blonde dove for the floor. Matt struggled to bring his pistol around.

The room throbbed with energy a split second before the scarred man was thrown violently backward across the room, crashing through a window into the night. Matt fired his pistol twice, each shot slamming into the African's skull with dull thuds. The African slumped to the floor. Rosecroft fell to one knee, drained. Matt continued to cover the room with his pistol, attempting to staunch the free flow of blood from his chin with his left hand. The blonde crawled to the far corner of the room and vomited.

"Shit, Rosecroft, I'm never drinking with you again."

It was the same nightmare Parker Hudson had over and over. Essentially the same. He is somewhere, anywhere, and when he looks into the sky, he sees a passenger airplane. *Gee, don't see those anymore,* he thinks, and then, as he watches it, it crashes. Sometimes just out of sight, sometimes right in front of him. But the plane always crashes, and Parker always screams, except he has no voice, and all he can manage is a choked whisper. And there's nothing he can do about it. Sometimes he turns to look away from the plane, knowing that if he looks, it will crash. But he always opens his eyes at the last minute and sees it go down; usually a lumbering double decker that is stalling on takeoff. He read an online about dream interpretation once, and it said that this dream represented some fear or doubt that he harbored in his subconscious but could not resolve. Whatever it meant, it usually ended with him waking up shaken. Now he sat up in bed, rubbing his temples. He glanced at the clock on the nightstand. *Just after midnight.* He could see the reflection of Karen's sleeping visage in the light of the clock face on the opposite nightstand.

Just as he lay down again, he heard the buzz of an incoming com. He reached across to the remote on the nightstand by his side of the bed and answered it. By the time he finished the conversation and returned the handset to its cradle, Karen was sitting up in bed.

"Who was that?"

"Flavius Blair. Matt Sheridan was involved in a shooting tonight."

"Shit, was he hurt?"

"Blair says he got nicked in the chin. Nothing serious."

"Why did he wake you up to tell you that?"

"We have cops involved in E.Z. shootings every night, but he figures I'm watching out for Sheridan. Which I guess is a little bit true. He says that Sheridan took down a couple of jazz gangsters trying to rob some bar. And his admin assistant, a teke of all people, took out one of the jazzers who was working. The assistant took a buckshot pellet through the leg. I guess he and Sheridan are both all right."

"I guess Mr. Sheridan's reputation has some foundation in truth."

"You know, I think I even heard a little admiration in Blair's voice. Which is saying a lot, considering Blair."

"Do you need to go in or anything? How do you handle this sort of thing with your subordinates?"

"You don't know? You're my boss; you tell me."

Karen returned to her pillow and rolled over with her back to Parker.

"All the good guys are alive, so I'd go back to sleep and deal with it in the morning."

"You're right," said Hudson. He lay down, his back to Karen.

Karen Russell's eyes were wide open.

Clark Rosecroft squirmed as the nurse applied a small clamp to the entrance wound on his right quadricep, midway between knee and hip, and off center by several inches. The laser technician stood patiently behind him. She was glad that it was twelve-thirty Friday morning rather than twelve-thirty Saturday morning. The six-bed trauma center at Carter Memorial in Arlington currently held only two patients. Thursday nights were usually quiet. Friday night the room would be full, with others moaning and screaming in the prep room. And Carter Memorial took in only cops and firefighters. The laser tech was glad she had Friday night off.

The nurse rolled Clark onto his left side, lifting the dressing gown that had draped down over the exit wound, and began to affix another small clamp to it. As Clark rolled over, he saw Sheridan was propped up on one elbow, watching the procedure.

"The dress is a good look for you, Rosecroft," said Matt sarcastically.

"Shut up!" Clark shouted.

The nurse glared at Sheridan and made it clear he did not approve. Matt shrugged his shoulders.

"All set, Ms. Baines," said the nurse, backing away from Rosecroft.

"Thanks, Todd," said the laser tech.

Clark watched fearfully as she approached with the laser instrument, which looked like a cross between a 1970s hair dryer and a revolver.

Ms. Baines smiled at Clark as she dialed down the "barrel" of the instrument and aligned it with the brackets on either side of the clamp. She flipped down the dark lenses she'd been wearing on top of her head. She looked through a viewfinder on the "hammer" end of the laser and depressed the "trigger" with her right index finger. There was a click and a flash of white light. Clark screamed. Ms. Baines looked up slowly from the laser. Sheridan chortled.

"Mr. Rosecroft, your leg is anesthetized. You couldn't possibly have felt anything," she said sourly.

Rosecroft pouted. Sheridan laughed louder.

"And, sir," she said, turning to Matt. "I wouldn't laugh if I were you, because, unfortunately, we cannot anesthetize your entire head."

Matt unconsciously touched his left hand to the pressure bandage taped onto his chin.

"I've had worse."

Ms. Baines shook her head and lased closed the exit wound on Clark's leg. He didn't scream this time; he just stuck his tongue out at Sheridan. Then the nurse lifted Clark's right arm and pressed what looked like a small pneumatic hammer in his armpit.

"Ten-day cycle of antibiotics, in case of infection. And this will hurt," he said before Clark could react. The tool chugged, and a gel was injected, which expanded in Clark's body to form a pea-sized, disintegrating time-release capsule. He howled.

Sheridan sat up and admired the two half-inch paper-thin lines that closed Rosecroft's wounds. Todd and Ms. Baines moved over to Sheridan, leaving Clark grimacing, left hand in his right armpit.

Nurse and technician worked wordlessly, professionally. They tried not to strike up conversations or friendships with patients, since it was likely that one day they would wheel a former patient from this room down the hall, into the elevator, down to the basement, and into the morgue.

Clamp in place, Ms. Baines approached with her laser. Matt

noticed she wore a wedding band, which meant she was really Mrs. Somebody. He couldn't help but notice the buttons on the side of her tunic straining to hold against her large breasts. *Bigger than Courtney's,* he figured. *Had I really noticed Courtney's breasts like that?*

"This will hurt, Mr. Sheridan," said Mrs. Somebody.

Matt only shrugged his shoulders.

"Please don't look down into the light," said Mrs. Somebody, and almost before the words were out of her mouth, the trigger clicked and the bright light flashed. The laser seared his flesh, and the pain was excruciating. His ears rang, and his head swam. He squinted his eyes and gritted his teeth. It was over in a second.

"Ain't so bad," he said. He watched Mrs. Somebody's breasts as they moved with her back to the laser cart, and he was rather unaware as Todd lifted his right arm and stuck the pneumatic injector into his armpit. He was off guard when it chugged, and he flinched.

"Doctor says you can leave tonight. Take a couple of days off; we'll process the online to your headquarters. Mr. Rosecroft, you'll be with us for a couple of days." Without a word, Todd turned and left, passing Flavius Blair as he entered the trauma center. Matt leapt off the bed and stood, his ears still ringing from the noise of the shooting and the pain in his skull. Rosecroft sat up.

"Gentlemen, relax," said Blair. Matt did not.

"I've just come back from the crime scene. I won't pursue what you two gentlemen were doing in that establishment, and frankly, I don't want to know. Fortunately, you were in a Yellow Sector E.Z., so there was only one lawyer to deal with. He says it was a good shoot. Thank Higher Powers that this doesn't have to go to the grand jury. Rosecroft, you ever kill a man before?"

Clark ran his finger along one of the tiny laser closures on his leg. "No, sir."

"Well, I know it's hard the first time, but I want you to know that your actions were also totally justified. I'll make sure that one of the department counselors gets in touch with you. You may want to talk to someone. . . ."

Matt was quietly incredulous. *Blair is actually behaving like a human being,* he thought.

"And you, Sheridan," said Blair, whipping around to face Matt.

"That was some fine shooting, and you showed some balls. And it also had to be one of the most ill-advised maneuvers I'd ever seen," said Blair.

Matt couldn't tell which way Blair was going, but at least he could tell he wasn't being reprimanded.

"Calculated risk, sir. From my interpretation of the situation, things were quickly going out of control, and I knew civilians were in danger, so . . ."

Captain Flavius Blair actually smiled at Sheridan.

"No need to explain, Sheridan, I'll read your report when you finish it. I have to admit that I may have been wrong about you. I'd seen your record, heard some stories about you. But I figured you were just some political payback getting transferred and promoted. I didn't figure you'd have what it takes. Maybe you do after all. But one thing I was completely correct about is that you are definitely the luckiest dumb sonofabitch in the world."

Matt responded with a wan smile. *My luck is only on the extremes: extremely good and extremely bad,* he thought. *I've had some very bad luck too.*

"You say so, boss," was his only reply.

"Well, if you can drive, Sheridan, I'll make sure Mr. Rosecroft makes it to his room. I had a patrol officer drive your car over here. Take three days each admin leave with pay, captain's discretion," said Blair as he held open the trauma center door for another nurse, bringing in a wheelchair for Rosecroft.

"Oh, Sheridan, one thing. I still want that fucking Bromberg report. I'll have Vo wire it to your home com in the morning. You're not off the hook on that one."

Sheridan nodded, fatigued. "Yes sir."

Clark hobbled over to the wheelchair.

"Rosecroft, give me a call tomorrow, will ya?" asked Matt.

"Sure thing," said Clark. He was tired too, but Matt could already see darkness in his eyes. The usual spark, the twinkle, was gone.

"Hey, Clark," said Matt, pausing for Rosecroft to look at him. "You saved my life tonight, you know that?"

When Rosecroft spoke, his voice cracked.

"Just doing my job," he said as Blair wheeled him out of the trauma center.

* * *

Matt shouldered open the door to his apartment, and had to step carefully in the darkness to avoid stepping on Pasha, who was waiting at the door. He clicked on a light in the kitchen, but left the living room in darkness. He slumped into his chair in front of the entertainment console, but didn't turn anything on. As he reclined, the Colt, still in the small of his back, jabbed against his spine. He reached around and removed the gun and holster. The weapon still smelled of gunpowder, and the smell triggered a powerful memory of the past evening. Only then did reality hit him. Carelessly, he threw the pistol to the floor and stared at his hands. *I killed two men tonight,* he thought. *Two violent, dangerous, worthless scums of the earth that deserved their fate, but nonetheless, I have taken away from them something that could never be regained.* The enormity of the situation, the finality, the wholeness, numbed him. He sank his head into his hands. *This is what I've been trained to do,* he thought. *This is what I do. This is what I do better than anything else, better than anyone else.*

Matt long ago stopped counting the number of men he'd killed; the number was meaningless. One was as significant as a thousand by the sheer fact that he bore the responsibility in his mind and soul for taking a human life. He never killed unnecessarily. But no matter how many times he'd faced this phase, when the adrenaline was out of his bloodstream and when his heart had stopped racing, he couldn't avoid the crushing emotional gauntlet he would undergo. The last time, most recent times, he'd simply obliterated his thoughts with alcohol. There was always an unsympathetic hangover to face, but the escape, albeit temporary, was enough to get him over the hump, when his psychological training could kick in and build a new section of the wall behind which he held such emotions. *And many others too,* he realized.

He wished he could talk to Jenny. Before she died, that was how he stayed sane. Talking on the phone, long letters, her hours at the hospital after he came back from Pakistan. He remembered for a long time being hung up about the wounded Chinese soldier he'd killed in mercy on the Karachi battlefield. How in another time and place they might have been friends, or maybe they never would have ever met each other in the course of a lifetime. But their paths had intersected, and each life was different thereafter. Jenny always had the right word, the right phrase, to soothe him. Since Jenny was gone, it'd been booze. And lots of it. Like with the CAP back in San Diego. No matter what the official story was, Matt knew he'd fired the shot.

He stood and went to the kitchen, where a virgin bottle of National Beverage Bourbon waited for him to take her. As he reached into the cabinet, he stopped. Instead, he closed the cabinet and walked out of his apartment.

Courtney Powell stumbled toward the rapping noise, trying to rub the sleep out of her eyes. It was after one in the morning, and in just a few hours she would have to get up to go to work. She stubbed her toe against the sofa on the way to the door in the darkness, and she muttered a mild expletive. Opening the door halfway (in her grogginess forgetting to check the viewer to see who it was), the sudden introduction of hallway light nearly blinded her, her pupils narrowing. As she squinted, she noticed who had knocked.

"Matt?"

"I'm really sorry to wake you, I just . . ."

Courtney tried to shade her eyes with her hand against the light.

"I'm sorry I disturbed you. Never mind . . ."

"Wait," Courtney said, grabbing Matt's arm as he turned to leave. "No problem, come on in."

Matt sighed. "Are you sure? I really shouldn't have—"

"Forget about it. I'm awake now," she said, turning back into the apartment. She located a light switch.

In the light, Matt saw she was wearing an oversized red-and-yellow New Columbia Presidents football jersey. And probably nothing else, he guessed, as her bare legs from the knee down poked out from under the jersey. Nice legs. Her hair was tousled, and she had lines on her face from her pillow. Matt felt a strange, warm sensation in his chest.

She took his left hand, almost startling him, and led him to the pastel colored couch in her living room. They sat at a respectable distance from each other. As she sat down, she put her feet up on the couch and stretched the jersey over her knees.

"What's wrong, Matt?" she asked sincerely.

"I . . . I need someone to talk to,"

"I'm listening," she said softly. "What's wrong?"

"I was involved in an . . . incident tonight."

"Oh, no! What happened?"

"There was a shooting . . ."

Watching his face and eyes as he talked, Courtney could see the bright pink crease across the bottom of Matt's chin. She touched it gently.

"You're hurt!"

"I was lucky. It only grazed me."

"You were the one who was shot?"

"I was one who lived," he said quietly, looking down at his folded hands.

The hair on the back of Courtney's neck and forearms began to rise.

"It was a robbery that went bad. I was in the wrong place, or maybe the right place, I don't know, at the right time. At a bar up in Coffin City. Couple of jazzers tried to rob some women who worked there. With all that paper money lying around, those places are magnets for stickups. The jazzers shot one of the bartenders. My assistant and I heard the shot; we ran to it . . ." His voice trailed off.

She moved over to him and put her hand on his forearm. His forearm was hard, his skin straining to hold in the large green veins that rippled his arms.

"I killed two men tonight. My partner killed another."

Courtney struggled to keep her mouth from dropping open. Chills ran up and down her spine.

"I—I've killed men before. In the Marines, as a cop. And there's this, uh, like, phase that I go through, where what's happened hits me, and, well, no more than for a day or so, until I can pack it away. I usually just get drunk, which must sound great, but it gets me by, and then I'm back to normal. But this time, I just . . . I wanted to talk to someone instead."

As he looked up, Courtney stared into his eyes.

"So keep talking," she said softly yet firmly. "'Cause I want to help you. But you've got to let me inside your head a little. All I know is that you love your cat, drink red wine, played a little football in high school, you're a cop and you used to be a Marine, and you speak some languages, and some are harder than others, and we need more rain, and traffic is getting bad, and you alphabetize your food. That can't be everything that you are, Matt."

Matt was a bit stunned, but he started. "My middle name is Xavier, which I hated as a kid, but now I think is pretty cool. I was married to a beautiful woman whom I didn't deserve, named Jenny. We had a son, David. Davey. They were killed in a car accident five and a half years ago. I was driving, and we were making a turn. . . . There was this cement truck. . . . It flipped over onto our car . . ."

"I'm so sorry, Matt."

"Yeah, me too. I, uh, I never got over it, I guess. I didn't . . . I couldn't go to their funeral. I just couldn't. I guess I just refused to believe they were dead. Like me not showing up would somehow make them alive somewhere. So I didn't go. I haven't seen my parents since then, 'cause they're mad at me for not going. We haven't spoken since. I've got a brother who's . . . well . . . I haven't heard from him in two, three years. I was Catholic back before they lost their tax exempt status and had to go underground, but I seem to pray to Higher Powers only when I need something, or when I'm in trouble."

His heart was racing, and his common sense was telling him to shut up. *Some sections of the wall are crumbling. You'll drown if the floodwaters are released.* But his heart was bursting with a mixture of sorrow and joy that he had never quite experienced before.

"I guess there's a lot more, but I'd bore you mostly. And right now I'm hurt bad, and I still miss my wife more than anything, and I've known you for only a couple of weeks, but . . ."

"Matt?"

Don't make me ask you, he thought, *please.*

Almost as if she read his mind, she reached out to him, wrapping her arms around him and pulling his head to her chest. He sighed as he put his arms around her, holding her tightly. His head swam a bit as her scent intoxicated him, and he could feel the floodwaters receding; the wall was holding.

Courtney ran her right hand through his short hair, and then ran her fingers lightly across his back. *He felt . . . contented. Some sense of . . . resolution?*

"Thanks. I needed that," he said, raising his head and loosening their embrace.

Courtney looked into his eyes for what seemed an eternity. She squinted, almost as if she thought she saw something in the recesses of his mind but couldn't quite make it out. Then she kissed him.

She had kissed him before, to say good night after their sterile Russian courting sessions, but now she kissed him tentatively but warmly. He kissed her back, unmistakably responding to her. He held her tightly now, almost restricting her breath. She ran her hand along his chest and stomach, and farther, and she knew he was responding in other ways.

"I can get my health card," she said, since it was still a misdemeanor not to exchange health plastic before any sexual contact.

"No need. I trust you," said Matt. *When was the last time I said that to anyone?*

They stood, lips still pressed together. He ran his hands up under the football jersey cautiously, slowly. They came to rest on her breasts, neither large nor small, but firm, unmistakably welcoming his touch.

"I have to warn you," Matt whispered, "it's been over five years for me."

She smiled at him. "Five years? That's even longer than me!"

His hands moved around to her back and down to her firm buttocks.

"I just can't promise any . . . endurance," he said, a little embarrassed.

She laughed, then looked him in the eyes mischievously. "We've got all night. I'll call in sick tomorrow."

Karen excused herself from the crowded quarterly meeting of her district directors. She'd already heard all the information she needed, and the rest of the presentations were boring, pats on the back by old cops who'd turned into bureaucrats somewhere along the way. She walked along the curving corridor to her office and gave her best sickening smile to her secretary, because she knew old Betsy hated it.

"No interruptions, Ms. Holleran," instructed Karen.

Betsy scowled her acknowledgment, as usual.

Karen closed the door behind her, locking it. She darkened the windows' glass and flipped on the small light on her desk. She sat at her terminal and logged online with public information. She punched in an address code, and seconds later was online with the North American Philatelic Society. She ran through the menu and touched the screen for information. The information screen came up, with a space for a category code. She entered the code for North American—eighteenth century. *How creative,* she thought. *The computer security guys at External must have a lot of time on their hands.* The North American—eighteenth-century screen came up and requested a collection code. She typed in the numerical sequence she'd memorized but had not used in years. It took three tries for her to get it right, transposing a couple of the numbers. On the third try she was dumped into a blank screen with a six-space box in the center. At this point she split the screen on her monitor on the horizontal, and placed the Read-Write containing Matt Sheridan's records in the CD drive. She pulled up the general information section and scanned down to the educational history. There was something . . . something . . . that nagged at her—something she'd missed, something she needed to know. She had a hunch, and this was the only way to find out.

There! While his records showed continuous assignment to NROTC (Naval Reserve Officer Training Corps) from the time he started his undergraduate studies to the time he graduated, no mention was made of his summer assignments. In the educational section, unless he was taking courses, summer months were not accounted for. Since he was in NROTC, the employment history, because he was enrolled as a full-time student, would refer back only to the education history. Four summers of Matthew Xavier Sheridan's life were missing from his official file—at the confidential level. She knew that persons with secret or sensitive supplements were annotated as such in the confidential file. But a person with a top secret or eyes only supplement was not; their file was identical to those with no supplement. Therefore, one would have to know the TS or eyes supplement existed to request it. Karen didn't know, but she had a hunch.

"Woman's intuition," she chuckled, realizing that remark would get a male three days in a local lockup.

She removed the large opal ring she wore on her right index finger and looked inside the band. Recording the access code was a felony, but no one ever thought to look on the inside of a ring band, where it had been obligingly inscribed by a thoroughly confused jeweler. She hadn't looked at it in years, since her brief stint with the Office of Internal-External Intelligence Liaison. She remembered "convincing" the director of the office for a weekend in Maine not to deactivate her access code. She knew she'd need it someday. And now she did.

She entered the code, remembering how that weekend really hadn't been all that unpleasant, and a "wait" message flashed on the screen. Shortly, it flashed "access granted," and the screen for the Department of Security—External, Master Personnel Archives appeared. Looking at the bottom half of the screen, she typed in Matt's social identification number. Another screen appeared and her machine beeped: "Warning: Record contains top secret supplement. Further access requires acknowledgment of liability to Wagner statute on classified information and its associated penalties."

Karen pressed the "acknowledge" bar onscreen.

The monitor flashed.

Reading the first paragraph, Karen smiled.

Matt stared through sleepy eyes at the clock, which was buzzing. Seven A.M. They'd slept for, maybe, ninety minutes. His head sank back into the pillow. His first two efforts had been underwhelming, both ending extremely . . . promptly. But Courtney was a patient and unselfish lover, and on the third and fourth, and then after a short nap, the fifth attempts, she too experienced explosive, shuddering resolution.

He sat up in bed and looked at her, deep in sleep, unfazed by the alarm. Her hair had fallen over her face and was quite a mess, but he could feel the stirring again. While she might not have been video-star beautiful, Matt was amazed at how sexually attracted he was to her.

Only then did Matt realize his head still ached, and his lower jaw was extremely stiff and sore. He ran his finger along the latest addition to his scar collection.

He leaned down and kissed Courtney's bare shoulder, and she stirred.

"Hey, it's time for you to call in your sore throat," he said softly.

She rolled over, brushing the hair out of her eyes with the back of her hand. "That's not the only part of me that's sore this morning."

Matt grinned a little as she rolled over to the nightstand on her side of the regent-sized bed, grabbing the com set. She called in to the principal of her school, who wished her well and told her not to worry, because they had two teaching assistants available to fill in for her.

She hung up and rolled over to Matt, her head on his chest, left arm on his stomach. Morning's light was beginning to peek through the blinds, which stood three-quarters closed. She began to trace an invisible line up and down his stomach and chest with her long index fingernail.

"I guess when you get shot they give you the day off, huh?" she asked.

"Better than that. When you shoot someone else, you get three days off," he said. He was over the sick feeling that had possessed him the night before. He was thankful for three days off, which would give him a five-day weekend.

Courtney wasn't sure how to respond, so she continued to draw silently on his skin. She traced a thin line of hair down his stomach, then drew her hand upward along his right rib cage. She felt something . . . out of place.

"What's this?" she asked, rubbing a large lumpy area just out of sight.

"Compound fracture of the fifth and sixth rib," he said matter-of-factly.

"My God, how . . ."

"Sort of a long story, but the thumbnail version is that when you raid a jazz house in a bad part of town, don't volunteer to go in first. I took a full load of triple-ought buckshot in the side at point-blank. My Borlon suit and flak vest saved my life. However, I still absorbed the shock of the blast," he answered.

She propped herself up on her right elbow now, taking a look at his body for the first time in the light. In the process, the covers fell to her waist, and Matt couldn't help glancing at her breasts out of the corner of his eye.

Courtney traced her fingers over a thin but pronounced ridge of hard, off-pink skin in the middle of his nearly hairless chest.

"And this?" she said without looking up.

"Bayonet in Tijuana. The tip of the blade lodged in my sternum, and he couldn't run me through."

She wanted to ask Matt what happened to "the other guy," but she figured she already knew the answer.

She now shifted in bed, leaning on her left elbow, her body across his chest, and ran her right hand over his slightly larger than normal pectorals. Her fingers came to rest on the small hole in his left shoulder, the rim of the circular scar puckered almost like a pair of lips.

"And this?"

His blood was truly stirring now as she pressed against his torso. He looked into her deep brown eyes, and his heart ached.

"Aren't you bored with show-and-tell?" he asked, and she pouted as if chastised.

"Karachi, back in 'fifteen. Chinese nine-millimeter at point-blank nearly killed my ass," he said. He sat up abruptly, drawing her to him, and kissed her, holding her tightly. The warmth of another soft human body felt good against his skin.

The covers had been pulled down to his mid-thigh by sitting up, and as she broke from their kiss, the brushing against her elbow was distinct. Her eyes widened, and she laughed, laying her head against his shoulder.

Her hair still smelled wonderful.

"I don't believe you," she said.

"You've set out a gourmet buffet before a starving man. What else would you expect?" he said, kissing her neck.

She tossed her head back, half moaning, half growling, eyes closed.

"And aren't buffets supposed to be 'all you can eat'?" he asked, guiding her back to the mattress.

"You like Fettuccine Alfredo?" Matt asked.

Courtney was still half asleep in bed. He had already risen and showered, and was dressed except for his tunic. He still had the tunic he wore to work the day before, which, he realized just then, was actually splattered with blood, his blood, down the front. He simply folded it and tossed it over his shoulder.

"What?"

"Do you like Fettuccine Alfredo? I'll cook dinner for you tonight," he offered.

She rubbed her eyes and yawned as she spoke. "Sounds great. Do you, uh, have lunch plans?" she asked.

"Sort of. I'm behind by two reports, and despite the fact that they gave me three days off, my boss still expects the reports on time. I really need to get them done today, so I won't eat lunch."

She accepted that. "Well, then I'll go buy wine . . ."

"White wine. Something sweet, maybe, and cold," Matt suggested. "To be honest, I'm . . ."

"Getting sick of red wine," Courtney said, finishing his thought for him. They both laughed.

"Well, I'm gonna sneak down the hall into my apartment," said Matt. "And I'll probably just burn this outfit," he said.

Courtney nodded. "How about sixish?" she asked.

"Sounds good to me," he answered. He walked to the bed and kissed her gently. "Later."

He turned to leave, tunic over his right shoulder. She couldn't help noticing the huge jagged scar across his left shoulder blade, roughly in line with the small puckered scar on the front of his shoulder.

"See you later."

7

Matt was a little surprised by the knock on his door at eleven that morning. He'd been working diligently, and had not only finished the Bromberg report, but was now going through the instructions for reporting the shooting the previous night (only ten hardcopy pages for an E.Z. Yellow Sector shoot).

Pasha looked on scornfully, tucked comfortably into his basket, as Matt answered the door. He was half expecting to see Courtney—although he needed some rest just then—and was shocked to see Karen Russell standing at his door.

"Ms. Russell . . ."

"Karen, please. May I come in?" she said, entering his apartment. After the fact, Matt said, "Sure."

"I heard about last night, and since I was in the neighborhood, I thought I'd just stop by to say hello and see if you were okay."

Matt's eyes narrowed ever so slightly. He waved at his chair in the middle of the sparse living room. "Please, sit down." He noticed her perfume drift subtly under his nose as she passed, her soft blouse brushing against his bare upper arm.

"Thank you," she said, surprising him again.

He spoke what he should have been only thinking to himself. "Quite an honor for a narc lieutenant to be checked on by an appointee-level executive."

She smiled at him but did not respond. "Got any coffee?"

"Sure. Cream and sugar?"

"Black is fine," she said, standing in front of the chair but not sitting.

In a moment he was back from his kitchen with two steaming mugs of freshly processed coffee. As he handed a mug to her, he noticed for the first time how tall she was; though he was barefoot and she wore understated ankle boots, she was definitely eye to eye with him. He pulled a chair from his dinette and swung his leg over the seat, facing her, seated backward in the chair.

"I'm not going to beat around the bush, Matt. I'm here for a different reason. I need to speak to you very candidly," she said, sipping the coffee but never breaking eye contact.

Matt was thoroughly confused. "Yes?" His eyes finally wandered, focusing on the top two buttons of her blouse, which were open. She shifted the weight on her feet and the blouse began to open a bit more.

"Let me start by saying that I was the one who brought you back east, Matt. You were on a shortlist of mine when I read the onlines about the CAP shooting there in San Diego."

Matt was getting a bad feeling, but he didn't respond. He hadn't touched his coffee.

"I know you killed the CAP, Matt. The cover was my idea, and I had some favors coming to me."

Matt exhaled loudly. Pasha had sprung from his basket, and now climbed into Matt's lap.

Karen stood and walked to the dining room table behind him, setting down her coffee. Matt noticed her jeans fit tightly. He smelled her perfume again, then shook his head to clear his thoughts.

"What do you know about the Confederation of American Patriots, Matt?" she asked.

He didn't turn around. He shrugged. "Bad guys. Terrorists. They attack government, media, and business targets. Kill innocent people. Shoot up a bunch of people. Neo-fascists."

"They are a threat to our way of life," said Karen.

"I suppose so," Matt responded.

"Matt, I need to invoke the Engler Protocol," said Karen, staring at him, knowing he would turn around.

Matt's heart palpitated. He turned to face her.

"Excuse me?"

Karen smiled. "Are you trying to fool me?"

"About what? I just don't know what you're talking about," said Matt.

"What did you do between your freshman and sophomore year in college, Matt. In the summer?"

"Uh, let's see. I was in NROTC, so I had a summer obligation. But I guess that was the summer I did OCS at Quantico."

"For eight weeks. What about the other eight weeks?"

Matt shrugged. "Don't remember."

"The summer between your sophomore and junior years?"

"Uh, jeez, I guess . . . that was advanced infantry at Camp Lejeune maybe? Or was it language school . . ."

"Eight weeks. The other eight weeks?"

"That was years ago. I can barely remember what I did last week."

"Summer between your junior and senior years?"

Matt did not respond.

"As I remember," Karen said pedantically, "that was the summer when the Mexican Insurrection was really heating up. Two years later you led a platoon into Tijuana, did you not?"

Matt turned to sit forward in the chair, setting his coffee on the table.

"And after you graduated you were transferred to San Diego, correct?"

Matt looked at his feet. "Yes."

"Because you volunteered for the newly formed Shock Marines?"

"Yes."

Karen grabbed his other dining room chair and placed it in front of him, sitting face-to-face. She smelled really good, Matt thought, despite the fact that he knew the disastrous end to which this conversation was heading.

"You've heard of the Marine Corps' Force Recon?"

"Of course."

"And what happened to it?" Karen continued in Socratic method.

"It was disbanded in '01."

"Publicly," Karen stated. Matt did not respond. She rose from the chair.

"Force Recon was disbanded, to the American public. But we both know it still existed. And we both know that some special Marines were still accepted as volunteers into Force Recon, on a top secret basis. And we both know that these volunteers were language and intelligence specialists, and they were trained to be the most efficient killing machines on earth, do we not?"

Matt did not answer.

"We know that the CIA, and later External Intelligence, took volunteers from Force Recon to serve as support on covert missions. The bad kind, you know . . ."

"Look, I don't know what you're getting at," said Matt, rising from the chair.

"You sure as shit do, Matthew Xavier Sheridan. I've read your TS supplement. All that missing time in the summers, you were with Force Recon. Training first, learning the ropes, then going on ops, short-term summer projects. When they formed the Shock Marine groups, they took their officers almost exclusively from Force Recon. They put you guys up against the SEALs and Green Berets as far as being professional killers. You worked Tijuana, Saudi, Tehran. You were on the beach in Karachi weeks before the invasion."

Matt was completely silent.

"All the time you spent in Tehran, you were going behind Chinese lines, sometimes Russian lines. TS file says you even picked up some Farsi 'cause you're a fucking tape recorder when it comes to languages. Your reports helped convince the JCS that a frontal assault on the Chinese lines was foolish. You probably saved tens of thousands of lives. And only a small handful of people on earth knew what you were up to, not even your family. Not even Jenny."

His head whipped around, and fire burned in his eyes. *She was right.*

"When you volunteered, and again when you retired, you signed documents acknowledging the Engler Protocol. You agreed that not only would you refrain from discussing your activities with anyone besides other Engler signatories, but also, due to the nature of your clearance and the information you know, that you could be called back to serve your country at any time. And you know the potential consequences of refusing."

The words rang in Matt's head, and deeply suppressed memories, almost forgotten, came rushing back to him. He stood and walked up to Karen until he almost stood on her toes.

"So what the fuck do you want . . . Ms. Russell?"

Matt looked through the passenger-side window as Karen Russell's VIP-issue hummer strained at sixty miles an hour. They were on the inner loop of the Capital Beltway, headed toward Western Fairfax County, out of the E.Z. At Braddock Road, they exited the beltway westbound and proceeded through an aging strip mall area, entering more prosperous suburbs.

This trip was actually refreshing for Matt. Here he was, driving through northern Virginia, not being shot at, not having to call in corpse sightings, not seeing the pathetic long-haired walking skeleton slaves of an Asian narcotic. Instead, he glimpsed manicured lawns, clean cars, and clean citizens, intoxicated with the notion that they were safe. In reality, they were no more than a five-minute drive from the worst of human depravity. And their intoxication was the true goal of Matt's job. While the few small, independent, local police forces operated in the suburbs, issuing traffic tickets, reporting accidents, and the odd late-night street patrol, the true crime control effort was in the E.Z. And their concern was simply keeping crime from spilling out into these suburbs.

"Here we are," said Karen, turning into the parking lot of a small restaurant, its jaunty red-and-white awnings faded by years of brutal Virginia summers. There were few cars in the lot, and she was able to park near the door. Between breakfast and lunch, only one customer, one irritated waiter, and a largely disinterested kitchen staff were in attendance.

The decor was early eighties brass and ferns, a style regularly ridiculed in the videos. Even the name of the restaurant, Super Tuesdays, was tongue in cheek, ridiculing the primary system of the old Democratic party. Matt followed Karen to the darkened corner booth, where the lone patron was seated.

The patron rose, a fiftyish man with a powerful build and a crooked nose. He extended his hand to Matt without acknowledging Karen.

"Lieutenant Sheridan, glad you came. Dan Reilly," he said in a polite voice.

"Mr. Reilly," Matt said, returning the courtesy.

The three sat awkwardly in the semicircular booth, Matt across from Karen, Dan in the middle.

Without instruction, the irritated waiter appeared with three mugs of coffee, then disappeared.

"I'm glad that Ms. Russell was able to convince you to join us today," said Reilly falsely.

"I had no choice, Mr. Reilly," replied Matt. Reilly cast a sideways glance at Russell questioningly, and she shook her head almost imperceptibly. He raised an eyebrow and returned to his interlocutor.

"Lieutenant, I'm sure you're sensitive to the fact that today's meeting must be held in the strictest of confidence. No one but the three of us can know about this meeting. Not any of your supervisors, friends, or acquaintances."

Matt nodded.

"Ms. Russell and I both have regular jobs that we report to, but they're not our primary jobs. Since you don't know where I work, that fact isn't that important. But it's extremely important, since you work in Ms. Russell's organization, that her primary employment can never be revealed, under any circumstance."

Matt nodded again.

Reilly paused for effect. "Lieutenant, my position is with the Department of Security, Internal. I run the counterintelligence branch of Internal Intelligence. Ms. Russell works for me."

Matt offered no response. He sipped his coffee, but did not break eye contact with Reilly.

Reilly narrowed his eyes, tilting his head slightly to look down his crooked nose at Matt, and continued.

"My office is responsible for neutralizing internal threats to our government, generally terrorist organizations, and specifically the Confederation of American Patriots. I know you're familiar with that group," said Reilly, smiling.

"My reputation precedes me," said Matt, looking at Karen. Incongruously, she winked at him.

"Matt, if I may call you Matt, we have been attempting to infiltrate the CAP organization for the past two years. We've had people get inside, but never for very long. We just lost two senior men in the New England area. . . . They were cops too."

"Cops or I.I.?" Matt challenged, using the abbreviation made popular in the videos for Internal Intelligence.

Reilly shifted forward in his seat, resting his elbows on the table.

"Well, Matt, both, like Karen. But the problem is that we invested over a year in their infiltration, and almost as soon as they got in, they were compromised."

"That's supposed to make me feel good?" asked Matt.

Reilly scowled. "I'm getting to the point. I.I. operatives are being compromised at a high rate. Too high. That's why I decided to go outside the organization to find personnel. We're working on identifying the source of these leaks, but to be honest, we're coming up empty-handed. In the meantime, I can't just stop my infiltration efforts. We've got to get inside these guys' heads, see what makes them tick. Try to get some advance warning on their targets. They've already killed a lot of people, Matt."

"Indeed," said Matt, frowning.

"I know your background, and I know your abilities. That's why you were identified as a potential . . . assistant for us."

"Assistant?"

"All right, Sheridan, look. Let's cut the shit here, okay? You have talents that your country needs. And I need them. Now. I can't afford to lose any more of my own people, and my office is leaking like a friggin' sieve. I'd like to say that I'm giving you an option, but I'm really not, am I? So let's not play the game anymore, okay?"

Matt looked back and forth between Russell and Reilly. Reilly was leaning almost all the way across the table now. Russell was looking down at something. At nothing.

He rubbed his eyes and ran both hands through his hair. "Well, then, Mr. Reilly, what's my job?"

"It's very simple. Get inside and tell me everything. Anything. Your role is that of a disaffected cop. They like to target cops because of their access to weapons. There's a local cell that you'll be tapping into. Because of the proximity to the capital, the northern Virginia local cell is much more valuable to the CAP organization, and therefore for our purposes, than some of the other cells. We'll put you onto a contact who can get you inside. Then, all you gotta do is convince them you're one of them and keep feeding us information. Ms.

Russell will be your control. You'll see her on a work-related basis, maybe even on a social basis, and report through her. No data or hardcopy, all oral." Reilly handed a disk across the table to Matt.

"This is a background brief on what we know about local CAP operations. After you complete the read file, it's programmed to reformat itself, so the info will be lost. Don't take any notes; I trust you're smart enough to remember the data. Ms. Russell will fill you in on any other specifics."

Matt placed the microdisk in his tunic pocket.

"Are we through?" Matt said, standing, draining the rest of his coffee.

"Any other questions for me at this point?" asked Reilly.

Matt shook his head as Karen stood to leave.

"Well, then, Mr. Sheridan, it's most unlikely that we'll see each other again," said Reilly.

Matt lowered the coffee mug toward the table slowly, then, with just inches between the mug and the table, snapped his wrist downward. The heavy mug broke loose from its handle and skidded across the table toward Reilly. Matt flipped the handle aside.

"We'll see."

Matt bowed to an imaginary sensei, his eyes raised as he began the forms. He could not remember the full 1,024-form routine he displayed to earn his black belt. He could barely remember the 512-form routine that earned him his brown belt. Today, he would go with the full blue belt routine of 256 forms, which he did remember, and just improvise the rest. It had been several months since he ran through his forms, and he knew he was rusty, but he needed to think, to concentrate. Nothing else could clear his head as effectively.

He moved fluidly through the opening forms, a series of stances, blocks, and blows that initiated the routine. They were intended as much for stretching and warm-up as for actual combat, but all the forms of Shaolin Black Dragon kung fu were built on these basic forms. Black Dragon kung fu was a style closely related to the unorthodox, aggressive White Dragon "open hand" kung fu, but which incorporated additional throwing elements. The White Dragon style had been adopted by Chinese pirates and brigands, mainly for its incorporation of animal-like raking and striking maneuvers. Black Dragon style was adopted by the palace guards of the Ming emperors in the sixteenth century. It was extremely obscure in the Western world, which was its most attractive feature to Matt.

He moved quickly to the middle portion of the routine, picking up his half staff from the floor. Even using the practice staff, his twirling and striking movements came dangerously close to the entertainment center, which Matt was still paying off against his credit account. But his thoughts never strayed from the forms, and the staff portion of the routine was soon over.

The entire routine, including improvised moves for cool-down, took just over five minutes. Matt sank to a seated lotus position on the floor. He checked his pulse and was relieved to find that it was still around sixty beats per minute. He relaxed, exhaled forcefully, and, with a clear mind, could think.

His head was still spinning from the implications of the morning meeting. He had read the data provided and had memorized the name of his contact, Stanley Karkowski. Karkowski was the worst kind of lowlife Matt could imagine, and his association with the CAP made this impression all the more clear. Matt was somehow to make contact with him at, of all places, an Irish pub. The Pride of Dublin was not far from the substation, in the Old Town section of Alexandria. Karkowski wasn't himself an accepted member of the CAP, but apparently knew several members of the local cell. It was believed that to ingratiate himself with his would-be "friends," he would be eager to present a cop to the local cell leader. Once inside the organization, if Matt was successful, he was to stay in as long as possible, in an attempt to locate the national command structure. Taking down the local cell members, while potentially satisfying, would do little damage to the overall organization. I.I. needed to start at the bottom and work its way to the top. In two intense years, probing local cells across the country, I.I. operatives had gotten nowhere—and had often paid the supreme price.

Matt recognized the great danger, but at the same time took comfort in the fact that he believed only he, Reilly, and Russell knew about his operation. He remembered how his bowels had loosened reading about a secret American military mission in Tajikistan from a local paper while he was in Dushanbe. He was confident there would be no external compromise of this effort.

He was still troubled by the nature of his selection though. He felt betrayed, but realized that by invoking the Engler Protocol from a proper level of authority, there was nothing he could do. Violation of the Engler Protocol was potentially punishable by termination. The bad kind.

"Fuck me!" he shouted as he stood. He began his forms again.

Courtney took her last bite of pasta and looked across the table at Matt. He'd finished before her and was quietly sipping a California-imitation Frescati.

"I'm sorry I eat so slow."

"That's all right. Usually I'm the last to finish because I've been running my mouth. There's no hurry. Enjoy," Matt offered.

He gazed into her eyes, and their soft brownness almost hypnotized him.

"Something wrong?" she interrupted.

"No, sorry, you just have gorgeous eyes," he said, somewhat embarrassed.

She winked at him. "Well, at least you're not staring at my chest for a change."

He could feel his face flush, then he laughed with her. *Her laugh was deep and throaty, like her voice,* Matt thought. *I feel that warm sensation in my chest again.*

"Ms. Powell, I do believe you owe me something."

Courtney wrinkled her nose. "What's that?"

"Quid pro quo. I shared with you last night. Now it's your turn."

"Well, there's not that much to tell really . . ."

"Then I'll guess," Matt said, his eyes dancing. "You haven't always been a teacher, have you? What did you do before? I guess you did whatever you used to do in the place before you came here, right?"

Courtney covered her mouth with her hand.

"Have you been following me or reading my onlines?"

Matt grinned. "I told you I'm just guessing."

"As a matter of fact, I was living in New York City. Well, Connecticut . . ."

"No one actually lives in New York City anymore."

"Exactly. I was working in Manhattan. I was the personnel director for an online publishing company."

"And when you left your boyfriend/fiancé/husband, you changed careers and cities?"

"Do I know you from somewhere before?"

"Still guessing," said Matt, smiling.

Courtney sighed, then rose to clear the table. Matt felt somewhat stupid in his choice of attire for dinner: wrinkled khakis and a pressed but casual short-sleeved tunic. Courtney had worn a units-style black cocktail dress, with wide, sharp shoulders, gathered waist, plunging neckline, and hem just at the knee. *Obviously*, Matt thought, *I've forgotten the potential implications of a dinner invitation. I have a lot to relearn.*

"You're close. He was my boyfriend. We'd been dating for, like, eight years. We'd lived together for the last two. We'd talked about . . . well, we'd sort of made plans, but never quite got engaged. I came home from work one day, and he was taking the last of his things out of the apartment. All he said was 'I've changed my mind,' and walked away. I was sick of New York by then, so when I saw the online for the on-site teaching position, I picked up and moved here. Three years ago this Winter Holiday."

Matt sat in silence as she went to the kitchen with the dishes. As she disappeared around the corner from the dining area, Matt rose and topped off both their glasses. He carried them to meet her in the living room. She took her glass from him, and they sat on the sofa together. As she sat, she crossed her legs, which pulled up the hem of her dress to mid-thigh. Matt felt his heart palpitate. *Now I remember how much I like black stockings.*

Matt opened his mouth to speak, then stopped.

"What?"

Matt shook his head.

"What were you going to say?"

Matt could taste the stupidity that was rushing to his mouth, but he released it anyway.

"I'm glad he dumped you."

For a second that lasted an eternity, Courtney did not respond.

She was searching his eyes again, and he could almost feel her climbing into his mind. *What did she see?*

Finally she smiled. Not a happy or amused smile. More of a . . . naughty smile.

"Me too," she said. She put her wineglass down on the coffee table, and then plucked the glass out of Matt's hand, similarly disposing of it. Without another word they embraced, and he could taste the sweet wine on her lips. As his hand found her exposed right thigh, he met no resistance, and finally the irritation of the morning was slipping from his mind.

"Fuckin' Sheridan," muttered Detective Sergeant Noah Benning. He squinted in vain to see through the rain on the windshield. The wipers were purely ornamental, moving little water and making much noise. It was Sheridan's idea to have weekly supervisor inspections of some of the narco stakeout and undercover sites. It was Sheridan who scheduled the Sunday evening drive-by. And it was Sheridan who plugged two guys Thursday night. So Benning, being the new Deputy for Operations, had the privilege of riding around on this miserable night, missing the second half of the Seattle–New Columbia game. *No big loss,* Benning thought, *since the Presidents would undoubtedly lose to the five-year-running Super Bowl champion Seahawks. And besides, Kathy liked the couple of extra bucks raise in the plastic account Sheridan had gotten him.*

He was cruising the streets of North Alexandria, near the transitional zone called Arlandria for its proximity to Arlington and Alexandria. Public housing stood in the area many years before, was briefly encroached on by town homes and condominium buildings, then deteriorated into slums with the rise of jazz. Despite the promise of guaranteed employment, the jazz epidemic had driven many to crime. Because one dose would consume an average weekly wage, few could afford the habit without resorting to crime.

Benning drove north on Alfred Street, then made a right on Montgomery, heading east toward the river. Just as he swung onto Montgomery, he noticed a large figure sprawled on the sidewalk in front of a decaying town house. He pulled to the sidewalk and rolled down the front passenger window for a better look. From what remained of the head, Benning could see it was a corpse, DAS. He rolled up the window and continued his route. He called in the corpse to the station on the remote com on his collar. *No sense getting wet to look at that one,* he thought.

He was shortly approaching the old Montgomery Park, now just a patch of littered dirt. Detectives Valdez and Jackson had been posing as homeless for a little over a month, gathering information on the largest of the organized jazz gangs in northern Virginia, the Gutters. Led by an Asian known only as Cha, they had adopted their name from their traditional practice of disemboweling rival gang members or delinquent junkies. Little had been seen or heard of the Gutters in the few days since one of Cha's most powerful lieutenants, Black Rod, as he was known on the streets, was killed in the gunfight with Sheridan. Word on the street was that Cha had put a price on Sheridan's head.

Benning slowed as he approached the park, driving slowly enough to get a visual contact from the detectives, but not so slow as to raise suspicion from any onlookers. He could see the detectives' impromptu cardboard lean-to, tacked to the only remaining tree in the park, soaked and drooping from the steady rain. He could see legs sticking out from under the cardboard, and he guessed the detectives were sleeping.

Sleeping! Both of them wouldn't be asleep; one always had watch.

Instinctively, Benning slammed on the brakes. Too late for stealth. He screamed into the com.

"Nova, this is N–4! I need backup, code three. Montgomery corner Royal. Looks like two officers down. Need medical. I'm going EVA!" He leapt from the car, initialing his extra vehicular activity without awaiting response.

He blinked against the rain as he sprinted from the car, which now blocked Montgomery, to the tree, some fifteen yards away. Despite the rain, Benning could smell a faint odor of cordite in the air. His Standard 9 was quickly in his hand.

He ripped the cardboard away from the tree, panting from his brief exertion. He dropped to his right knee and cursed.

Detectives Valdez and Jackson lay oozing life into Montgomery Park. Valdez groaned slightly, and Jackson's chest rose and fell very slowly. Valdez had been shot at least three times that Benning could see, once in each arm and once in the stomach. Jackson had taken at least one round in the upper chest, and as Benning looked more closely, he could see the bullet hole drawing in air as Jackson struggled to breathe. "Fuck, Nova, where's the goddamn backup!"

He felt a slight pressure on his trouser leg, and he turned to see Valdez pulling at it. He knelt and pressed his ear to Detective Valdez's mouth, which was moving silently.

"Set up . . ."

Benning shuddered. *This is Sheridan's patrol.*

"Gutters?"

Valdez nodded weakly.

Benning stood and spun around. Emerging from a burned-out town house across Royal Street, he saw several gaunt figures moving slowly, purposefully, toward him. He could not make out the faces of the four, but he could definitely make out the red glow from their cigarettes. Machine pistols, probably Fuegos, hung loosely from lanyards around their necks.

Benning glanced down at Valdez and Jackson, and realizing his only course of action, ran for his car. As he sprinted, cigarettes were tossed and Fuegos brought up as the four figures raced across the street.

I have a minimal chance of getting to the car and driving away, Benning thought. *But even though Valdez and Jackson look terminal, they might have a minimal chance to survive. I can't leave brother officers to a certain death. Even at my own peril. We don't do that.*

Benning skidded to the far side of his car, crouched behind the front fender, and opened fire in the direction of the advancing figures. They too opened fire, bullets raking the body of the hummer, bright muzzle flashes lighting up their vacant faces; two Africans and two Europeans, each with scarred foreheads.

Benning ducked behind the car, crouching behind the right front tire, and changed magazines. The Fuegos were tearing up the car, and from the passenger cabin to the rear of the vehicle, slugs were traversing completely through the thin fiberglass of the car's frame. Benning had some cover, putting the motor area between him and the shooters, but he knew they would be on top of him soon. He braced the Standard 9 on the hood of the car and fired.

The four gunmen did not flinch, but slowed to a trot. They changed magazines in staggered time, never letting up the hail of bullets. They were close enough to Benning now that he was nearly deafened by the roar of the guns. None of the four had even looked back at the two wounded officers.

Just as the four shooters were fanning out within ten yards of the car, Benning heard the sharp wail of a siren, followed by tires squealing. He looked back through the shattered rear window of the hummer to see a Tactical Response Team van leap the curb at the far corner of Montgomery and Royal. Six black-uniformed, masked, and helmeted federal officers jumped out. The four shooters redirected their attention.

As Benning watched the ensuing action, it seemed to take hours, in slow motion, but in reality lasted only a few, violent seconds. The four shooters were caught from the flank, trying to turn the Fuegos on the officers. Five of the six officers opened up with M16A4s, locked on automatic, the muzzle flashes creating a strobe effect on movement in the street. The bullets slapped into the four shooters, tearing them from crown to crotch. The four managed to squeeze off shots that flew harmlessly into the night sky. The sixth officer, armed with an American Arms automatic twelve-gauge shotgun, fired one round into each falling body for insurance. As the last shooter fell, his dead finger spasmodically tightened on the trigger of the Fuego, emptying the clip into the body of his partner next to him.

Benning watched the roaring spectacle breathlessly. He never heard the short, slender Asian, otherwise know as Cha, walk up behind him and fire both barrels of the ten-gauge shotgun into the back of his head. Cha disappeared into the night.

Matt slid onto the barstool at the Pride of Dublin. He wasn't more than two miles from the substation, but he didn't feel like checking in. He and Courtney had spent a quiet day in her apartment; she had disabled incoming coms, and they watched some old classic videos. He'd ignored the com flashing in his apartment when he went there to change clothes, three messages from the substation—two from Blair, and one from Rosecroft. *Screw 'em*, he thought, *they'll be there when I get back.* He didn't even put on his paging unit.

Of course, he told Courtney he was going to the station, and he was uncomfortable having to lie to her, but the sooner he finished up his "extracurricular" assignment, the better. He made a promise to himself that he would never lie to Courtney otherwise.

The bar was quiet, almost deserted in the late afternoon. It was Monday, so the sparse crowd wasn't unusual. Matt had timed his arrival with the change of the station's shifts. *Plausible deniability,* he thought.

The stool was in the middle of the long, dark oak bar, putting him within earshot of any conversation that might arise. He threw his plastic across the bar to the bartender—a tall, muscular European young man, with curly brown hair.

"Stout. And a tab," said Matt.

The bartender nodded, and shortly a pint glass with an opaque black liquid appeared. Matt sipped it, concentrating not to frown or wrinkle his nose. *National Beverage Stout undoubtedly was made from the same tap water they used in their regular beers,* Matt thought, *with black crayons thrown in. It only mildly tasted like the good Irish stout which, until just a few years ago, was legally imported.*

Matt glanced around the bar, noticing its scattered tables for any who might want to eat, and a small raised area for a stage. The Pride of Dublin offered live entertainment nightly, a rotating group of Irish folk artists. It seemed sinful to Matt, proud of his own Irish heritage (one half, on his mother's side), to listen to soulful ballads from Ireland while drinking brown pig swill from St. Louis. *Oh, well.*

Matt nursed his beer for nearly twenty minutes, and was about to give up, when a round red face, which he had seen a dozen times on video, entered the bar. *Stanley Karkowski. Stosh. Target.*

Karkowski entered noisily, making everyone aware of his presence. He swiveled his five-foot-eight, two-hundred-fifty-pound body through the doorway; a black trench coat swirled around him. His nose and cheeks were red, and likely he had already patronized a similar establishment previous to this one. His eyes were two small black dots behind a pair of thick eyeglasses. His thinning brown hair was slicked back flat against his round head. He strutted toward a seat at the near end of the bar, and pointed a short, beefy finger at the bartender. He spoke in a high, nasal, almost whining voice.

"Skip! Vocka!" he shouted, slightly slurring his words. Matt forced himself not to laugh. The character and psychological profiles in the dossier were nearly perfect.

Karkowski was three empty stools away from Matt. As he sat, his huge buttocks draped over either side of his seat, the stool nearly disappearing.

"Skip, let me tell ya. If it weren't for these blacks and Orientals getting arrested all the time, I wouldn't be getting rich defending them from all the Jew prosecutors," laughed Karkowski, using three of the most repugnant slurs for members of the groups he assailed.

Skip did not laugh, but shook his head, sliding a small frosted glass of clear liquid to Stanley. Stosh downed it in one pull, wiping his mouth with the back of his left hand. "Again!"

Matt watched as he downed a second, then a third.

"Skip, have I ever told you what the real problem is?" asked Karkowski, his head rotating to locate an audience. From the corner of his eye, Matt could see Karkowski's gaze settle on him briefly, then continue back to Skip.

"Probably, Stosh . . ."

"The problem, Skip, is that the Jews and the blacks and the Orientals have taken over this country. And the Hispanics. Did I say the Hispanics? This whole country is outta control. That's why there are so many jazz junkies, no control. What we need is a little more order, a little more toughness," Stosh ranted.

"Whatever you say, Stanley," said Skip with a sigh.

Matt raised his index finger to get Skip's attention.

"Another stout, please, and one of whatever your friend is drinking, on me."

Skip laughed, but followed his directions. Chilled vodka was soon in front of Stanley.

"From the gentleman down there," Skip said to Stanley, pointing toward Matt.

"Hey, no shit?" asked Stanley.

Skip nodded and turned his back, wiping some glasses with a dishrag.

"Hey, buddy, thanks!" shouted Karkowski, raising his glass to Matt.

"*Na sdrovya!*" Matt offered back.

"To what do I owe this honor?" asked Stosh.

"I just like a man who's not afraid to speak his mind," said Matt. The line had the desired response, and Karkowski flopped off the barstool, shuffling toward Matt. He came to rest on the stool directly next to Matt.

"Thanks. Stanley Karkowski," said the big small man, extending his plump hand to Matt.

"Matt Sheridan," said the detective lieutenant, returning the gesture. As he reached out, his synthetic leather jacket fell open, revealing his badge, now clipped to his belt.

"Oh, shit, are you Sufficiency?" asked Karkowski, taking a half step backward.

Matt laughed. "Do I look like a complete fag?" he asked, using a term to put Karkowski at ease. "Narcotics."

Stosh whooshed. "You fuckin' scared me there."

"Sorry. Those assholes in Sufficiency wouldn't understand what you're talking about. They don't spend a lot of time on the street. So why is it that you're defending these blacks and Orientals anyway?" Matt asked, using the slurs.

"Look, it's like this," said Karkowski, leaning on the bar so as not to fall down, pushing back his glasses with the back of his hand. "I know these fuckin' blacks and Orientals are guilty, just lookin' at 'em. And I apologize to you, 'cause I realize you cops are the ones who suffer, but I gotta help put these guys back on the street."

"Why, so they can shoot at us cops?"

"No, not exactly. If I can keep these bastards on the street, it's gonna keep cops busy, distract 'em from . . . other things."

Matt looked up, his confidence rising. *This was going to be a piece of cake,* he thought. "Two more, please," he said to Skip. He'd taken only a sip of his second tepid beer, but Karkowski had drained his drink.

"Like what, Stosh?"

"Well, I can't tell you, you see. It's secret." Karkowski's words were markedly slurred now. Skip returned with the drinks, and Stanley's was quickly downed. Matt pushed his aside.

"Well, Stanley Karkowski, I can't say that I like what you do for a living, but I like the way you think," said Matt. *I need to take a shower after dealing with this guy,* Matt thought. Matt stood and pushed back from the bar. "Uh, Skip?"

Skip turned back to see Matt making writing motions in the air. Though one didn't sign anything to close a tab, it was just traditional. Matt fished in his pocket and withdrew three scrip notes and put them on the bar. Skip passed Matt's plastic back. Then he held out his hand.

"Thanks." They shook.

"No problem. The name's Matt."

"Pleasure," said Skip, turning to greet a customer who had just entered the bar.

Matt turned toward Karkowski. "Nice to meet you, Stanley. See you around sometime."

"I'm in here all the time," said Stanley.

Matt smiled and nodded. *I know.*

Matt was still patting himself on the back as he walked down the hallway to his apartment. The fall's early darkness had stolen the ambient light in the hallway, and he squinted to see. What he did see at the end of the hallway was his apartment door open a crack, light seeping out. He reached to the small of his back and put his hand on the butt of his pistol.

He moved slowly down the hall, past Courtney's door, and approached his own. As he neared, he could hear Courtney's voice, and one or two others, speaking in hushed tones. He entered the apartment and looked into the living room. Courtney was seated on the floor, her eyes shimmering with sadness. From the corner of his eye, he saw Rosecroft and Blair seated at his dining table.

Without a word of salutation, Blair rose and walked to Matt.

"It's Benning."

The rain beat down mercilessly on the policemen as they stood in silence around the fresh grave. There were nearly one hundred of them crowded around the grave site, and hundreds more who waited respectfully at the road, amid the long line of patrol cars and motorcycles that stretched off into the distance. There were four civilians at the grave site—Kathy Benning and her three young sons. Matt cursed the world's irony that today was his first day back off administrative leave. The rain ran in rivulets off his uniform cap, which he hadn't worn in over a year, and trickled past his face, mockingly. He didn't wear his slicker, and now his dress blue uniform was soaked. The rain beaded on the still-shiny lieutenant's bars atop his shoulders, their glean taunting him from the corner of his eye. He wondered if there was some rookie detective walking through Nova Narco this morning, wondering where all the cops were.

A department counselor was droning on, recalling Detective Sergeant Noah Benning's record, his devotion, even recounting a bittersweet anecdote. No one listened. The Benning boys were poking and prodding each other, old enough to know that something bad had happened, yet not old enough to understand the significance of forever. Kathy Benning held her composure. She betrayed no maudlin emotion, but rather showed something different.

The counselor's drone stopped, and six cops, among them Oscar Vo and Flavius Blair, moved the casket containing the remains of Detective Sergeant Noah Benning from the temporary dais to the lowering apparatus above the grave. The casket was draped with the flag of the Federal States of America, a single blue star against a background of one white and two red stripes. The policemen removed the flag in unison and began to fold it. From a nearby hilltop, the Comarva honor guard, five men and two women, fired three shots each from their rifles. When the last shot was fired, the three-man honor band softly played the lilting strains of the national anthem, "America United" (it was much gentler than "The Star-Spangled Banner"). Though Matt could not see him, Parker Hudson stood a few yards behind the honor band, alone, and behind rain-splattered sunglasses wept in silence.

The officers achieved a crisp, triangular fold of the flag, signaling Matt's turn to step forward. He moved to Mrs. Benning, who shivered slightly beneath an umbrella held for her by a patrol officer.

"Mrs. Benning . . . Kathy, I promise you with my life that there will be justice for Noah," Matt said.

She looked up at Matt and simply cried.

Captain Flavius Blair detached himself from the group of pallbearers and approached Matt with the flag. The hard man was not crying, but Matt could see a softness in his eyes that he had never seen before. Blair handed Matt the flag and stepped back.

Matt turned back to Kathy Benning, flag held loosely in his white-gloved hands. He could hear the pulleys beginning to whir as the casket was moved into place for its final descent to earth. Matt handed the flag to Kathy Benning, and she took it reluctantly with one hand. She looked down at her sons, then at her husband's casket, then back at Matt. Her lips barely parted as she spoke, almost in a whisper.

"And just what the hell am I supposed to do with this?"

Owen Thomas grumbled as he stumbled toward the command center along the forest path in the dark. *This better be good,* he thought. Tonight had been one of the few nights when the prospect of eight uninterrupted hours of sleep had been real. *Goddamn!*

Judy met him at the door to the gymnasium, its floodlights illuminating a fifteen-yard circular area.

"Good news, old man," she announced, her face animated.

"If it isn't good news, someone will be executed tonight," he said. Judy looked into his eyes. She really wasn't sure if he was joking. He would make his pronouncement good if he felt like it.

As they entered the gymnasium, he squinted against the lumens being cast by the huge fluorescent bulbs. It took a few seconds for his eyes to become fully adjusted to the bright light.

Judy took his free arm, and he hobbled along with her. They moved past the large cluster of partitioned "offices" to a single cubicle, somewhat isolated from the rest of the gym. The man could see Jimmy White Horse standing behind the cubicle's seated occupant.

Judy and the middle-aged man rounded the near partition of the cubicle, nodding to Jimmy. Arthur James was seated at a desk in the cubicle. He wore a computer resolution terminal visor, covering his eyes and forehead. His hands flew across the keyboard in his lap, and corresponding images flashed across the computer monitor on the desk. He was grinning from ear to ear.

"What have you got, Arthur?" asked the middle-aged man.

The visored young man chuckled. "Ah, if you weren't my old man's friend, you'd be shit outta luck tonight."

The middle-aged man did not appreciate the attempt at humor. "If your old man wasn't my friend, you'd still be cleaning toilets in Tahoe," he said sternly. The levity among the onlookers was stifled.

Arthur cleared his throat. "Just joking, of course. I've found the data store, and I've copied and downloaded it," he said. He turned as if to look at the middle-aged man, but his eyes were lost behind the heavy plastic visor, which fed the CRT image to his eyes without the distraction of peripheral motion.

"It was in a congressional committee slave node, in a file marked for deletion but never purged. There are plenty more files like it, so I've also established an identity in the system. So, while I've downloaded all the data we need for now, I can access the data real time, pretty much whenever I like, based on the fake identity."

The middle-aged man looked closely at the data displayed on the monitor, titled simply Electoral College 2016. The man looked at Jimmy White Horse, then Judy, then Arthur. Then he smiled. He smiled from ear to ear. It was the first time that Jimmy White Horse had, in the past four years, seen Thomas smile. Judy could not say the same, but her relationship with the man was different.

The general clasped a viselike hand to Arthur's shoulder. Arthur winced but did not dare make a sound.

"You've done well, Arthur," said Owen.

Without a further word to all those assembled, he spun on his good leg and began to limp away. He called back over his shoulder.

"Judy, I'll need to see you in my quarters."

And without a word to any of the others assembled, she followed, responding, "Right away."

Though only in existence for a few years, Visireal technology already had dramatically changed the world of electronic media. Visireal was developed at the Federal Pacific Institute for Technology to provide an advanced data recording medium. The project was specifically geared toward visual recording, to provide digitized video for clarity. The medium would be designed so that it could not be altered or tampered with after recording, so that it could be used as evidence in federal courts. To that end, Visireal was developed as a purely digital medium, whereby images were recorded to microchips in the form of data. The data would then be assigned to individually encoded bits of memory, which could then never be edited, changed, or recorded over. To do so would require decryption of each bit of a Visireal chip's one gigabyte of memory, each one with a unique encryption based on random noise patterns taken from soundings on the floor of the Pacific Ocean. The project took over ten years to complete and cost over ten billion then-year dollars. But in the end the federal government had a recording medium that could present irrefutable proof in courts of law of visual recordings, audio recordings, or even keystroke records of monitored computer activity. Visireal technology had given the federal justice systems tens of thousands of crucial arrests in criminal, narcotic, and social offense cases.

The middle-aged man was looking over Arthur's shoulder as he finished the last of his downloads to one of their precious Visireal chips. They lost good men in Buffalo during the raid on the federal center where they had confiscated the system, consisting of a visual recorder, a data recorder, a playback station, and a dozen chips. But without the equipment, they had no hope of achieving their goals. . . .

Arthur leaned over backward in the chair, a string of hollow crunching sounds rippling down his spine. "This should just about do us, shouldn't it?"

Thomas shook his head sadly. "I'm afraid not. There is one more set of data . . ."

"Which is?" fished Arthur. Generally, he made it a point not to ask potentially sensitive questions of the middle-aged man like this, but it was worth a shot.

"You'll see in a couple of weeks."

Jimmy White Horse stared across the fire at Owen Thomas. The crackle of the fire blended with the murmur of the nearby brook, and the sound had a sedative effect. Owen held a small, straight glass in his bad right hand, and poured two shots worth of single malt Scotch with his left. He stood and handed the glass across the fire to Jimmy, impervious to the flames that licked at his hand. He sat again and, taking a similar glass from the knapsack at his feet, poured a second glass for himself. Pain was shooting up and down his leg, as it always did on cold nights like this, but he knew that soon the twelve-year-old Scotch would soothe him. He rubbed his good eye with his right hand and slowly sipped the Scotch from his left.

"So it's the Manassas Federal Penitentiary, in your opinion?"
Jimmy nodded. "Lowest casualty probability. Best ingress and
egress routes. Good targets."

"Best targets are at the Kennedy pen in Boston," said Owen.

"And nearly a brigade of Special Services guarding it," remarked
Jimmy.

Owen nodded, sipping the Scotch and staring out at the brook.

"How soon?" he asked Jimmy.

"Two weeks, soonest."

"We're running out of time for the big event."

"That's why I'm saying two weeks. Ordinarily, I'd say this operation would take at least four weeks to plan and implement."

"Ah, but that's why I hired you, James," said Owen. White Horse
hated to be called James.

"And the data?" asked White Horse.

"Manassas fed pen will be the last. Mr. Horace has made his statement, and by now, I hope, he's getting fat and drunk at my col-
league's home in Madrid. Arthur has finished the downloads, and
those are probably the most important. We just need this final piece
of the puzzle. Everything after it would be gravy," said Owen. He
stood and walked to the edge of the brook. He knelt and scooped
up a handful of the cold water. He sipped most of it, then rubbed
his face with the remainder.

"Young James, I used to fish this stream, years ago. I used to hunt
this land too."

White Horse grunted his acknowledgment.

"I wish I could fish and hunt again, but I probably never will."

"Who knows what we'll all be doing in a few months?" Jimmy said.

Owen turned to him and spoke quietly. "I'm afraid I know exactly
what we'll all be doing."

Matt Sheridan sat with his feet propped on the edge of his desk. He stared through bloodshot eyes at the video monitor, split into four screens. Flavius Blair scowled from one quadrant. Sam Goldberg, Chief of Narcotics, Vice, and Sufficiency Detectives, appeared blandly in the second. James "Jimmy" Franklin, Director of Comarva Detectives, stared from the third. Parker Hudson grimaced from the fourth.

"Lieutenant, this is a most unusual conference com," announced Hudson, breaking the temporary silence.

"Yes, Lieutenant, I wish we could have followed a more normal chain of command in this instance," noted Franklin, an African who had once been the New Columbia Chief of Police.

"Well, sirs, I apologize for the irregularities, but I felt the urgency of the situation overrode protocol," Matt remarked, dropping his feet to the floor and leaning forward.

"Detective, I've taken the liberty of forwarding your request to Chief Goldberg, Director Franklin, and Director Hudson," announced Blair.

"Yes, thank you. Since all four approvals are required . . ."

"Let's just get right to the point here, Lieutenant," interrupted Hudson. "Exactly what is this all about? The overtime budget you've requested is nearly half of next year's entire budget."

"Sir, in the short time I've been in this position, I've discovered that the narcotics situation in northern Virginia, and particularly the Arlandria portion of the E.Z., is particularly dangerous, with tendencies—"

"Mike," interrupted Franklin. "The E.Z. has always been dangerous," he said, still rubbing sleep from his eyes.

"Sir, respectfully, I've looked at the arrest and street distribution volume estimate numbers from the past two quarters . . ."

Goldberg, a man with coarse, graying black hair and dull eyes, took his turn to interrupt.

"Lieutenant, Detective Sergeant Noah Benning, he was one of your people?"

Matt cleared his throat. "Yes sir."

Goldberg just nodded.

"Mike, I'd have to raise the objection that I think there is an emotional content to this request that we just can't overlook," said Franklin, waking up now.

"Look, Mike . . ."

"Matt, sir," added Blair.

"Matt . . . you've just lost one of your men, and we all feel terrible about it, believe me, but . . . tripling street patrols, dedicated Tactical Teams . . ."

"And, Lieutenant, I need not remind you that Homicide is carrying out the official investigation of Benning's murder," interjected Blair.

Matt scowled.

"Detective," said Hudson. "This has been filed as a bona fide request, and we must treat it as such, which means I'll take it forward to my supervisor. But it will go without my support. We don't need a vigilante operation going on. We have constitutionally mandated personnel ceilings to deal with. And besides, the best we can do, from a narcotics standpoint, is destroy product and take it off the streets. That's about the best we can ever do. If we start making arrests, all the courts will do is return the suspects to our E.Z. Which leads me to the conclusion that you have no intention of simply arresting people."

"Sir, we've had unprecedented increases in narcotics traffic in the E.Z., particularly Arlandria, in the past two quarters. Narcotics-related gang violence has sharply increased, and if you'll look on-screen at my report, you'll see that narcotics arrests and incidents of unregistered telekinesis outside the E.Z. in northern Virginia, directly traceable to Arlandria jazz gangs, have quadrupled in the same period. Detective Benning's death is coincidental, and frankly symptomatic of the problem," explained Sheridan. He paused to let the information sink in.

"Well, gentlemen, if you all agree, I will send this forward to Ms. Russell without comment," announced Hudson, bringing the discussion to a close.

Each head on the monitor nodded concurrence.

"Lieutenant, your request will go forward as such. Is this acceptable to you at this point?" asked Hudson.

"Yes sir," said Matt. One by one, the heads on the monitor blinked out, and the com returned to standby.

Sheridan looked across at Rosecroft and Oscar Vo, seated in the guest chairs in front of his desk. "Why don't you two draft up the online requesting volunteers in advance. I've got a good feeling about this one."

The two grunted in the affirmative.

"And you are dismissed . . . gentlemen," said Matt, his eyes glancing toward the door.

Rosecroft and Vo both raised their eyebrows in surprise, but nonetheless dutifully followed their instructions.

As the door closed behind them, Matt punched a speed access code into the com. The hostile expression of Betsy Holleran filled the monitor.

"Ms. Holleran, could you put Ms. Russell on the line, please. This is Lieutenant Sheridan in Nova Narco. It's important, and I'm sure she'll take my call. . . ."

Matt slipped into the Irish pub just as the sun was setting. With the recent time change, the days were getting much shorter, and he seemed to be seeing less and less daylight. He was there for two purposes tonight: first, to make contact with his new "friend" Stanley; and second, to drink a toast to himself for Karen Russell's approval, without comment, of his narcotics emergency plan. By tomorrow morning he would begin picking out volunteers for the Narcotics Response Team. But, nonetheless, he had a job to do tonight, and until he finished this job, he couldn't concentrate on his new task of cleaning house in his sector of the E.Z.

The bar was crowded this evening, patrons elbow to elbow at the bar and clustered around the scattered tables. The first band of the night, of course, an Irish folk band, had already started their first set of mournful dirges. Matt could remember an Irish pub back in State College that offered much more lively and spirited Irish folk music. However, with so many of the songs written in times of insufficiency, it was no longer appropriate to suggest a proclivity for alcoholism and fornication by people of Irish descent. He could still hear a song about a drunken sailor in his head.

He spotted Stanley easily, seated at his corner stool, holding court. His voice seemed to be at a moderate volume, so he wasn't yet completely intoxicated. Matt grabbed a seat several stools away as a man and woman got up to leave. He caught the bartender's attention, who he remembered as Skip.

Matt passed across his plastic and ordered a draft stout for himself and a "vocka" for "Stosh," mimicking the Eastern European's slurred pronunciation. That earned Matt a laugh and a wink from Skip as he stepped away. The stout arrived in a moment, and shortly thereafter Stanley waddled to Matt's stool.

"Hey, thanks, friend. You're Mitch, right?"

"Matt. Sheridan."

Stanley clasped one of his swollen hands on Matt's right shoulder. "You're the cop, right?"

Matt glanced around for effect, then nodded.

"Yeah, yeah, that's right. You said you like a man who speaks his mind."

"That's right."

"And I'm glad you're not one of those Sufficiency detectives or I'd be up shit's creek!" laughed Stanley loudly.

"Well, you've got nothing to worry about from me," said Matt. "I'm on your side." Matt raised his glass to toast.

"Here's to men who aren't afraid to speak their mind."

Stanley raised the shot glass of vodka, gold-ring-encased pinky finger sticking out delicately to the side.

"Na sdrovya!" he shouted, downing the drink in one gulp. He slapped Matt on the arm and moved back toward his stool. Matt gulped down his stout much faster than stout was meant to be consumed, and pushed it toward Skip.

Several other patrons were pointing empty glasses at Skip, but he took Matt's glass first.

"That guy is too much, huh?" said Matt.

"Yeah, but he spends a shitload of money in here," said Skip as he poured a new draft.

Matt nursed this stout, swiveling in his seat to watch the soulful trio on the stage. Dinners were being ordered and served, and Matt's stomach rumbled as the hearty aroma of shepherd's pie wafted toward him. He realized he hadn't eaten all day, but he did drink six cups of the road sludge that Oscar Vo called coffee. *I must be getting over the nausea,* he thought. He hoped he could still have dinner with Courtney, but he was definitely going to be home late this night. He didn't tell her he'd be home late. *Am I supposed to tell her?* he asked himself.

Two slow stouts and ninety minutes later, over the noise of the crowded bar and crooning Europeans, Matt finally heard Stanley's voice reach a shouting volume level, indicating that he was truly and thoroughly drunk.

Matt signed his cash account slip and gave it to Skip with a generous tip. He would have to ask Karen for some sort of an advance or reimbursable account; *this is getting expensive for a limited budget,* he thought.

He walked slowly toward Stanley, affecting his own gait to appear less sober than he really was. Stanley was shouting some story about "blacks this" and "blacks that," waving his arms wildly.

Matt shoved his way next to Stanley. "Well, Stosh, I gotta get outta here, but I'll see you around."

"Yeah, sure thing, Mitch."

Matt started to walk away, then turned back to Karkowski. "Oh, yeah, and, Stanley, hey, just let me know if I can . . . you know, help you out sometime."

Stanley stopped in midsentence, and his jaw dropped slightly.

"Watch my seat," he instructed one of his groupies, then heaved his body off the stool. He walked quickly to Matt's side, grabbing his left arm, and directed him toward the front door.

"What's wrong, Stanley?" said Matt, slurring for effect.

Stanley steered Matt as best he could, in his impaired state, away from the door and toward a section of the building outside the overlap of the streetlights.

He spoke now in almost a whisper.

"Hey, what do you mean, if you can help me out sometime?"

Matt glanced left and right. "You know, if I can help you out. You have some friends and all . . ."

"What friends? What do you mean?" Stanley asked, his tone bordering on desperation.

"C'mon, Stosh . . . I been hearing the stories. You're an important man," said Matt.

Stanley released Matt's arm and visibly relaxed. He was buying it.

"Well, I don't know if I'd say important . . ."

"Sure as shit are important. You have a very important . . . cause," said Matt.

"Yeah, I guess I do have some important causes."

"Well, I thought, being a cop and all, I could help you out," said Matt.

Stanley suddenly stiffened. "Hey, look, I don't know just who the hell you are. I've talked to you twice . . . you're a cop, you could be with Sufficiency, you could be setting me up!"

"Stan, if I was with Sufficiency, I'd have busted you already. Do an ID on me if you want; I don't mind. I just want to help. I've heard the rumors, Stanley. You're in the big time."

Stanley stood quietly, considering the situation.

"Look, do you have a pen on you?" asked Matt.

"A pen? What would I do with . . . oh, wait. Yeah, I do," said Stanley as he fished one out of his sweat-stained suit jacket pocket and gave it to Matt.

Matt took a business card out of his wallet, as well as his plastic, which he handed to Stanley.

"You read the numbers to me, I'll write them down, you double-check them, then ID me. No problem."

Stanley squinted and struggled with the card, but managed to read off the numbers. Matt handed the card to Stanley, and he confirmed them. Matt and Stanley swapped back the plastic and the pen.

"See you in a couple of days, Stosh," said Matt as he strolled away.

Stanley stared down at the card. "One way or another."

Matt shuffled down the hallway, his shoulders stooped. He glanced at Courtney's door as he passed it, but did not stop. He opened the door to his own apartment and found Pasha waiting patiently.

"Hey, little man," Matt said as he entered, holding out his hands. Pasha, on cue, jumped into Matt's arms. Matt scratched the back of the cat's neck and was rewarded with a warm nuzzle against his cheek.

He entered the living room and set Pasha down. He saw that his com was flashing, so he powered up and pressed Display Incoming. Two messages from Courtney. He pressed Reconnect. A moment later Courtney's face appeared on the screen.

"Hi," he said evenly.

"Hi, Matt," she said. "I called before, but you weren't home yet. It's later than you usually get home."

"Yeah, I, uh, was working on something. Did you eat yet?"

"I had a little dinner about an hour ago. I was starved," said Courtney. They ate dinner together nearly every night. *Was I supposed to call?* Matt wondered. *Are we supposed to eat together every night?*

"Would you like to come over and watch me eat? Maybe watch me drink some lousy bourbon?" asked Matt. *That's a pretty lame offer.*

Courtney smiled. "Sure would. See you in a minute."

She appeared just minutes later, and watched Matt lifelessly stuff down an instameal and two fingers of bad bourbon. She talked about her day at school, and Matt nodded politely, following the conversation but not listening. After he ate, he retired to his chair in front of the com. He turned on the CNA news, sound off, and selected some obscure pieces by Buxtehude. Courtney sat in his lap.

He closed his eyes and sighed his under-pressure sigh, and Courtney began to rub his temples.

"You've had some late nights this week."

"Yeah, well, we're planning for a major narcotics operation and—" Matt paused. *Should he tell her?*

"I, uh, I've been working an undercover assignment that's very sensitive. I guess I should have called tonight if you were waiting for me, I just didn't know—"

"That's okay, Matt. I understand. You have enough to worry about."

"Well, I'm glad you're not angry. I'm gonna be running a pretty tough schedule for the next couple of weeks, so I don't know—"

"Matt, I'm here whenever. Don't worry about it," she said. Matt felt the warm sensation in his chest. She pressed her lips to his, and Matt could feel himself stirring.

She stood and took his hand. "Your bed is too small. Come over to my place."

He stood next to her and they embraced. "If you insist," he said.

Pasha meowed in complaint as they left, but to no avail.

They were soon in her apartment and went directly to the bedroom. He tugged at her jogging suit, and she pulled on his tunic. They embraced and kissed, a firm, hungry kiss. He pulled her top over her head, and his fingers traced a delicate path across her cheeks, down her neck, and onto her breasts. She held him by the upper arms, and they kissed again. His mouth slid from her lips to her cheek, and shortly to her neck. She tossed her head back.

"Oh, Matt, I think I'm falling in love with you," she purred.

He froze as if a switch had been thrown and his body shut off. He pulled away from her. He stared at her, his jaw slightly slack. *What did you expect her to say, Matt? You knew this might happen. Didn't you want it to happen? Are you ready for this now?*

"Matt, what's . . . what's wrong. I . . . thought . . ."

"Courtney, I'm sorry, I, uh, I forgot about an online I have to file tonight. I really ought to get back. . . ."

She crossed her arms across her chest, raising her right hand to her mouth. Tears began to well up in her eyes.

"Matt, I'm sorry." Her voice cracked and wavered. A single tear rolled down her right cheek.

Matt swallowed hard and resnapped the flap of his tunic.

"No. I, uh, it's just that . . . I forgot all about this report, and the captain will have my butt in a sling. I'm sorry. I'll call you." With that he turned and walked out of the apartment.

Courtney sank to the edge of her bed, buried her face in her hands, and wept.

"Goddammit, why did you do that?" screamed Parker Hudson. His back was to the window, and the lights of New Columbia reflected in Karen's eyes.

"I'll tell you why," she said, turning her back to him. "Every other day, I'm getting calls from Senator This or Congressman That, complaining that kids from their districts are going into the E.Z. and buying jazz, or the jazzers from the E.Z. are going out to the malls and selling. I've been waiting for someone to do something, to take some action, but all I see are people sitting on their hands, reacting to crime instead of fighting it."

"That's a load of bullshit, and you know it. What Sheridan has planned is revenge, pure and simple. He's gonna take my cops and detectives, go out there with the APCs (Armored Personnel Carriers) you granted him, and take a fucking bloodbath."

"Feeling sorry for the bad guys, Parker?"

"Karen, when his personal twenty-man army starts rolling up and down the streets of Alexandria, what do you think is going to happen? The whole area will be one big free fire zone. And, granted, while it is the E.Z., you still can't get away with wholesale slaughter in the streets. Besides, you know there are plenty of good people who live in the E.Z. How many bystanders are going to get killed? How many of my cops are going to get killed?"

"Parker, calm down. Maybe I agree with some of your points, but I'm willing to give it a chance. For a couple of weeks. See what happens. Besides, I give the lieutenant a lot more credit than you do, and you should give him more."

"Why?"

"Come on, Parker. He's a war hero; he was an officer. He's led men in battle," she said, and Hudson didn't miss the subtle dig at his own military career. "He's a good cop, conscientious."

"Karen, I don't like it a bit, and I'm pissed!"

She pulled him toward her and he fell onto the bed. She straddled him and pulled open his tunic. "I think you just need to take your mind off work for a little while," she said. She kissed his chest, then his stomach, then unsnapped his pants.

Parker didn't think about work until the first rays of dawn peeked through the curtain the next morning.

The chirping of the alarm was most unwelcome as Matt forced his heavy, swollen eyes to open. He hadn't seen or spoken to Courtney in three days, and they'd missed the entire weekend. He watched football, drank two bottles of National Beverage Bourbon, and now he felt as though someone had run a steel rod through his skull during the night. He slowly rose to his feet and staggered to the bathroom, where he was mercifully relieved of the remaining contents of his stomach. He turned on the shower and stepped in with his underwear on, then slowly peeled the wet clothes from his body. *The drinking hasn't been this bad since I came out to Virginia, before I met Courtney. I've got to go talk to her, or something. What do I say? This has all been very immature, Matt,* he thought.

After a painful shave, a forced cup of coffee, and a merciless commute, Matt arrived at the substation. Today, he would make the final selection of his Narcotics Response Team members. He hoped that within a week they would be out on the streets.

He had recovered enough to compose himself, in case Captain Blair showed up, but he knew that he must still reek of stale liquor. At his office, he shooed Rosecroft out, whom he caught with his feet up on the desk, reading the online comics on Matt's machine. Matt forced down another cup of coffee, then called Rosecroft and Oscar Vo back in.

"Please assemble the volunteers in the ready room. Get me a hardcopy of all their file synopses and have them ready for me. I'll be down in a few minutes."

Sergeant Vo nodded and excused himself from the office. Rosecroft spoke.

"Sir, perhaps it's not my place to say—"

"Rosecroft, can you tekes read minds?"

"Not actually, sir, although we can sense energy patterns that the brain emits—"

"Rosecroft, first of all, when no one else is around, don't call me *sir*. Second, I don't give a shit about your opinion."

Rosecroft swallowed.

"Yes, uh, Matt."

"Well, maybe you tekes can't read minds, but we drunkards can, so go fuck yourself, and then I'll see you in the ready room," Matt snarled. Seeing Rosecroft's frightened reaction, Matt added a slight smile and rolled his eyes.

"Thanks for your opinion, Clark. Now go away."

Rosecroft returned the smile, and, with a sigh of relief, left the office whistling the atonal melody that always seemed to be banging about in his head.

Shortly, Matt forced himself out of his chair and down the hallway to the elevator. He couldn't help thinking about Courtney, and her face seemed to flash before his eyes. He rode the elevator down one story and exited to his right, almost directly into the ready room.

The ready room was where the regular roll call meetings were held for the patrolmen who operated out of the substation. As he entered, Matt saw nearly forty men and women, uniformed and plainclothes alike, lined up to await his arrival. Vo and Rosecroft stood proudly at the front of the room, like two elementary-school hall monitors. Sheridan walked directly to the desk at the front of the room and sat down. As he had asked, hardcopies of each cop's file sat before him.

"Ladies and gentlemen, I want to thank you sincerely for your response to my call for volunteers for the new Narcotics Response Team. I'm sure that each of you has read the job description online that I processed, so I needn't spend a lot of time telling you about the danger and risk of personal injury involved."

Matt stood and let the comments sink in. He walked to the line of police officers. As he walked along, he noticed that five of the forty cops were women.

"Officer Rosecroft, would you bring me the files?"

Rosecroft scampered over to Sheridan with the stack of files. Matt quickly thumbed through them and came up with the names of the five women officers.

"Officers Petry, Walsh, D'Agostino, and Detectives Freeman and Saunders, you are dismissed," he said.

Detective Saunders, a hardened veteran of New Columbia Homicide, spoke out. "Lieutenant, respectfully I submit that our dismissals seem to be the result of a gender-based decision—"

"Incorrect, Detective Saunders. I stipulated in my online a minimum height requirement of six feet. None of the five of you qualifies."

"Lieutenant, that is patently—"

"Detective, it is completely within your prerogative to file a grievance against me. Dismissed!" Matt shouted. The five female officers left, their heads hung low.

Matt then walked down the line of remaining cops. He noticed four wore wedding bands. He dismissed each.

"I'm sure you are all fine police officers," he offered. "But I am not accepting married men for this position."

Without further explanation, he returned to the desk and glanced at the remaining files. These remaining men were physically the most impressive of the substation. He was particularly interested in a six-foot-six-inch African named Kwasi Jamaal, a patrol officer, and a six-foot-five-inch, three-hundred-pound European, also a patrol officer, named Earl Klingler. Both men were in their late twenties.

"Gentlemen, before I make any final selections I want you to know that what you have volunteered for is not glamorous work. I assure you it will be dangerous, it will be violent, and it will be thankless. You can expect long hours with short praise, and I can offer you little beyond the personal satisfaction of a job well done. And also, I must inform you that I just received word that the overtime and dangerous conditions pay that I requested were rejected just this morning," he lied. "Now, if you are no longer interested in the Narcotics Response Team, I will think no less of you, and your record will bear no notice if you wish to leave now."

Twelve of the older men left the room. Nineteen remained, including Kwasi and Earl. Matt nodded to Oscar Vo, and he closed the door to the room.

"Well, gentlemen," said Matt. "Shall we talk business?"

Marty Granger had seen good days and bad, but lately he had seen mostly bad. He thought he'd be next in line as lieutenant after Black Rod got iced, but Cha had yet to pick a successor. Marty could win big points if he took out the cop Sheridan, whose death sentence Cha had proclaimed weeks before. No one knew much about Sheridan; he was from the West Coast and definitely an outsider, but Marty had been following him around for almost five days now.

Marty looked over at Skinny Jefferson, who was dozing in the front passenger seat of the hummer they had stolen. Marty hated working with a partner, especially an African, but Marty recognized that Skinny knew the streets of Alexandria better than anyone else in the E.Z. A twelve-gauge pump shotgun lay across Skinny's lap, pointed down at the floor. Marty touched the handle of the Fuego 10mm automatic under his arm for reassurance.

They'd followed Sheridan almost night and day, and Marty was playing a hunch that they'd see him tonight at the Irish pub he'd been poking his head into lately. He looked back at Skinny and figured there was no need to wake him up yet.

Matt left the substation later than he wanted, but he was in a good mood because his hangover had finally gone away, and more important, he had picked out an elite nineteen-man force to work with him. Unfortunately, Matt realized, he had to go to his second job, and would head over to the Pride of Dublin to catch Karkowski. He wanted to go home to try to talk to Courtney, although he had no idea what he would say. *Something. Anything.*

Matt parked his hummer a few blocks from the bar and walked the rest of the way. It was drizzling, and the moist cold seemed to penetrate his overcoat directly into his bones. He entered the bar and was not surprised to see, directly in front of him, the usual sad trio of folk singers. The Monday night crowd was sparse. He hoped he would be able to do his business and get home before kickoff of the Monday night game.

Turning to his left, he instantly saw Stanley and company in their usual spot at the end of the bar. As was his custom, Stanley was regaling his admirers in some fantasy turned reality that he just made up.

As Matt walked toward the bar, Stanley noticed him and stood immediately. "Lieutenant Matthew X. Sheridan! Please be my guest for a drink," he hollered in his drunk voice.

Matt nodded and joined the group. Introductions were made all around, but Matt could not remember the names of any of the sorry crew whom Stanley had just presented.

Stanley thrust a shot glass into Matt's hand, and he could guess by the clear liquid the glass contained that he was in for a shot of "vocka." Matt accepted the shot gratefully and drained the glass.

Stanley unlimbered himself from his barstool and stood, pausing to adjust his boxer shorts, which had ridden up on him. He grabbed for his overcoat.

"Matt, do you mind if I speak to you outside for a minute?"

Marty nudged Skinny. "He's here. He just went into the bar."

Skinny stirred a bit, then yawned, sitting up in his seat. "Say again?"

"Sheridan just went into the bar. Let's go get a closer look, see if our friend will be coming out anytime soon."

Skinny rubbed his face with his right hand. "Whatever you say, boss."

He swung open the car door and stood, carefully concealing the shotgun under his coat. He quickly attached it to the shoulder sling he had built into the coat, and was ready to roll. Marty emerged from the driver's side, pulling his overcoat tight around him. They moved swiftly across the street and into a nearby doorway, where they could easily observe the comings and goings of the Pride of Dublin patrons.

Matt and Stanley emerged from the bar and strolled to the spot where they stood just a few nights before. Both men turned up their collars against the continuing drizzle. Stanley was first to speak.

"You checked out clean as a whistle," he said.

Matt shrugged his shoulders. "Of course."

"Well, I'm inclined to think you may be able to help some friends of mine."

"Your friends being?"

"Matt, you've heard of the Confederation of American Patriots, haven't you?"

"CAPs? Of course."

"Well, I have some certain . . . connections with the CAPs. You understand?"

"Sure," said Matt, his heart racing.

"If you can give them a show of good faith, they may be interested in inviting you to join their group."

"And what sort of show of good faith are they interested in?"

"Matt, can you get your hands on some guns?"

"Uh, well, yeah, sure. . . . It may take a little time though," answered Matt.

* * *

They stood for just over a minute, and Marty figured they would have no other company. Sheridan was talking to some fat-assed suit and seemed oblivious of his surroundings. If Marty could bring Sheridan's head to Cha on a silver platter, Cha would definitely make him the next lieutenant. Marty nudged Skinny with his elbow, and the African straightened from his leaning posture. Skinny, well over six feet tall, towered over Marty, and he stretched a bit, almost as if to show off the height difference. They walked side by side down the street, Skinny's right hand resting on the grip of the twelve-gauge shotgun slung in his coat.

"Well, the sooner the better, of course, but the people I know are usually pretty patient," said Karkowski.

"Okay, it'll take me a little while, but I think I can come up with something. Do they want pistols or rifles or what?" asked Matt. He buried his hands in his pockets as the damp evening air was numbing his hands.

"I think they need just about everything, but—" Stanley paused as he looked down the street, past Matt's ear. Matt caught his gaze and followed it over his shoulder, turning around. He saw a tall, thin African and a short, scruffy European walking directly toward them.

Matt turned his back to Stanley to face the two men, who were closing on him very rapidly. Not more than ten feet away, Matt could see the muzzle of a long-barreled pump shotgun peeking out from the liner of the tall African's jacket. Ignoring Stanley, Matt stepped toward the man.

The African, as if half asleep, reacted very slowly. As Matt stepped toward him, the African started to raise the shotgun, hesitated, then started again. The hesitation was all the time Matt needed to close the distance between himself and the African. The small European was digging for something under his arm as, at point-blank range, the African managed to raise the barrel of the shotgun to waist level and point it at Sheridan.

Matt stepped again toward the African with his right foot, driving his right knee into the African's shin. Matt swung his right arm across his body and caught the barrel of the shotgun, pointing it just outside his left hip as the African squeezed off a round of buckshot. The gun roared and Matt felt the shock against his body, but the pellets smashed into the window of the Pride of Dublin just feet from Stanley. Stanley threw himself to the sidewalk.

In the next instant, Matt reached forward with his left hand and jammed his left middle and ring fingers into the shotgun's open receiver as the African cycled the weapon for his next shot. The slide slammed hard against Matt's fingers, cutting them wide open, but the weapon would not feed another round into the chamber. Simultaneously, Matt drove his left knee forward into the African's groin, doubling him over.

By that instant, the small European had drawn and pointed his weapon, with difficulty at very close quarters. As he squeezed the trigger, Matt pushed hard on the African's shotgun, turning him toward the small European. As the European fired twice, the African was rotated directly in front of the Fuego 10mm. The small man's first shot pierced the African's back between the shoulder blades. The slug emerged just above his sternum, and continued on to slam into Matt's left shoulder. The second shot passed through the African's right shoulder, ricocheted upward off the second right rib, and caromed into the sky. Matt pulled on the shotgun as he fell backward, keeping the already-dead African between him and the European.

The European fired a third time, this shot missing Matt and the African, and crashing into the window of a fast food restaurant next to the Irish pub. Matt, by then, had landed on the pavement on his seat with the dead African on top of him, but had wrestled the old .45 from the small of his back. He snap-fired from the hip a split second after the small man had taken his third shot. The heavy .45 roared, the slide working as loud as a freight MagLev. The slug struck the European in the groin and plowed through his intestines to his hip, where the shock of the blow shattered his pelvis. The European dropped his gun and fell screaming to the pavement. Three seconds had elapsed.

Matt rolled the African's corpse off him onto the sidewalk. He pulled his fingers free of the twelve-gauge, dropping it to the pavement. He then returned the .45 to its holster and pulled his badge out from under his tunic, on its familiar nylon cord. Reaching under his tunic near his left shoulder, he felt a 10-mm slug trapped in the fibers of his Borlon vest. He pulled it out and dropped the slug into his pants pocket. He slipped his fingers under the vest and felt a small but angry hematoma already starting to swell, just above the entrance wound scar he'd received at Karachi. *That's gonna hurt,* he thought.

Matt turned to make sure Stanley was all right and saw that he had crawled almost all the way back to the Pride of Dublin. The unmistakable scent of feces in the air made Matt realize that Stosh had been truly frightened by the whole incident.

Finally, Matt stepped over the African's body, eyes wide open though dead. He moved over to the European, picked up the Fuego, and dropped the magazine to the street. Then he knelt over the small man.

"You work for Cha, asshole?" he asked.

The small man was rocking slowly on the ground, clutching his groin, sobbing. "I need an ambulance, man."

Matt bent his head toward the European's scraggly face. As he bent over, he drove his knee into the man's groin and leaned all his weight on it. The European emitted a high-pitched scream.

"Maybe with all the screaming you didn't hear me," said Matt through clenched teeth, almost in a whisper. "I asked you if you work for Cha." He let up the weight from his knee for the small man to talk.

"Fuck you, Sheridan," growled the small man.

Matt pressed down again, putting his face close to the small man's. The small man screamed and kicked his feet.

"I'm afraid I didn't hear your response, citizen," said Matt. "Are you working for Cha?"

Matt did not let up this time, and the small man continued to scream. Finally, he turned to look Matt in the face and shook his head yes.

Matt smiled. "When Cha comes to visit you in the hospital, tell him that I said he's a dead man."

Matt stuck the Fuego into his front waistband. He took two side steps and picked up the shotgun. With one hand he cycled it clear and carried it against his shoulder. He noticed that blood was streaming from his fingers and that the ache in his shoulder had spread to his back and lungs as he breathed.

Stanley was still on all fours in the doorway of the Pride, his suit pants in desperate need of dry cleaning. Skip, the bartender, was the first person out the door to meet Matt.

"Call nine-one-one. Officer needs assistance. Two down, one DAS."

Skip turned back toward the bar. Matt knelt next to Stanley. "Give me a week, Stosh."

Matt's left hand and shoulder seemed to throb in unison as he reclined in his armchair. The com was off, but he saw a message from Courtney flashing against the dark screen. He eschewed prerecorded music tonight and selected instead an uncomplicated late-nineteenth-century piano protocol for random generation.

He clinked the two ice cubes in his bourbon against the sides of his glass, but he was too tired to drink. He tried to flex his injured fingers, as they were stiff against the laser closures the paramedics made at the scene. Against his own better judgment he had refused treatment for his shoulder. He just wanted to get away from everyone. He just needed to be alone.

The com began to chirp, signaling an incoming, and he opened one eye to see who it was. He could see it was Blair's number, and he cursed himself for not filing an interim online, as procedures required. He braced himself as he powered on the screen and selected Receive.

Detective Captain Flavius Blair's grimacing face filled the screen.

"I'm waiting for your goddamn online, Sheridan. Could you please tell me what the hell happened tonight?"

"Well, sir, I was outside the Pride of Dublin over in the Old Town Yellow Sector and I was accosted by two armed men. . . ."

"No shit, Sheridan, I heard that much. My question is, who were the perps? Did you recognize them?"

"No sir," Matt said, mostly telling the truth.

"Witnesses in the bar said you spoke to the wounded man."

"Just advising him of his rights," Matt lied.

"I seriously doubt that you've ever advised a set of rights in an E.Z. in your career, Sheridan," snarled Blair.

"First time for everything, sir."

"Bullshit, Sheridan. I've also seen an initial statement from the wounded man. He claims you tortured him."

"Purely exaggeration, sir."

"Bullshit again, Sheridan. I think you should know that this incident has already raised some eyebrows with the regional civil liberties office, and it's not more than what, five hours old?"

Had it been five hours already?

"I thought we had an understanding with those people about what we do in the E.Z."

"We do. And you're lucky this happened in the E.Z., or we'd all be up on charges right now. But this is two public shootings in the last two months that have your name attached to them, Sheridan. That triggers a flag in the civil liberties database, and they can't *not* investigate."

"It was a righteous shooting, Captain. Those two bastards were gonna do me. Shit, they almost did. I had to defend myself."

"So you're saying you think you were targeted? If that's the case, we can pull you off the street, send you over to admin for a few months . . ."

"No, sir, I don't believe I was personally targeted," Matt lied again. "I believe these two were probably jazzed up, looking for trouble. I just happened to be in the wrong place at the wrong time."

Blair frowned. "You're in way over your head, Sheridan. I don't know what you're up to or what you're trying to prove, but there's a world of hurt about to come down on you."

"Advisory acknowledged," said Matt.

"You're a smartass sometimes, Lieutenant, and I don't appreciate it," said Blair, pausing. "You refused treatment at the scene? Report says you were shot."

"Yeah, well, I had a couple of slices on my hand closed up, but I refused for my shoulder."

"And because I'm talking to you right now, I can assume you were wearing your vest."

"Never leave home without it."

"You are the luckiest shit alive, Sheridan. I will talk to you to-morrow."

"If you say so, sir," said Matt. Blair blinked off the screen without further word.

Matt leaned back in the chair and closed his eyes.

9

Matt had the dream again. Jenny comes through the door of his apartment, wearing her wedding dress. The dress in which she was married and buried. She comes to Matt, reaching out her hand to him, her green eyes wet and shining with tears.

"I love you, Matt," she says.

Matt tries to speak, but has no voice.

Jenny reaches toward Matt, moving toward him, but as she gets closer, blood starts to stream from every pore, and her face and dress are covered with gore. She reaches for Matt with bloodied hands. "I love you, Matt."

He screams again and again, until he screams loud enough to wake himself.

The clock read three A.M. *Was I asleep three hours or six or one?* Matt stood, his body stiff from the unnatural position of sleep in his chair. He was sweating profusely, his tunic clinging to his body. He stood and walked to the bedroom, shucking off the wet tunic and putting on a comfortable short-sleeved pullover. As he grasped the tunic, the pain in his fingers reappeared, and when he shrugged the tunic over his frame, an ice pick stabbed him in the left shoulder. *A very familiar ice pick.*

Sitting on the edge of his bed, Matt noticed he was shaking. Not uncontrollably, but hard enough to notice. Running his hands through his hair, Matt stood, then looked through his wallet. He still had the key card that Courtney gave him. He stared at it a moment, then walked back into the living room. He retrieved his own key card and slipped it into his pants pocket. Without shoes he left his apartment and walked down the hall to 805.

He didn't knock, but simply inserted the key card and pushed open the door. Locking the door behind him, he walked quietly back to Courtney's bedroom and pushed open the door.

She was asleep, in her Presidents' jersey, hair strewn across her face. Matt moved into the room and stood at the foot of the bed, watching her. He kneeled on the bed.

As he did, the sensation of motion and slight groaning of the bed-springs woke Courtney with a start. She called out "Who is it?" in a very soft, sleepy voice just as Matt lay down beside her.

"Matt?" she asked in a very startled voice.

He said nothing, but clasped her outstretched hands. He folded her hands across her stomach, and lay with his chest pressed firmly against her back. He moved his right arm across her stomach and held her tightly. He buried his face in her hair at the base of her neck.

She relaxed now, smelling his familiar scent, and ran her hand along his right arm, interlacing her fingers with his. They both fell asleep.

Kwasi Jamaal and Earl Klingler were the first two cops to greet Matt as he entered the roll-call room. Eight other cops were assembled as the first shift of his new Narcotics Response Team. He would ride with them today as they supported the ongoing narcotics enforcement activities taking place.

All the men nodded at him and he nodded back. He felt rested despite the fact that he had just three hours of uninterrupted sleep the night before. He'd left a note on Courtney's com asking her join him for dinner, and he looked forward to her response.

Clark Rosecroft walked in just behind Sheridan, looking ridiculous in the Narcotics Response Team standard issue: Fritz helmet with com shield, Borlon external body armor, gray and khaki standard issue urban combat fatigues, and high black synthetic leather boots. Sheridan had relented after much cajoling and allowed Rosecroft to join the team as his assistant. The other ten men assembled were much more impressive. Exactly the image he wanted.

Outfitted identically to his team, Matt stood at the front of the room. After he called roll, he spoke.

"Gentlemen, good morning. I want to thank you all personally for your participation in Nova Narco's response team. We have a lot of work ahead of us, work that may never be completed. But we've got to get a handle on what we all perceive as a very bad situation becoming completely out of control.

"Be prepared to face the facts: The people we arrest will at best be shipped off to another E.Z. Most likely, they will simply be returned to our E.Z. We will be in constant danger, and the fact that we are wearing uniforms makes us targets as much as anything else. Realize that you will be called upon, in the course of your duty and to protect your brother officers and yourselves, to kill if necessary. Also realize that there are still plenty of good folks who are forced to live in these Yellow and even Red sectors, and who could get caught in the cross fire if we are not careful. We must not lose sight of these people, because beyond ego gratification and the remaining twenty-five percent of our paychecks, it is for these people that we are out there. And for the people outside the E.Z.s, who also get twenty-five percent of a paycheck, some portion of the balance of which pays our salaries.

"Now, many of you don't know me very well. Some of you do know me and think I'm an asshole. Well, perhaps some of that opinion is deserved. I really don't need you to like me; I've got a cat at home who's got that job. But you've got to at least respect me, and me you, if we're all gonna stay alive. So, there you have it.

"Today and tomorrow, I intend to initiate our program by educating our target audience. We'll be touring the main open air markets and neighborhoods on foot and in the Schwarzkopf, handing out hardcopies of a circular we've had printed announcing the new effort and giving what the department attorneys tell us qualifies as fair and reasonable warning, under the Urban Emergency Act. After that we will begin our expanded patrols and aggressive support and response to narco teams in the field."

Matt looked around the room at his men. None had so much as blinked.

"Mr. Rosecroft will be joining our team for some backup from the telekinetically enabled aspect. Any questions?"

No man spoke.

Matt nodded to Rosecroft. "Then follow me to the garage." He flipped his helmet onto his head, wincing at the pain streaking through his hand and shoulder, and secured the chin strap. The other men did the same and followed him out of the briefing room. The men marched almost in unison to the large elevator that took them down to the lower garage. They followed Matt's lead toward the latest addition to the substation's motor pool, on loan from a local National Guard unit: an M-121, Schwarzkopf Urban Conflict Defense Vehicle. A Schwarzkopf for short.

The M-121 was state of the art in Urban Conflict Defense Vehicles, outpacing the M-120 Assault Vehicle and the ubiquitous M-99 Armored Van. The Schwarzkopf was a six-wheel, all-wheel-drive three-axle-steering vehicle. The solid rubber tires were nearly four feet tall, giving the vehicle over three feet of clearance. The chassis design was similar to the Soviet BMP of the mid-eighties, with reinforced rolled steel, and a minimum plate thickness of four inches.

The personnel compartment could carry twelve fully armed heavy assault troops, standing. The front cab held space for a driver, the commander, and a com operator. The front cab had only two tiny slits for emergency vision; normally, the vehicle was driven by video sensors mounted on the front chassis. The vehicle was fully programmable for "drive by wire," which allowed an operator to turn over directional functions to the onboard computer, but most operators stuck to the video.

An elevated platform in the personnel compartment allowed a troop to enter the roof turret of the vehicle, where an Eraser was mounted on a demand-sensitive 360-degree-arc rotating turret. Just to the rear of the turret and slightly to the side was anchored the small surveillance drone, known as a 'bot, short for robot. When launched, the com operator could maneuver the drone to make Visireal recordings, take visual surveillance, or perform infrared scans on dwellings.

Detective Sergeant Oscar Vo was waiting for the team at the personnel compartment door, standing next to a large metal crate.

"Gentlemen, compliments of the Assistant Secretary of Security—Internal. Log in your personal ID numbers as you make your withdrawals." He supervised as each man approached the trunk and removed a brand-new M16A4, four loaded magazines, two stun grenades, a spring-loaded telescoping steel baton, and two loaded magazines for their Standard 9. Matt selected the same equipment for himself, with the exception of the Standard 9 magazines, as his 1911A1 Colt was in its familiar place at the small of his back. Sheridan forced Rosecroft to carry a Standard 9.

When the last man had finally outfitted himself, Vo produced a stack of the hardcopies of which Sheridan had spoken:

"Attention northern Virginia residents of the Comarva Emergency Zone: In accordance with the Urban Emergency Act, a narcotics alert has been issued for this area. Possession, distribution, sales, or intent to possess, distribute, or sell, or conspiracy to possess, distribute, or sell, illegal narcotics, specifically the hallucinogenic *xin ji*, or jazz, will be considered crimes of utmost gravity, and offenders and/or potential or suspected offenders will be handled with extreme prejudice. If you are now, or have been, a witness to any activity described above, please contact the Northern Virginia Narcotics Detectives at the com address below. There will be no other warnings."

The big vehicle lumbered north along Washington Street, through the downtown district that had once been a popular and high-priced shopping area. On this brisk morning there was very light traffic, persons going here and there, past boarded-up stores. The team was headed farther north, into a more residential Yellow Sector, bordering on Red. Just blocks away from where Noah Benning was murdered.

The vehicle turned left on King Street, then right on Alfred into a neighborhood of decaying town homes. The machine was getting glances from everyone on the street, and Matt knew that the sight of the Schwarzkopf alone would send a strong message.

Several blocks into the neighborhood, Matt tapped the driver, a National Guard specialist called up for this specific active duty, and he slowed to a halt. From the front cab, Matt spoke "com four," into the vehicle's internal intercom, and the ten men in the rear tapped their com sets to channel four. Matt would then be able to speak without yelling.

"All right, I'm gonna go EVA here and hand out some hardcopies. Jamaal and Klingler, I want you two outside with me. Jones, I want you up in the turret. Rosecroft, you stay standby with the com, and I want your eyes on my backside."

"I bet that's not the only part of me you want on your backside," taunted Rosecroft. Matt drove a stiffened index finger into Rosecroft's fleshy right upper arm.

"Oww!" Rosecroft yelped.

Without further ado, Matt slid out of the front cabin. He reached in and pulled out the M16A4, which he slung over his right shoulder, and then the stack of hardcopies. Jamaal and Klingler shortly joined Matt at the front of the vehicle, their weapons at the ready. Matt walked between the two, who were about ten feet apart, down the middle of the street.

Some faces began to appear in windows along the street, mostly Africans, but with Europeans, Asians, and Latins scattered among them. For those who came out of their houses, Matt provided a hardcopy. For those who did not come out, he handed a hardcopy to Jamaal or Klingler, who then ensured that the paper made its way into the houses.

The streets were very quiet, and through the course of the day there were no incidents. Matt handed a hardcopy to a middle-aged African woman who had waved him to her home.

"You know, Officer, not all of us who live down here are bad. But we're stuck. They won't let us move somewhere else. They won't let us take jobs outside the area. Lots of us are scared to death. How are we supposed to raise our kids like this?" she asked, staring Matt in the eye.

He swallowed hard. "That's why we're here, ma'am." The woman's young son ran into the building from behind Matt. "For you and for him."

Matt unsnapped his helmet as he went back out to the Schwarzkopf. *This is going to be the hardest part,* he thought.

As they rolled toward the substation, southbound on Washington Street, they passed a few more cars than earlier in the morning. Mostly the same beat-up hummers, a couple of patrol cars, and one shiny new hummer parked in front of a former department store.

Two blocks down the road, something clicked in Matt's mind. He directed the driver to make a right, another right, backtrack a few blocks, then run right back onto Washington Street. As they did, they swung onto Washington several blocks north of where the shiny new hummer was parked.

"Rosecroft, how many folks in the E.Z. do you know who could afford a new North American Motors touring sedan?"

"Only jazz dealers, but why would they buy something dull like that?"

"Exactly," said Matt. Over com four he shouted, "Jones, back in the turret. Jamaal, Klingler, get ready to go EVA. We're making a stop on that hummer up ahead. Rosecroft, call it in."

The driver responded, and the diesel intercom engine growled. It was infinitely quicker, even with its huge load, than any privately owned hummer. It reached the parked car in seconds. The driver swung the Schwarzkopf in front of the hummer. Two men, an African and an Asian, who had been standing on the sidewalk speaking to the two European occupants of the hummer, fled on foot in opposite directions as the Schwarzkopf scraped the front bumper of the sedan.

Matt was already out the front door, leaving his rifle in the vehicle. The rear doors were opening and the two giant cops were emerging.

"Watch them," shouted Matt, pointing to the hummer as he took off after the Asian running north on Washington Street. The African had too great a head start for Matt to catch him. *Besides,* Matt thought, *I want one of these guys to get away so he can start telling the stories. . . .*

After a half-block sprint, Matt caught the Asian, who, though very skinny and wiry, was obviously in poor physical condition. Matt tackled him from behind, and the two spilled to the sidewalk. The Asian tried to stand up, but Matt quickly buried a knee in his kidney. Pinned to the ground, the Asian flailed his arms uselessly. Matt looped a set of nylon restraints around his wrists and yanked him to his feet. He wore Gutters colors. Matt frisked him and found nearly four ounces of a liquid substance in a sealed plastic bag. Matt opened the bag and carefully waved his hand over the opening. Just enough of the odor of the contents reached Matt's nose, and he could feel his intestines spasm involuntarily.

"Looks to me like a good four ounces of liquid, friend. This much could almost actually get you sent to prison," said Matt. As he looked into the Asian's face for the first time, he noted the prominent J-shaped scar on his forehead.

"Fuck you, cop. You gonna waste your time takin' me in? They'll just let me go this afternoon. Gimme a break," said the Asian, sneering.

"No, you'll find I have something else in mind," said Matt, leading the Asian back toward the hummer.

At the hummer, Jamaal and Klingler had each secured one of the European passengers. As Matt approached, he could see they were teenagers, probably just out of high school for the day. He turned his Asian suspect over to Jamaal and Klingler, and they each held an arm.

Rosecroft hopped out of the vehicle with the handheld ID reader and started scanning IDs.

Matt turned to the two young Europeans.

"What are your names?"

"James Hunter."

"Mark Weston."

"And where do you live?"

"Fairfax, sir," said James, shaking.

"Fairfax, huh," said Matt. "Refresh my memory. That's not in the Comarva E.Z., is it?"

"No, sir."

"Suburbs. Nice. Grass and stuff, right?"

"Yes, sir."

"Well, I'd say you boys down here in a Yellow Sector of the E.Z. are really out of place. Wrong turn somewhere?"

The boys didn't answer, but hung their heads.

"Or was it that you were bored and came down here to score some jazz? You've heard of that, haven't you? The leading cause of death by overdose in the country? The instantly addictive drug that's got two hundred thousand slaves in the mid-Atlantic alone? The drug that people are killing each other and my cops over?" said Matt, the volume of his voice rising to a shout.

The boys did not look up.

"No answer? You figure nothing is going to happen to you 'cause your middle-class dads make more money than the people who live in the E.Z.? Why do you think these poor Africans and Asians and

Latins and yes, even Europeans, are killing each other? To sell this shit to your sorry white asses. So I arrest the Africans and Asians and Latins, but what about you boys? You don't live in the E.Z. We don't have jurisdiction to come out to the suburbs and kick in your doors and arrest you. But guess what . . . you're in my world now!" shouted Matt. James began to cry.

"Well, you're big men to come down here in Daddy's car with Daddy's money to be tough and score some jazz. How big do you think you'd be in the penitentiary, huh? The two of you'd get your asses ripped in a heartbeat. Well, I'm gonna make a deal with you," said Matt, pulling the Colt .45 from its place of honor. He pointed it at the new hummer.

"You boys get the fuck outta my E.Z.," said Matt. He then fired three rounds through the hood of the car. "And you explain to Daddy where the bullet holes came from. Then I won't arrest you."

Both boys nodded, then they scrambled into their car. Without a word they backed out of the parking spot and disappeared down the road. Matt shook his head. *Odds are they'll be in a federal rehab center in a couple of months anyway. Or dead in the street. Or somewhere in between, like Tommy.*

The rear door of the Schwarzkopf had flung open at the sound of Sheridan's pistol, but he waved the remaining men back into the personnel compartment. He tapped the com on his helmet.

"Rosecroft?"

"Here, sir."

"Take the vehicle for a slow trip around the block. I need about five minutes. Understood?"

After a short pause, Rosecroft responded.

"Gotcha."

The armored vehicle slowly pulled away down the street. Matt turned his attention back to his Asian suspect, held firmly between Jamaal and Klingler. He nodded to his men, then walked into the narrow alley that ran next to the building. Jamaal and Klingler followed, dragging their prisoner bodily behind them. Matt led them behind a Dumpster, unattended for probably over a year, just out of sight from Washington Street. Matt stood in front of the Asian.

"What's your name, citizen?" he asked.

The Asian spat on Matt. "Fuck you!"

"Well, Mr. You, I need to ask you some questions before I am forced to release you."

"Fuck you."

"Yes, Mr. You, I did get your name. But I need to ask you who your supplier is."

The Asian did not respond.

"Officers Jamaal and Klingler, do you notice Fuck You here attempting to resist arrest?" Matt asked.

Jamaal looked puzzled at first, then Officer Klingler smiled.

"Lieutenant Sheridan, I definitely see this suspect attempting to resist arrest."

A light suddenly went on in Jamaal's head. "Now that you mention it, he sure is trying to resist."

Confused, the Asian looked between Jamaal and Sheridan.

Sheridan withdrew the telescoping stun baton from its holder on his belt. He placed pressure on the grip and the baton telescoped outward, from six inches to a full eighteen inches in length. The baton was topped with a small solid-steel ball.

"Ya know something that really hurts?" Matt asked the Asian, then swung the baton viciously. The steel rod rapped the Asian across the shins just below the knees. With a yelp, he fell to his knees.

"That hurts like hell, don't it, Mr. You?"

The Asian gasped for breath.

"The name of your supplier," growled Matt.

The Asian was still on his knees wincing and gasping for breath, his arms stretched backward by Jamaal and Klingler.

"I'm sorry, I didn't hear your answer," said Matt as he swung the baton again, landing it across the center of the Asian's right upper arm. He screamed.

"You're killing me," wailed the detainee.

"No, I'm torturing you," said Matt. This comment made both Jamaal and Klingler squirm. "If I was killing you, you wouldn't be in so much pain right now. If you'll just give me the name of your supplier, I'll stop."

"They'll kill me," groaned the Asian.

"Your choice," said Matt. He swung the baton again, this time striking the man's upper left biceps. The man cried out loud.

"Please, stop!"

"You ever heard of Noah Benning?" snarled Matt. He nodded to Jamaal and Klingler and they released the Asian's arms. Matt then kicked him on to his back and smashed the baton across the man's lower legs again. The Asian cried out.

"Liebovic. A guy named Liebovic. European. I meet him for distribution. Once a week. And I don't know nothing about any Benning."

Matt applied pressure to the baton again, and the rod slid back down into its housing. "Good, well, Mr. Fuck You, we've made some progress. When the Schwarzkopf comes back, you'll take a little ride back to the substation with us, we'll get some more specifics on Mr. Liebovic, and then you'll be free to go on your miserable way."

The Asian, still sobbing, had curled up into a ball. Jamaal and Klingler had backed off a few feet and turned their backs.

Matt knelt beside the Asian as he heard the rumbling of the Schwarzkopf coming around the far corner.

"And when you see Cha again, you tell him Lieutenant Matt Sheridan says he's a dead man."

Matt emerged from the Schwarzkopf as it was still rolling slowly into the motor pool. He was a bit disturbed that the men had been so quiet on the return trip. He knew himself that he was dangerously close to going over the edge, and he was sure that he had affected the men. *No one said it was going to be pretty,* he thought.

As he cleared the vehicle, Oscar Vo was waiting for him.

"Lieutenant, problem. Blair just called from headquarters. He wants to see you downtown ASAP."

Matt unsnapped his helmet. "What for?"

"East Region civil liberties inquiry into the shooting last night. Blair is sitting with the lawyers and the independent counsel who's investigating. They need you over there immediately."

"Shit," said Matt, slouching in exasperation. The Schwarzkopf was now emptying, and Jamaal and Klingler emerged with Fuck You, who was walking with great difficulty. Rosecroft trotted to Matt's side from the front compartment.

"Rosecroft, I want you and Oscar to take Mr. You up to one of the interrogation rooms and get the dump on this Liebovic," said Matt, loud enough for the detainee to hear. "If he cooperates and gives you good info, release him. If he doesn't, or he gives you a hard time, just hold him till I get back."

The Asian glared at Matt as Jamaal and Klingler manhandled him to the door past Sheridan.

"They've got a chopper waiting for you on the roof," said Vo, following the prisoner with his eyes.

"Chopper? They must have a real hard-on about this one," said Matt.

Vo looked away.

"Problem, Sergeant?" asked Sheridan, taking a step closer.

"Yeah, problem," said Vo. "Respectfully, sir, I don't like what's going on here. It's not right. You've turned narcotics into a vigilante squad. You've been granted your own little army, complete with armor. You bring in a prisoner who's obviously been beaten in custody. An Asian at that, I might add. It's just not right."

"How long did you know Noah Benning?" Matt asked.

"That's not a fair question, and that's not the issue here. . . ."

"I knew him only a couple of months. How long did you work with him? Something like six years, right?"

Vo looked down at his shoes.

"We are in an E.Z. One of the worst in the country. We aren't narcotics detectives, because we never send anyone to prison. We destroy the narcotics, and turn the bad guys loose. To shoot at us. To deal more narcotics. To create new addicts. For someone who's been in this environment for as long as you have, I have to say I'm astounded at your attitude."

"These people are still human beings. . . ."

"No!" shouted Matt, driving his index finger into Vo's chest. "Kathy Benning is a human being. Seth, Benjamin, and Noah Junior are human beings. People with no respect for life are not human beings!" He turned toward the door to the elevator.

Under his breath, Vo mumbled, "What does that make you?"

The distance from the Alexandria Substation to Comarva headquarters in Northeast New Columbia was only a few miles, but could only practicably be reached by metro or helicopter. Located in the center of one of the most dangerous Red Sector E.Z.s in the country, road travel by anything less than armored vehicle was suicidal. This Red Sector E.Z. was for all intents and purposes a free fire zone, for both sides. Police efforts in this area were much closer to guerrilla warfare than crime fighting. But the headquarters had been built years before the sector had deteriorated so rapidly, and it was thought that any move of the regional police headquarters would give a negative indication of federal will to enforce the law. As a result, it was impossible simply to drive to headquarters.

The chopper, an upgraded UH-2000, rose from the roof of the Alexandria Substation and hopped quickly across the Potomac. This was Matt's first chopper ride since Iran, but the sensory memories of the typical chopper ride rushed rapidly back to him.

He was seated on a bench, facing out of the aircraft sideways, in the personnel area, by himself. He didn't have time to change out of his fatigues, but he did leave the helmet in his office. In the front of the aircraft were seated a pilot and a copilot, required by regulation rather than by the capability of the aircraft. In the wide, open sliding door frame of the personnel compartment, feet on the landing skids, sat a door gunner. He swiveled a frame-mounted Eraser, staring down its raised Plexiglas sights, scanning the ground.

As they neared the headquarters building, occupying a city block at Second and W streets, the copilot threw a body armor vest back to Matt. He pointed to the com set on his helmet, and Matt picked up one of several headsets lining the wall, putting it to his ear.

"Put that on and return it to one of the admin types once you're inside," said the copilot.

Matt had heard some stories about going to headquarters, but he hadn't believed any of them. Now he did, and he wished he'd kept his helmet.

He had just fastened the side panels of the armor when he felt the craft start to lower. The large building looked like it belonged in 1945 Berlin rather than 2021 America. It was pockmarked with innumerable bullet holes, and its original coat of white paint was graying. The row houses that surrounded the headquarters on all sides looked even worse for wear, many of them literally bombed out, most burned out. As the UH-2000 neared the roof landing pad, small orange sparks appeared in the top floor window of a house some three blocks away. Matt heard the rounds impact the fuselage, followed shortly by the ripping sound of the Eraser as the door gunner returned fire. Gun smoke began to fill the personnel compartment.

"Go, go, go!" shouted the copilot, waving Matt out of the helicopter.

Matt located the roof exit door through the front windscreen, ducked his head, and dove for the doorway.

As Matt passed, the door gunner held his fire. Standing on the landing skid, he noticed he was still four feet off the roof. But there was no time for landing. He jumped to the roof without incident, then ran to the roof door. The opposing gunner had been silenced. As Matt turned to wave at the chopper crew, they were already ascending rapidly. The chopper's gunner let loose one last burst for good measure, then the craft rolled left, toward the river.

"Shit," Matt said to himself, exhaling. Just inside the door, he was met by a uniformed patrol officer, who took his body armor.

"Lieutenant Sheridan?"

"Yes."

"Good. They're waiting for you downstairs." The officer, an African woman, hung the armor on a peg by the door.

"Lieutenant, are you carrying any weapons?"

Matt reached for his Colt at the small of his back and presented it with the safety clicked on. He dropped the magazine and handed the firearm to the officer.

"Thank you, Lieutenant," she said, leading him down the hall to a small office, inside which were numerous small lockers. She ran a card through a reader on the stack of lockers and opened one. She placed the pistol inside and closed the door. Matt noticed that her holster was empty as well.

"Number twenty-three, Lieutenant. You can claim it on your way out."

She took him to a secured door just beyond the small office and placed her palm against the Optics 200 plate, speaking her name into the small microphone on the doorjamb. The door swung open.

Without comment, she walked Matt to the end of a hallway that ran beyond the secured door, past rooms that looked like storage closets. At the end of the hall was an elevator, which seemed to be waiting for them, because it opened immediately when the officer pressed the call button. There were ten floors to the building, judging by the call panel, and the officer pressed eight. Seconds later the doors opened at the eighth floor.

The corridor there was well lit and tastefully carpeted. They walked past several empty meeting rooms, and finally the officer showed Matt into a large conference room. Immediately Matt recognized the frowning faces of Captain Flavius Blair, Director Jimmy Franklin, and Chief Sam Goldberg. There were three other individuals in the room, who Matt guessed would be the department lawyer, the civil liberties lawyer, and the independent counsel hired for the investigation.

Without invitation or a chance for anyone to speak, Matt went directly around the end of the conference table to the man he determined would be the independent counsel. He was a short, corpulent man with a red nose, thick glasses, and a pinky ring on his bloated right hand. Matt looked him directly in the eyes as he spoke. He nodded purposefully.

"Good afternoon, my name is Matt Sheridan from Nova Narco."

The little fat man swallowed hard. He cast a sideways glance at the men around the table, then spoke, blinking. "Good afternoon, Mr. Sheridan. My name is Stanley Karkowski." They shook hands. Matt nodded again, his eyes locked on Stanley.

Blair stood at that point, but Matt continued the introductions by himself. He walked over to a slight, mature African man, perhaps seventy years old. "Lieutenant Matt Sheridan."

"Afternoon, Lieutenant. I'm Edward Thompson, department counsel."

Matt turned and extended his hand to the third lawyer. The tall, slim, middle-aged European with a neatly trimmed mustache and beard did not extend his hand.

"Lieutenant, my name is Carlton Beck and I am here from the East Region Civil Liberties Agency."

Matt dropped his hand and smiled at Beck. "Pleasure to meet you."

"Lieutenant, would you please take a seat," said Blair, motioning to a seat on the far side of the conference table. No one sat next to him. From left to right, facing him across the table, sat Karkowski, Beck, Thompson, Blair, Franklin, and Goldberg.

"Lieutenant, I realize that you have been very busy today, but the reports of the shooting you were involved in last night have flagged the national civil liberties database as the second in a ninety-day period," said Blair, beginning the proceedings without ceremony. "Mr. Beck was assigned as counsel for this case, and he requested an emergency preliminary inquiry, and for that reason, we have called this meeting."

The mature African spoke. "Lieutenant, as department counsel, I will represent the department during today's discussions. Based on today's discussions, there may be further investigation, or even a call for a grand jury. The grand jury would then decide whether or not to indict you on any charges they might deem applicable. At this time, to proceed further, however, I am required to obtain your signature, as well as Counselor Beck's, agreeing to the binding terms of the independent counselor. You may decline to submit to the directions of the independent counsel, but I must forewarn you that refusing to sign will require further investigation by a grand jury."

"I'll sign," said Matt. A hardcopy of the agreement was passed to him along with a pen, and he signed. Beck then also signed.

As they signed, Karkowski was setting up his portable terminal on the conference table. He was obviously fumbling with applications and files. Next he produced what looked like an old-fashioned cassette recorder. The device was actually an automated court reporter, which could record, then transcribe into text, the conversations that would take place during the hearing. Finally, he scanned in the signed agreement and gave the original to Beck.

Beck spoke in a contemptuous baritone. "Lieutenant, we are about to discuss the events of last night. The report received in our database indicates that a complaint has been filed by a Mr. Martin Granger of Alexandria. His report indicates that following an incident outside the Pride of Dublin restaurant, he was shot by you without provocation, and subsequently tortured by you while awaiting medical assistance. We at CLA are treating this as a serious matter, hence this procedure. Mr. Karkowski has been hired as independent counsel for this matter. Mr. Karkowski, for your information, has worked with us on numerous occasions, and he has been very . . . successful in his efforts. He has read the police reports, medical reports, and victim's statement . . ."

"Victim?" Matt interrupted loudly. His interjection earned a cold stare from Beck.

"Victim's statement and eyewitness reports. He has not read your statement because you have yet to file one."

"I'm still within the twenty-four-hour window before disciplinary action," countered Matt.

Beck smiled. "Well, it seems you are quite familiar with these reports, then, aren't you, Mr. Sheridan?"

"I have no comment for that statement," said Matt. He could feel the arteries in his neck beginning to constrict.

"So, in the case that you do not have a report filed, I suggest that you might offer Counselor Karkowski a verbal of your side of the story, and we can go from there."

"My pleasure," said Matt, turning to look at, in turn, his superiors, and then Karkowski.

"Last night, around seven o'clock, I left the substation and went over to the Pride of Dublin to have a beer before I went home. It's the only place around the area to get good stout on draft," said Matt, lying.

"After I had my beer, I stepped outside to go home. I exchanged some words of pleasantry with an intoxicated patron, warning him about driving home, when I saw two men approaching me, an African and a European. As they got near me, I could see that the African was carrying a shotgun inside his trench coat. He aimed the shotgun at me, at which point we fought for the gun, and, I believe, one round was fired. Then the European, who I assume to be Mr. Granger, drew a pistol from beneath his jacket and fired two or three times. At that point, while I was still struggling with the African, he had gotten between Mr. Granger and me, and Mr. Granger's shots killed the African. One of the shots passed through his body and struck me in the left shoulder. I was wearing my vest at the time, and I was fortunate to get only a bruise from it. I fell to the pavement and pulled out my pistol, which, as an off-duty officer I am required to carry, and fired a single shot at Mr. Granger. When Mr. Granger went down, I went over and secured his weapon, ensured that he was carrying no other weapons, advised him of his rights, and then waited for police and medical units to arrive. When they arrived, I declined treatment and went home."

Beck chuckled. "I have a few questions I'd like to ask to clarify some of your story for Counselor Karkowski. Do you mind?"

"Go ahead, Mr. Beck."

Beck turned to Karkowski. "Any objections?"

"No, go ahead," said Stanley.

"Lieutenant, I guess I can almost see your point that you felt Mr. Granger was firing at you, although we know that he shot a Mr. Walter Jefferson. What I would like to focus on are your actions after the shooting. Can you tell us where you shot Mr. Granger?"

Matt smiled. "Alexandria."

Franklin and Goldberg snickered, but Beck was clearly not amused.

"On his person, Lieutenant."

"It was in the groin area, as I remember."

"Very painful, wouldn't you imagine, Lieutenant?"

"I would guess so."

"So explain why Mr. Granger charges that you knelt on his groin."

"Well, I knelt next to Mr. Granger to secure his weapon and to check to see if he had any others. I guess the pain was so bad that he thought that I was kneeling on him."

"And who is Cha, Mr. Sheridan?"

Flavius Blair leaned forward in his seat, glowering. Matt shrugged his shoulders. "Don't know."

"Mr. Granger claims that you were asking questions about Mr. Granger's relationship to him."

"Mr. Beck, this is the first I've heard that name."

"Don't patronize me, Lieutenant. Is not the suspect in the death of one of your detectives, Sergeant Noah Benning, named Cha?"

"Mr. Beck, that investigation is being handled by our homicide division, and I don't have access to that sort of information."

Beck frowned and turned to Stanley.

"Are there any other questions you would like to ask?"

Stanley thumped on his computer and read from the screen. "Yeah, Lieutenant, are you the same Captain Matthew Sheridan, USMC, honorably discharged?"

Matt nodded. "I guess that would be me."

"You won the Silver Star at Karachi in 'fifteen, didn't you?"

"I wasn't competing for it, so I wouldn't say I won it."

"You've been cited for bravery by the Federal Police Force how many times in the past five years?"

"Sir, I guess I never kept count."

"Seventeen times. Mr. Beck, do you recall how many times Mr. Granger has been arrested before this unfortunate incident?"

Beck looked incredulously at Karkowski. "I don't recall . . ."

"Twenty-four. Seven felony convictions, all resulting in remand to the confines of the Comarva Emergency Zone for probation."

Beck growled under his breath. "Karkowski!" Thompson, Blair, Franklin, and Goldberg were now on the edges of their seats.

"Based on the reports filed by police and eyewitnesses, and Lieutenant Sheridan's testimony today, I can see no evidence that would support the probable-cause requirements to send the claims of brutality by Mr. Granger on for further review. Furthermore, it appears to be a justifiable shooting in self-defense. Therefore, I see no point in pursuing this investigation further and wasting a lot of national investment. As arbiter, I am dismissing this case."

Matt let the nearly scalding water stream over him, and he recalled one of the very few pleasant memories of recuperation in Germany when he spent a weekend at a spa in Baden. However, the substation shower was a far cry from a European sanitarium. The day's events were still spinning and jumbled in his head, but he could still grasp the fact that he had been incredibly lucky at the inquiry. Now he owed Stanley.

Matt heard his name called from behind and he turned.

"Rosecroft! What do you want?" he asked.

Clark had poked his head into the three-place shower room. "Sorry to disturb you, but Joey Woo, the guy we hauled in today, gave us some good info on this Liebovic character."

"Good. Go ahead and release Mr. Woo. Let's run some ID checks and AKAs on Liebovic. Have Bromberg work through some of the details tonight. We'll go visit Mr. Liebovic tomorrow morning."

"Sir, with the information hot like this, I thought—"

"Rosecroft, you're really getting into this cop shit, aren't you? Unfortunately, I have a meeting tonight that I cannot avoid. And I'm hungry, and I've had only three hours sleep. We'll collect him tomorrow." Matt reached to the wall and turned off the water.

Rosecroft frowned.

"Sorry, Clark, but I'm putting only ten hours in today."

Rosecroft thought for a moment as Matt reached for his towel. "I see it is true what they say about you Europeans," he said, now laughing.

Matt reached to the soap holder and removed a large bar, which he promptly and vigorously threw at Clark, bouncing it off his head. Clark attempted to deflect it telekinetically, but was too late.

"Oww!"

Madison, Wisconsin, January 2004

The morning snow crunched beneath Roy Horace's feet as he walked toward the physical sciences building. He pulled the hood of his heavy parka tighter around his face, but it was no use against the thirty-degree-below-zero wind-chill factor. His glasses had fogged over and were nearly about to freeze, so he was forced to squint through two tiny clear areas on the lenses near the bridge of his nose. His left hand was pressed tight against his chest, hoping to keep warm the precious cargo he carried against his body.

Reaching the door to the building, he found it locked, which he expected. It was only the second of January, and classes would not begin for another week. The few students who remained on or near campus would still be hung over this early in the morning after Wisconsin's last-second victory over Washington State in the Rose Bowl the previous day. The building would be empty, so he would have no interruptions or distractions.

Being a teaching assistant afforded him the privilege of a key to the building, and he used his key to open the door. The lock was partially frozen, but with a few practiced jiggles he was able to coax it open. Inside, he did not turn on any hallway lights, but groped his way along the dim corridors to Lab A. He picked another key from his key ring and opened the door. Inside Lab A, he did turn on the lights. On one of the dozen tables in the room sat a glass box that looked rather like an aquarium, filled with clear liquid. Lying beside it on the table was what would look like, to the untrained eye, a set of automobile jumper cables that led toward to an electric outlet in the wall.

He went to the desk, then reached inside his coat to remove what he had carried so carefully. He produced two slender pieces of a silver-colored metal approximately six inches long by two inches wide and one inch deep. He set them on the table carefully. He removed his coat, then unlocked his private drawer in the lab table. His notebook and some back issues of various scientific journals were inside. He skimmed through his notes, but he knew the contents by heart. He breathed deeply, then put away the notebook. His hands shook slightly as he picked up one of the metal pieces and carefully attached to it one of the "jumper" clamps, sheathed in red plastic. He thought about the scientists in Utah from the early days, and how he would champion their reputations. He also thought about how angry he was that the government and the university turned down his requests for funds to conduct his experiment; and how he had ended up peddling marijuana on campus until he had enough money to buy the two pieces of beautiful metal on the table. And he thought that in just a few days he would be the most powerful sixteen-year-old Ph.D. candidate in history. And that there was a good chance that he'd finally get laid.

He attached the black-coated clamp to the second metal sliver, then lowered both slowly into the water. He thought he saw a few bubbles in the water already, but he didn't expect any major results until the apparatus had been powered for at least forty-eight hours. Or even seventy-two. There was an element of uncertainty in his experiment design, but it was groundbreaking. Roy Horace's heart was racing. Dramatically, almost theatrically, he followed the cable toward the electric outlet. The cable ended in a three-pronged grounding plug. He held the plug in his hand.

He plugged it into the wall.

Just as the prongs of the plug touched the outlet, the lights in the lab dimmed, flickered, then went out. *Another power outage,* he thought. The severe weather had a drastic effect on the local power grid, and as a result the Madison area was having brownouts and power outages. Shortly, Roy noticed that the emergency exit in the darkened hallway had returned to life, but the lights in the lab had not.

"Shit," he muttered, cursing aloud, knowing that his mother was hundreds of miles out of earshot.

He made sure the plug was all the way in the wall socket. When the power went out, some of the old circuit breakers must have been thrown, he thought, as they often did in power outages. It would be easy enough to flip the breakers. He had done it often enough that he knew exactly where the breaker box was located. But that was on the far end of the west wing of the physical sciences building, and here he was, with his experiment, in the far east wing of the physical sciences building. At least the apparatus would be powering up for a few minutes after he flipped the breaker, before he could return to the lab, he thought.

Again he groped along the darkened halls, not wanting to turn on any unnecessary lights. His glasses had unfogged, and he would have to deal only with pushing them back on his nose.

It took almost five minutes for Roy to reach the main breaker panel, located in a basement utility room in the west wing. He flipped open the panel door and saw that all the breakers for the east wing were thrown. He began to flip them one at a time. The last breaker for the east wing was the one that controlled Lab A. With a bored sigh he flipped it from the off to the on position.

The east wing of the physical sciences building was vaporized in a brilliant, searing flash of white light.

10

Matt played with the stirrer in his drink as he waited for Karen Russell to arrive. He'd sent her an emergency online requesting the meeting, which he was sure she would not like. He picked the New Orleans Café as their meeting place; it was just down the street from Karen's Skyline office. Later he was meeting Courtney there for dinner, to which she had agreed when he called her on the com after his shower.

Almost on time, Karen Russell slid into the semicircular booth next to him. She was clearly angry. Matt couldn't help notice her perfume again.

"This stunt could get both of us killed," she snarled under her breath.

"Sorry, but it's been a busy twenty-four hours, what with getting shot, shooting a guy, and having a civil liberties inquiry. How was your day?"

"I've read all the onlines. We've also started getting some reports on the activities of your praetorian guard today."

"Already?"

"Driving an armored vehicle through the streets of northern Virginia would raise some eyebrows, wouldn't you think?"

Matt did not respond.

"So you'd better not be asking for any more favors, because I have no more to give. First of all, I've expended every bit of political capital I have in the department, and second, our relationship will very soon become obvious. You realize that we will be in grave danger if that happens?"

"I'm in grave danger already, Ms. Russell."

She sighed. "Cut the 'Ms. Russell' bullshit." She waved at a waiter and ordered a vodka martini. The restaurant was nearly empty despite it being the dinner hour. In addition to the fact that the New Orleans Café had been deteriorating for several years, the restaurant industry itself had been sagging. While food and produce were subsidized by the federal government to keep prices relatively low for consumers, restaurant meals were taxed heavily. Twenty-five percent of a paycheck did not buy many restaurant meals.

"Our friends want guns," Matt said without introduction.

Karen's eyes widened. "They want guns?"

"I promised Karkowski I'd get him some."

"What?"

"Come on, Karen, you're the professional. I've got to prove my bona fides to them. I'm a cop; cops have guns, et cetera. This shouldn't be a surprise."

"I'm just surprised that they approached you this soon."

"Well, I'm still dealing just with Karkowski, so I haven't met any of 'them.' But if I can come up with some guns, I think I'll be on the fast track."

Karen smiled at the waiter as he returned with her drink.

"I don't like the idea of giving them guns. We usually try money or information first."

"Then let's give them guns they can't use."

"Explain?"

"All the data we have on them is that they use standardized ammunition. Nine-millimeter, five-five-six, and seven-six-two. Obviously, since there is no ammunition in the country available for private sale, they're undoubtedly manufacturing and reloading their own. Never find any brass at a CAP shooting, but we know from ballistics that they're shooting brass cartridges."

Karen shook her head slowly, concentrating on Matt's explanation.

"So let's give 'em something like the American Arms two-six-five . . ."

Karen smirked. "Caseless ammo."

"Exactly. None of the reports across the country ever show them using caseless ammo or weapons that fire it. They can't supply themselves with caseless, so they don't bother with it."

Karen plucked the olive from her martini and chewed it thoughtfully.

"Mr. Sheridan, you've got a great idea. How many and how soon?"

"The more and quicker the better. And they've got to have serials that can be traced back to the department. I'm sure they'll run them."

"Doable. I need to check with, uh, well, you know," said Karen, realizing they were rattling on about a top secret initiative in an uncleared public place. "How about five days?"

"That'll work."

Karen emptied her glass and stood. "By the way, take it a little easy with your Narcotics Response Team. Makes it hard to cover for you. And besides, I can't afford for you to get killed now."

"I'll think about it," Matt lied. As she passed, she drew her fingernails across Matt's back. He looked up at her, and she winked as she left the restaurant.

Courtney arrived some twenty minutes later, and Matt was on his third drink. He would need the false courage. She slid into the booth next to him, but not too close. She surprised him by ordering a draft beer.

"I'm glad you came."

"Did you think I wouldn't?"

"I wouldn't have blamed you."

Courtney sighed. "Look, Matt . . ."

"Wait. Please. First of all, I want to apologize for the other night. The way I acted, what I did, was wrong, and I am sorry."

"No, Matt, I'm sorry. I shouldn't have . . . Well, I . . ."

"Look. Let me try to explain. Maybe if I hear it come out of my own mouth I'll understand too. It's been five and a half years since Jenny was killed," said Matt. He paused and exhaled with a rush. "People get over things, move on with their lives, and mostly I have. So it's been over five years since I've been in any sort of a relationship, or even attempted one. And I care very much for you, Courtney, I really do. You have to know how special you are to me. But I've realized that I'm still not over Jenny. And not her dying, I've accepted that by now. But . . . I still love her, and I always will. Part of me died when she died, and I just don't know that I could ever love anyone again as much as I loved her."

Courtney slid over next to him and took his right hand. "Matt, I realize how much you love your wife, and I don't want to take that away. I don't want to take her place."

Matt squeezed her hand and felt his face flushing. "I need to do something, and I need your help, please."

"Whatever you need."

"I need to go up to Pennsylvania. To see my parents. And I've never visited Jenny's and Davey's graves. I need to—"

"I understand. I'll be happy to go with you."

"Thanks," said Matt. Almost on cue, the waiter arrived with Courtney's beer.

Owen Thomas watched in silence as the staff dismantled the gymnasium setup. Most of the equipment would be sent off to regional command centers, mainly west of the Mississippi. They would still need quite a bit of the equipment to support the upcoming operations in Virginia. After "the Big Show," as they had all started calling it around headquarters, it would be a long time before another permanent national headquarters could be reestablished. And who knew what the organization would look like afterward.

Judy strode next to Owen. "You're sad about leaving this dump, aren't you?"

"I guess I've grown attached to it. There is comfort in familiarity."

"Well, Murcheson says that his group has picked out a nice spot for us down in Virginia. He says it won't be quite as spacious as this place, but then again, this is like working in a barn."

Thomas chuckled. "You complain about everything, don't you?"

"That's my job," she replied. "Whoa, take those over there!" she shouted at a young man carrying a box full of computer equipment apparently in the wrong direction. She ran off after him.

Thomas turned and limped toward the far corner of the gym, which was as yet undisturbed. In a small conference area, consisting of a desk, four chairs, and a computer terminal, four men were putting the finishing touches on plans for the Manassas Penitentiary raid. Jimmy White Horse was doing the most talking, and Arthur was typing frantically on the computer keyboard. Dominic Passarella and Vince Miles, formerly Federal Police captains in the Boston area and currently tactical advisers, were reviewing hardcopy blueprints.

"How's it look, James?" asked Owen.

Jimmy White Horse turned in his chair. "I wish I had more time."

"We've got only a week left."

"I need another month to plan this properly. But we're just going to have to do our best. And we gotta move our operation, which really has me nervous."

"That's been in the works for months though."

"Yeah, well, I still don't like it."

"But just think, James. The move means we are getting close to the big show."

"Which is what I should be working on right now too. I need a whole other me to get all this done."

"James, we've got all the cells in the country working on that one. You have the easy part."

White Horse glared at Owen, then turned back to his blueprint.

Matt grimaced as he swallowed Oscar Vo's bad coffee, and looked, with a puzzled stare, at the information that Bromberg had pulled together on Liebovic. Bromberg found him in the local com directory, since he had no priors, and he didn't turn up in the known offender files. Rick Liebovic lived in the west end of Alexandria, not far from Skyline, in a middle-class "transitional" Green Sector neighborhood just inside the E.Z. Bromberg was able to access his plastic codes, and by tapping in, uncovered his entire life story, where he'd lived and worked and gone to school, his health records, and his cash and credit accounts. The only anomaly in the records was that he had no outstanding credit balance, which was generally unheard of. *So how did someone so clean come to be associated with jazzers, and why did some street punk name him as his supplier?*

Matt split the screen and selected the intercom function from the com menu. He entered Oscar Vo's office code and called him to the office.

"Close the door, Sergeant," said Matt. Vo stiffened on being called by his rank.

"I've been considering what you said yesterday in the garage."

"Sir, I'm sorry if I was out of line, but—"

"No, don't apologize, Oscar, I respect that you are a man of convictions. That's why I'm giving you the team today."

"Sir?"

"I'm going to follow up on the Liebovic thing personally today. We still don't have a replacement for Benning. You're next in command."

"But, Lieutenant, I have very little experience. . . ."

"Look, it'll be cake. Just cruise around in the Schwarzkopf for a couple hours, hand out some fliers, and kick some ass if necessary. The men have all had Tactical Response Team training and experience. They can run themselves for a day. But I want you to do it. I'm doing this because a) I have confidence in you, and b) I think you need to see a little more of the streets," said Matt evenly.

"Sir . . ."

"Thank you, Sergeant," said Matt, returning to the computer screen.

"But, sir . . ."

"Could you find Rosecroft and send him in here on your way back to your office?" asked Matt, ending the discussion. Vo stormed out of Matt's office, slamming the door behind him.

With mid-morning traffic it was a ten-minute ride out to the Alexandria Arms apartments, just inside the city's western boundary. Rosecroft rode with Sheridan, his nose buried in one of the hardcopy comic books he loved to read: cyber-slasher super-hero pulp put out by the handful of approved comic presses. Sheridan glanced over at him several times during the trip, but Clark was too engrossed to notice. Matt laughed and shook his head.

They arrived at the apartments, which were in three-story gardenstyle buildings. There were dozens of the buildings at the top of a rather steep hill, off the main street, Beauregard. The hummer strained as it attempted to carry the two men up the hill.

Matt located the building number they were seeking and parked in the lot in front. Rosecroft put down his comic book.

"This certainly doesn't look like the environs of a jazz dealer," Matt remarked.

"Jazz is an equal opportunity narcotic," quipped Rosecroft.

"We still need to be careful. The online said that Mr. Liebovic works as a programmer, so I'm thinking there's a good chance we might find him here," said Matt. He exited the vehicle, patting at the small of his back. Rosecroft followed. The November morning was crisp, and the men's breath steamed from their nostrils.

Liebovic's apartment was on the first floor of the building. Inside the hallway, Matt guessed that one set of sliding doors out to a small patio in front of the building belonged to Liebovic. In front of the door, Matt reached inside his overcoat and withdrew his badge. Rosecroft fumbled with his wallet for a moment, then finally shrugged his shoulders, empty-handed. Matt rolled his eyes at him.

As they stood on either side of the apartment door, Matt rapped on it. There was no immediate answer. He knocked again, harder this time. After thirty seconds there still was no answer.

"Do your thing, Rosecroft."

Clark stood in front of the door and concentrated on the knob. The knob began to jiggle at first. Then the door began to shake, then suddenly, with a terrific ripping sound, was blown inward off its hinges.

Matt looked at Clark, the Colt now in his hand. "Jeez, Rosecroft, I just wanted you to take a turn knocking," he said, winking.

"Federal Police!" Matt shouted as he entered the apartment. He entered the living room, which seemed fairly neat for a reported bachelor. He noticed the leather furniture, the extensive entertainment center, and the fine artworks hung on the walls. *These are not the effects of a workaday computer programmer.*

Down a carpeted hallway leading out of the living room, a door opened, and a skinny young man, half asleep and in his underwear, emerged.

"What the hell?" he mumbled, trying to force his pupils to narrow to the sunlight streaming in through the sliding glass door.

Matt rushed up to him, grabbed one of his arms, and tossed him to the floor. "Secure him, Rosecroft," he ordered. Clark walked slowly up to the man lying on his stomach, and concentrated on his back. The young man was pinned to the floor.

Matt slid next to the open door, then swung into the room in a crouch. A blond woman, probably in her early twenties, lay in bed, the sheets pulled up to cover her nakedness. She screamed as Matt entered the room.

"Put your clothes on and get outta here," barked Sheridan. He watched her dress to make sure she did not have a weapon, then with the Colt directed her out of the room. She was visibly shaken, and she screamed when she went into the hall and saw the young man lying on the floor.

"Rick! What's going on?"

"I said, get outta here!" shouted Matt. This time the girl obeyed and she ran for the front door.

Matt scanned the bedroom. It was sparsely but elegantly furnished, with a regent-sized water bed, an antique rolltop desk, and a computer terminal. He was then back in the hall, and moved to a second door. He swung it open and ducked in to discover the bathroom.

He moved slowly toward a final door to avoid any surprises. He turned the doorknob slowly, then swung the door inward. Crouching in the doorway, he noticed the curtains were drawn and the room was dark. He flipped on the light switch, then whistled.

"Jackpot!" he shouted. The room held three fifty-five-gallon drums and numerous cardboard boxes. There was a small table in the room with measuring devices for liquids and powders. In a corner of the room was a two-foot-high stack of scrip notes. And propped against the wall was an M16A4. Sheridan walked back to the living room. "Mr. Liebovic, I presume?"

"I want an attorney," said the prone man.

"All right, Rickie, we can do that, but I've got two quick questions to ask you before we call. First, I want the name of your supplier, and second, I want to know where Cha is."

"I have nothing to say without my lawyer."

"Well, Mr. Liebovic, in my world there are two ways to do things, the easy way and the hard way. I detect you're choosing the hard way."

Liebovic did not respond.

"Sheridan . . ." Rosecroft began to interrupt.

Matt straddled the man. "Let go of him, Rosecroft."

Without awaiting confirmation of his order, Sheridan yanked the man to a standing position by his full head of hair. The man screamed.

"I want my goddamn attorney now!"

Matt spun the man to face him, and then cocked his right arm. Rosecroft jumped between them, grabbing Matt's arm.

"Rosecroft!"

"Matt, hold up! You're in enough trouble already. We're in a Green Sector and this guy has no priors. You'll be in deep shit if you work him. Unless you're gonna kill him, we gotta take him in."

Matt pushed Rosecroft aside and his pistol suddenly emerged in his hand. Liebovic's look of smug satisfaction turned to abject fear. Matt worked the heavy slide and pressed the barrel to Liebovic's forehead. Tremors ran through Liebovic's body.

"I want Cha!" Matt screamed, spittle flying from his mouth. He shoved Liebovic's head backward with the barrel of the pistol, the hammer of which he then cautiously lowered with his thumb. Matt exhaled.

"Okay. Rosecroft, two calls. First, we need Crime Scene out here to take care of all this shit. Second, call, uh, Sloane and have him run in George Bender for questioning. Usual suspect sort of thing."

Rosecroft exhaled too, relaxing. He grinned. "Be happy to."

Matt began to drag Rick Liebovic out to the car.

"Can't I get my pants or some clothes?"

"No."

Sheridan dragged Rick Liebovic from the rear passenger seat when they reached the substation garage and pulled him toward the elevator. His bare feet scuffed against the pavement.

"When am I gonna get my lawyer?"

"As soon as we're at the detention area, you can get him on the com."

Matt and his prisoner, followed closely behind by a breathless and speechless Rosecroft, elicited many strange glances from the substation occupants. The three men rode the elevator to the top floor, where the short-term holding cells were located. They passed through two security doors, then approached a third, where a uniformed officer collected Matt's pistol. Through the third door they entered the large holding-cell area. There were ten cells, side by side, each occupied. The cells served as a temporary holding facility, keeping suspects for several hours while being processed, or for the odd overnight stay.

In the middle of the 150-foot room was a single, lonely desk, at which a corrections officer normally sat. At this moment, however, he was kneeling next to a plainclothes police officer, Doug Sloane, who sat on the floor. Both were perspiring heavily and breathing hard. A trickle of blood ran from Officer Sloane's lower lip, which was split. They both looked up as Sheridan, party of three, approached.

"Sheridan, you owe me big time for this one," said Sloane, the killer of the killer of Lieutenant Solinsky.

"I already owe you, Sloane," said Matt as he approached.

Matt led Liebovic over to the desk, and immediately hoots and catcalls directed at the new detainee began to emanate from the ten cells. There was a com on the desk, and Sheridan allowed Liebovic to send his one com. Liebovic shuddered as his lawyer told him it would be at least ninety minutes before he could make it to the station. Matt looked on, amused.

"Well, Rickie, as soon as your lawyer gets here we can move to one of the interrogation rooms downstairs. But until then, I'm afraid I'll have to incarcerate you."

Liebovic rolled his eyes. "Look man, I'm freezing. Can't I get a uniform or something?"

"Mr. Liebovic, you've not been convicted of any crime, so you're not a prisoner of the federal government's. Right now you're a suspect who won't talk, who is waiting for his lawyer. I wouldn't want to demean you by putting you in a prison uniform."

"You're Sheridan, right? That's what they called you. Look, Sheridan, I think you're making a big mistake. . . ."

"Officer McGarrity," Matt called to the corrections officer. "We need to put this suspect into a cell. Let's put him in, uh, seven, shall we?"

Sloane and McGarrity gave Matt knowing grins. "Oh, you mean with George Bender? 'Back door' Bender? 'Bend over' Bender? Well, Lieutenant, these cells do hold two persons, and no other is available. Wouldn't want to be insufficient about it . . ." said McGarrity as he grabbed Liebovic by the upper arm and led him to cell seven. Liebovic stared wide-eyed as they approached the cell, its occupant currently handcuffed through the bars.

George Bender, an angry man, stood only five feet nine inches, but weighed over two hundred pounds, not an ounce of it fat. His face was nearly disfigured from numerous scars, physical records of his many violent encounters with his fellow man. He was dressed in a T-shirt and jeans, and his huge biceps rolled back the sleeves of the shirt. He, too, was perspiring.

Sloane turned to Sheridan. "Took both of us to get him in there, with cuffs on him."

"I'm not surprised," said Matt.

"Wait a minute, what's going on now?" shouted Liebovic, trembling.

"Rickie, you're not very swift. I'll repeat. We're putting you in a cell to wait for your lawyer to get here so you'll talk to us."

Standing in front of cell seven, they were close enough for George Bender to hear. He smiled a jagged, semitoothless smile from ear to ear.

"Got some company for you, George," said McGarrity.

"Wait . . . wait . . ." stammered Liebovic, his eyes filling with tears.

McGarrity ran a key card through the reader on the cell door, then flipped the toggle. The cell door slid sideways. George Bender tugged against his handcuffs. As McGarrity shoved Liebovic through the door, Matt used his restraint tool to slip the nylon fetters from his wrists. McGarrity slid the door closed.

"Officer McGarrity, Officer Sloane," said Matt, loud enough for everyone in the room to hear. "You two have obviously been in an altercation. Why don't you leave your keys with me and head on down to first aid and get looked at. I'll keep an eye on the prisoners."

McGarrity laughed as he handed over his handcuff keys and his key card and walked toward the security door. Sloane approached Sheridan.

"What's this guy in for, Lieutenant?"

"He had a six-month supply of jazz for all Comarva in his apartment. Paraphernalia. Assault rifle."

Sloane looked the shivering Liebovic up and down.

"Have fun, George," Sloane shouted as he walked for the door, blowing a kiss to the muscular man.

"Rosecroft?" asked Matt.

"Uh, Lieutenant, I have to file some forms before Mr. Liebovic's attorney gets here."

"Well, get on with it, Rosecroft," ordered Matt. Rosecroft, too, shuffled out the door.

When the door had shut, Liebovic began to scream. "You can't do this to me! Let me out of here!" George looked over his shoulder and snarled at Liebovic.

"Well, Rickie, the time for cooperation has passed, I'm afraid. I only needed answers to two simple questions and you wouldn't help me. I just can't help you now, especially since you requested your attorney."

"Sheridan!" he screamed.

Matt ignored him. "Now, George, do you think you've calmed down enough that I can uncuff you?"

George nodded vigorously.

Liebovic sobbed. "No! Please, don't!"

Matt continued. "All right, nice and easy, George, I'm gonna uncuff you."

"Thank you, Officer," said George, a thin line of drool dripping from his lower lip.

"Dear God . . ."

"Liebovic, if you're praying in there, I'll have to send someone up from Sufficiency to question you," said Matt. He unlocked Bender's handcuffs. Bender smiled and turned toward Liebovic.

"Stop! Stop!"

"Oh, you know something, Rickie," asked Matt. "I forgot to tell Rosecroft to book us one of the interrogation rooms for when your lawyer shows up—in ninety minutes. I'd better go tell him. I'll be back in just a little while." He walked away without another word.

As Sheridan neared the door, he heard Liebovic screaming for him to come back, his pitch and volume rising with every word. He passed through the security door, and just before it shut he could hear Liebovic screaming his name from cell seven.

Matt accepted his pistol from the officer at the security station, then motioned for the officer to follow him back into the cell area. Liebovic wailed, "I'll talk! I'll talk!"

Liebovic, wearing a new federal corrections uniform and holding a cup of coffee, sat in a visitor's chair in Matt's office. Matt sat at his desk, typing into his computer. Rosecroft stood in front of the door, and Oscar Vo sat in the other visitor's chair.

"All right, one more time. I hold for Cha. I keep it because I've got no priors, and I qualified for the Green Sector apartment. I take delivery every month from an old Italian guy named Morelli. That's all I know about him, I swear. I meet him in a garage in one of the old buildings in Coffin City. I bring the stuff back to my apartment. Cha comes by, usually brings some of his lower ranking dealers with him. We package the jazz, he and his men take it, and that's it. They pay me scrip, and I don't ask any other questions." Liebovic drank from the coffee cup, and his hands shook.

"What about the Gutters?" Matt asked.

"I don't really deal with them. I do know he doesn't live with them; he's got some luxury condo up in Rosslyn. All I know is that you don't fuck with Gutters, and they're moving jazz big-time in Comarva. You made a small mistake, Lieutenant, before, when you said I had a six-month supply of jazz for Comarva. That was only two months' worth."

"Holy shit," Matt muttered.

"Really, that's all I have," said Liebovic.

Matt stared at him, then pushed the intercom application on his machine.

"Detective Saunders, would you please stop by admin and pick up a package they have for me there, then bring it to my office, please?" he said. He closed the application without awaiting a response. The room was silent for five minutes before Detective Saunders knocked on the door and entered the office.

"Your package, Lieutenant."

"Detective, can you hold up a minute?" Matt asked. He handed the package across to Liebovic.

"Rick, this is a one-way MagLev ticket to St. Louis. I suggest you take it before your lawyer gets here. I'll have Detective Saunders drive you by your apartment so you can get some clothes, then to the metro station. I suggest you disappear. No charges will be pressed. If you decide to wait for your lawyer, charges will be pressed, and you'll have to wait here until you post bond."

"Hey, I cooperated with you. I don't like—"

"Rosecroft, you and Detective Saunders take Mr. Liebovic back upstairs to holding until his lawyer gets here."

"No, wait! Wait a second. . . . Okay, I'll take the ticket."

"But before you go, I have one last request," said Matt.

Matt and Rosecroft slouched in the hummer, far across the parking lot from the apartment building. Officer Sloane's hummer was parked much closer. It had been a few hours since Liebovic's call had been routed from the substation through his home com to the online address where Cha picked up his messages. Sheridan had called up some technicians from technical support, but they were unable to trace or locate the address. They were still working the problem, and thought that within a few days they would be able to reverse-engineer the physical location of the com on the receiving end. But Liebovic had dutifully left his message, and by that time was probably halfway to St. Louis.

Matt's hunch paid off shortly thereafter. He noticed the battered hummer swing into the lot, parking just two cars away from Sloane. Two unkempt Latins emerged from the car, looked around carefully, then entered the apartment building.

"You got 'em, Sloane?" Matt asked into the com set on his collar.

"Yeah, two males, Latins, wearing Gutter colors."

"Don't lose them when they come back out," instructed Matt. Indeed, the pair soon emerged from the building, obviously angered by the discovery of the empty apartment.

"I haven't lost one yet," bragged Sloane.

"No need to break your streak, then."

The two Latins jumped back in their hummer, which whirred to life. The tires squealed as they backed out of the parking space, and metal ground as they hastily changed gears.

"All right, Sloane, go get 'em. Call in wherever they stop, and we'll get a surveillance team on them." Matt spoke into the com.

"Ten four, L.T.," said Sloane, pulling out behind the suspect hummer.

Matt smiled at Rosecroft. "This is starting to get good."

The president was not at all impressed as Bryan Carruthers swaggered into the Oval Office. The head anchor for the Central News Agency as well as the elected head of the Federal Media Council, Carruthers exuded more self-confidence than one would expect when meeting the President of the Federal States. But Carruthers thought he owned President Kersey, and had said as much on any number of occasions off camera. Carruthers was in his late forties, tall, handsome, and fit. His tan was still deep despite the fact it was the middle of November; he wore an imported handmade silk suit and a heavy cologne to match his personality. He strode to Kersey's desk, where the president stood, then sank into one of two real leather chairs without invitation. Kersey frowned at Carruthers, but the newsman simply smiled and crossed his legs.

"You rang?" dribbled from Carruthers's mouth.

The president sat. "Yes, Bryan. Thanks for coming. I called you in today because I need a favor."

"Of course," smirked Carruthers.

Kersey's teeth clenched and unclenched. "Bryan, the media play an extremely important role in the government of our country . . ."

No shit, thought Carruthers. "Of course."

"The American people long ago recognized the partnership between the three original branches of government and the media, and for that reason we officially created the fourth, the National Media Council."

Carruthers closed his eyes dramatically, then propped up his face with two fingers from his right hand. "And?"

Kersey coughed into his fist, his throat tightening. "And so there has been close participation by the executive branch, particularly, in contributing to the media.

I got you elected, didn't I, thought Carruthers. "So?"

Kersey walked from behind the huge oak desk and sat in the visitor's seat opposite Carruthers. "So that's why, from one arm of the federal government to the other, I am asking for your help. With the CAP problem."

Carruthers sat up in his chair. "What exactly do you mean?"

"We need to make the American people aware of what a threat these terrorists are to our way of life. They need to see more than just the cut-and-dried news items. We need to help them focus on the problem, to help join the fight against these bastards."

Carruthers leaned forward, elbows on knees, both index fingers pressed to his lips.

"The media has great power. I'm asking you, for the sake of the country, to consider using your editorial prerogative to tell the American people the truth. Help them see the problem in our midst.

And maybe win yourself another Emmy, thought Carruthers. "I see."

"If we can help the American people understand what the danger is, the Confederation of American Patriots will wither on the vine. The media can help us defeat the CAPs," said Kersey.

Carruthers nodded, then stood. "I will take that under advisement, and I will pass it along at the next meeting of the National Media Council." Without further notice, Carruthers strode out of the room the way he came in.

As the doors closed behind Carruthers, Kersey moved to the window behind his desk and stared out past the Ellipse to the Washington Monument. "I really hate that prick," he muttered to himself.

"A week?" Matt shouted into the com.

"Sorry, Lieutenant. That's the soonest we'll have any sort of good info. I gotta set up the stake, get people lined up to work it, then we gotta watch these shits for a few days to get a good idea of who's coming and going, and what's going on in the building," replied Sloane.

"What about the info from Valdez and Jackson? Can't we get anything from that?"

"Respectfully, Lieutenant, if we didn't already have all the intel from Valdez and Jackson, I'd say you'd be lookin' at three weeks to a month."

"Shit!" shouted Sheridan.

"Lieutenant, again, respectfully, sir, I want to kick in the friggin' door to this place myself. As much as you. But if we're gonna send men in there, we gotta know their habits inside-out. We don't want any of the good guys getting hurt."

Sheridan sighed. "Never tell anyone that I admit you're right, in this case." He did not wait for the laugh on the other end to cut the com line.

Matt looked down the hallway through his open office door and realized that the second shift was starting to filter in. *Time to go home.*

11

Matt was dreaming of Karachi again, when Courtney shook his shoulder. His conscious mind fought against the cobwebs and confusion of sleep, and he remembered that he was in his apartment, in his bed. Squinting against the darkness, trying to use the tiny amount of ambient light for sight, Matt noticed Courtney was holding the remote com handset out to him. He sat up and touched on a bedside light. He blinked violently against the sudden brightness.

Courtney closed her eyes and did not reopen them. *She is so sexy when she's rumpled like that,* Matt thought. The tone of her voice, however, was anything but sexy.

"Some woman needs to speak to you, and won't give her name," she growled. Matt looked at his nightstand clock. *Two A.M.*

He took the handset from her, then swiveled in bed to turn his back to her. "Hello?"

"I need to see you. Now." *It was Karen Russell.*

"What . . ."

"You know what."

Matt paused, his conscious mind finally winning out over his subconscious.

"All right, where . . ."

"Just go get in your car. I'll get you on your remote com."

The line went dead. Matt turned to Courtney, who had reopened her eyes and was pouting. Matt handed her the phone.

"And that was?"

Matt sighed. "I . . . can't tell you." He felt the warm sensation in his chest as he watched her react in the light. She was wearing the sheer red negligee she had bought from an underground mail-order company just a few days before and received today. *Yesterday, actually.* Despite the tension of the moment, Matt could feel the stirring . . .

"Bullshit!" she said. Matt's jaw dropped. It was the first time he'd heard her curse. Ever.

He lowered his head. "Look. I can't tell you everything. It's part of that . . . undercover assignment I'm working."

"Something to do with that jazz gang?" she asked, her frown lifting ever so slightly.

"Kind of, yeah," Matt lied. *I promised myself I wouldn't lie to Courtney, but I can't tell her the whole truth. It's too dangerous. Besides, I'm not telling a complete lie.*

He rose quickly from the bed, and, without a word, pulled on the sweatshirt and jeans he'd discarded on the floor the night before. He tugged on his boots and secured the Velcro straps on them tightly. He took his .45, still in its belt holster, from the nightstand, and clipped it inside the back of his pants. He looked over at Courtney, and she was watching him with sad eyes.

"Well, the sooner I get this project done, the sooner I can get out of it." He shrugged his shoulders.

"Will you be back before morning?" she asked.

He shook his head. "I really don't know. I will try."

She lay down silently, turning on her side with her back to him.

He sighed and turned out the light, then walked toward the bedroom door.

"Be careful," she called after him.

Matt slowed as he approached his car in the underground garage. There was someone in the passenger seat. The Colt was in his hand, held low against his right leg as he strode cautiously toward the car. He looked around, and over both shoulders, for any signs of additional parties, or an ambush. He saw none.

He ducked behind a large van, then doubled back toward the far wall of the garage. There, he crouched and duck-walked behind the various parked vehicles, toward the row in which his department-issue hummer was parked. It was in the front space of a two-car row, its tail next to the nose of the car parked behind it. There was a lane behind the second car, but Matt stayed close to the other cars aligned in the second space. He raised the .45 into a firing grip, then charged the passenger door of his car.

"Freeze!" he shouted, almost pressing the muzzle of the pistol against the window of the car. The person in the passenger seat jumped. Matt lowered his weapon.

"Holy shit, I think I pissed my pants," said Karen Russell, rolling down the car window.

"Good. What the fuck are you doing in my car?"

"Not so loud. Just shut up and get in."

Matt obeyed, and circled around to the driver's side. He slumped into the seat.

"What's going on, Karen?" he demanded.

"Not so loud."

"What's going on?" he repeated in a snarled whisper.

"I got your guns."

Matt was somewhat taken aback by her brusque pronouncement. "What?"

"Are you mentally challenged? I said I got the guns you asked for."

"Where?"

Karen smiled. "In your trunk."

Matt rolled his eyes and slammed his head into the headrest.

"In my trunk?"

"Yes."

"What am I supposed to do with guns in the trunk of my fucking department car?" Matt shouted.

Karen pulled back on the door handle and swung the door open. "I suggest you get them to our friends as soon as possible."

Matt was still cursing under his breath as he neared the Pride of Dublin. It was a little past two-thirty A.M. *Tomorrow, no, today, was Saturday. We're supposed to drive up to see my family in Pennsylvania. In fact, we're supposed to get up in a few hours to get ready. Shit.*

Before he left the garage, Matt had verified that, indeed, a crate with fifty American Arms Model 265 10mm machine pistols was in his trunk. He had checked the weapons on top of the stack and found that they had serial numbers beginning with three letters, D, S, I; Department of Security, Internal. He had assumed the rest were similarly marked. He was near panic wondering what he would do with the guns overnight, but realized that the Pride of Dublin didn't close until three. Maybe Stanley was there.

Just as Matt was maneuvering into a parking spot, across King Street from the Pride, he noticed a familiar bloblike figure stumble through the front door. Matt cut the starter and leapt from the hummer.

Looking both ways on instinct, he ran across the street and quickly caught up with the staggerer. He slammed his arm across the man's shoulders.

"Stosh, *vshistko v porzadku?*"

"*Tak, doskonale . . .*" Stanley slurred. His brain then catching up with his mouth, he glared at Matt.

"Sheridan! You speak Polish?"

"*Mooveeh mawo po polsku.* I took a semester in college."

"Well, I'm fuckin' impressed," Stanley snarled. Matt began to steer him in the direction of the car.

"Stanley, I need to talk to you over this way. It's very important."

"Sheridan, I'm drunk and I want to go home. . . ."

"Stanley, don't make me bust you for public intoxication."

Stanley harumphed, then complied with Matt. They crossed King Street and went to the rear of Matt's car.

"Okay, Stanley, I got your order. I want them out of my car tonight."

"You're shittin' me."

"Honest, Stosh. I got a crate in my trunk. If I have to open it up here on the street to show you, I might as well just kill the both of us right now," said Matt in a serious tone.

"Hmm . . . All right, wait here," said Stanley. He turned and started back to the Pride. Matt watched in confusion.

Matt leaned against his car. He began to shift weight from his right foot to his left; he left his apartment wearing only his sweatshirt, and the mid-November air chilled him. He hopped for almost ten minutes before Stanley reemerged, ashen-faced.

"What's up, Stanley?"

"You know where Lake Accotink Park is?" Stanley asked, his voice unsteady.

"Yeah, pretty much."

"Drive over to Lake Accotink Park. Go all the way in to the parking area. You'll be met there. Make sure you're not followed. And you must never come back here. And you must never contact me again."

Matt nodded and extended his hand to Stanley. They shook.

"*Biw meewi chee spokatch*, Stosh."

"You too, Sheridan."

With those words, Stanley turned and was gone forever.

Lake Accotink Park was nestled in a residential area of Springfield, Virginia. An access road into the park ran at an oblique angle from the closest state road. The park featured a modest lake, a dammed stream, and a small manmade beach. During the day in November, there would be few, if any, souls enjoying the park. At three A.M., it was deserted.

Matt stayed in the car, which he parked in the lot pointed toward the access road. He turned off his lights but left the motor running. The heater was on, and the car was warming up, but Matt's hands remained ice cold.

Shortly, a pair of lights appeared on the access road, just above and to the right of the parking lot. The lights were attached to a large van, and as it made the hairpin left into the parking lot, they were turned up to high beam. Matt was practically blinded, and he stepped out of his car. He tried to shield his eyes with his left arm, to little avail.

Matt could hear doors opening and a sliding door sliding. There was the sound of numerous feet on the gravel, and four figures emerged in the beams of the headlights. Three of the figures were massive and towering. They were the size of Jamaal and Klingler, or better. The fourth figure was smaller, but still tall. Matt could make out very little of the features of the three figures, but he could tell that the three giants were dressed in black, including masks, and carried old M16A2s, which looked like toys against their gargantuan frames.

The fourth figure stepped toward Sheridan, and Matt could see that he did not wear a mask. In fact, Matt was startled to recognize him.

"Skip?"

The fourth figure extended his hand. "Last name Murcheson," he said evenly. They shook.

"Stanley tells me you have something for us."

Matt's heart was pounding. "That's correct."

"Tell me why you want to give us something."

"Because I want in."

Skip was silent for a moment. He rubbed his face.

"Sheridan, you realize what you've done is very dangerous . . ."

"I'm no Person Scout, Skip. I've seen some of this world—"

"I know," Skip interrupted. "I can't guarantee you'll be accepted. You realize if you're not, you've just signed your own death warrant?"

"I signed that long ago, Skip," said Matt. *How ridiculous to discuss a matter of life and death with a man named Skip. From now on I'll call him Murcheson,* he thought.

"Then let's see what you have for us," said Murcheson, striding past Matt toward his car.

Matt followed, pointing toward the trunk. Matt opened the trunk, revealing the wooden crate. He lifted off the lid and pulled back a chamois cloth to display the first layer of ten machine pistols. Without invitation, Murcheson reached in and withdrew one. The American Arms 265 was somewhat larger than a standard pistol and slightly smaller than a submachine gun. Its standard staggered box magazine held thirty rounds of caseless 10mm ammunition. These weapons were equipped with extended fifty-round magazines. With rates of fire in excess of twelve hundred rounds per minute, the American Arms 265 was one of the most impressive firearms in the federal inventory.

Murcheson slid out the extending stock and shouldered the weapon, dropped the magazine, and checked the receiver. He fingered the fire-select switch, which had options of safe, single round, three-round burst, and full auto. He returned the weapon to the crate.

"Very impressive. Still have packing grease on them."

"Brand new out of inventory. They just got 'lost' this week."

Murcheson nodded. "What about ammo?"

"What about it?"

"We're, uh, a little low on ten-millimeter caseless right now."

Exactly, thought Matt. "I didn't know—"

"Can you get some?"

"Probably, but I may be pushing it—"

"How soon do you think you could get your hands on some?"

"Well, I'm going out of town later today, be a few days. Soonest would be late next week. And ammunition is a little bit tougher than guns."

"Shit," Murcheson muttered. "All right. This is still good, but I could really use the ammo sooner. I'll be glad to accept these weapons on behalf of the Confederation of American Patriots," said Murcheson, extending his hand again. Matt accepted it.

"Boomer, a little help, please," Murcheson shouted toward the van. One of the giant figures handed his rifle to another, then strode to the hummer.

Murcheson pointed to the crate, the lid to which he had just restored. "Let's get this in the van."

Matt opened his mouth to interject that "Boomer" might need some help. Before he could speak, Boomer, who, on closer inspection, Matt guessed was close to seven feet tall, lifted the crate out of the trunk effortlessly. He walked casually back to the van.

Murcheson closed the trunk. "Matt, I'd like you to meet some people. Will you be back next Saturday?"

"Most likely, yeah."

"Okay, next Saturday, around midnight, meet me here. We'll go for a ride."

Matt nodded.

Murcheson nodded back, then slapped Matt on the arm as he trotted back to the van. Doors closed, and the van nimbly turned in the lot, then disappeared down the access road.

The apartment was still dark when Matt returned at three-thirty. He stopped at his com and left a message on Karen's com that he had a report to file, and nothing more. He walked quietly to the bedroom. Courtney was still in bed, with her back to him. He undressed, carefully setting his pistol and holster on the nightstand, and gently got under the covers.

"Everything okay?" Courtney asked without turning to Matt.

"Yeah, fine. Everything went okay."

"Who's the woman?" she asked.

Matt sat up in bed and turned on the light. He tugged on Courtney's shoulder, and she turned over to him.

"Courtney, there are some things about me that I'd prefer you didn't know. They are things that I'd prefer *I* didn't know. But right now I'm between a rock and a hard place. I can't get out until I finish this project I'm working. And to be honest, it has nothing to do with my job as a cop. There's a part of my life that I've been trying to bury, and right now I've been dragged back into it. I can't tell you what's going on because I don't want you involved in any way, shape, or form. I won't tell you. I'm sorry. I'm in enough jeopardy myself right now as it is."

She sat up in bed and folded her arms, but said nothing.

"I don't mean to hurt you, Courtney. And I sure as hell don't want you to get hurt. That's why I don't want you to get involved in this other part of me. Not even as much as knowing what's going on. It's for your own good. . . ."

"I thought I knew you, Matt. Or I was getting to know you. But I don't know who you are at all, do I?"

Matt dropped his chin to his chest. "You do. You know the me that I've shown you. And it's all true. It's all very real. But the things I haven't told you, the me you've never met . . . I don't want you to know. Not even Matthew Sheridan, Cop. Everything I've told you, everything I've shared with you, I swear it's all true. But when I go through the door, go out into the world, I'm . . . different. I don't like myself that way. I know you won't like me either."

"So that's why you've been trying to get yourself killed?" she asked sharply. Matt's shoulders sagged.

"Matt, I'm sorry . . ."

"No, you're right, I guess. Partially. I guess, it's just that—" Matt sighed heavily. "After I married Jenny I realized that she could help me bury the things in my past. She was so good, such a good person, it seemed like she canceled out all the . . . evil that I'd been through. I got out of the service and got a job as a cop. Mainly because I didn't have any other choices. But mostly, I wanted to do good. I know that sounds pretty corny, but I was changing. I wanted to forget the bad side, the bad stuff. When she died, I knew what I would become again. And I did. So the only way to feel good again, to feel alive again, was to be with her again. Now, that really sounds stupid. But I've been emotionally dead since she died. I couldn't kill myself; there's no honor in that. But if I was killed in the line of duty, well, there's all sorts of honor in that, right? Well, try as I might, and as close as I've come, it never happened. Either I'm the luckiest man on earth, or I'm just not meant to go right now. Or a little of both. Jenny used to say that everything happens for a reason. I guess she's right, somewhat. So that's why I . . . have done the things I've done."

Courtney pressed her lips together tightly.

"But since I've met you, I feel different. I haven't felt like this since before Jenny died. You make the good side come back too. And that's why I need to go home this weekend. There are some things I need to resolve within myself. And I can't do it without you. You're very special to me. But I'm not free of my other life just yet. If you can't live with that, I won't ask you to. If you want out, I'll understand. I hope you don't, but I won't fault you for it."

"I hate myself for loving you right now," she said, then she wrapped her arms around him. They lay down together and slept until the alarm rang.

The trip north up Route 15 had been very quiet. Matt struggled at several points to keep his eyes open, and Courtney just stared out the window. Matt hadn't taken a long hummer trip in years, and now he remembered how tedious they were. With the vehicle's top speed of only fifty-five miles an hour, mandated by law, one could never make up time on the road. So he sat, his head propped up with his left hand, his right lightly touching the steering wheel.

Matt felt uncomfortable after his talk with Courtney the night before. He was also uncomfortable with the fact that he hadn't seen or spoken to his parents in over five years. He was going home unannounced, and he hoped that the surprise factor would work to his benefit. And he still wasn't sure how Courtney had reacted to last night, because she hadn't really said anything since. *She's in the car, isn't she,* Matt asked himself.

About an hour and a half into the trip, Matt's eyelids started to get heavy. Just across the Maryland-Pennsylvania border, he decided to try a cup of coffee. He took the very next exit, marked 15 BUSINESS STEINWEHR AVE, and drove a few miles into a small town. He made a hard right onto Taneytown Avenue, and he followed that to a pair of strip malls sitting astride the road.

Pulling into a convenience store lot, Matt went in for coffee and a Coke for Courtney. He emerged shortly, and as he did, staring beyond the strip mall opposite the one he was in, he noticed something. *The slope of the ground, maybe?*

Without averting his eyes, he handed the soda to Courtney through the window.

"What is it?" Courtney asked, finally speaking.

Matt did not respond but set his coffee on the hood of the car. He took off his overcoat and set it down as well. He looked around the lot, then noticed a large plastic garbage can in front of the convenience store. He dragged it from the plate glass doors to the edge of the storefront. He climbed up on the garbage can, and it gave him just enough of a boost to grab the bottom of the sloped metal of the storefront leading to the flat roof.

"Matt, what are you doing?" Courtney shouted, now getting out of the car.

The store manager, alerted by one of the clerks, also emerged and hollered at Matt, who was pulling himself onto the roof.

"Hey, what the hell are you doing? Get off the roof!" shouted the manager, standing in the parking lot, looking up at Matt.

Matt simply gazed at the field behind the opposite strip mall, criss-crossed with parking spaces and access roads, that sloped away for about mile, across Steinwehr, to a line of trees. He turned and looked behind him and saw a cemetery, by all appearances overgrown and untended. Looking to his north, farther into the town, he saw the cupola of what had once been a Lutheran seminary, rising above squat public apartment buildings.

"Matt, what are you doing?"

"Get off my roof, asshole!"

Matt reached inside his sweatshirt and pulled out his badge. "Police business."

The store manager frowned.

"This is Gettysburg, isn't it?" Matt asked the manager.

"Yeah."

"Thanks, citizen, I won't need any more of your help," said Matt, dismissing the man. He grumbled as he went back into his store.

Courtney had reached the edge of the parking lot, where she could look up to see Matt.

"Matthew Sheridan, have you lost your mind?"

"This is Gettysburg, Courtney. I've never been here before."

"So what? Get down off the roof."

"Court, Gettysburg. As in the Battle of Gettysburg."

"Oh, yeah, right. I remember that from grade school, I think. They still taught the European-American Civil War back then."

Matt continued to scan the area and saw two hills to his left, the farther one larger than the nearer. Judging by the town and the cemetery, he thought, looking back to the parking lot, it should be right . . .

"There!" he shouted.

As he lowered himself from the roof, Courtney yelled, "Be careful." He walked slowly toward a group of trees that stood in a small patch of grass at the far end of the strip mall. There was a garbage pail chained to it, as well as several bicycles. Courtney followed a few paces behind.

"This is it, can you believe it?"

"What?"

"The Angle, the copse of trees, 'High-Water Mark of the Confederacy.'"

"I haven't the faintest idea what you're talking about."

"Back when I was in NROTC, we took a military history course. The professor accidentally assigned us an insufficient book. It was a history of the Civil War, as they still called it then. He had gotten the call numbers transposed, and while the library didn't carry it, I was able to get hold of it through some, uh, connections I had. It recounted the Battle of Gettysburg."

"How could you be so fascinated by a war for social dominance by fratricidal Europeans? There's a reason why the courts made them take down all the markers and monuments, what, twenty years ago," Courtney stated.

"Well, I know that's what they say about it in school these days, but this text I read was remarkable. The text said the fight was over the form of government at the time, and slavery."

"We don't teach it in school anymore. The war changed nothing in the old United States government, and it is humiliating for African students to discuss a time when they were second-class citizens. The war really meant nothing to our federal history."

Matt stood at one of the trees and ran his hand along its rough, raised bark, still resilient after nearly three hundred years.

"Six hundred thousand men died during the Civil War. Americans. More than any other single American conflict. That many people don't give up their lives for nothing."

"Sure. To see who would dominate society. To see who would exploit women and people of diversity. To see who would reap the massive profits of the growing industrial society. That's why the courts declared the subject insufficient and made them take down all the markers and monuments," Courtney repeated in an exasperated voice.

Matt smiled. "Well, I guess we'll just disagree on this one. One day, a hundred and fifty some years ago, there would have been over seventy thousand men lined up from around that cemetery back there, all the way down through here to the top of that smaller hill down there," Matt explained, pointing with sweeping gestures.

"Right here, there used to be a little stone wall and these trees. A bunch of tired, scared men and boys hunkered down and watched as some fifteen thousand other scared men and boys came out of those trees way over there. Both sides were pounding each other with artillery, and they'd been fighting for three days. Then those fifteen thousand men and boys walked across that field; it was empty then, pretty much, and they marched in the open toward all those men in this area up here. The men up here fired down on them, and in less than an hour, nearly ten thousand men from both sides were killed or wounded. But a handful of the fifteen thousand made it as far as here, these trees. The two sides fought hand to hand, with muskets, with pistols, with rocks. You'll never convince me that there wasn't something more that made these men lay down their lives."

Matt walked past Courtney silently, but she caught up to him and took his hand as they walked back to the car. When they were ready to leave, Matt decided to drive north through the city to get back to the highway. This route took them past the cemetery, its great wrought iron gates rusted and hanging loosely from their hinges. Matt looked in at the rows upon rows of graves. "They must have believed in something."

Three and a half hours later, Matt parked the hummer in front of an old house. The paint had turned gray from years of hard winters and was cracking from years of dry, hot summers. The house was not more than two miles from Interstate 81, in Wilkes-Barre, Pennsylvania. Nestled in the Wyoming Valley, Wilkes-Barre was an aging town, and the house was aging with it. When the coal mines were still in operation, the Wilkes-Barre/Scranton area rivaled the larger industrial areas of the Northeast in jobs and commerce. But now Wilkes-Barre, like most of its senior citizen residents, was making itself comfortable to die. With the repeal of the Sherman and Clayton Antitrust acts, in exchange for big business accepting the Universal Employment Act, the small textile and other light industries that had flourished twenty years before had vanished. With few jobs offered to young people, most were moving away. Not unlike Matt, some years before.

Courtney's mood had lightened, and Matt's had darkened, as the trip progressed. Now they sat in the hummer as Matt stared at the front door. He reached over and squeezed Courtney's hand.

"Wish me luck," he said. She kissed him lightly on the lips.

They exited the car and walked up the front steps of the house. The wood protested loudly under the modest weight, as did the front porch as they approached the door.

"Let me go first," said Matt, and Courtney obligingly stood behind him. He rang the doorbell.

Shortly, a silver-haired woman in her late fifties opened the front door, then pushed open the screen door, which had the winter glass in it. She peered over thick bifocals, not quite seeing Matt yet.

"Hi, Mom," he said quietly. She looked up at him now, and her mouth dropped open. Matt propped open the screen door with his left arm, and without a word his mother wrapped her arms around him and squeezed. After a moment of silence Matt heard a booming voice from within the house.

"Who's at the door, Grace?"

With the telltale squeak of a prosthetic leg and the heavy footfalls of a two-hundred-forty-pound man, James Francis Sheridan emerged from the kitchen to the living room and looked to the door. Grace Sheridan stepped away from her son, tears streaming down her cheeks. The elder Sheridan approached, standing a head taller than his oldest son. They looked into each other's eyes for what seemed an eternity, the elder Sheridan frowning severely. Finally, Matt extended his hand to his father. James Sheridan looked at it, then at his son's face. He took his son's hand, and nearly yanking him off his feet, pulled Matt into a bear hug.

"Welcome home, son."

12

Grace Sheridan carefully handed the cup of hot tea to Courtney. Courtney was seated next to Matt on the sagging, overstuffed couch with a faded floral print. Grace sat in the armchair next to the couch, to Courtney's left. James Sheridan sat on the brown sleeper sofa directly across the living room from Matt and Courtney. The video monitor was off, and Matt remembered that was a rarity in the Sheridan household. And Sheridans had lived in this house for well over one hundred years.

"So, Matt, you said you're living in New Columbia now?" asked Grace.

"Well, just outside New Columbia. It's actually Alexandria where I live."

"And that's where you live too, Courtney?"

"Yes, well, uh, actually, we're neighbors. We live on the same floor in the same building."

"Pretty convenient," growled James, followed by a wink.

"James Francis!" Grace reprimanded. She always used his given and confirmation names when she was angry.

Matt smiled, but could see that Courtney was squirming a bit on the couch.

"So what brought you back east?" asked the elder Sheridan.

"Department of Security. I got a promotion, and they sent me out here."

"No shit, uh, I mean, no kidding?" asked James, sipping his tumbler of bourbon and ice.

"Yeah, I went from plain ole detective to detective lieutenant."

"How did you manage that?"

"Wasn't my idea, really. I had very little choice in the matter. I was ordered to accept it."

"Why would you have to be ordered to take a three-level promotion?"

"Long story, Dad," said Matt, sipping his matching tumbler of bourbon. *James Sheridan may be my father,* Matt thought, *but we're Marines together as much as father and son. He won't press me.*

"Well, Matt, I'm thrilled to see you," said his mother.

"I'm glad to be back. It's been too long. I'm sorry."

"No apologies are necessary, Matt. You know your father and I love you no matter what."

"I know," said Matt. He could feel his ears burning, and changed the subject.

"Where's Tom? Is he around?" he asked.

Grace bit her lip and looked down into her teacup. James cleared his throat.

"We haven't heard from your brother in two years."

"What happened?"

James frowned. "We don't know. He was doing well after he got out of the clinic. He had a job at the grocery store for a while. Things were going fine. We really felt like we were reaching him, getting him back, you know? Then one morning he was gone. He just up and left. No note, nothing. He took some clothes and a few things and left. I traced charges against the joint plastic account we set up for him to New York City; then there was nothing. No more charges, nothing. We tried the police, hospitals, missing persons, morgues, but there's no sign of him. He's an adult. The police won't find him. . . ."

Matt shook his head slowly. He looked over at his mother and saw her cheeks were streaked with tears.

"While we're on the topic of good news," grumbled James, "your grandfather Sheridan passed away this summer."

Matt lowered his head and ran both hands through his hair. Courtney placed her hand on his shoulder softly.

"Died in his sleep. He asked for you just the night before he died."

Matt looked up and sighed. "I wish I could've seen him."

"Well, don't worry about it. The old bastard was tough; he understood."

"He was your father, Dad."

James paused. "Yeah, I'm your father too, and you'll say the same about me when I go. Sheridans don't mourn the dead. They celebrate the living."

Matt drained his glass and pressed his lips together tightly. He tried to read his father's eyes. "Fuckin' A. Oops, sorry, Ma!"

His father scowled at him, but as Matt held out an empty hand to him, James emptied his glass and handed it to him. "Refill." Matt left the family room and went into the adjacent sitting room.

"Courtney, can I ask, what do you do for a living?" said Grace after an awkward silent moment, changing the subject.

"Oh, sure, I teach mentally and physically challenged children at an on-site school in Arlington."

"Oh, that's wonderful. It must be rewarding."

"It really is. At the end of the day I feel like I've accomplished something."

Matt returned from the sitting room, where the bar was located. He handed his father a refreshed tumbler.

"So, Lieutenant, I guess that big promotion got you off the streets, at least," James said.

"Yes and no. I work the Comarva Emergency Zone. I still spend a lot of time on the streets."

"Oh, God," Grace exclaimed, looking out the living room into the dining room, at nothing.

The room fell silent, and everyone stared into his or her drink. After a moment, Matt reached for Courtney's hand. He cleared his throat.

"They're, uh, up at Mount Olivet, right?"

His mother shook her head questioningly for a second, then her mouth opened. "Oh, well, yes. Yes, just where we discussed . . ."

Matt bit his lip. "I'm gonna go up, uh, tomorrow."

"If you remember where your grandmother is, Grandpa Sheridan is next to her. Then they're just at their feet. . . ."

Matt nodded and squeezed Courtney's hand. She bit her tongue to keep from crying out; he was crushing her fingers.

"Uh, you've been getting the money I've wired for flowers, right?" said Matt, his voice beginning to waver.

Grace's eyes began to fill with tears. "Every week, son." She set her teacup on the coffee table and went to Matt. He stood as she approached, and they embraced. After a moment, Grace stepped back and wiped the tears from her eyes with the palms of her hands.

"Come on, dinner's ready. We were getting ready to eat. There's plenty."

Matt held out his hand to Courtney, and she accepted it with the one that wasn't throbbing, and stood with him.

"Thank you so much, Mrs. Sheridan. I'm sorry we're imposing on you like—"

"Imposing? You're not imposing. And please call me Grace."

"Then, thank you. Grace."

After dinner Courtney went to the kitchen to help Grace with the cleanup. They both muttered tongue-in-cheek complaints about male exploitation laws, but the Sheridan men went off to the living room. James went via the sitting room and creaked back into the living room with two more tumblers of bourbon. It was their fourth or so, and Matt could sense the feeling slipping from his extremities.

"How's the leg, Dad?"

"Eh, good days and bad." The senior Sheridan had lost his right leg in the Second Gulf War as a thirty-eight-year-old master sergeant. From that day forward, he had vowed that no Sheridan would again be an NCO.

"How about your shoulder?" James asked.

Matt smiled and rubbed it unconsciously. "Good days and bad."

They stood in front of the plate glass window in the living room, looking across the street at another sagging, coal mine–era house, and just beyond it in the distance, the purple-gray mound known as the Back Mountain, which made up the western rim of the Wyoming Valley. Snow was beginning to fall.

"Snow tonight?" Matt asked.

"Yeah, we're supposed to get two or three inches."

"Kinda early for snow, isn't it?"

James laughed. "You've been living in southern California too long. It's almost December. Of course it's gonna snow up here."

"You're right. Hey, did Penn State play today?"

"Yeah, they beat Michigan twenty to three. In Michigan. It was a good game."

"You know, State College is probably halfway between here and New Columbia. If I got some tickets through the Alumni Association, would you like to catch a game?"

James punched his son on the arm. "Sounds great."

They stood quietly for a moment, watching the scattered heavy flakes falling.

"You still got the old forty-five?" asked James between sips.

Matt reached to the small of his back and drew the pistol. He handed it grip-first to his father. "It's safe. I don't have a round chambered."

James set down his drink precariously on the arm of the sofa. He then looked the gun over, dropping the magazine, then working the slide. He handed it back to Matt, who returned it to its holster.

"Your grandfather left you something in his will. . . ."

"Dad, I can't take anything. . . ."

"No, no, it's, uh, well, it was your great-grandfather's. That old buzzard had it till he died, then he left it for your grandfather with specific instructions that it was for you. You were maybe a year old when your great-grandfather died, but he remembered you in his will. I didn't even know the thing existed until I heard about it in your grandfather's will. It's upstairs; I'll dig it out tomorrow."

"Sorry about Grandpa, Dad."

"I miss him a lot, Matt. I really do. But I know that when he died, he knew how much I loved him, and that's what really matters."

Almost on cue, Courtney and Grace appeared from the kitchen. "Well, gentlemen, while you two weren't helping us, Courtney and I decided on some mushy romantic comedies to dial up tonight."

In unison, James and Matt rolled their eyes. It was a genetic trait.

"The good news is I still have plenty of bourbon," said James, emptying his tumbler as he creaked back to the bar.

The hummer slid on the fresh snow for a few feet as Matt spotted the tall Houseman gravestone that had always been the marker indicating the row of plots in which the Sheridans were buried. Matt hadn't been to the Scranton Diocesan Cemetery since they buried

Grandma Sheridan some fifteen years before. But he remembered the place.

Courtney sat quietly in the passenger seat. Matt opened his mouth to say something, then stopped. He was silent for a moment after, then said, "I'll be back in a few minutes."

Without further word he left the car. He walked around the Houseman marker and began crunching through the three inches of new fallen snow. He walked about twenty yards until he saw the first of the Sheridan gravestones, dating back to the 1920s. He paced to the plot where his grandmother was buried and stopped to notice that the information on the right side of the marker had been filled in. JAMES XAVIER SHERIDAN, 1935–2021, MSGT, USMC. Matt lay his hand gently on the marker.

"Grandpa," he whispered.

He then looked to his left, to the foot of the grave, and saw the blank back of a squat, wide gravestone. He swallowed hard and walked to it. He moved to the front of the marker; it was covered with snow. He cleared his throat and squatted on his haunches. With a gloved hand he cleared away the snow from the middle of the stone.

DAVID FRANCIS SHERIDAN, 2014–2016.

Matt cleared the left side of the stone.

JENNIFER BAILEY SHERIDAN, 1988–2016.

There was still room on the right side of the stone covered with snow. Matt cleared that too.

MATTHEW XAVIER SHERIDAN, 1988–20.

Just the way they used to sleep in that big bed together.

Tears began to blur Matt's vision, and he blinked them back.

"Uh, hi, guys. It's me. I, uh, don't know exactly what to say right now, except I'm sorry," Matt whispered through a constricted throat.

"I know I'm five years late. I'm sorry. So sorry. But I . . . it's just that . . . I always thought that if I never came here, then it was like you never died. And I've kept you alive, inside of me, all this time. And I, uh . . . ." Matt swallowed hard.

"I know I can't do that anymore. But if I can't keep you alive, I know that I can keep the love alive that I have for both of you. Big guy, you know Daddy loves you very much. . . ."

Tears began to fall from Matt's eyes. One or two at first, but they fell.

"Jenny . . ." Matt fell forward to his knees and touched both hands to her name, carved in stone. Now he wept, openly, loud.

"I love you so much. I love you . . ."

It was five or ten minutes that he wept like that, his entire body shaking. Finally, the tears slowed, the racking sobs stopped. He wiped his eyes and blew his nose in his handkerchief. He composed himself and brushed the snow from his knees.

"Okay, guys, I gotta run," he said, sighing. "Save my spot."

As he walked to the car, he noticed that the hummer was partially blocked from view by the Houseman marker. Courtney could not have seen him.

When he reached the car, he smiled weakly as he got in.

"Ready?" he asked.

That night, the four stayed up late, laughing, telling embarrassing stories about Matt's childhood, and looking at old family photographs. Finally Grace shooed James off the sleeper sofa so she could make it up for Courtney. The night before, Grace made up the sleeper for Courtney, and Matt's old twin bed for him, in his old room. Matt winked at Courtney, and later apologized for his mother being old-fashioned, but Courtney said she didn't mind. Matt told her he would come downstairs after his parents had gone to sleep, but after the bottle of bourbon he and his father had consumed, he'd promptly passed out in his bedroom. He apologized again to Courtney before they left for the cemetery, but she shushed him.

He whispered now in her ear, "I won't forget tonight."

Courtney looked at his tumbler, which had been emptied and refilled several times.

"We'll see about that."

Grace soon chased the two men upstairs and kissed Courtney on the cheek good night. In his room, Matt put on a pair of sweat pants and a T-shirt. Then he lay back on the bed, and fell asleep.

Jenny came to Matt that night. In bed, he opened his eyes and he saw her come to him, sitting beside him on the bed. She wasn't wearing the wedding dress, but rather had on jeans and that ratty PSU sweatshirt she always wore around the house.

"Jen?" Matt called out.

"I'm right here, Matt."

"Is that you?"

"Who does it look like?" she said with a smile.

"This is a dream," Matt announced.

Jenny put her hand on his forearm. He felt warmth.

"Thanks for coming today," she said.

"I'm sorry it's been so long. . . ."

Jenny put her finger to his lips. "I know. You told me."

"You know I love you, Jenny."

"I always knew you loved me, Matt. Always."

Matt was silent.

"Do you love her, Matt?" Jenny asked.

"I don't know . . ."

"Matthew Xavier Sheridan, I know when you're lying," Jenny said, smiling.

Matt looked away for a moment. Jenny put her hand aside his cheek, and he turned to her.

"Matt, it's okay to love her. I understand."

Matt moved his mouth, but no words came out.

"Matt, I know that you always did, and always will love me. But that doesn't mean you can't love her too. We'll always be soul mates."

He tried to sit up in bed but couldn't. Jenny stood. From behind her, he could hear Davey's voice, and a young boy of about eight ran up beside her. Her tugged at her hand.

"Come on, Mom. Oh, hi, Dad!" he said, pulling her arm toward the darkness.

Jenny smiled and nodded at Davey. "Your son," she said.

"Wait!" Matt shouted.

"Good-bye, Matt," said Jenny. She turned and disappeared into the darkness.

Matt sat up in bed with a start. He looked at his watch. *Three A.M. I was asleep, wasn't I? Wasn't I?*

He rose from bed and went into the hallway. Just across from his room he could hear his father's trademark snore. He padded down the steps to the first floor, where Courtney was sound asleep on the sofa bed.

He watched her for a few minutes, just sleeping. Her hair was tousled, as usual. *I can't believe that tousled hair turns me on so much,* he thought. Courtney grasped the covers close to her body. He sat down next to her, and she woke with a gasp.

"I hate when you do this to me," she said in a sleepy whisper.

He smiled at her, then took her chin in his right hand. He pulled her to him and kissed her, once quickly, then once longingly. He looked at her for a moment, then took her face in both hands, pressing his lips tightly to hers.

"I love you, Courtney," he said quietly.

She smiled at him. "I love you."

He slid under the covers with her, and they made love slowly, quietly, passionately, until the first rays of dawn began to spill through the living room window.

Matt was waving good-bye to his mother and father, the car packed and running, when his father yelled out, "Oh, wait. C'mere!" His father disappeared upstairs as Matt went back into the house.

In a moment his father was downstairs again. In his left hand he carried an old ammunition can; in his right he held what looked like a trombone case.

"Almost forgot the stuff from your great-grandfather," James said. He first handed Matt the ammunition can.

"I think there's about a thousand rounds of forty-five in there," he said as Matt's arm sagged from the load his father had carried so effortlessly.

"Grandpa Sheridan must have learned his allegiance to the forty-five from his father."

"And don't you forget it," said James as he swung the trombone case level. He opened it, then turned it to reveal the contents to Matt.

"I had heard stories about this . . ."

"All true. And it's all yours," said James.

"Well, I sure as hell will take this," said Matt, closing the case.

The muscular, mustached man named Dominic left Route 15 at the exit formerly intended for Disney America in Haymarket, Virginia. When Disney abandoned its theme park plan, it sold the land it had purchased for the park to the federal government. On the southern end of the tract, the Manassas Federal Penitentiary was built. Named for the closest county seat, the Manassas Federal Penitentiary was built to house the ever-increasing volume of prisoners entering the federal penal system. Just a few miles east down Interstate 66, which intersected Route 15 where the prison grounds stood, the Federal Department of Corrections was building another extension to the prison. It was on an unused tract of land formerly owned by the National Park Service, which was bordered by a small stream called Bull Run.

Dominic slowed the light green Department of Corrections bus as he negotiated the 360-degree circle of the exit ramp. At the end of the ramp, an access road stretched three hundred yards to the front gate of the penitentiary. The huge floodlights and searchlights shined brightly on this cold November night; it was two A.M., Sunday. Dominic rolled to a stop at the first checkpoint, an automated guard station. Beyond it was the double electric outer fence of the prison. Just inside and to the right of the gate he saw the second checkpoint, a manned guard station, in which lights were now being turned on.

He reached a card out to the higher port on the automated station, which was installed to accommodate the frequent bus and truck traffic at the prison. He held his breath as he saw the six barrels of an Eraser swivel upward as he ran his card. Seconds later, a green light blinked on the card panel, and the first gate on the electric fence rolled to the left, opening. Driving now due west into the prison compound, Dominic saw, two hundred yards ahead, the seven-story main complex of the prison, surrounded by an inner electric fence. Just seventy-five yards ahead to his right, the north, was the administrative and visitor registration building. Directly opposite to that, to his left, the south, was a parking area and a modest motor pool garage. But directly next to him now was the first manned guard station.

Twenty-four-year-old Chucky Bailey, Department of Corrections, emerged from the guard shack, hitching up his pants as he walked to the driver's side of the bus. Dominic rolled down the window.

"What the hell are you doin' here this time of night?" Chucky asked in a thick Southern accent.

"I'm down from Ithaca for the prisoner transfer."

Chucky surveyed the empty passenger seats located behind the locked cage of the driver's area. "You ain't expected until tomorrow mornin'."

"Yeah, I know, sorry about that. But we're supposed to get some snow up north later tonight and tomorrow morning, so I figured I'd get down here ahead of it, and not get stuck. I left this afternoon just as soon as I heard about it."

"Why didn't you call to notify us?"

"I sent my online, and it was approved. Did you read the onlines for tonight?" Dominic challenged. "I'd be hamburger meat back there if it wasn't approved."

Despite the fact that Chucky Bailey had finished tenth grade before he dropped out of school, he was still completely ignorant of computers. He hitched up his uniform pants again as they slipped from his skinny waist.

"You got a hardcopy I can take a look at?"

"Sure," said Dominic. He reached into his uniform jacket and withdrew a printout of the online, handing it to Chucky.

Chucky's breath was visible in the cold air, and he was starting to shiver slightly, as he had left his station without his jacket.

"Okay, you go on straight to the admin building, right over here," he said, pointing with a spindly finger. "I think Wanda's in there tonight to check you in."

"Thanks," said Dominic as Chucky handed him the hardcopy. "Oh, and, uh, one thing."

Dominic opened the folding door to the bus on the passenger side, motioning with his head for Chucky to step over. Bailey did as he was gestured and walked around the front of the bus to the door.

"Good night," Dominic said as Vince Miles sprang from his crouched position on the stairwell and tackled Chucky through the open door of the guard station. Vince drove his two-hundred-pound body into Chucky as he landed on top of him. Before Chucky could scream, Vince had clasped a chloroform-soaked rag over his face. Chucky Bailey was quickly unconscious without a struggle.

Vince dragged Chucky completely into the station and pushed him under the control console out of sight. He sat down at the control console and toggled the second gate of the electric fence. With a thumbs-up, Dominic drove through the gate. Vince returned the sign, then looked at his watch. Zero plus three minutes. He pushed the admin building's icon on the computer screen built into the control console and spoke into the microphone.

"Hey, Wanda, I got a prisoner transfer coming to see ya," he said in his best mimicked Southern drawl.

"Gotcha, Chucky," said Wanda, who then closed the line.

Dominic parked directly in front of the door to the administrative building, which was a squat, temporary, trailer-type structure. During the day it would hold nearly a dozen admin officers and clerical staff. But early Sunday morning, it held only two: Wanda Devins, the overnight duty officer, and Wayne Rowland, the twelve-to-eight shift facilities control officer. Dominic strode into the building, leaving the door open. It consisted of a large open area divided by numerous partitions for offices. At the very rear of the room, to the north, was a walled office that housed the facilities control area. A large counter ran across the width of the building, behind which was standing Department of Corrections Officer Wanda Devins. She was a tall, skinny redhead in her late forties, who must have smoked heavily when it was still legal. Her voice was raspy.

Dominic approached, wearing an identical Department of Corrections uniform, with the standard issue insulated jacket. He tipped his cap.

"Hi, I'm Jerry Walls, down from Ithaca. I'm here early for my transfer tomorrow."

"Yeah, I saw it in the online. Let me call it up," she rasped. She began pecking at a keyboard in front of the monitor that stood on the counter. While she looked down, Dominic reached into his pocket.

"Can I ask one question?" Dominic said. When she looked up from the monitor at him, he grabbed her hair with his left hand and jammed a rag over her face with his right. Wanda slumped to the counter. Discarding the rag, Dominic quickly waved back at the bus. As he did, ten men dashed into the building. Each was clad entirely in black, wearing a helmet and body armor. They were equipped similarly, each one carrying in a right hip holster a silenced pistol, and in a left hip holster, an unsilenced pistol. Numerous magazines for each hung from their body armor on webbed slings. The tenth man, very tall and skinny, carried a strange-looking camera. He shook from head to toe.

Dominic hopped over the counter, then raised his left hand to hold up the men. He crept toward the facilities control area and produced two pistols from under his jacket. The one he carried in his right hand had a long silencer attached to the barrel. The one in his left did not. As he neared the door to the facilities control office, he saw it was open a crack. Standing just to the side of the door, he pushed it inward.

"Hey," called a voice from within. In a second, a rumpled, middle-aged man emerged, his eyes heavy in the fight against sleep. In a split second he saw Dominic, and Dominic saw the Special Services crest on his uniform. Dominic fired the silenced pistol once into the man's heart. The man's mouth fell open in a look of amazement, and he clutched at his chest. He mouthed some unintelligible words, then fell to the floor, dead.

Dominic waved to the men, and each hopped the counter in turn. A man from the group of ten, known as Gizmo for his fondness for computers and electronics, ran forward past Dominic into the control room. He sat down at the facilities control desk. He popped his helmet off and set it on the floor beside him. As he did, two men dragged the body of the Special Services guard into the room with Gizmo. Two other men had moved Wanda to her desk, leaning her backward and propping her feet up in a feigned posture of sleep.

Dominic and the other nine men waited at the rear exit door of the admin building. Through the reinforced glass, beyond a short patch of ground bisected by a concrete walkway, lay the utilities building, which contained the local transformer, emergency generators, water pumps, and com net equipment for the complex. Seventy yards beyond the utility building to the northeast, at a height of about twenty-five feet, stood a manned guard tower. In the distance to the northwest, they could see a second manned guard tower, which they knew stood in the middle of the northern east-west perimeter fence. A third tower stood in the far northwest corner of the complex, the third on the northern east-west perimeter. Each tower had a stationary floodlight which, with their overlapping fields of illumination, lit up the entire inner compound from the main building to the perimeter, and some thirty yards out into the surrounding fields.

From behind them, Gizmo croaked, "Fences down in four, three, two, one, mark." He looked up and nodded at Dominic. Dominic reached for a small transmitter on his belt, and turned it on and off twice in rapid succession. *Objective secured. Time for B Squad to go into action.* Gizmo then croaked, "Lights out!"

Jimmy White Horse scanned the prison complex with his night vision binoculars. He was careful not to look directly at the floodlights, lest he be blinded. He and his ten men lay prone in the field just beyond the range of the floodlights. His three sharpshooters lay with their eyes closed behind their .300 Winchester Magnums; they would not have time to let their eyes adjust when the lights went out. The other six observed, resting quietly. The last dog patrol of the area had just passed. That gave them about ten minutes until it passed again. Jimmy was grateful that they wouldn't face the same security tonight that he had when he went into Chase. The geography of the location, mainly open fields, inhibited such extensive, active, automated security.

He glanced around at his men, all, like himself, wearing black fatigues, helmets, and body armor. This would be the first major, organized military strike by the CAPs, and it would be a serious test for their organization. But Jimmy was confident that the men taking part in the evening's action, hand-picked volunteers from among all the cells on the eastern seaboard, would perform admirably. And unlike previous actions, he expected to take casualties tonight. That weighed heavily in his heart. But the prize was too great to beg off the raid. *Tonight, they could secure the information and prisoners to advance their cause to the American people. Without tonight, the "big show" could not take place.*

Then the clicks came in on his transceiver. "Show time," he said, stowing the binoculars in a pocket on the outside of his body armor. His men rose to a crouch, with the exception of the sharpshooters.

The floodlights on the guard towers went out. Two seconds later, the sharpshooters had opened their eyes, acquired their individual targets with laser scopes, and fired. Aim for the Special Services crest was the instruction. The three big rifles fired within a half second of each other, and three guards slumped out of sight.

"Go!" shouted Jimmy, and the ten men sprang to their feet, sprinting for the fence. One volunteer ran in front of the others, carrying a tungsten-toothed chain saw. He push-started the motor, and the saw growled to life. Without art, he cut a wide hole in the fence, which the rest of the men filed through. He then dropped the chain saw and unslung his M16A2.

Inside the fence, the three sharpshooters each sprinted for a guard tower. They entered the fence at the middle guard tower in the perimeter, and one sharpshooter climbed into it. The other two dispersed east and west, sprinting for their stations.

Shouts began to emerge from the main building and from the other guard towers across the complex. The sharpshooter who had reached the middle tower station took aim on the tower that stood in the middle of the western north-south perimeter. He held his rifle steady against the roof supports and sighted in on the guard. With the tower lying just past the northwest corner of the main building, it was a tricky shot. But the guard in that far tower, panicked in the darkness, was spraying his M16A4 randomly into the grounds on the north side of the complex. The sharpshooter exhaled and squeezed the trigger. The rifle roared, and a little over two hundred yards away, the back of the Special Services guard's head exploded in a shower of pink gore. A little over twenty seconds later, the other two sharpshooters reached their positions, taking aim on their secondary targets, the guards in the towers directly to the south of each, in the southeast and southwest corners. These shots were nearly six hundred yards long. The rifleman in the northwest tower fired first, then, ten seconds later, the rifleman in the northeast corner fired. Two more Special Services guards fell dead. Only one guard tower remained, the one in the middle of the southern east-west perimeter. Because of its position, line of sight was blocked from everything but the south side of the complex.

The rest of B Squad ran to their southwest, to a temporary building in the northwest corner of the complex. Here they took up positions of cover and began to fire sporadically at movement. They were making a lot of noise.

Dominic heard the night erupt with gunfire, and he set his squad in motion again. He sent Pete Stevens to guard the utilities shed, and left Andre Washington to guard the admin building. He took the remaining seven men through the rear door. They quietly walked around to the front of the admin building and down the service road to the inner fence gate leading to the main building. Dominic heard the lock click open, and he swung it to the side. Then he and A Squad walked into the main building area.

As the squad approached the door to the main building, Larry Cohen ran forward, next to Dominic. He concentrated on the handle of the central entrance door. With a slight squealing of metal stripping metal, the handle depressed and the door opened. Dominic raised the pistol without a silencer, holstering the silenced pistol. Cohen drew his silenced pistol. Dave Brock, Bill Conlan, and Andy Skiba also drew silenced pistols. Gary Martell and Enzo Lindo drew unsilenced weapons. Dominic motioned to the last man: the tall, thin man with the recorder.

"All right, Arthur. Start recording."

Arthur's hands shook violently as he lifted the recorder to his shoulder, put the viewfinder to his right eye, then depressed the record button. He then depressed a second button to lock record on. He exhaled slowly in an unsuccessful attempt to steady himself.

"Ready," he said, his voice cracking.

Dominic Passarella silently swung the main entrance door wide open.

Heavily armed corrections officers were spilling out of the main building from the west and north auxiliary exits. After seven or eight had fallen in their tracks at the north door, the remainder were rerouted to the west. The sharpshooters in the guard towers alternated their ammunition clips based on whether their targets wore the Special Services crest or not. The Special Services officers were targeted with 250-grain hollow-point rounds. The officers without the crest were fired on with special plastic-coated gel rounds. If fired at the head, these rounds could kill. Even a shot in the torso or limb could cause an entrance wound. But the round contained a strong anesthesia that would cause unconsciousness in seconds. The sharpshooters were the best in the entire organization, and no regular-duty federal corrections officer would be killed.

Jimmy White Horse and the remainder of B Squad were having a difficult time of it. Their position, now inside and outside of the temporary building, was under withering fire from the guards who were spilling out of the main building, now numbering almost thirty. The plan called for a holding action of only ten minutes. Ten minutes might as well have been ten days, Jimmy thought. While the sharpshooters in the towers were able to put down guards as they presented themselves, Jimmy and his men were firing only blanks.

A Squad entered the lobby area, which was dimly lit. There were two doors in the room, one that read VISITING AREA, and the other that read AUTHORIZED PERSONNEL ONLY. They went to the latter. Cohen again concentrated on the door, and its lock was forced open. There was a set of stairs leading downward, which the men rapidly descended. They came to another secured door, which Cohen similarly opened. The men then spilled into a small anteroom, and Cohen shattered the lens of a ceiling-mounted surveillance camera as the door opened. On a control panel just a few feet away, three red lights were now flashing: Main Entrance, Main Access, and Camera One out. This was where it would get hairy. Cohen concentrated on the next locked door, and the handle crunched as it was depressed. Dominic nodded at Martell and Lindo, and they came forward. They stood giving just enough room for Cohen to swing open the door. Dominic held up his left hand, showing four fingers. Silently, he folded down number four, number three, and number two; when he folded number one into a complete fist, he shook it. Cohen yanked open the door, and Martell and Lindo dove through the doorway onto their stomachs. Lindo dove low, Martell dove over top, and they landed left and right of each other in the next room. As they hit the ground, they both fired their pistols, which made sharp hissing sounds rather than bangs. A loud report from the far end of the room sounded simultaneously, and Martell rolled over, grabbing his left leg. Dominic was next in the room.

The room ran about forty feet north to south and was about twenty feet deep east to west. The door that the teke had just opened was in the middle of the east wall. Just to the north of the door was the semicircular control station, at which two corrections officers were now slumped. One sat with his face on the control panel. The other was slouched in his seat, with a Standard 9 in his right hand. The feathered ends of small darts stuck out of each man. Directly opposite the door in the east wall was a heavy door. The rest of the west wall was made of thick clear Plexiglas. From the control room, one could see the small transition room to which the heavy door led, then a retractable wall of bars just a few feet opposite the heavy door. Beyond that lay cell block one, with two stories of cells, thirty in all, along the south wall. The north wall was just ten feet from the bars of the cells and consisted of cinder blocks, all the way to the ceiling. There were two tiny openings for windows near the top of the ceiling. At the far end of cell block one, another transition room could be seen, which led to the kitchen, recreation, and shower facilities.

Dominic went directly to Martell and waved the rest of A Squad into the room. Skiba stayed in the anteroom to cover the squad's rear. Lindo sprang to his feet and rushed to the control station. Without ceremony, he dumped the two guards to the floor and took up a seat at the panel. He first shut down the emergency lights for this sector of the building. He then locked the doors and bars at the far end of cell block one. Finally, he flipped open the heavy door, and the wall of bars retracted from the far side of the transition room.

By then, Dominic had helped Martell administer his personal trauma kit, which consisted of one morphine and one antibiotic syringe. The bullet had entered the back of Martell's left leg as he lay on his stomach, and had exited just above his knee, ricocheting off somewhere in the room. Dominic saw there was extensive bone damage, and the bleeding was severe. But there was no time, just then, for any further medical assistance, and both men knew it. Martell nodded at Dominic.

Arthur had entered the room with the team, and despite shaking violently, he dutifully recorded all the events. Martell's leg wound made Arthur queasy and a little bit dizzy, so he propped himself against a wall to remain standing.

When the heavy door swung open and the bars opposite had retracted, Dominic, Brock, and Conlan ran into the cell block. Arthur moved to the far end of the transition area, where he could record the entire cell block. As they entered, Lindo flipped the master switch that opened all the cell doors. Brock ran to the far end of the cell to cover for intruders.

As a few frightened heads began to peek out of the cells, Dominic spoke in a basso profundo. "My name is Dominic Passarella, and we are from the Confederation of American Patriots. You will be coming with us tonight. Please file out through the east doors, and please walk, do not run. As you pass the man with the recorder, please speak clearly your name, where you are from, when you were brought here, and why you were brought here. When we get out to the bus, please sit two to a seat and keep your heads down."

There was little response at first from the inmates. Dominic shouted, "Now . . . please!" his voice magnified and echoing within the stone walls. This brought an immediate response, and the forty prisoners of cell block one, men and women, young and old, of mixed nationalities, began to stream from the cells. One by one they passed Arthur, providing the information that had been requested. Dominic helped the last inmate out, an obese, elderly African man who limped badly. A Squad left the building as they had come in, escorting the prisoners to the bus, which Vince Miles had by then brought up to the inner fence gate to the main building. Lindo and Brock carried the pale Martell to the bus. To the northwest, on the other side of the building, they could hear the furious gun battle taking place between B Squad and the corrections officers.

Arthur was last on the bus, recorder running. Vince took the wheel and backed up onto the service road that was paved in a circle around the main building, just outside the fence. As he drove north, he blew the horn three times in quick succession, then slowed as he reached the bend in the road to the west. Two sprinting figures emerged from the darkness, Stevens running from the utilities building, and the sharpshooter from the northeast guard station. Vince swung the door shut, and they continued to the west, toward B Squad.

The corrections officers had moved forward from the main building, and a few had crossed the ground between the inner fence and the near, south side of the temporary building. The sharpshooters in the north central and northwestern towers had put down over a dozen guards, but with the corrections officers now wearing helmets and body armor, the shooting was very difficult. It also made it impossible to distinguish between regular duty and Special Services guards, and therefore, the gel rounds were being fired exclusively. With only leg and arm shots available, and with the targets moving, dodging and acquiring cover, the situation was becoming desperate. Three of the seven men who had split off with Jimmy White Horse had been wounded, one fatally. The six living men still fired furiously, making as much smoke and noise as possible. But each was down to his last clip of blanks, and their firing would of necessity be reduced to single shots. Each man did have a Standard 9 loaded with live ammunition, but that was for emergency. They were almost there.

Then Jimmy heard the triple burst of the shrill bus horn. His sharpshooters were then climbing out of the towers and heading for the service road.

"All right, B Squad, prepare to evacuate," he ordered. Two men continued firing, and the wounded men helped one another to the northeast corner of the temporary building, near the service road. Jimmy heaved the two-hundred-pound body of Mack Fullwood onto his left shoulder and moved to the corner of the building. Just then the headlights of the bus illuminated the temporary building.

"All right, heads down, everybody!" shouted Passarella. The inmates and A Squad complied. Arthur ducked in his seat but kept his recorder running.

Vince drove the bus around the corner of the main building and turned to the south. Doing so, he interposed the bus between the rest of B Squad, crouched behind the northwest corner of the temporary building and the remaining guards. The guards held their fire for a moment, confused over the appearance of a Department of Corrections bus. They were unaware that this bus, stolen almost a year before, had, in the last month, been refitted with bulletproof glass, solid rubber tires, and triple reinforced steel plate paneling. As they held their fire, the two remaining sharpshooters of B Squad piled breathlessly onto the bus. Finally, the remains of B Squad limped onto the bus, the last being Jimmy White Horse and the late Mack Fullwood.

The bus was full now, and men were lying prone on the floor for room. As the bus began to back up, the corrections officers began to open fire on it. The bullets and shot pellets at best made dents or impressions in the steel plating and glass. Most ricocheted harmlessly away. Making his K turn, Vince drove the bus east down the service road.

Vince took the turn south at a precariously fast speed, the bus's right wheels lifting slightly off the ground. He ground the gears as he steadied it, slowed, and turned east toward the main gate. Andre Washington was waiting in front of the admin building, on the passenger side of the bus. Vince swung the door open and slowed. Andre jumped onto the bus at a full run. Guards were beginning to emerge around the corners of the main building perimeter, firing after the bus, rounds thudding into the rear door.

Vince slowed again as they passed through the main gates, which he had locked open before he left Chucky Bailey's station. The bus roared out of the complex and turned onto the ramp for Route 15 North.

As the last echo of firearm reports died off to the south, the bus was silent, with the exception of the soft groans of the wounded. About a mile north of the prison, Vince slowed the bus and turned onto an almost invisible dirt road that ran off the interstate. The bus lurched from side to side as he did, and soon he was driving over a rutted farmer's field. As he drove on the field, he flashed his high beams on and off three times. His signal was returned by a single flashlight, which flickered on and off three times. He slowed, then smiled broadly as the cabin lights and engines of a dozen VTOL aircraft came to life.

13

Matt strolled into Super Tuesdays a little after two. As soon as he returned to his apartment, after his long trip from Pennsylvania, he checked his messages. Karen left an emergency contact request in the form of an online saying "need to review policy manual." She expected him at one-thirty, but he took his time and unpacked first.

She glared as he approached, looking around the restaurant to double-check that the lunchtime crowd had dwindled to nearly nothing. I.I. had long since cleared Super Tuesdays for such meetings at prescribed hours of the day, given its anemic business.

"You're late," she growled.

"So fire me."

"I'm in no mood for sarcasm, Sheridan, so keep it to yourself," she instructed. "What happened Friday night?"

"Saturday morning, you mean. Well, I passed the, uh, properties, and they were gratefully accepted. You can guess what they asked for immediately, and I told them I'd have to work on it. I've got one name—"

"Who?"

"Skip Murcheson. Works as a bartender down at the Pride of Dublin. He's Stanley Karkowski's connection to the whole thing. Stanley told me I was never to go back to the restaurant, and I was never to contact him again."

"Just as well. The name Murcheson is familiar. I'm sure we've already got him in the files. What I need now, more than the names of members, is activity. I need any operational intel, movement of personnel, and any contacts between the local cell and their national command."

"I'm supposed to meet some more people on Saturday night."

"Good. What did you hear about yesterday?"

"Yesterday?"

"Did you hear anything about Manassas when they spoke?"

"No. They didn't say very much, really. The only thing Murcheson said was that he wished he'd have the ammo sooner."

Karen stared into the distance and chewed on the stirrer from her iced tea.

"So you heard nothing at all about Manassas?"

"Should I?"

Karen leaned across the table toward him, and the low neckline of her blouse revealed the white lace of her bra and the smooth curves of her breasts. She whispered. "We had what we consider a major assault on the Manassas Federal Penitentiary early Sunday morning by CAP commandos. Looks like nearly fifty of them judging by the damage they inflicted. Federal corrections officers took high casualties. CAPs left with about forty maximum security inmates. These people are very dangerous. . . ."

"Shit! Nothing in the news about it."

"It's being played very low-key right now. And consider that classified information, by the way."

Matt shrugged.

"I need you deeper inside this group, Matt. Time is running out." She leaned across the table again. "We have reason to believe that a major CAP assault is planned in the next sixty to ninety days. We need a heads-up."

"Get me the ammo, and they'll tell me anything."

"Just stall them on that for a while. I don't want to get that drastic yet."

A waiter approached the table, but Karen waved him off.

"Your government is counting on you, Matt," she said.

After a silent pause, she said, "Is there some other incentive I can use to get you to move more quickly on this?" She placed her right hand over his.

Matt looked at her and slowly removed his hand but did not respond. He stood and walked away from the table without a word.

Matt noticed that there were quite a few more open parking spots in the substation garage than usual. He rode the elevator to the third floor and walked down a quiet hallway to his office.

This looks like my first day, he thought. Then his heart began to pound. He rushed to his office, shouting for Rosecroft and Vo. There was no answer.

In his office he flipped on his computer and saw the message, the first one on his screen. Officer Burt Jackson died on Saturday night. The first viewing was today at two o'clock. He looked at his watch. It was two forty-five.

Matt leaned back in his chair and ran both hands through his hair. He looked at the left and right walls of his office, but he was looking at nothing. He stood, hands on his hips, shuffled a few steps in place, then cursed to himself.

"Fuck."

He ran his hands through his hair again and lowered his head. This time he screamed at the top of his lungs. "Fuck!"

Courtney sat in Matt's lap, in the easy chair, and Pasha sat in her lap. Beethoven's Ninth spilled softly from the entertainment console speakers. Matt's eyes were closed, his head lay back against the head-rest. Courtney massaged his temples.

"We buried Burt Jackson today," he said finally, after nearly a speechless hour in the apartment.

"The one who was wounded when Noah was—"

"Yeah. He's got a wife and a teenage daughter. It really sucks. It's days like this that—"

"What, hon?"

"It's, I don't know, it's . . . I want to quit. I just want to give up. But I can't."

When he opened his eyes, he saw Courtney was looking into them. "So what would you do?"

Matt chuckled.

"What?"

"It's stupid—"

"No, tell me."

Matt sighed. "I think I'd like to teach French literature. Maybe at a magnet school. That's pretty stupid, isn't it?"

Courtney was beaming. "I never knew you'd want to be a teacher. And French literature?"

Matt closed his eyes again. *" 'Où sont les neiges d'antan?' Montaigne."*

"So why not?"

Matt laughed again. "I ask myself that question all the time." He kissed her unexpectedly. She jumped at first, then pressed her lips to his in return. Matt lifted the cat out of the chair.

"To your basket, Pasha," Matt commanded. The feline lowered his head, and, dragging his tail, did exactly as he was told.

Owen Thomas breathed in the fresh country air, supervising as the last of the communications equipment was loaded into the barn. Not that it was very barnlike now, with its sophisticated telecommunications and computing resources nestled within a specially designed secure shell within the structure. But from the outside, the barn retained its run-down-early-twentieth-century look. It matched the run-down-early-twentieth-century farmhouse they adopted as the temporary national command center.

He bent and picked up a pebble with his right hand, moving it with difficulty across the backs of his aching fingers. *Good for dexterity.* He looked at the smiling faces of his staff, regulars and volunteers, who were still basking in the success of the past weekend's efforts. While Owen recognized the results as positive, he still focused on the casualties, one of whom would never again report for duty. He realized that he was sometimes too much of a perfectionist, but he had never been able to forgive himself for the death of any of his men. He knew it was inevitable, and necessary to advance the cause, but ever since Iran, he vowed he would never let himself get used to it.

Judy strode next to him and ventured to loop her right arm through his left. She was smiling too. She had let her hair out of the tight bun she usually wore, and her dark locks spilled over onto the hood of her parka. The weather had turned decidedly crisp, and with the time she spent outside ordering the equipment installers around, her nose and cheeks had turned pink.

"You're going to freeze out here," she said, drawling her words ever so slightly in her gentle Mississippi accent.

"Not for a while yet," said Owen. He smiled, but sadly.

"What's wrong?"

"You should know me by now, Judy."

She put her hands on her hips. "Owen, the operation was almost a week ago. It was a huge success."

"Tell Mack Fullwood's mother what a success it was."

"You're not being fair with yourself, Owen, and you know it."

Owen turned and looked across the rolling hills of northern Virginia. They had chosen Lucketts, Virginia, for its relative isolation, with access to major roadways, namely Route 15.

"We debriefed the last inmate today. They're scattered to the four corners of the country. You saved their lives, Owen. And you know that now we can start the final preparations for the 'big show.'"

Owen threw his pebble, and pain shot from the tips of his fingers up almost into his neck.

Judy tugged at his arm, turning him. She was almost thirty years younger than he, and though they had virtually nothing in common but the cause, Owen loved her desperately.

"C'mon," she said. "I'll fix you some cocoa."

Matt stood outside his hummer and unconsciously watched the steam from his breath rising against the dim parking lot lights. He would rather have been at home tonight, for more than just the reason that he was bone tired. The past week since his return from Pennsylvania had been a very busy one for the Narcotics Response Team, assisting on nearly a dozen jazz busts, from North Arlington to South Alexandria. All the suspects were eventually turned loose, but the team had destroyed a significant amount of jazz. Combined with the amount they confiscated from Liebovic, the street price of jazz was skyrocketing in Comarva.

He was thinking about Courtney, and how she asked that he not go tonight. He explained that he had no choice. He still hadn't given her the full story, and he figured he never would. Then the lights of a van appeared on the park access road.

The van swung into the lot as it had the previous Saturday morning, but this time did not blind Matt with the high beams. Matt approached it at a trot, and the side door slid open. Inside, in one of three captain's chairs, was Murcheson. Next to him was a giant African, *one of the two giants from last week,* Matt guessed. The third captain's chair was empty, reserved apparently for Matt. Just behind the captain's chair was an empty bench seat. A squat, powerful Asian drove the van, and one of the other African giants sat in the front passenger seat.

Silently, Matt hopped in the empty captain's chair. He nodded at all four men. Without ceremony the Asian turned the van around in the lot and headed out.

"Matt, I need to ask you if you are armed," said Murcheson politely. Matt reached for the small of his back and drew his pistol. Quickly, the nearest giant reached out from his seat and grabbed Matt's right arm. But just as quickly, Matt flipped the pistol from his right hand to his left with a snap of his wrist. Instantly, he dropped the magazine into his lap.

"Whoa, whoa, whoa, Neil, take it easy," Murcheson said to the African. The African looked uneasily at Matt, then released his arm.

Matt flipped the pistol with his left hand and caught it by the barrel. He then extended the weapon grip-first to Murcheson.

"That won't be necessary, Sheridan. I just need to know if you're armed, that's all."

Matt winked at Neil, who was frowning. He flipped the weapon to a proper grip and returned the magazine to its previous position. He then holstered the gun.

"Matt, there are a couple of people I'd like you to meet tonight. For security reasons, and this is nothing personal, this will be a rolling interview. It's still a bit early for us to take you to any of our fixed installations. . . ."

"Not a problem. I understand."

"Good," said Murcheson. They rode in silence for nearly a half hour, driving in a random route through the suburbs of northern Virginia.

At a traffic light in downtown Fairfax, the side door slid open without warning and two men hopped into the van. One was an older man, in his sixties, short and lean. The other was a tall, thin man who had to duck as he entered the vehicle. As the light changed to green, the van rolled on.

Murcheson made the introductions. "Matt, this is Rick West, my deputy," said Murcheson, introducing the older man. *My deputy,* rang in Matt's head.

"And this is a man we'll just call Arthur. He's with the national organization, and he'll be observing tonight." Matt shook hands with both men.

"Tell us why you're interested in joining the Confederation of American Patriots, Matt," said Rick West. *Because I want to bust you up,* Matt thought. *The government doesn't like you, and they own me. And I'm not too enamored with your extremist right-wing horseshit myself.*

"Well, for one thing, I believe in a lot of the things you guys stand for. . . ."

"Such as?"

"Well, I know you guys speak your mind. You're not afraid to say what's on your mind. Nowadays, most people are afraid to say just whatever comes to mind for fear of insulting someone. Your people are against the sufficiency laws and that sort of thing. You know, like Stanley Karkowski . . ."

Murcheson interrupted. "Karkowski is a joke. He's not one of us. Racists and bigots don't have a home with us. Blowing up school buses and beating up homosexuals have nothing to do with patriotism. If that's what you think this is all about, you've got a bigger problem . . . from us."

"Oh, no," said Matt, straining so as not to stammer. *I wasn't expecting that. I thought they were all like Karkowski.*

"So what else, then?" West asked.

"I don't think the New Liberty party is all it's supposed to be. I think they've broken a lot of promises and hurt the country," said Matt. He was beginning to recall some of the catch phrases he'd been briefed in the chip that Dan Reilly had given him. "Social justice through industry is bankrupt morally and politically."

"Have you ever been involved in any political organizations?" West asked.

"No," said Matt.

"So why join one now?" West said.

"Because I decided it was time to take a stand," Sheridan said.

West pressed his lips together tightly, then rubbed his face with his left hand. "Well, I'm sure if you care enough to get us those beautiful weapons, then you've got some idea of what we're about."

"I have some idea."

"Matt," continued Rick, "would you be willing to let our national organization do a data search on you?"

"No problem at all," said Matt. He reached into his wallet and extracted his plastic. He handed it to West, who then turned it over to Arthur. Arthur, in turn, fished a handheld ID scanner from his jacket pocket and copied the information from Matt's data strip.

"Our national organization has much better resources to handle this sort of thing," said West.

"Have at it," said Matt with a smile.

"Great," said Skip. He handed Matt a CD Read-Write case. "From now on, if you want to contact me, use an online. This Read-Write has the encrypt/decrypt protocols for my personal com line. Of course, don't give it to anyone. I'm putting my trust in you, Matt."

Matt slipped the disk into his inside pocket. "You got it."

"Matt," said West, reinserting himself into the conversation. "About the 265s you gave us. Has Skip briefed you on the, uh, logistics problem we have with them?"

"Yeah, he said you were a little short on caseless."

"Matt, we can't use those weapons without the ammunition. Can you get some for us?" asked West, looking Matt directly in the eyes.

"Rick, you know, the guns were fairly easy. I just changed the inventory records, then signed for them myself. Comarva has one central supply source for ammo, and we have to account for every single round we use. I could lose my job very easily if anything questionable came up with ammo. . . ."

"And not for walking off with fifty machine pistols?"

"Look, guns are lost and misplaced all the time. They usually turn up somewhere, so the department isn't gonna worry about fifty guns, out of several hundred sent to the mid-Atlantic, for a couple of months. The guns themselves are harmless, unless you hit someone with one. But ammo is another story. Missing ammo sends up a red flag in a hurry."

Rick frowned and stared out the front window.

"What if we gave you a job?" asked Murcheson.

"What?"

"We have numerous supporters who would be willing to hire you for a shadow job. You'd report to work, they'd keep all the records and papers on you, and you'd draw a regular paycheck. But you'd spend most of your time working for us."

This is getting better by the minute, Matt thought. "I'll think about."

"Good. Keep in touch, then," said Murcheson. The van slowed as the Asian exited Route 50 into the Fair Oaks Mall parking lot. The van rolled to a stop near the movie theaters, just in the shadows of the Fairfax District federal administration building. A small red hummer sat idling.

"Donna will drive you back to the park," said Murcheson. Matt nodded, then shook hands all around. Arthur slid the side door open, and Matt backed out of the van. As he stepped out, he was patting the small of his back.

Parker Hudson smiled as he strolled unheeded past Betsy Holleran into Karen Russell's office. She frowned at him as he entered, but he continued smiling.

"That's quite a shit-eating grin," she said.

He flipped a disk case onto her desk, followed by several papers.

"I really have to hand it to you," he said.

"What's that?"

"Biweekly statistics. Northern Virginia shows dramatic increases in jazz busts, destruction of narcotics, and a huge increase in the street price in the area. Of course, we've had a significant increase of brutality complaints, but since they got shit on their face the last time, civil liberties hasn't filed any new charges against us. So I have to say that I was wrong and you were right."

"About the Narcotics Response Team?"

"Well, that and Sheridan. He's really made an impact since September. You've backed him up all the way since he's gotten here. And I've gone against you every time. But he's produced, and I have to say I was wrong."

"Well, I hope you're feeling very humble right now." Karen grinned.

Hudson made an exaggerated bow. "I am your most humble servant."

Karen applauded his histrionics.

"Lunch is on me," said Hudson, straightening.

* * *

Dan Reilly smiled pleasantly to passersby in the mall. They could not see that where he grasped the back of the bench with arms outstretched, his knuckles were white. He continued smiling as Karen Russell sat down beside him, placing her packages on the bench between them. The Tysons Corner retail outlet was crowded for a Monday night as shoppers took advantage of the Winter Holiday sales. Karen glanced over her shoulder at the bench directly behind theirs and found it empty.

"What is going on with Sheridan," said Dan, skipping small talk.

"He hasn't reported since his meet Saturday night."

"Why not?"

"How the fuck should I know, Dan? I haven't been able to contact him."

"You realize that people are going ape-shit over Manassas."

"No kidding?"

"Look, Russell, I got called into the Oval fucking Office this morning to be personally sodomized by the president. And Sheridan meets the local cell commander, has a follow-up, and has heard nothing about Manassas."

"I believe him. You know he's got a woman friend he's seeing. He practically lives in her apartment. Maybe they were busy this weekend. . . ."

"Very cute, Russell, but I'm reading from the same source as you. I don't like it a bit. I want Sheridan turned off."

They both smiled politely as two mature women tottered past the bench.

"Not yet, Dan. I think we're close to a major breakthrough."

"The fuck we are. I want him turned off."

"No. I'll run him on my own if I have to. I have the means to do it, and you know it, Reilly."

"Are you fucking him too, Russell?"

She narrowed her eyes. "Not yet."

Dan grunted and crossed his legs.

"Then I suggest you turn him off."

Matt had just finished blousing his camouflage trousers into his boots when he heard the com signal an incoming call. He straightened and looked at the monitor. It was an audio only from a conventional telephone, with an Alexandria interchange. Audio only was selected by default, and he touched the line to answer.

"Sheridan, Narcotics."

"Is this Lieutenant Sheridan?" asked a woman's hushed voice.

A snide remark leapt into Matt's mind, but he resisted it.

"Yes, it is. Can I help you?"

"Uh, you gave me this here paper a few weeks ago, and said to call—"

Must be from one of the hardcopies I distributed, he thought.

"Yes?"

"There's been . . . something going on next door to my house. People in and out at all hours of the night. Loud noises and shouting from next door. Cars in the street all the time. I saw the guy who lives next door, well, it was vacant until just a couple of days ago, and he just . . . appeared. He's selling some brown stuff all day long. Weird-lookin' people."

"Go on, ma'am."

"Well, I like to keep to myself and all, but they started bothering with my son. He's only eight, and he's got to walk past that house going to and from the education center."

"Where is this house located? I can have an unmarked car swing by and check it out."

The woman gave him an address on Alfred Street.

"Thank you for your help, ma'am."

"Thank you, Lieutenant," said the woman, disconnecting.

Matt immediately buzzed Sloane.

"What's the address on your target again?"

"I've got the block of Royal west of Montgomery Park under surveillance."

"Anything on Alfred?"

"No, that's a new one. You got something?"

"I just got a tip. Looks like some squatters in a vacant house, selling."

"Could be. We've really shook up the usual markets, so they're moving around a lot."

"Can you send someone past for a look-see? I'm riding with NRT this morning, so I'll roll past later myself."

"Can do, Lieutenant."

Matt grunted, then disconnected. Just as he did, he saw an incoming from Karen's number. She had a couple of days to mull over his latest report. She wanted more, he knew. He started to touch the screen, then withdrew his hand.

"To hell with her," he muttered. "She can wait." He patted the small of his back as he headed for the motor pool.

The Schwarzkopf had barely cleared the garage when the com set crackled.

"This is N–3, Norton. I've got shots fired at 346 Alfred. Need backup, code three."

Sheridan reached over to the com, past Rosecroft's usual place. Clark had taken a day of sick leave. *Just as well,* Sheridan thought. *He may have been an accomplished teke, but he was generally a pretty poor cop.*

"Norton, this is NRT. What's your twenty?"

"I'm on the floor of N–3, stopped in the street in front of 346 Alfred."

"Hold tight, Norton. We're rolling on you," said Sheridan. The street location and directions had appeared on the driver's HUD, and without instruction he was turning the heavy machine in the proper direction. Matt tapped the com on his helmet and relayed situation information to the rest of the squad. In the next few moments that they traveled, Matt could hear the dispatcher redirecting additional units.

The Schwarzkopf turned onto Alfred very quickly, and Matt could see the brown unmarked hummer, N–3, stopped in the middle of the street. The side windows had been shot out, and the front and rear windows were shattered. Matt directed the driver to position the vehicle between the car and the building.

This was quickly accomplished, and Matt hopped out of the Schwarzkopf behind, to the far side of the vehicle from the building. The shooters had paused, and Matt realized, looking back at the building, that he could be hit from the third floor if the assailants were there.

He duck-walked to the door of N–3 and yanked it open. Detective Yarmo Norton was still sprawled on the floor.

"Let's move, Norton," Matt commanded.

The detective obeyed and crawled to the Schwarzkopf. He slid into the front cabin seat, next to the driver. Matt sat next to him. Matt directed the driver to move to the far sidewalk, which he did. Matt tapped his helmet. He ordered Officer Jones into the turret to man the Eraser. He told the rest of the team to sit tight.

"All right, Norton, what's the scoop?"

Yarmo Norton was a young European, disheveled, a little bit flabby and short, with a vacant look in his eyes. He wasn't particularly smart or strong or good with a firearm. But with the aid of his own vapid personality, he was one of the best undercover agents in the department.

"I made a couple of passes, and I saw two Latin males handing bags with a brown substance in them to certain passersby on the street. These people would then put something into the hands of the Latin males. I guess on my third pass, they made me, and opened fire. One of the rounds killed the motor, and I stopped."

Matt looked across at the car. He winced.

"Gee, Norton, do you think on your third pass they noticed the triple array antennas on the roof? You figure that gave you away?"

Matt shook his head and spoke to the squad.

"All right, I need two volunteers to close either end of the street off. I need two men to get into the alley behind the house. The rest of you will come with me into the house. Jones, you'll cover with the Eraser. As soon as we get some more backup, we should try to evacuate the block."

Without further command, Klingler and Jamaal were the first two out of the vehicle. Klingler went behind the Schwarzkopf to close the north end of the street. Jamaal went south. As they exited the personnel compartment, Jones kept his finger on the trigger of the Eraser, just in case.

Sheridan looked at Norton. "Norton, get the 'bot in the air, and keep an eye on the alley."

Norton nodded.

Matt leapt from the cabin, M16A4 slung over his shoulder. "Jones, get ready to cover."

As Sheridan rounded the corner of the vehicle, Detectives Gomez and Hong had already separated, headed for the rear of the building. Patrolman Corporal Don Allen, and Detectives Mike Blackstone, Jack Mueller, and Pete Venski met Sheridan, weapons at the ready. They darted across the street, although the house had grown quiet. As Sheridan and his group reached the stone staircase leading up to the door of the suspect building, they heard a pop as the 'bot was ejected from the roof of the Schwarzkopf. Its air scoop deployed, and the drone sailed into the air.

Matt leveled the A4 at the two front windows in the building, just to the right of the doorway, as he climbed the stairs. Venski and Mueller also watched the windows from the cover of the stone staircase, and Allen and Blackstone climbed the steps behind their lieutenant. Sheridan pressed himself into the corner of the doorjamb. Allen and Blackstone crouched on the steps.

The com crackled and Norton spoke. "Sheridan, I've got a perp in the alley behind the house, looks like an Asian male headed, uh, north, toward Madison."

"Shit!" shouted Matt. "Gomez, Hong, what're your twenties?"

"Turning the corner toward the south end of the alley," reported Detective Gomez.

"End of the alley!" shouted Hong.

"Look for a perp!" shouted Sheridan.

"Got him on the screen, Sheridan. Watch it, Hong!" shouted Norton.

A gun roared from the north end of the block.

"Shit! Norton, where's backup?"

Klingler's voice broke in. "Hong's down. I'm covering him. Perp is headed north, turning west on Madison. Armed with a double barrel shotgun."

A second-floor window shattered, raining glass on Sheridan's helmet. The barrel of a Fuego machine pistol appeared, spraying shots down on the stairs. Blackstone groaned and fell to his seat on the steps. Sirens began to approach from all directions.

Matt kicked the doorknob with his heavy boot, and the old hardware snapped on impact. The door swung open and he ran into the house. Allen and Mueller were right behind him as Venski assisted Blackstone back to the Schwarzkopf.

Inside the building, Matt stood at the bottom of a steep flight of steps leading to the second floor, running along the wall to the left of the doorway. He looked directly into a living room area, which contained a moldy couch and plenty of glass from the two broken front windows. With a nod of his head, Matt directed Allen into the living room.

"Front room clear," said Allen.

With his gun barrel Matt directed Mueller down the hallway to the area beyond the living room. Mueller slid along the inside wall and whipped around the corner into the next room.

"Clear," he said. "I got a doorway to the front room back here. There's a kitchen beyond."

Matt nodded to Allen, and he entered the second room from the living room. Together, they entered the small kitchen area, which sported little besides a nonfunctional sink.

"Clear," said Mueller.

Moving back into the hallway, Mueller noticed the door to the rear of the building was open.

"Exit here where the first perp got out," said Mueller.

"Anything else back there?" asked Matt.

"Not that I can tell," said Allen.

"I'm going up," said Matt. Allen and Mueller ran to the bottom of the steps, rifles pointed upward. Sheridan began to climb the steps.

The stairs groaned and creaked as he walked. Halfway up, his com crackled and he jumped.

"Holy shit, Norton!" he whispered.

"Trouble, Lieutenant. Sloane just called in. They just had a 'bot do an infrared on the stakeout target. It's empty. They had nine suspects in there earlier this morning. . . ."

"How did they get away from there?"

"Sloane says they must have snuck out—"

"Snuck out of the stakeout target! Let's get an IR on the second floor."

Matt looked up the stairs, his grip tightening on the forebarrel of the rifle.

"Crap! Sheridan, I'm getting eight signatures."

"Shit!" exclaimed Matt. He turned to order Allen and Mueller out of the building, when a door at the top of the steps opened and two Latin males emerged, firing Fuego machine pistols down the stairs. Matt gasped as he felt two rounds pound into his upper chest, stopped by his body armor. He heard Allen and Mueller shout behind him as he squeezed his rifle's trigger, sending a burst of 5.56mm slugs up the steps. Beyond the orange flame spewing from the barrel, Matt saw one, then the other man crumple. Before the second man hit the splintered wood floor, a door opened from the room in the front of building, which overlooked the stairwell behind Matt. Three men emerged. Two were burly Africans armed with Fuegos; the other, a European, his forehead scarred with the letter J, was unarmed.

Three rounds slammed into Matt's back as he turned. Bullets bit into the staircase and walls all around him. Allen had crept back to the step just below Matt and fired up through the floorboards into the second floor. The two armed Africans dove left and right, but the scarred European stood his ground, focusing on Matt's rifle. Matt squeezed off a three-round burst that dropped the armed man who broke left. Then the rifle was wrenched from his grasp. It flew directly to the feet of the scarred man.

Matt gasped to catch his breath as he grabbed his pistol from its holster and snapped off two rounds. Hastily aimed, both slammed into the knees of the scarred man, who collapsed with a yelp. As he did, the man who broke right squeezed a burst at Matt, one round of which sliced through Matt's right biceps. As his right arm was dropping, he flipped the pistol to his left hand and fired three times, two rounds striking the standing man in the forehead. Matt grimaced and wheezed as he scrambled to his feet.

A thick haze of gunpowder hung in the stairwell, and the house now smelled of cordite, sulfur, and feces, as dead bodies voided themselves. Matt ventured a quick glance at Allen, who was crouched on the steps. Mueller was dragging himself toward the front door. Matt could hear tires screeching outside and voices shouting.

Matt charged up the stairs. He thought of Noah Benning, Burt Jackson, Hong, Blackstone, and Mueller, then completely cleared his mind. At the top of the stairs he stepped over the bodies of the first two men he'd dropped. They were wearing gang colors. Gutters. He kicked each in turn, and they did not respond. He looked into the room at the top of the steps from which they had emerged, and he saw that it was empty. There was a door to his left that was closed, and to the front of the building the door was open to the room from which the three men had burst.

He crept along the wall, pistol pointed forward as Allen climbed the steps beside him. Matt watched the teke at the far end of the hall out of the corner of his eye. He was screaming, holding his legs. Allen positioned himself to the left of the unopened door by the hinges, Matt to the right by the knob. Sheridan kicked the door in and Allen swung his rifle barrel in.

A shotgun roared, and ten buckshot pellets flew between the two cops into the wall above the staircase. Allen squeezed off a three-round burst from his A4, which crushed the chest of the tall, skinny European inside the room who had fired out. The European died on the floor.

Reports from outgoing shots now emanated from the front room, overlooking the street. Men shouted in the room as the Eraser opened up on the windows, and Sheridan and Allen hit the floor. Slugs whistled through the air over their heads, tearing up the house around them. As Matt aimed his .45 toward the front room, the teke propped himself up on one elbow and screamed at Sheridan.

"Motherfucker, I'll kill you!"

Just then Matt felt a slight pressure on his pistol. He fired once. The round burrowed into the teke's forehead at the very top of his scar.

"Not today, asshole," snarled Sheridan.

He dropped his pistol's magazine with one round remaining and, with intense pain, slammed another one home with his right hand. He worked the slide, then ducked as the Eraser opened up from the street onto the building again.

When the Eraser stopped, Matt rose to one knee, still covering the open door. Allen followed suit. An instant later, two Asians with Fuegos ran from the front room into the hall in front of the officers. All four men opened fire simultaneously.

Corporal Allen held down the trigger of his weapon. His first shot pierced the shoulder of the Asian to the left. The second shot passed just above his shoulder. At that instant, the first round fired by the

Asian to the right struck Allen high on the helmet, knocking him over backward. The second shot shattered the face shield, and the third shot plowed into Allen's body armor at his sternum. The Asian to the left squeezed off a three-round burst as Matt was firing the Colt. The first shot hit Matt low on the right side of his stomach. Sheridan knew from the pain that surged through his body that the round had found the tiny band of his torso not covered by the body armor, where it wrapped downward over his groin. The second shot creased his right thigh, and the third shot missed altogether.

Matt's first two shots struck the Asian to the left in the heart, the third in the right eye. As Corporal Allen was just hitting the floor, the Asian to the right had turned his weapon on Matt, and fired three rounds into the wall next to Matt. Matt fired once, striking the Asian on the bridge of his nose, the crushing shock of the slug blowing his eyeballs out of their sockets. Matt fired again, and again, and again as the body fell, sending each shot into the head as it dropped to the floor. The slide clanked open on the empty magazine.

Matt slid to the floor with his back to the wall, pressing his right hand to his stomach.

"This is Sheridan. Clear. Need medical," he grunted.

Matt could hear the tromp of footsteps coming into the house below. He looked down at his side and saw his hand was covered with blood. He noticed Allen stirring on the floor next to him. Then Matt stopped being conscious.

Owen Thomas strode among the partitions as he always did, looking over the shoulders at his computer specialists, as though he understood most of what they were doing. He was relieved that "the barn," as he now called his information center, was finally operational. Now he just had to get used to the feel of the floor, count the steps from wall to wall, and estimate the angles of the sunlight streaming through the windows at dawn and dusk. He walked past Arthur's cubicle, looking at him from the corner of his eye, and patted the younger man on the shoulder. He had reached the adjacent cubicle when his conscious mind received a signal sent previously from his subconscious. He took two steps backward to Arthur's cubicle. He squinted at the screen.

"What's this, Arthur?"

The younger man took off his CRT visor. "Oh, I'm helping out the northern Virginia cell. They asked me to do a National on a guy they're interested in. . . ."

Owen was now leaning across Arthur's body to read the screen. He smiled.

"Get me a hardcopy ASAP, Arthur. And get hold of Murcheson. Tell him I want to talk to this Sheridan comma Matthew Xavier."

14

Matt stared vacantly at the com. Bryan Carruthers of CNA had been droning for ten minutes already.

"Tonight's feature item is a look at the Confederation of American Patriots, or CAPs. In light of their brutal attack at the Manassas Federal Penitentiary, the CAPs have seemingly become an armed threat to this country, rather than just a dangerous group of outlaws. With four federal corrections officers and eight CAP terrorists killed, this was the bloodiest confrontation yet with the CAPs."

Video of the yard surrounding the Manassas Federal Penitentiary appeared on the monitor.

"This dramatic video, just released by the Department of Security, was taken only a few hours after the raid. As you can see, the bodies of the eight CAPs are strewn about the compound. Officials believe the CAPs were attempting to free several violent felons housed at the facility, felons whom they regularly target for recruitment to their cause. . . ."

"Bastards," grumbled Matt as he powered off the monitor with his remote control. *But that doesn't really seem like Murcheson and his group. Are they separate?* He was sitting up in the hospital bed, trying to get comfortable. Courtney dozed in a chair next to his bed, having spent nearly forty-eight hours awake.

He fought against the intravenous tube in his left arm to pop a few acetaminophen tablets into his mouth. His right arm was heavily taped from shoulder to elbow, and he could barely move it. He swallowed the pills with a cup of water, warmed from its time on his bed tray. As he shifted his weight, hot irons prodded him along the length of his torso, front and back. He smacked his lips, his mouth very dry from the massive antibiotic cycle on which they started him. He had asked for more water over an hour earlier, but the surly nurse who was on shift had stated plainly that he had ten other patients to attend to, then disappeared.

Just as Matt was returning his head to his pillow, a middle-aged African in a long white coat entered the room, reading the screen of a portable patient file system.

"Mr., uh, Sheridan, good evening. My name is Ken Lonney, I'm the physician on duty this evening. How are you feeling?"

"I've had better days," said Matt. Courtney awoke and sat up in her chair to listen. Her hair was flattened on the side where she had rested against the chair. Matt looked away quickly, feeling the initial stirring of arousal that her mussed hair always caused. *I bet even that would hurt right now,* he thought.

"I've read through your file and looked at your ultrasounds. You were brought in—"

"I guess it was, what, two days ago?" Matt finished.

Courtney glanced at her watch. "A little over forty-eight hours."

"Well, Mr. Sheridan—"

"Matt, please."

"Okay, Matt, the reports from your tests today indicate that the damage to your small intestine was successfully repaired, and your blood work indicates that the steroid introduction has already started to reinforce the muscle reconstruction that was performed. I had to look at those ultrasounds twice. You were extremely lucky that the bullet passed through your body and missed your spine and your kidneys."

"I was also extremely lucky to get shot in the half-inch uncovered portion of my body. It was just bad luck."

"Well, ninety-nine percent of the injuries we see like this result in permanent spinal, kidney, or intestinal damage. Our computer model projects seventy-percent recovery for that injury in about a month. One hundred percent in two months. The microsurgeon and the laser surgeon did some exquisite work."

"Remind me to send some flowers," said Matt, smiling.

"It also looks as though your arm will be fine too. The bullet passed through your biceps and missed the humerus. Again, you'll have muscle damage to heal, but the reconstructive surgery and the steroids should have that healed fairly soon. A month or so. The fractures in your ribs seem to be simple hairline ones. There's not much we can do for those, so you'll just have to take it easy for a while."

"When do you think I can eat again?"

"Well, we want to give your system some time to recover from the shock, and we also want to make sure that there's no infection, although we have no reason to be concerned that there will be. A few more days, probably."

"Doctor, I'll pay you handsomely if you'd just smuggle me a beer," said Matt.

Dr. Lonney shook his head and chuckled, then headed for the door.

"Dr. Finkleman will be by tomorrow morning to see you."

Matt was gingerly snapping up a fresh tunic when Officer Doug Sloane entered his hospital room six days later. As usual, Sloane's straw-colored hair was windblown and unruly, and his clothes looked slept in. Of medium height but powerful build, the twenty-eight-year-old would have seemed more to be a blocking fullback than a detective. He rubbed a pink scar on his left cheek as he spoke.

"Lieutenant, I'm sorry to bother you—"

"No trouble, Sloane. I'm getting ready to go home this afternoon. I can't wait to get out of here."

"Good. How're you feeling?"

"Pretty good, for getting shot and all. Everything's really sore, and it hurts just to sit on the toilet. But at least I can walk around, do a few things. The reconstructive and laser surgeons did a great job. It's a good thing I was a priority trauma case though. The guy in the bed next to me here died last week waiting for a surgeon. Anyway, I just need to get my strength back now."

Sloane was still standing in the doorway, hands shoved in his pockets. Matt motioned him to the chair beside his bed with his head. Sloane sat.

"What's up?" Matt asked, wincing as he swiveled to face Sloane. He rubbed his right biceps.

Sloane sat with his elbows on his knees, hands clasped.

"I, uh, just wanted to, uh, apologize—"

"For what?"

"For blowing the stakeout on the Gutters place."

"Why do you think you—"

"Look, Lieutenant, I had nine guys in that place, and they just walked out from under my nose. I never even saw them. You guys walked right into a trap."

"Sloane, look, yeah, they got out of the place, but shit happens. They had a teke with them. Who knows what kind of shit he coulda pulled to fool the sensors or get out of there. I've seen it happen."

"Four guys got shot because of me."

"Sloane, four cops got shot by jazz punks, not by you. Hong just got decked, he's all right. Blackstone took one in the nuts, but he had his extended body armor on, same as me. And Mueller got a through-and-through in the thigh. He's already home. So, Sloane, don't sweat it, all right."

"The, uh, the teke that killed Lieutenant Solinsky, he was my collar. I was in the room."

"And you killed him. What's your point?"

"I should have known he was a teke. I fucked up."

"How were you supposed to know unless he was working? C'mon, Sloane. Be realistic."

Sloane did not answer, and had not looked up from his feet.

"Well, I'm not going to give you a big hug so you'll feel better, so just take my word that it wasn't your fault, okay?" said Matt, grinding his teeth as he slid off the edge of the bed to stand.

"I got something for you though," said Sloane.

Matt raised his eyebrows.

"You know the digging Bromberg was doing on the name Morelli?"

"Yeah, he was supposedly the supplier for Cha and Liebovic."

Sloane looked back to the hospital door, and seeing it was slightly ajar, rose from his seat and closed it tight. He walked to Matt's side and leaned against the bed. Sloane spoke in almost a whisper.

"Bromberg got a match on an old Sicilian from Baltimore, currently of Great Falls, Virginia, name of Antonio Morelli. He goes back to the old days of organized crime, and I guess he used to be a small-time local hood moving heroin up in the projects in Philly. Anyway, since he's outside our jurisdiction, we sent a request through Division asking for permission to stake him. Permission denied. Next day, Blair called the chief of detectives for northern Virginia to get some help. Request denied. So I did some research. It turns out Morelli's name has come up as a target in a dozen investigations over the past two years. But the investigations keep getting turned off at the division level. For this reason or that. So, anyway, I thought, screw 'em. I staked him on my own."

"What?"

"Last night and the night before, I've been sitting on him. Huge house for a nickel bag wise guy, by the way. So, last night, a truck, a six-wheeler, shows up at his place. Old Tony and about six muscle guys came out of the house and got into his limo. They followed the truck. So did I."

Matt sat back on the edge of the bed. "And?"

"They drove all the way up to the friggin' Baltimore harbor. They pulled into one of the big warehouses, everybody got out, then about fifteen minutes later, they started loading fifty-five-gallon drums into the truck. Shitloads of 'em. Just like the ones in Liebovic's place."

The hair on the back of Matt's neck was standing on end. "Did you see anything else?"

"No, that was the best I could do. I didn't get too close, so I wouldn't blow the tail. And the warehouse was in a compound of some sort, behind a barbed wire fence. Looked like it was guarded, double gates, the works. I was working with a nightscope that I, uh, borrowed from the department."

"Log it out to me, I'll vouch for it. You know that I can't ask you to continue this, officially. Especially if Division has denied it. Actually, I'm a little surprised Hudson wouldn't play ball on that one. But at any rate, there's no way I can restrict you from what you do on your own time, as long as it's legal, and I'm not well enough to join you myself," said Matt, grinning.

Sloane nodded. "Gotcha." Without a word he stood and strode to the door. Just as he was opening it, Courtney was walking in.

"Oh, excuse me!" she said, bumping into Sloane.

"My mistake," said Sloane, slipping past her into the hallway. He disappeared down the corridor.

"You're early," Matt said.

Courtney turned toward the door. "Oh, do you want me to come back later?"

"No!" he shouted, and she giggled.

"I was just remarking that you're here early. That's good."

"I told the principal that I threw up in the girls' bathroom this morning, and she let me leave."

Matt nodded, then his eyes widened. "You didn't really . . ."

She laughed. "Relax. No, I didn't."

Matt exhaled with conviction.

"So, Lieutenant, are you ready to go home?" she asked, picking up the travel bag she'd packed up for him the night before.

Grunting, Matt pushed himself away from the bed. "Absolutely."

Skip Murcheson sat across the heavy oak desk from Owen Thomas. Jimmy White Horse sat beside Murcheson. The day was deceptively bright, as an early December frost had frozen the ground that morning. Through the window behind Murcheson and White Horse, Owen could see a pair of quarter horses trotting in the rolling pasture beyond.

Owen picked up the hardcopy file from his desk without looking at it. He addressed Murcheson but did not look at him.

"Tell me, Skip, not to interject myself into your command structure, but just how much do you know about Detective Lieutenant Matthew X. Sheridan?"

"Well, sir, we confirmed that he's a detective with the Comarva E.Z. Federal Police command, new to the area, decorated cop, and a decorated Marine."

"Shock Marine, yes. And what else?"

"He's gotten us some firearms. . . ."

White Horse interrupted. "Caseless ammo firearms."

Owen glared at White Horse. "Thank you, James. I'm addressing Mr. Murcheson here. And what else?"

"Not too much else, I guess. Sometimes you have to go with a gut impression."

"James here has a gut impression that Sheridan is a plant," said Owen.

Murcheson looked at Jimmy, who was scowling.

"I am myself actually quite familiar with Mr. Sheridan, though we've never met," said Owen. Both Murcheson and White Horse stared with wrinkled brows.

"I used to know Mr. Sheridan, in a past time, in a past life, as Mynah. That was his code name. He was one of our most valuable assets when I was with the Joint Command in Iran. As I said, I never met him, never spoke to him, and maybe he's never heard of me. He pulled off some of the most incredible projects . . . Russia, Iran, China, Central Asia. We used him again just before Karachi. He was on the ground in Iran when we were gearing up for Operation Liberty Strike. He wrote the final analysis from his own raw data that canceled the operation. We would have lost fifty thousand men the first day. . . ."

Thomas's gaze finally returned to Murcheson. "And he has published numerous times in *Proceedings* for his articles on force doctrine, grand strategy, and an overhaul of the foreign military sales process. Mr. Sheridan is a very complex man."

With elbows on the desk, Owen pressed his hands together, then pressed his index fingers to his lips. The three men sat in silence for nearly a minute.

"Owen, with the 'big show' coming up, and with the national headquarters relocated here, I just think that this Sheridan is dangerous to the organization!" said White Horse.

"Sheridan is dangerous period. While I back you fully, James, I also know that a man like Sheridan could be a major asset for us. And you'll not raise your voice again."

White Horse cleared his throat. "Sir, respectfully, if you think he's a plant, we'll get rid of him."

Thomas did not respond.

"Sir, what do you think?"

Thomas pushed back in his chair and placed his feet on the desk. He returned his attention to the quarter horses. "I'll tell you when you bring him out here tomorrow."

Matt walked very slowly down the hallway toward Courtney's apartment. She held his left hand and carried his travel bag. He'd slipped his right arm into a sling, which helped ease some of the aggravation of the raw tissue in his arm.

"Did I ever tell you I think you're great?" Matt asked her.

She smirked. "Not standing up, that I recall."

"Very funny. Well, if I haven't said it, I think you're great."

She ran her key card in her apartment door lock and pushed the door open. She nudged Matt into the darkened room first. From somewhere within, a light was thrown, and a living room full of people shouted, "Surprise!"

"Oh, shit," Matt grunted. The room was filled with detectives and officers from the Alexandria Substation. Matt was startled to see Flavius Blair.

"Why aren't you people out catching bad guys?" Matt asked.

"'Cause you killed 'em all," shouted Rosecroft from the back of the room, near the hors d'oeuvres tray. Matt rolled his eyes.

"No thanks to you, Mr. Sick Leave," countered Sheridan.

The group erupted into general laughter. *I killed seven men, and I haven't thought twice about it,* Matt thought. *Why?*

Courtney closed the door behind them and led Matt into the room. His entire Narcotics Response Team was there, including Mueller, sporting a cast and a cane. Oscar Vo was also in attendance, and he smiled when he greeted Matt.

Matt pointed at Courtney. "I'll get you for this."

"Promises, promises," she said. The police officers all oohed like grade-schoolers.

"I thought you guys all hated me," said Matt.

"We do," said Detective Saunders, thrusting a beer bottle at him. "But they said there'd be free beer." The group cheered again.

Matt threw his left arm across his eyes and faked a swoon. He then looked at his watch. "Hey, it's only twelve-thirty."

Blair stepped forward. "Don't worry. Nova Narco officially has the afternoon off. This is an official ceremony."

"Ceremony?" asked Matt. Courtney stood very close to him and gently looped her left arm through his right.

"That's right," said Blair. "Could everyone gather around here for a second, please? And, Rosecroft, put down the chicken wings for a minute?"

Each head turned toward Rosecroft, who was caught with his mouth stuffed with food.

"Sorry, sir," he mumbled.

"Very well. Detective Lieutenant Sheridan, it is my honor to read to you a letter passed to me, to forward to you, by Mr. Louis Hathaway, Assistant Secretary of Security, Internal. 'Lieutenant Sheridan, It is with gratitude and respect that I write to you today, to commend you for your actions of the past November 23. Your bravery, dedication to duty, and dedication to your subordinates are exemplary of the finest qualities of a federal detective. Your action, after suffering serious bodily injury, is indicative of your commitment to law enforcement and the people of the Comarva region. Your initiative resulted in the largest confiscation ever of the narcotic *xin ji*, or jazz, on the East Coast. While we have a long way to go, by your action the streets of America are a little bit safer today. Sincerely, Louis Hathaway, Assistant Secretary of Security, Internal, Federal States of America.'"

Blair handed the letter to Sheridan, which had been placed in a small wooden and glass frame.

"What's this about 'the largest jazz bust on the East Coast'?" Matt asked.

Detective Venski spoke up. "Lieutenant, do you remember checking the door underneath the stairs to the second floor in that building?"

Matt wrinkled his brow. "No."

"Exactly. When we cleared the house—you were already on your way to Carter Memorial at the time—we realized that a door under the staircase hadn't been checked. It was the steps to the basement. We found ten fifty-five-gallon drums down there. Looks like they were planning on moving out of the house at Montgomery and Royal and were gonna set up shop in that place."

Matt nodded in appreciation.

"Sheridan, the rest of your team has also received personalized letters from Parker Hudson, along with commendations for bravery in their permanent files," said Blair.

"Good," said Matt. "Thank you. Everyone, thank you for everything."

After an awkward silent moment, Courtney said, "Everybody eat and drink; there's plenty."

Rosecroft approached her, still swallowing food. "Can I take that bag over to Matt's apartment for you?"

"No thanks, Clark. Matt will be staying here for a while, I think."

Matt and Courtney sat on the couch under a thin blanket watching Bryan Carruthers explain the growing menace of the Confederation of American Patriots. Matt had stretched his legs out to rest on the coffee table, a respectable distance away from the bottle of gewürztraminer they were enjoying. There was a knock at the door.

"Stay put. I'll get it," said Courtney, shrugging off the cover. Matt watched her walk to the door. Tonight she wore a flattering pair of jeans instead of baggy sweats. As Courtney opened the door, Matt rolled his eyes and threw his head against the back of the couch.

"Sorry to disturb you, but I'm looking for Matt. Is he here?" said Karen Russell, though she could see him on the couch.

Courtney held the door with one hand and propped the other on her hip. She frowned. "Is this important? You know he just got out of the hospital today. . . ."

Matt was beside Courtney. "It's okay, Court. It'll take just a minute." He brushed past Courtney and narrowed his eyes at Karen.

"Let's go down to my apartment," he said, and walked slowly in that direction. He heard the door slam shut behind him. Karen walked directly next to Matt.

"How did you know I was there?"

"Don't be naive, Sheridan. I've been in this business for a while, you know."

Once at his apartment, Matt keyed it open and nearly tripped over Pasha in the darkness. The cat meowed and ran in circles.

"Hey, little buddy. Courtney been taking good care of you?" He reached down and scratched the animal behind the ears. He then flipped on a light and closed the door.

"What's going on, Karen?"

"That's what I'm supposed to ask you."

"Well, about a week ago I got shot about ten times in a gun battle with drug dealers. Other than that, Mrs. Kennedy, what did you think of Dallas?"

Karen pointed a finger at him. "Not funny, Sheridan. You could go to jail for that."

Matt shrugged.

"What's going on with the CAPs?"

"I've been in the fucking hospital, Karen, I don't know! I've given you everything I've gotten so far."

"Reilly is pissing his pants that you missed the Manassas raid."

"I didn't miss the Manassas raid. It never came up. I had no idea they had an op planned, and I don't assume that they automatically tell brand-new members all their secrets. I'm making progress though. I've given you Murcheson already. I've got the encrypt/decrypt protocol to contact Murcheson. I just haven't had a chance to report since the last meeting. Wouldn't you consider eight days in the hospital extenuating circumstances?"

Karen sighed and leaned against the wall.

"So report."

"Fine. I got two new major players. One goes by Rick West, and he's supposedly Murcheson's deputy. European, in his sixties, short, no real distinguishing features—the other they said was with the national organization. He read my plastic; he's gonna do a search on me too. I figure I'm still clean."

Karen nodded.

"This West guy pressed me on ammo for the 265s I gave them. He says they're 'very short' on caseless. When I told him that I could lose my job for trying to steal ammo, they offered me a job. . . ."

"Offered you a job?"

"Yeah, they said that they have numerous people in what they call 'shadow jobs.' I guess they report an income and so forth, but the people do just CAP work. What, I'm not sure."

"Very interesting. Do you think you could get one of these jobs?"

Matt laughed. "It's not exactly like the National Employment Online, you know. They said they'd give me a position if I lost my job with the department for stealing ammo."

"What if you just quit the department and told them you were fired?"

Matt shook his head no. "First of all, they're not gonna believe me if I show up without the ammo. Second of all, I'm not quitting. Not for this."

Karen pointed at him again. "You'll quit if you're instructed."

"And when I refuse?"

"When you refuse, you will be terminated."

Matt reached to the small of his back and drew the Colt. In the fluorescent light it gleamed from the new polish job he'd given it in the hospital. It was the first thing he asked for when Rosecroft came to visit. He quickly worked the slide and pressed it to Karen's chest. She had gone for her purse when he reached, but he beat her to it. She trembled ever so slightly. He ground his teeth together as fire spread through his right arm, and he could feel the synthetic muscle connectors pulling against his own tissue.

He released his grip on the pistol, and it pivoted upside down on his index finger, in the trigger guard. He pressed it grip-first into her right hand.

"Then go ahead and terminate me right now. I'll quit your little bullshit scam before I quit the police. So if I'm gonna get terminated, why don't you just go ahead and save us both the time and trouble," he said through clenched teeth, staring into her eyes.

She did not break eye contact, but pushed the pistol back at him. "Not yet."

He lowered the hammer on the weapon and returned it to its holster.

"Are you finished?" she sneered.

"Hardly."

"Well, we're still waiting for the other shoe to drop. We're expecting another major action very soon. We need that information. I need you to contact them and get back with them as soon as possible."

"Wait here," he said. He walked over to his com and powered up the screen. As he did, he noticed a message flashing. He recognized the number.

"Perfect timing," he said softly as he called up the message. *Thursday night, the park, eight o'clock.*

"I'll have something for you the day after tomorrow."

Matt had to knock a second time before Courtney opened the door. As she did, she quickly turned and walked away toward the living room.

"I'm sorry about that, Court," he said.

Without responding, she sat on the couch. The reflection of the video in her eyes shimmered.

"It won't happen again, I promise."

"Is that the woman who called that night?"

Matt sat beside her. "Yes."

Courtney folded her arms across her chest. "Do you see a lot of her, when you go on your little night missions?"

Oh, shit, Matt thought. "No. Look, don't get the wrong idea."

"Why won't you tell me the truth!" she shouted. When she looked at him, she saw blood dripping from the little finger of his right hand. "And what happened to your arm?"

Matt glanced at the blood, then rolled up his sleeve. The bandage around his upper arm was bloodstained. He sighed, then took her face in his left hand.

"Courtney, I want you to understand that if I tell you, and you ever repeated it, I could get killed. And you could get killed too."

She pulled away from his hand. "I'm not afraid."

He sagged a bit, then ran his left hand through his hair. He spoke in a soft voice, almost whispering. "I'm working undercover for Internal Intelligence. It's got nothing to do with the department. I am infiltrating the local Confederation of American Patriots organization. That's what I've been doing at night. That woman is my control officer, whom I report to. The situation with the CAP is very dangerous right now, and I'm trying to help our country. Because of what I used to do in the service, they called me back, and I couldn't refuse them. So now Internal Intelligence has me until I finish the project."

She closed her eyes and dropped her chin into her chest. Matt could see goose bumps on her bare arms.

"Look, as soon as I get them what they want, I'm out. And I'm thinking about quitting the department too."

She looked up at him and spoke with an unsteady voice. "Really?"

"We could get out of this area, go somewhere else, do something else . . ."

"*We?*"

Matt swallowed. "Yeah. *We.* If you want to . . ."

She leaned over, wrapped her arms around him, and squeezed.

Matt's face contorted. "Aarrgh!"

She let go of him. "Sorry. I forgot."

Matt waited patiently at the park. Boredom was something to which he had never grown accustomed, and with a minimum mandatory thirty-day health suspension from the department, he was facing two and a half more boring weeks. *Tonight should be interesting though,* he thought. He drove his hands into the pockets of his overcoat, which was much warmer since he'd zipped in the winter liner.

This night an unfamiliar dark blue van arrived, but Matt recognized Murcheson in the front passenger seat. The squat Asian was driving. As the car rolled to a halt, Murcheson got out of the car, and he opened the sliding door for Matt to climb in back.

"Hope you're feeling better," said Murcheson.

Matt grunted as he forced his way into the backseat. "I've been better."

"I read about your incident the other day in the police blotter. Unfortunately your event rated only about two inches onscreen."

"Those are the breaks, I guess."

"So you got hit in the arm and the stomach?" Murcheson asked as the Asian drove them out of the lot.

"And a bunch of times in the chest and back. And a little slice in my leg. Body armor saved my ass."

"Glad you made it."

"Me too."

"Uh, Matt, if you don't mind," said Murcheson, pointing to the van's compartmented interior. "No windows in this unit; of course the rear is closed off from the cabin. You won't be able to see where we're going. Security reasons, you understand."

"No problem, but what's up?" Matt asked.

"We have a very special meeting tonight," said Murcheson.

Matt shrugged his shoulders and settled back into his seat.

They had traveled on a dirt road for nearly a mile, at about thirty-five miles per hour, by Matt's estimation. The vehicle made a half-circle turn, then stopped. Matt had finally lost track of where they were when they turned east off Route 15, around Lucketts, he guessed. *This used to be his favorite game as a child, lying down in the back of the old station wagon with his brother, coming home from somewhere at night with his parents. He'd close his eyes and imagine the streets, the turns, the distances, then he would open his eyes just before they would turn into the driveway. It made it that much easier when they taught him to do it as part of his trade craft.*

"Okay, Matt," said Murcheson. The Asian cut the motor.

Matt saw a brightly lit farmhouse. It was white, two stories, and huge. Just beyond the farmhouse was a barn, and bright light spilled from beneath the barn door.

Matt was between the Asian and Murcheson as they walked to the front door. Just before they reached it, Arthur opened it.

"Good evening, gentlemen. Please come in."

He opened the door, and they entered the house. It appeared to be early twentieth century in design and construction. The floors were hardwood, and the walls were half walnut panel and half print wallpaper. Standing in the vestibule, Matt could see large sitting rooms just to the right and left. A hallway ran straight ahead into what looked like a kitchen. Immediately in front of them was a wide, curving staircase that led to the second floor.

"We'll be headed upstairs. Mr. Sheridan, are you armed tonight?" asked Arthur.

Matt nodded, and with a grimace, started to reach for his holster.

Arthur waved him off. "No, keep it. We just like to know, that's all. If we didn't trust you, you wouldn't have made it this far."

Arthur turned and headed up the steps. The Asian peeled off and quietly sat in an overstuffed armchair in the left sitting room.

"Matt, this is a very special occasion. The leader of the national organization has asked to see you."

Matt could feel the hair on his arms rising, and his heart was racing.

"Why would the national leader want to see me?"

Arthur turned and smiled. "You'll see soon enough."

At the top of the stairs, Matt could see what looked like six large bedrooms and one bathroom. They walked along a tasteful red runner carpet to the farthest bedroom. The door was slightly open. Arthur swung it completely open, and the three men entered.

The bedroom had been converted into an office, and a single desk, facing a large picture window overlooking the rolling hills behind the house, was located in the center. A man in his fifties with an eye patch and silver hair, pulled back into a ponytail, stood behind the desk. An angry-looking Native American with long black hair stood in front of the desk.

Arthur took Matt's coat, then led Murcheson out of the room. He closed the door behind him, leaving Matt alone with the two men.

"Please, Mr. Sheridan, come in, sit down," said Owen Thomas, gesturing to one of the chairs in front of his desk.

Matt walked to the chair, and Owen met him there. He grasped Matt's right hand carefully. "I understand you've been wounded recently."

Matt nodded, then eased himself into the chair. "Still pretty sore."

"I know what you mean," said Owen returning to his seat. Jimmy White Horse remained standing.

"It turns out that I know you very well, Mr. Sheridan, but we've never met. My name is Owen Thomas."

Matt's eyes widened. "Owen Thomas? Owen Thomas was assassinated five years ago in Las Vegas."

"Well, I was shot, but, as a famous Missourian once said, the rumors of my death are greatly exaggerated."

Matt leaned forward and stared at Thomas. "What if I don't believe you?"

Owen chuckled. "Always the cynic, aren't you? At least that's what they said about you when you went by the code name Mynah."

Matt's jaw dropped.

Owen smiled at himself. "Now, only General Owen Thomas, former XVIII Corps Commander, would know that, wouldn't he?"

"You read my reports. . . ."

"I've read a lot of your work, Mr. Sheridan. Classified and unclassified. And I've heard the stories about your exploits. Reads better than fiction."

"Just a second though," said Matt in a strong voice. "You were shot on campaign in Las Vegas. You were buried. It was in the news. President Kersey spoke at your funeral."

Thomas smiled and shook his head. "This may take a while. James, are you sure you won't sit?"

The Native American shook his head.

"Suit yourself." Thomas pulled open the top right hand drawer of the oak desk and produced a bottle of amber liquid, three small glass tumblers, two metal tubes, and two books of matches. He pushed a metal tube toward Matt, along with a pack of matches.

"Cuban?" he asked.

Matt salivated like Pavlov's dog, but shook his head no.

"Keep it for later, then. Scotch? It's a single malt."

This time Matt said "Sure" before he could stop himself. Owen poured three glasses, pushing one to Matt, and handing the other to Jimmy. White Horse accepted the glass and leaned against the desk.

All three sipped simultaneously. Owen licked his lips, then continued. "I was dead to the world, for all intents and purposes. But the party was very upset that one of its own would dare to run for the nomination against the incumbent president. They bought the party line I gave them when I retired, and they liked the idea that a military man was joining the party."

"You're rambling, boss," snickered White Horse. Thomas glared at him.

"Thank you, James," Owen said. "Let me ask you this, Mr. Sheridan, being yourself a man of strategic thought. Why was the American-Arabian Protectorate formed?"

"It was formed after the Second Gulf War to protect the Arabian peninsula and Iran from encroachment by external forces on America's significant interests in the region."

"Then three years later it was announced that the Saudi oil reserves were starting to dry up, wasn't it?"

"Yes."

"And the government established an emergency program to expand its nuclear power facilities, to prepare for the cutback in oil. Private ownership of internal combustion engines was outlawed?"

Matt sipped his Scotch. "Yes."

"If the wells were running dry, and we had expanded our nuclear power at a dear cost to the American taxpayer, then why did we fight the Chinese when they tried to take the gulf?"

"We had long-standing bilateral defense agreements—"

"Do you believe that bullshit, Sheridan? Come on, you're intelligent, and you're a cynic. Why did the government kill all the brave boys to keep the Chinese out of the gulf?"

Matt squirmed painfully in his chair and looked into his drink. He had no answer.

Thomas drank again. "Because the oil is still there. They have as much oil in the ground now as they did sixty years ago."

"But if we weren't using the oil—"

"They just stopped pumping it. People are eating rats in Paris right now because the little bit of oil that's available is astronomically expensive. And that's one of the reasons why I resigned. I couldn't be part of the lie that the federal government was perpetuating."

"Now, wait a minute. If the oil was still there, does it make sense to spend hundreds of billions of the taxpayers' money to convert to an all-electric society?"

"It does if it actually costs them next to nothing."

Matt put his glass on the edge of the desk.

"Excuse me?"

"Mr. Sheridan, have you ever heard of a man by the name of Roy Horace?"

Matt shook his head no.

"Have you ever heard of cold fusion?"

A chill ran down Matt's spine that made him shudder. He nodded yes.

"Roy Horace discovered the secret to cold fusion way back in 2004. The key to the reaction was lunium. The properties of lunium were still a very new commodity, but he recognized its molecular similarities to palladium, which had previously been used to attempt cold fusion reactions."

Matt leaned forward in his chair, nodding. "I took some physics classes in school."

"Deuterium atoms in heavy water were so violently attracted to lunium rods arranged in a charged reaction cell that the nuclei fused at an exponential rate. Remember the explosion at the University of Wisconsin back in 2004 they said was a bomb?"

Matt nodded.

"World's first massive cold fusion reaction."

"So?" Matt asked, his brow wrinkled in confusion.

Thomas sighed, then gesticulated with his hands. "Don't you see? All the reactors they built, conveniently along the West Coast are cold fusion reactors. They are powered by seawater. Filtered goddamn seawater!" Owen shouted, nearly shrieking.

Matt sat back in his chair, dizzy.

"So, in a very roundabout way, this is why I was 'assassinated' in Las Vegas. I knew the truth about Saudi, and I knew about cold fusion. I told the party bosses what I knew, and that if they wouldn't let me challenge Kersey for the nomination, I'd talk to the media. So they 'assassinated' me and gave me a hero's funeral. But they needed me alive to find out who else I had told, who else knew the truth. That's how I met James here. He was my cell neighbor in solitary in the jail on Nellis Air Force Base. When the CAPs broke me out, they took him with me. So, to make a short story very long, that's how I'm Owen Thomas, not deceased."

Matt stood and gulped down the Scotch. "Pretty overwhelming," he said truthfully.

"So tell me, Mr. Sheridan, if you're so skeptical of what I have to say, and a true believer of what New Liberty tells you, why did you approach the CAPs? I'm very curious now. James thinks you're a plant."

Matt's heart was pounding. He cleared his throat so it would not crack. He could see that White Horse had a Standard 9 in his hip holster and had unsnapped it.

"I don't believe in the way the government limits the freedom of speech, and I think they're too easy on criminals."

"But you don't believe what I've told you tonight?"

"I'd have to say that if I can't see it with my own two eyes, I can't believe it," said Sheridan.

"From you, Mynah, I know that's true. Perhaps you will have a chance to see some of it for yourself. And I hope, very soon, the rest of the country. But in the meantime, I'd like you to consider joining my staff. . . ."

"What?" snapped White Horse.

"Calm down, Jimmy."

"This guy is a fucking plant! I know it!" shouted White Horse.

"No," said Owen. "I know Mr. Sheridan. Even with his injuries, if he was a plant, he'd have killed me by now. And maybe you too."

White Horse scowled.

"As I was saying, Mr. Sheridan, I'd like you to consider joining my national staff. You'd have to go underground, of course, but I think that you would be well suited here. I want you to think about it."

Matt set his glass down and steadied himself against the edge of the desk. Owen pressed a button under the desktop, and in just a few seconds Arthur appeared at the door. Matt stumbled a bit as he headed toward the door.

"Oh, Mr. Sheridan?" Owen called after him.

Matt turned to him.

"You forgot your cigar."

Matt paced Courtney's living room floor for nearly an hour the next morning before the knock came at the door.

At least Courtney has already left for work, Matt thought as he opened the door. Karen Russell breezed past him.

"All right, Sheridan, what do you have?" she asked, making herself comfortable on the couch.

"Well, fortunately for you, I can't get comfortable sleeping in her bed. It's too new, and my body aches. So I got up and wrote you a report on the contact last night."

"You wrote a report?"

"Yeah, I know it's against policy, but last night was very eventful. I met Owen Thomas."

Karen stood. "Owen Thomas?"

"Yeah, he's the leader of the CAPs' national organization."

Karen's face was suddenly flush. "Owen Thomas is dead. And besides, all the reports we've gotten on the national leadership puts them in Pennsylvania."

"Could be. This guy claimed to be Owen Thomas."

"Where were you?"

"I don't know," Matt lied. "They had me in the back of a closed van so I couldn't see where I was going."

"Shit! So what did you get?"

Matt walked over to the disk drive of Courtney's com. He extracted a Read-Write, put it in a plastic case, and flipped it to Karen.

"Read the report. It's all there. Now, if you'll excuse me . . ." He brushed past her and slowly stretched out on the couch. "I haven't slept in twenty-four hours, and I'm gonna try to get some shut-eye."

"This better be good, Sheridan," Karen growled as she headed for the door.

"This is it?" shouted Reilly.

"That's what he gave me," said Karen.

"'Met Owen Thomas, drank Scotch, and talked about the service.' What the fuck kind of report is that!" he shouted, the cigarette in his lips jumping up and down.

"I brought it right over as soon as he gave it to me. He said he had too much to give me a verbal."

"Shit!" Dan said as he rose from behind his desk. He paced back and forth in front of his picture window, which had been darkened.

"You know I got word that one of Sheridan's buddies is staking out Morelli."

"Morelli?"

"Russell, you turn this fucking Sheridan off, or there's gonna be a massacre!"

15

Matt walked cautiously toward his office. The detectives on the floor came out to greet him, and he spoke briefly with each man and woman. He entered his office and sagged slowly into his chair. He powered up his com. Rosecroft shortly stuck his head in the office.

"Hey, boss, you're supposed to be on sick leave."

"I am. I'm not working. I'm here relaxing. Besides, I'm bored out of my skull."

"How're you feeling?"

Why does everyone ask me the same question, Matt thought. "Getting a little better, I guess."

"Good. Hey, do you want to do lunch in about an hour? The owner over at Shanky's has been asking for you."

Matt smiled. "It hurts me to get a hard-on, Rosecroft, but I'll think about it."

"Cool," said Rosecroft.

The door was pushed wide open, and Officer Doug Sloane entered, visibly upset.

"Lieutenant, I gotta talk to you. Closed-door."

"How did you know I was here?"

"Heard your voice in the hall."

Matt shrugged. "Come in and sit down."

Sloane entered but held the doorknob. He looked at Sheridan, then at Rosecroft.

"It's okay, Sloane. Rosecroft is safe," said Sheridan. Sloane closed the door, then sat. Rosecroft sat beside him.

"Lieutenant, I got busted."

Matt frowned. "What do you mean?"

"Somebody found out that I was staking Morelli's place. The order came down from way up, and Captain Larimer won't tell me where it came from. But not only am I off Morelli, Larimer said he was taking me out of plainclothes. They're sending me down to fucking Roanoke to work highway patrol. Fucking traffic detail."

Matt whistled. "No explanations?"

"Nothing. Absolutely nothing."

Matt whistled a single low note as he leaned back in his chair. "Rosecroft, you go on to lunch by yourself. I need some time with Officer Sloane here."

Courtney was not at all pleased that I'm going out, Matt thought. *She told me I still wasn't well, and I need more rest.* Matt went anyway.

He met Sloane at a bar in North Arlington, and from there they rode in Matt's hummer to Great Falls, one of the few remaining exclusive suburbs of New Columbia. They stopped the car just up the block from the Morelli home. The house had few lights on. They watched the house for nearly two hours with no activity, when the telltale headlights of a large truck appeared at the end of the street. The two slouched in their seats.

The truck pulled into the Morelli drive, and the limousine pulled in close behind. Six men unloaded two dozen heavy barrels, while Tony Morelli watched, shivering against the cold night air.

"You say this is going on every night?" Matt asked.

"Every fucking night," said Sloane.

Matt shook his head. "I think I'll be taking it from here."

It was just past one A.M. when Matt made his way down the hall at the River View Towers. His body ached all over now. As he neared the end of the hallway, he saw that the door to Courtney's apartment was open. His spine tingled, and his heart skipped a beat. *Thank Higher Powers that we decided to try to sleep in my bed tonight,* Matt thought.

The Colt was in his hand, and he felt adrenaline surge through his body. He sidestepped to the doorway, then knelt. He ventured a slow look around the corner.

He could see a single figure, all the way in the bedroom, silhouetted against the moonlight pouring through the bedroom window.

The figure was moving in and out of sight through the doorway to the bedroom.

Matt crept into the apartment slowly, keeping both hands on his pistol. He moved to the couch and knelt behind it for cover. A heartbeat later the figure emerged from the bedroom.

"Freeze!" Matt shouted. Noticing a long object in the figure's hand, he shouted, "Drop the gun!"

The figure jumped in place, but did not raise or drop the weapon. Weapon still trained on the figure, Matt moved to the end of the couch and flipped on a table lamp.

The figure blinked against the light. Matt saw a small, slight Asian, clad in black, carrying a silenced 9mm pistol.

"Cha," Matt said evenly.

The Asian squinted. "Word on the street is that you're looking for me. I thought I'd make myself available to you."

"Nice try. What are you doing in this apartment?"

"Had a hunch."

Matt stepped from behind the couch, weapon still aimed, and stood directly in front of Cha, just ten feet away.

"Drop the gun, Cha," he commanded.

"You drop yours, Sheridan."

"I've got mine aimed already, you don't."

"You don't really want to shoot it out with me, Sheridan, do you?"

"I don't intend to shoot it out with you, Cha. If you move a muscle, you'll be dead before you hit the floor. You drop the gun and you've got a chance to live."

Cha smirked at Sheridan and did not move.

Sheridan growled in a voice from deep within his body. "Now."

Cha dropped the gun at his feet.

"Kick it over here, real gently."

Cha did so. Matt bent at the knees and picked up the gun, his eyes and pistol never moving from Cha's direction.

"Nice equipment," said Matt as he held the silenced pistol in his left hand. He quickly tucked his Colt into his waistband and moved the 9mm into his right hand. As he did, Cha's knees flexed, as though preparing to move, but Matt's action was too quick.

"Don't even think about it," Sheridan growled. He pulled the slide back partway to verify that the weapon was loaded.

"Look, Sheridan," said Cha, his voice now shaky. "I can give you information. I'm valuable to you."

"You are the most worthless piece of shit on the planet right now, Cha."

Sheridan raised the 9mm and pointed at a spot between Cha's eyes. He took two steps closer.

"You are a worthless piece of shit who doesn't have the guts to look a man in the eyes when you kill him."

Matt thumbed back the hammer. He stopped, looking down the barrel past the front ramp sight, and stared into Cha's black eyes.

"Fuck you," he said, and pulled the trigger. The silenced pistol coughed, and the far wall was spray-painted red and pink. Cha's body dropped to the floor in a heap, a pool of blood spreading on the floor.

Matt stood over him. "That was for Noah Benning, motherfucker."

When Courtney opened her eyes, Matt was standing over her, shaking her with his right hand and holding one of her suitcases in the other.

"What's wrong?" she said through a yawn.

"Court, you gotta get up. You need to get out of here."

"What? What time is it?"

"Uh, about a quarter to two. Look, Courtney," he said, turning on a bedside light. She blinked against its brightness. He sat on the bed next to her.

"Something really bad is going down, and I'm not sure what it is. But I do know that if you stay here, your safety will be in jeopardy."

"Matt, you're scaring me. What . . . you've got blood on your face!" she yelped.

Matt wiped his face with his left sleeve. "It's not mine."

She covered her mouth with her hand.

"Okay, look, now, Court, you need to stay in control right now. Listen to me. A man came to kill me tonight. He was in your apartment when I came in. I'm sure he didn't just stumble in there; someone sent him. Please. Get up and put on some clothes. I've packed some things for you. I also went to a machine and scripped out my cash account. It's in the suitcase. It's not a lot, but it'll help for now. I put Pasha in his carrier; he's out by the door." Matt extracted an envelope from his pocket. "Here's a MagLev ticket to Philadelphia. It leaves at five this morning. We'll get a cab to take you to Union Station. Be careful there; it's extremely dangerous. When you get to Philadelphia, call my parents. I wrote the number on the jacket of the ticket. Out of Philly there's a local line that'll run you up to Scranton. Sit tight there until I can contact you."

Courtney bit her lip. "What . . . is . . . happening, Matt?"

"I'm afraid I'm on someone's shortlist for termination."

Matt was dozing in the small, uncomfortable chair at Betsy Holleran's desk. He had been there since seven in the morning. Karen Russell finally came to her office at nine.

"Ms. Russell, I'm sorry, but he insisted on waiting to see you," said Betsy as Karen strode into her office. Matt awoke and sat up with difficulty.

"Can I help you?" asked Karen, her eyes afire.

"I just need a minute in your office," said Matt, standing. He rubbed his face for circulation.

Karen had already begun to shuck off her long coat. "Come in, then."

Matt entered the office behind her and closed the door.

"What are you doing here?" Karen hissed.

"Well, actually, I came to see Parker Hudson, but since I've got a couple of questions for you, I just thought I'd kill two birds with one stone."

"What?"

"Why did you call off the Morelli stakeout?"

Karen turned her back to him and hung her coat on the rack behind her desk.

"That's not a concern of yours. . . ."

"Sure it is. I'm a narcotics detective. You are the supervisor of all the narcotics detectives in the eastern region of this country. Why would you consistently shut down operations against a man who has been named as a jazz supplier over the past two years?"

"It's above both our pay grades, Sheridan, so give it a rest," she said. She stood arms akimbo, very close to Matt.

"Fine. Question number two. Who sent Cha to kill me?"

"I have no idea what you're talking about. What's a chaw?"

"Don't give me that bullshit, Karen. Cha, the leader of the Gutters, remember, you authorized me a task force to shut him down? He paid a visit last night. Who sent him?"

"I still have no idea what you're talking about."

"Very well, I guess that's all I wanted to ask," said Matt, turning and walking to the door.

"Wait, I need to—"

"Sorry, Karen, I quit."

Matt opened the door and smiled at Betsy Holleran. He walked to Parker Hudson's office door, where Christopher Dino intercepted him.

"Sorry, Mr. Hudson is on the line right now—"

Matt pushed open the door, and Hudson stopped speaking in midsentence.

"Can you hold a minute?" he asked the screen, touching the hold icon. "Can I help you, Lieutenant?" he growled.

Matt reached into his overcoat and withdrew a Standard 9 pistol, grip-first. He dropped the magazine and placed it on the desk. He reached into his tunic and removed the cord around his neck.

"My shield and my weapon. I am resigning my position effective immediately. Since I reported to you from San Diego, I figured I ought to quit to you as well."

Parker wrinkled his brow. "What the hell is going on, Sheridan?"

"Pretty simple, actually. I'm quitting. My department car is downstairs in the garage," Matt said. *With a small, dead Asian in the trunk,* he thought.

Hudson's mouth was moving, but no words were forming.

"What brought this on? Was it the—"

"Ask your boss about it," said Matt. He turned, walked past Christopher Dino, and was gone.

Hudson was down the hall and at Karen's door in a flash. As Betsy opened her frowning mouth to speak, Hudson pointed at her. "You keep that trap shut, you old bat!"

Parker burst into Karen's office. She was talking to her monitor in a hushed voice.

"What the fuck is going on with Sheridan?"

"I think there's been some misunderstanding, and he's bent out of shape. Don't worry. We'll find you a new lieutenant."

"Don't worry? Don't worry? You brought this guy across the fucking continent, forced him on me, gave him a private army, and then when he quits, you say we'll find you another one! I want an explanation."

"If you want the truth, dear, Sheridan has been making romantic advances toward me for the past three months. I didn't tell you before because I knew how upset you'd get. But when I finally told him that if he didn't cease and desist, I'd fire him, he flew off the handle and said he was quitting. That's all I can figure."

Hudson shook his head and stormed back to his office.

Matt sat in the parking lot of the Daingerfield Island Marina, the icy Potomac flowing serenely past him. He'd taken the trombone case and ammo canister out of the department car after quitting, took a cab to National Airport, and rented a car courtesy of the wad of scrip notes he'd "confiscated" from Cha. Confident no one was around to observe him, he opened the trombone case and viewed his great-grandfather's legacy.

Model 1927A Thompson submachine gun. Original issue. His great-grandfather had carried it in the Pacific and brought it home after the war. The stock had been nicked a bit. *Gives it character.* He traced his finger along the wood stock, across the receiver, and up to the vertical foregrip. His grandfather had replaced the military horizontal foregrip with the vertical foregrip. Matt's grandfather had always said the Thompson was a weapon to be fired from the hip.

In the bell area of the case were two circular magazines, called C drums for their 100-round capacity. He withdrew one of the drums and flipped up the lid to the ammo can. It was full of factory-loaded .45 ACP bullets. He pressed one after another into the C drum.

"Yello," said Clark Rosecroft to the monitor as it signaled an incoming call. He didn't recognize the originating number, and the caller had disabled the video.

"Shanky's. Now," commanded a familiar voice.

Rosecroft shivered as he entered Shanky's. The bouncer waved him past, the two men being well acquainted. The crowd was somewhat sparse for a midweek lunch, and Rosecroft spotted Sheridan instantly, seated facing the stage at the bar. Rosecroft passed the stage as he walked, and the dancer, a redhead he remembered, cooed, "Hi, Clark."

He flashed a forced smile at her and joined Matt at the bar. Sheridan was drinking coffee.

"What's up?" asked Clark, sitting next to Sheridan.

Sheridan put down his coffee cup but did not look at Rosecroft. "Have you heard that I quit?"

"What?"

"Good. I guess you haven't."

"You quit?"

"Just this morning. Since I'm sure there is no standard operating procedure for processing someone who quits while on extended medical leave, they probably have to process my circuitwork manually."

"Why did you quit?"

"You mean in addition to being shot up by junkies? I quit on principle because they called off the Morelli stake and fired Sloane."

"Shit," mumbled Rosecroft.

"Rosecroft, I need you to do something for me."

"You name it."

"Go back to the substation, go down to Property. Log out a scope for me. You know the model, day/night, IR, telescopic. Put it in this," Matt said, pulling a small black gym bag from under his stool and shoving it into Rosecroft's hands.

Rosecroft looked at it incredulously.

"I need it ASAP. So, please, go get it, will you?"

Rosecroft's eyes were dulled with amazement.

"I could get fired if I—"

"Look, you still haven't gotten word that I quit, right? Bernie in Property will take care of you."

Clark was still staring vacantly at Sheridan as Matt pushed him gently with his left arm. "Go."

Rosecroft quickly slipped off the stool and stumbled out of the bar.

Matt reached into his pants pocket and pulled out the wad of scrip. They were all very large bills. Almost fifty of them left. He peeled off two and walked to the stage. The redhead smiled at him.

"What's your name?" he shouted to her.

"Leslie. What's yours?"

"Matt. Here," he said, tucking the two bills into the garter, high on her thigh. "Enroll in junior college or something."

An hour later Rosecroft returned, black bag in his right hand. He hopped onto the stool next to Matt, who was still drinking coffee, and handed him the bag.

Matt opened its Velcro closure and peeked inside quickly. "Excellent. I owe you. Any trouble?"

"None. You were right. No one has heard anything at the station. Not even Blair."

"The miracle of modern technology . . ." Matt muttered. He got off the stool.

"Where are you headed?" asked Clark.

"I've got some business to attend to. I'll call you later." Matt turned to walked away, then turned back to Rosecroft. He had another of the large bills in his hand.

"Here," he said, pressing it into Rosecroft's hand. "Give this to the redhead when she comes out. Tell her to make it two semesters."

"Huh?"

How convenient, Matt thought. He had just found a lot full of brand new American Motors sedans, identical to the late model he'd rented, waiting to be loaded onto a freighter in the Baltimore harbor south terminal. He'd simply waved to the rent-a-cops guarding the lot as he entered, then slapped them on the back and asked them how they thought the Ravens would do in the playoffs this year as he walked out. They didn't seem too concerned with the gym bag he carried.

He followed Sloane's description of the warehouse location from memory. It abutted one of the loading areas, among numerous similar warehouses on this south side of the harbor. From three blocks away, he could see the barbed wire fence Sloane had described and the guards, who were posted along the fence perimeter and at the entrance gate. Sheridan wandered the terminal for almost a half hour before he found a suitably deserted and run-down warehouse building. He went to the rear of the building and located a narrow metal service ladder leading up to the roof of the three-story structure.

Sheridan put the handles of the black bag in his teeth, then patted the small of his back. He reached up with his left hand, then with his right, to pull himself up the few feet from the ground to the bottom rung of the ladder. Pain stabbed in his arm and his side, but with a muffled grunt he pulled himself onto the ladder. Slowly, he climbed the remaining thirty feet to the roof.

Though the building seemed run-down, at least the cement roof was intact. He crossed the roof in a crouch, almost duck-walking, to the roof access door. The door formed a "hut," which opened to a staircase down to the warehouse. Matt stood on an idle exhaust fan and boosted himself, with difficulty, onto the roof of the "hut." He pressed himself flat on his stomach against the roof. He felt an uncomfortable pulling sensation along his lower right side, and he imagined that his laser closures were ready to open.

From this vantage point, however, Matt had a good view of the south side of the harbor and this portion of the terminal in general. He fished the scope out of the black bag and focused on the warehouse.

Finding first the barbed wire fence, then the guards, then the warehouse, Matt directed his view to the ship moored at the loading dock just behind the warehouse. He could see two ramps leading up to the hull of the huge, rusty freighter, and it appeared that one ramp was for offloading cargo and the other for loading. Both activities were under way. Matt noticed scores of fifty-five-gallon drums being offloaded. So far everything was tracking.

Sloane hadn't reported seeing a ship, so it must have recently arrived, Matt thought. He tracked the scope from the hull of the vessel to the superstructure atop. He looked to the ship's flag mast and found it to be flying the banner of the People's Republic of China.

A chill ran up, then down his spine. *Jazzers weren't making this shit in their little laboratories. The Chinese are shipping it here.*

Matt shook his head as if to clear it. *This is ridiculous,* he thought. *They're unloading in broad daylight. There should be customs agents, federal narcotics agents, coast guard cutters swarming on that ship like flies on crap. All those online "conspiracy" sites talked about the Chinese and jazz. The government said it was nonsense and shut those sites down. No one ever really believed those rumors. It couldn't be true!*

Matt rubbed his eyes, then looked through the scope again, this time at the warehouse. For the first time, he noticed the men on the dock working in dark pea coats. White hats. He focused on the building itself, painted a drab gray. He worked his way from the ground to the roof, where he saw a logo painted just above the one-story-tall sliding door. *There were no lights near it, so it wouldn't have been illuminated on the nights that Sloane staked the place,* Matt thought.

He rubbed his eyes a second time and looked again. The lettering was unmistakable.

Matt dropped the scope and rolled onto his back, balling his hands into fists and pressing them against his eyes. "Holy shit," he said aloud. "Holy fucking shit!"

The lettering above the warehouse read FEDERAL STATES NAVY SUPPLY CENTER—BALTIMORE.

Matt sat cross-legged now, blended in with the night but shivering from its chill. He spent the day waiting, hoping against hope to spot Morelli's limousine arrive at a different warehouse. As night had fallen, a procession of trucks, vans, and cars into the warehouse had begun. They entered the gates after a check by the guards and pulled in to the large open doorway. Hour after hour, they came and went.

Finally, the truck and limousine combination bearing the license plate numbers Sloane had described to him appeared at the gate. The two vehicles entered the compound, and the limousine idled outside the building as the truck entered. Twenty minutes later, the truck emerged.

Matt's mind swam a bit on the roof of the hut, and he realized that he had stopped breathing. He finally exhaled, and his breath came in huge gasps. He had only one option now.

Matt let the truck and the limousine get a full minute ahead of him on the trip down Interstate 95. *I know where they're going anyway,* he thought. The trip to Great Falls took nearly an hour, and as the wee hours of the morning were now upon him, Matt struggled to stay awake at the wheel. He rolled down the window, and the rushing cold air woke him quickly. He had to roll down the window four times before he reached Morelli's house.

He parked down the block from the house, but much closer than he had parked before. As he stepped out of the car, he could feel his heart rate begin to increase, and he felt a sudden urge to urinate. *I haven't felt like this since the old days. It was a feeling of . . . anticipation.* Matt held the Thompson in his right hand, barrel against his right shoulder. In his left he carried Cha's silenced 9mm. He strolled down the sidewalk, not hiding his presence, but avoiding streetlights all the same. He approached a small shack next to the gate closing off Morelli's driveway.

A muscular man in his forties with black hair, a single thick eyebrow, and a shotgun slung in his long coat, shouted to Matt, "Hey, yo!"

The man was raising the shotgun when Matt fired the pistol. It barked softly once, driving a 9mm Parabellum slug through his forehead. Matt stepped inside the shack and looked over a crude instrument panel. He pressed a button marked Gate, and the driveway gate swung open.

Matt walked slowly up the drive toward the truck and limousine parked in front of the garage, attached to the huge house. Eight men stood around the limousine and truck, watching two other men unload fifty-five-gallon drums. Matt had gotten within twenty yards of the group, when one man turned and yelled, "Who the hell are you?"

Matt stuck the pistol in his waistband and leveled the Thompson with both hands. "Nobody move," he said quietly.

He then had the attention of all ten men. The two moving the drums froze on the ramp leading down from the truck. The other eight stopped in place.

"I want to see some hands," Matt commanded. He did not get an immediate response.

"Now!" he screamed, and jerked the Thompson back in his hands. The motion was enough that most of the men flinched, then raised their hands.

Matt walked toward the truck, sidestepping, keeping himself between the men and the house, but without turning his back to either. He continued toward the back of the truck.

A mature white-haired man spoke. "What's this all about? Do you know who I—"

"Shut up!" Matt screamed. He turned toward the two men stopped on the truck ramp.

"You two goombahs bring one of those barrels over here. Nice and slow."

The two manhandled the heavy barrel, which they had loaded onto a two-man handtruck. With difficulty they rolled it from the driveway across the lawn. When they were about fifteen feet from Sheridan, he commanded, "Stop." The men obeyed. Waving the barrel of the Thompson, Matt directed them back to the truck.

Matt set the Thompson on his right shoulder again and withdrew the silenced pistol. He walked to within five feet of the barrel and fired once. The slug made a dull thud against the side of the drum, and soon a syrupy brown liquid began to pour from the hole. He took a step closer to examine it, but he didn't have to go any farther. The telltale smell made his intestines spasm, and the pain that caused in his right side made his ears ring.

"You bastards!" he growled through clenched teeth. One of the ten men then dug inside his trench coat for a pistol. Matt saw the barrel clearing leather from the corner of his eye. He dropped the silenced pistol, wheeled, and lowered the Thompson. The world moved in slow motion.

As Matt brought the submachine gun around, the man squeezed off a wild shot that sailed over Matt's head into the night. Seven of the other men now also began digging for weapons, inside coats, under arms, and in waistbands. One of the men tackled Morelli to the ground and covered him with his body.

Matt squeezed the trigger of the Thompson, and the weapon came to life in his hands. As the bolt on the top of the receiver flashed back and forth like a sewing machine needle, Matt walked a line of slugs from the ground next to the driveway, up the first man's left leg, then diagonally across his body to his right shoulder. A second, then a third man fired pistol shots at Matt, one of which tugged at the collar of his overcoat, the other striking the ground by his right foot.

Matt walked forward as the Thompson created a deafening roar. The endless stream of spent cartridges from the gun traced a bronze arc in the house floodlights illuminating the lawn. He moved his aim from the right shoulder of the first man, and swept the gun left and right in an infinity symbol pattern along the line of men. Some dove, others fired futile shots, each missing Sheridan. His face was by now almost completely obfuscated in the flame spewing from the muzzle of the Thompson. In five seconds it was over.

Matt picked up the silenced pistol, then walked to the limousine. He kicked each body to ensure its mortality. Even Morelli, under his bodyguard, was riddled with bullets. Matt released the drum magazine and saw there were still a few rounds left.

Lights were coming on in the neighborhood, and sirens were wailing in the distance as he walked toward the rented hummer. He got in and drove the speed limit just a few blocks to a convenience store as police cruisers and ambulances raced past him. There was a pay com at the convenience store. He bought a soda in the store, breaking one of his large bills, then phoned Rosecroft.

"Yeah," said Rosecroft, answering groggily.

"Tell 'em down at the station that I closed the Morelli stakeout. And then tell them our government has betrayed us."

Karen Russell was waiting at the door when Dan Reilly rapped softly at Parker Hudson's apartment. She opened it immediately, and Reilly stepped in. An unlit cigarette dangled from his mouth, and he smelled of whiskey.

"Nice outfit," he muttered to Karen, who stood wrapped in a silk robe and nothing else.

"Shh. What the hell is going on? What are you doing here?"

Reilly pushed past her and went in to the living room, where he slumped into the sofa. The fluorescent bulb in the kitchen threw a bit of light into the hallway and living room. "It's all over. If we're lucky, we go to ground for a few years. If we're lucky," he said, slightly slurring his words.

Karen sat beside him "Shhh! What are you talking about?"

"Sheridan snapped. He went up to Baltimore. He saw the warehouse. Looks like he followed Morelli. He shot the fuckin' place up. Ten guys dead, at least, what they say."

Karen slumped in place, her head in her hands. "Shit. Where did you get this?"

"That little black twerp that works with Sheridan; he's Special Services. He's one of ours. Sheridan called him like, maybe an hour ago."

"Holy shit," Karen muttered. "We've got to terminate him now."

"What do you mean, now? I been trying to whack the bastard for three weeks."

"Why didn't you tell me?" shouted Karen.

"I told you. You just weren't listening."

"Do you think they turned him?"

"Who knows. All I know now is that he's got a fucking nuclear bomb in his head, and he's ticking."

Karen buried her head in her hands.

"I've got a dozen assets on him right now, looking for him. Five more coming in from the West Coast tomorrow."

Reilly now buried his face in his hands, then he and Karen looked up almost simultaneously. They had not heard Parker Hudson walk down the hall in his bare feet. He stood holding a Standard 9 at his side.

"Someone want to tell me what's going on here?" he announced.

"Oh, shit, Parker!" Karen exclaimed with a start. Reilly simply looked him up and down.

"He doesn't look all that impressive," he muttered from the side of his mouth.

"Look, Parker, what this is—"

"What happened to Sheridan? Who is this guy?" shouted Hudson.

Karen stood and walked toward Parker, stopping just between him and Reilly.

"Parker, you've got to listen—"

"No!" he shouted. "You listen. I want an answer. Why is Sheridan being 'terminated'?"

Reilly dove to the living room floor from the couch, rolling. Parker raised his pistol for a shot, but Karen was in the way. Hudson pushed her aside with his left hand, tracking and firing with his right. Reilly rolled past where Hudson had aimed with surprising agility. He came to a kneeling position and fired the pistol now in his hands, also a Standard 9. Parker fired his second shot simultaneously. Karen bolted for the kitchen.

Reilly's shot hit Hudson in the right thigh as Hudson's shot hit Reilly high on the left shoulder. Both men fired again simultaneously, Hudson buckling. Reilly's shot hit Hudson in the upper left arm, while Hudson's shot struck Reilly in the stomach. Both men fell to the floor now, both to their own right, firing as they went. Reilly's third shot hit Hudson in the right chest, and exploded through the middle of his back. Hudson's final shot hit Reilly in the Adam's apple. Reilly gurgled for only a moment before dying.

Hudson lay on his side on the floor. He wanted to press his hand against the hole in his chest, but he couldn't move his arms. *I know Mom figured out I was smoking after school. And it was an accident that I killed Daddy's tropical fish.*

He laid his head against the soft carpet. *Mommy would make him better.* He called for her.

"Karen?" he gasped.

Russell stood over him now, staring at him down the barrel of a stubby pistol.

"Sorry, Parker," she said, and fired a single round into his brain.

16

Matt drove the speed limit all the way west on Route 7, then followed Route 15 north at Leesburg. It had started to drizzle, but he had not yet turned on the wipers for fear that their steady rhythm would put him to sleep.

He was concentrating closely, trying to match the hum of his engine to that of the van that had previously carried him there. He matched the sound of the engine, then tried to match the sounds of pavement changing, bridges, stoplights.

When he finally reached Lucketts, he slowed as the van had slowed. He remembered turning right, traveling on pavement for a short distance, maybe half a mile, then turning onto a gravel road. It took Matt three right turns from Route 15, but he finally found the sound he remembered. He turned on the gravel road at the sign that read PRIVATE—NO TRESPASSING.

Next was about a mile of slow travel over hilly ground. This he matched as well. Finally, cresting a small hill, in the distance he could see a partially lit house, very large, standing on a hill overlooking the ground he remembered as the horse pasture. He turned on his hazard lights and proceeded slowly.

Soon enough, from an unmarked farm road, a four-wheel-drive utility vehicle appeared to his right. Then another appeared behind him. Finally, a truck pulled across the dirt road in front of him. He immediately rolled down his window and thrust out his hands.

Matt could see a man emerge from the vehicle behind, and another from a vehicle to his right. They were both armed with M16A2s, and they were definitely aiming at him.

"Open the door from the outside," the figure behind him commanded in what Matt realized was a female voice. Matt did as he was instructed.

"Step out slowly and turn your back to me. Hands over your head."

Matt followed instructions again, his right arm sagging lower than his left.

"Now walk backward to me. Slowly."

Matt walked backward. This woman must have been a cop, he thought to himself.

Just past the rear bumper of his car, the woman instructed, "On your knees, hands on top of your head."

Once again Matt complied, and in an instant four people were on him. The person from behind stepped across the soles of his feet.

"You're on private property, asshole," she barked.

"My name is Matt Sheridan. I'm here to see Owen Thomas."

As he uttered the word "Owen," he heard four rifle bolts being worked. *Uh-oh,* he thought.

"He knows me. He asked me to join the organization. He'll vouch for me."

One of the figures from the right peeled off and jogged back to his vehicle. Matt could hear a radio call being made, a response, then silence. After about a minute, more static came across the radio.

"Take him up in your jeep," said the figure returning to the scene.

At that point, the figure in front of Matt safed and slung his rifle. He then drew a pistol and held it on Matt.

"Back to the jeep," he grunted.

Matt stood, hands still on his head. He saw the face of the woman now, a tall African dressed in black fatigues. She motioned him to her jeep with the rifle barrel. The three walked back to the vehicle. She got into the driver's side. The man with the pistol opened the rear door and told Matt to slide across. When Matt was seated, he got in to the seat next to him.

All the vehicles roared to life, and they pitched and heaved across the rutted ground, driving offroad directly to the house. They rode in silence.

The three exited the jeep in the reverse of how they entered and walked to the door of the house. The door was opened by the man Matt remembered as Jimmy White Horse, one hand behind his back. The Native American frowned when he saw Matt.

"Yeah, it's him. Leave him with me."

"Hey, I've got some, uh, valuables in the car. Couple of weapons."

White Horse looked at the woman. "Kim, could you bring them up here, please. Just move the car off the road for now."

"Got it," the woman said, and she and the faceless man trotted back to the jeep.

Matt stepped in and White Horse closed the door. As he did, he lowered the hammer of the pistol he held. He turned his back to Matt and looked to the staircase landing, where Owen Thomas, still in shirtsleeves, stood. White Horse shook his head slowly.

"You could have been killed, you idiot," White Horse said, turning back to Matt.

"I doubt it," said Matt, opening his overcoat and revealing the silenced 9mm still holstered under his left arm. "They forgot to frisk me before they put me in the car."

White Horse lowered his head, then slammed the palm of his right hand into the wall. On the stairs, Thomas chuckled.

"You think this is funny?" shouted White Horse.

"No, I think you amuse me. Mr. Sheridan, please, step upstairs."

Matt walked silently past White Horse and climbed the steps to Thomas.

"Sorry I didn't contact you, but—"

"We've been hearing and reading all sorts of things on the coms and onlines tonight. Please, let's go into my office."

As they entered the office at the end of the second floor hallway, a middle-aged African, seated in front of Thomas's desk, stood. The man was in his late forties, Matt guessed. While he was some four inches shorter than Matt, he had broad shoulders, a powerful chest, and huge biceps that Matt envied instantly.

"Matt, this is Wallace Stoker. Wallace, Matthew X. Sheridan."

"Pleased, Matthew," said Wallace in a deep bass voice.

Matt nodded and smiled politely.

"In fact, this is somewhat fortuitous. I'm glad you have a chance to meet Wallace. He's my deputy within the national command structure. He joined us by way of Compton, the Naval Academy, and Stanford University. Mr. Stoker is the western coast commander of our organization, and we've been trying to browbeat James into going back west to take over operations out there. Mr. Stoker's operations commander is unfortunately deceased of late. So we've been up all night, and here you are."

"Yes, I'm sorry I didn't contact you, but, under the circumstances . . ." Matt stammered.

"We've been listening in on the emergency communications net out in the barn tonight. Among others. I heard about Morelli and company getting whacked. One man, they say."

"I guess . . ."

"He's been moving more jazz for the government on the East Coast than anyone else. They will sorely miss him."

Matt blinked his eyes slowly. "May I sit down?"

Thomas nodded, and Matt slid into one of the guest chairs.

"You know about Morelli, and the jazz shipments? And the government being . . ."

Thomas chuckled. "We've known about that for a long time."

"But . . . why doesn't everybody . . . how come . . ."

Thomas pointed to the other chair and nodded at Stoker. He then sat behind his desk. He dug into the top drawer and removed a new bottle of Glenlivet.

"You forget, Matthew, that the electronic and online media are now represented in the federal government by the National Media Council. They always claimed to be the fourth estate, didn't they?" asked Thomas.

Socratic method again, thought Matt. He shrugged.

"They were the fourth estate because they had to keep the government honest. But when good President Kersey acknowledged the institution of the media, and created the National Media Council, they finally had their rightful place at the head of the country."

"And?"

"And they became partners in government, along with the executive, legislative, and judicial branches. And, of course, then with the National Industrial Council."

"So why bring down the government they're now part of?" Matt said out loud. Thomas touched his nose with his index finger, then pointed at Sheridan.

"And besides, all their individual causes, socially sufficient behavior, social security, small *s* mind you, peace in our time?"

"All platform positions of the New Liberty party," said Matt, nodding.

Owen produced three glasses and poured three equal portions. He handed a glass each to Sheridan and Stoker, keeping one for himself. Matt sipped the Scotch, then set it on the floor next to his chair.

"But why would the federal government peddle jazz? The dangers . . ."

"To necessitate two things: first, the creation of the emergency zones, and therefore second, the requirement for a huge national police force," interjected Stoker. Thomas nodded his concurrence.

"Okay, I'm lost again," said Matt, shaking his head.

"Why do we have emergency zones?" quizzed Thomas.

"Because the crush of jazz-related arrests overburdened a system that had not caught up . . ." Matt spewed department policy.

Thomas leaned across the desk and pointed at him. "Every person you ever arrested in an emergency zone, where did they end up?"

"Back in the E.Z. of course."

"So why are all the prisons full?"

Matt stared blankly.

"You heard about the raid at Manassas, didn't you?"

Matt nodded.

"We took forty people out of Manassas. Can you guess their crimes?"

"They said they were violent criminals."

"That's right. *They* said. We released two freelance journalists, three Catholic priests, a lesbian, a Baptist preacher, two stand-up comics, a radio personality, and on and on. Eighteen of the forty were there for social sufficiency violations. There was one woman in there who had been arrested for distributing antiabortion literature way back in the nineties!"

Matt sat quietly, unable to respond.

"And the other twenty-two? Substance addicts. Heroin, cocaine, methamphetamine—all of the highly addictive drugs they legalized.

All these addicts nearly crushed the universal health care system, so the government had no choice but to ship them off to the penitentiaries. The legalization of narcotics failed so dismally that our New Liberty stewards had no choice but to hide these people. And they created the jazz epidemic to cover their tracks."

Matt dropped his head into his hands, propping his elbows on his knees.

"So we need the huge police force to control the E.Z.s."

"That's part of it," said Thomas, rising from his chair. He reached into another drawer and pulled out a fistful of cigar tubes. He extended his hand to Stoker, who waved him off. He offered cigars next to Matt, who hesitated, then took one of the tubes. He tapped it against his left hand with his right. Owen lit his own cigar.

"You need the huge police force, fighting the legitimate danger of jazz and the crime it causes, to hide the political enforcers they've spread across the country. What do you think the cops in Special Services do? The prison guards from Special Services? Sufficiency detectives? Not to mention the operatives of Internal Intelligence."

Matt could feel his face flushing, and he hoped it would not betray him.

"So you don't believe in the Social Sufficiency Act?" Matt asked.

"Do I believe in respect for individuals? Yes. Do I believe in protecting minority rights? Yes. Do I believe in civil and human rights? Yes. But what I don't believe is that the founding fathers could have ever dreamed of a time when a self-appointed political and cultural elite would take it upon themselves to determine and establish what speech or behavior was correct, and what was not. Or that the free media, which the founding fathers cherished, would go hand in hand with this group and fan the flames of hatred and intolerance."

"But the American people voted these politicians, this president, into office. Isn't this what they've asked for?"

Stoker jumped into the conversation. "Not quite. At first, New Liberty had something for everybody, with guaranteed health, employment, education, and social sufficiency. And we bought it. But they used these institutions to quell dissent. I'm an old liberal Democrat myself. I cheered back in the nineties when the Supreme Court decided that racketeering laws could be used to prosecute abortion protesters, and go after the old Ku Klux Klan, and the skinheads, and so forth, if you even remember those things. But nobody was paying very close attention when the same laws were upheld against the homosexual rights activists. Or the environmentalists. Or the war protesters. They were all troublemakers as far as New Liberty was concerned."

Thomas sat on the edge of his desk in front of Matt. "You see, Mr. Sheridan, in reality, the New Liberty party never actually took over this country. We gave it away ourselves, little by little, until we realized too late that everything America stood for was gone."

Matt clasped his hands to keep them from shaking. His voice trembled as he spoke. "But the people voted—"

"Some people voted. In the early elections, New Liberty won through massive vote fraud. They created and registered literally millions of new voters in key districts and key states. They captured just enough electoral votes to squeeze by. Now, the last three . . ."

"They were landslide victories . . ."

"Have you seen the actual popular votes? Or the actual electoral college ballots? Or the returns from any of the congressional races?" asked Wallace.

Matt shrugged.

"They got lazy in the last two elections, Matt. It was too much trouble to organize and control their phantom voters. So they just lied about the elections. Henry Kersey and New Liberty didn't win," said Owen.

"Then . . ."

"Why do you think the Confederation of American Patriots was formed?" asked Stoker.

"When in the course of human events . . ." started Thomas.

"You know, Abraham Lincoln said, 'At what point shall we expect the approach of danger? By what means shall we fortify against it? Shall we expect some transatlantic military giant to step the ocean and crush us at a blow? All the armies of Europe, Asia, and Africa combined, with all the treasure on earth, could not by force take a drink from the Ohio, or make a track on the Blue Ridge, in a trial of a thousand years. If destruction be our lot, we must ourselves be its author and finisher. As a nation of freemen, we must live for all time, or die by suicide,'" recited Stoker.

Hands shaking, Matt put the cigar tube on Thomas's desk, reached into his coat, and withdrew the tube he'd been given just days before. He fished out the matches, opened the tube, then lit the cigar. He puffed it until the end glowed orange. He stowed the matches and retrieved his Scotch from the floor. Matt sipped it, then exhaled. "So . . . we're committing suicide."

"No, Mr. Sheridan," said Thomas, puffing on his cigar. "We are fighting to live as free men."

17

Saturday, January 27, 2022, began the same as all the other days in the past two months for Matt Sheridan. The gravel crunched beneath his feet as he ran in the sharp, cold morning. He was breathing smoothly, in through his nose and out through his mouth, and he had fallen into a comfortable four-steps-inhale, four-steps-exhale rhythm. He was breathing deeply with no pain, and it seemed that the synthetic muscle restoration in his arm had healed completely. The wound in his side had healed as well, leaving behind only an entrance wound in his stomach, and an exit scar in his back.

The two months had been demanding, some days bordering on brutal. He and his team trained daily, endlessly, tirelessly. But he had accepted his assignment and was determined to finish it. He and White Horse still had trouble communicating, but both realized that they were not put together to be friends.

Matt rounded a bend in the road and could see the farmhouse at the top of the hill, two hundred yards ahead. He then saw Judy flagging him from the rear deck.

"Sheridan! They've got a line on the scrambler!"

Matt's eyes lit up, and he began a sprint that burned his lungs and his legs. He was back up to five miles a day, but the last half mile was still tough.

A little less than thirty seconds later, Matt slowed behind the farmhouse, near the main entrance to the barn. *Not bad for uphill,* he thought. He was breathing heavily, and he held his arms over his head to make room in his chest for his lungs to expand. Judy trotted up to him from the house.

"You boys need to stop smoking those nasty cigars," she lectured, leading him toward the barn.

Inside the barn, the activity was furious. Keyboards were popping, data lines ringing, and hardcopy printers spitting out endless reams of paper. Judy took him to a large, nonpartitioned area where four technicians sat around a common table. They called the area the corral, since, being the most junior of the technicians, they did not yet rate individual partitions, and were "herded" into this area. Janey Hazera, technical coordinator of the national headquarters, flitted from person to person, glancing over shoulders.

Judy waved to Janey as she led Matt to the workspace of a young Latin woman. "Matt, have you met Anita?"

Matt extended his hand, and the woman shook it. "I've seen Anita around quite a bit."

"Nice to meet you, Matt," said Anita.

"So you've got a line into the Wilkes-Barre organization?" asked Judy.

"Just got it. I've had a federal techie following my signature all night. I just dumped him. Their algorithms are getting better, but they're still unimaginative," said Anita. Judy and Matt nodded.

Anita stood from her chair and touched her monitor. "All yours, Matt. You've got about . . . five minutes left before I'll have to disconnect."

"Thanks," said Matt. He took her seat and saw Courtney's face on the monitor.

"Hey, gorgeous," he said, smiling.

"Hi, sweetie," she answered, also smiling.

"I have only a minute on the line. How was Winter Holiday?" Matt asked.

"It was nice. Your father is teaching me how to cook. He and I cooked Holiday dinner."

Matt laughed. "I believe it. Mom?"

"Uh, she's fine. She's still a bit . . . overwhelmed by everything."

"Me too. Are you staying busy?"

"Well, I'm spending a lot of time here at headquarters. I mean, local headquarters. I'm doing mostly busywork, but I guess it has to get done."

"Every bit helps."

"I miss you, Matt."

"I miss you, Court."

They were silent for a moment, looking at digital images of each other, two hundred and fifty miles apart. Matt noticed that the barn had grown quiet as well.

"I, uh, I think I'll be headed north in a few weeks. Hopefully we can see each other."

"I hope so too," said Courtney.

Matt bit his lower lip, then blurted out, "When I see you, I want you to marry me."

Courtney jerked her head backward and blinked her eyes in mock surprise. "Wow. Was that a proposal or an order?"

Matt's face was burning as it flushed. "Well, both."

Courtney folded her arms across her chest.

"And you've known me only a few months?"

"Gotta go with your instincts sometimes."

Courtney's smile drooped. "You are in a position to make me a young widow."

Matt held his breath. *I know what you mean,* he thought.

"So you'll find some rich old guy and kill him with the honeymoon. Will you marry me, Courtney?"

She sighed. "Yes, Matt. I will."

A loud cheer went up in the barn. Matt spun in his chair, his face bright red.

"Hey! Don't you people have a government to overthrow or something?"

The smiles and snickers continued as he turned back to the monitor. Courtney had turned red as well.

"You are red as a beet," she said, giggling.

"Yeah, well, I guess everyone got a big kick out of that. I gotta disconnect now."

"I love you, Matt. Be careful, please."

"I love you. I'll be lucky instead."

Matt Sheridan took communion for the first time in fifteen years. Rick West, deputy of the northern Virginia cell, *Father* Rick West, celebrated mass and gave communion to the CAP troops as the sun fell that Sunday afternoon. West came out to headquarters the night before, as the two squads operating from the headquarters base assembled. Matt was a little uncomfortable that he had been chosen to lead one squad, over Dominic Passarella, but the Boston native had been very understanding. Jimmy White Horse was none too pleased, but Owen had intervened in the final decision. Matt spoke with West for nearly an hour before Sunday mass and gave him a full confession. Matt told West everything, and although the veteran CAP was clearly uncomfortable, he granted Matt complete absolution.

Matt stood with his squad now, assembled just outside the main door of the barn. The activity in the barn was the most frenzied Matt had seen in his time at headquarters. Every technician, day and night shift, was on duty, and they were stepping on each other, running from station to station.

This evening Matt would lead the squad that Passarella had commanded at Manassas, without Gary Martell. Martell had recently returned to headquarters, finally free from the large cast on his leg, but still he could walk only with difficulty. He was in the "war room," formerly one of the sitting rooms in the farmhouse, converted to a national situation room. He was assisting Wallace Stoker, who would be provisionally in charge of the organization during the operation.

Owen Thomas, Arthur, and Judy soon emerged from the lower level of the farmhouse. Owen and Arthur were dressed similarly to Matt's squad, wearing black neoprene skin suits and the ubiquitous kevlar helmet with com visor. Matt's squad wore body armor and black balaclavas as well. The squad was equipped with M16A2s, Standard 9 pistols, concussion grenades, and combat knives. Matt toted the Thompson and his old .45.

As Thomas left the house, Jimmy White Horse, and the squad he would lead, emerged from a line of trees just a hundred yards from the house. They were outfitted identically to Matt's squad. They had chosen to wait separate from the rest of the group.

The whine of turboprop engines from the horse pasture below the house signaled the group that it was time to head down. With a jerk of his head, Matt energized his men, and they strode toward the sound, neither quickly nor slowly. White Horse's squad approached from their left, and Owen, Arthur, and Judy trailed behind.

Waiting for them in the horse pasture were two large federal com-

muter VTOLs, shipped north from Texas in pieces and recently re-
assembled. These two aircraft would carry the two squads. On air
traffic radars, these two aircraft had left Dayton, Ohio, a little over
an hour before, and were making all their way points. The people
in the barn were working furiously. The aircraft were due in to National Airport in about thirty minutes.

The men gathered silently around the aircraft, and the lights had
not yet been turned on. Judy held Owen's hand, and as she neared
the planes, the wash from the turboprops blew her hair across her
face. She reached over and squeezed Thomas's left hand. He looked
at her and nodded. She stroked his cheek lightly with her fingertips,
then turned back to the house.

"You got the chips?" Owen asked Arthur, who trembled only
slightly.

Arthur nodded.

"All right, men," Owen shouted over the engine noise. "I don't
have a speech for you. You're all professionals, and that's enough.
You all know your assignments. And you all know that five thousand
of your brothers and sisters will also be in action tonight. Make no
mistake though, we are the fulcrum. If we fail, 'big show' fails."

Owen slid between Enzo Lindo and Andre Washington, entering
the nearest aircraft and sitting in the empty copilot seat. Arthur followed him and sat facing backward in the attendant's seat on the
cockpit bulkhead. The passenger cabin of the craft would normally
seat twenty, but half the seats had been removed to accommodate
the heavily armed troops.

Jimmy White Horse took his squad to the other VTOL, which they
boarded. Matt's squad filed aboard the near plane. When all were
seated, the doors were sealed and the throttles were opened. First
one, then the other aircraft lifted, almost staggering, into the night.
Operation "big show" was under way.

"Buckeye One to National Tower, over," spoke Fred Moore, pilot
of the lead VTOL.

"National Tower to Buckeye One. Go ahead, over."

"National, request approach instructions, over."

"Buckeye One, we've got a bit of weather tonight. We're landing north to south tonight. You're cleared on 18L, over."

"Copy National, over."

Moore knew that Sue Crocker was less than one hundred yards behind him in the second VTOL. With the gusting wind and heavy rain that had just blown up, their next maneuver would be extremely dangerous. He looked over at Owen Thomas, who nodded. Moore touched the encryption module on the radio and punched in Crocker's frequency. "CAP 2, we're going down in five, do you copy?"

"Copy. Let's do it."

"Four, three, two, one . . ."

Moore dropped the nose of the craft and began a dive from his starting altitude of one thousand feet. Crocker followed directly behind him.

"Mayday, National, Mayday! Lightning strike, we're going down!" Moore shouted, then killed the radio.

The VTOL was in a vertical dive for the Potomac River, just below the Key Bridge, which connected Rosslyn, Virginia, with New Columbia. At a hundred feet, he rotated the engines and leveled out the plane. Behind him, Crocker followed suit.

In the air traffic control tower at National Airport, Buckeye One went off the radar screen.

In minutes dozens of emergency and police vehicles were headed for the Potomac River.

The New Columbia broadcast center and headquarters for the Cable News Agency were housed in a sparkling new steel and glass building at L and 20th streets. In the news center, Bryan Carruthers watched the Ravens take a four-point lead over the New Columbia Presidents with four minutes left in the first half of Super Bowl LVI. Carruthers would be doing a special half-time news update for the network, which was carrying the Super Bowl. He would give his special report to over two hundred fifty million Americans, and it would be viewed in subtitles by another five hundred million around the world. Not to mention armed forces radio and television.

"Damn planes are flying awfully low tonight," he said to no one, looking up at the ceiling in the direction of the sound.

Matt closed his eyes and gripped the barrel of the Thompson tightly as the commuter dropped to the roof of the building. With the radio tower in the northwest corner and the satellite uplink equipment in the northeast corner of the roof, the landing was extremely tight. As they touched down, the cabin door opened, and Matt led his squad out of the aircraft and into the driving rain. There was little time to waste as Sue Crocker was hovering nearby, awaiting her turn to land. Matt and the ten effectives raced for the roof access door. Arthur helped Owen hobble out of the plane onto the roof.

The squad ran to the access door, which was locked. Wasting no time, Gizmo slung his M16A2 and slapped a small ball of plastic explosive onto the door handle. He inserted a pencil timer, set for five seconds. The squad drew back as the charge exploded, the door swinging open.

By the time Matt's squad had entered the access stairwell, Fred Moore had vacated the roof and Crocker had landed. Jimmy White Horse's squad spilled onto the roof.

Matt took his squad down the steps to the sixth floor of the building. The door to the floor opened with some encouragement, and they found themselves in a narrow corridor that ran due north to due south. Just a few feet to the south, the narrow corridor crossed a wider corridor running west to east. He took half the men with him and entered the wider corridor to the east, the other half following Dominic Passarella to the west. At the far west end of the corridor was a stairwell, and to the far east, two elevators. He trained the Thompson on the elevator doors as the rest of his half-squad checked the numerous doors on the floor, all leading to vacant sales offices. Passarella's men checked the offices to the west and secured the stairwell.

Right on cue, Jimmy White Horse and his ten men appeared in the roof access stairwell and exploded onto the floor. Without hesitation, they turned to the west at the wide corridor and headed for the stairs. They were headed for the lobby to secure the building.

When the last man in White Horse's squad had entered the steps, Arthur and Owen then emerged from the roof stairwell.

They, too, turned to the west and headed for the stairs. Passarella's half-squad took the lead, descending in front of Arthur and Owen. When those two had entered the stairs, Matt and his men backed down the hallway onto the steps.

The echoes of the footsteps from White Horse's squad were still pounding far down the stairwell. Dominic emerged first on the fifth floor, and thoroughly surprised the overweight European security guard standing with his back to the stairs, pistol drawn. A quick butt stroke from Passarella's A2 put the man none too gently on the floor. Just ten yards ahead and on the left was the door to the main control room. Matt took the remainder of the squad and emerged on the fourth floor, where they strolled unopposed to a door marked BROADCAST FLOOR.

Bryan Carruthers stood with a start when he heard the muffled explosion. The workers in the broadcast center stopped their various preparations, despite being five minutes from airtime, and stared with puzzled expressions at the ceiling. The explosion was followed by what seemed like an endless parade of feet down the back stairs. He looked up to the director in the control room on the fifth floor above, who simply shrugged her shoulders. Bryan moved around the anchor desk and started for the door to the hall, when he heard a door being kicked upon, a dull crack, a groan, a thud, then silence.

Carruthers stained the front of his imported Italian trousers when Matt Sheridan kicked the door in off its hinges.

"Nobody move!" Matt shouted as his men spilled into the broadcast floor. Cameramen, technicians, and assistants all froze, raising their hands into the air. Simultaneously, Passarella led his half-squad, plus Arthur and Gizmo, into the control room overlooking the floor. Owen Thomas limped quietly toward the anchor desk.

"All right, camerapeople, you stay put. Everybody else I want along the back wall. Hands on your head!" Matt shouted. The trembling staff did as they were told, and Carruthers raised his hands, headed for the back wall as well. His body was shuddering, and sweat was pouring from his face. Matt poked the barrel of the Thompson into his chest.

"Not you, Carruthers. You're going back to the anchor desk."

Carruthers, wide-eyed, nodded his agreement. He turned and walked slowly to the desk.

On the monitors, the play-by-play announcer could be heard saying ". . . we are going to our New Columbia headquarters for a special update on the news from Emmy-winner Bryan Carruthers . . ."

As he did, Owen was seated at the main anchor chair, Carruthers sitting down next to him. Owen looked up to the control booth and received thumbs-up signals from Gizmo and Arthur, seated in the director's chairs.

Matt sent Andy Skiba to cover the employees along the wall. He sent Enzo Lindo and Andre Washington to guard the elevators. He sent Pete Stevens to guard the stairwell. Matt himself stood at an angle to cover both the cameramen and the anchor desk.

Owen was adjusting the strap on his eye patch, when Arthur's voice emanated from the booth intercom, "Four, three, two . . ."

"Good evening, ladies and gentlemen. My name is Owen Thomas, and I represent the Confederation of American Patriots. There's been a slight change in programming for the half-time news update, and I will be speaking in place of Mr. Carruthers. I promise I won't run over, though, and you'll certainly see if the Presidents can make up those four points from Baltimore in the second half.

"Also a quick word if you weren't watching the Super Bowl and I've just appeared on your monitor. CAP operatives across the country, in key areas, have taken over local satellite data switching stations and old cable network uplinks, and are temporarily feeding this broadcast to every frequency. They, too, will relinquish their positions shortly, and you'll be returned to your regular programming.

"Now then, many of you, perhaps, already know me. Despite what you've heard from the government and the likes of Mr. Carruthers here, I am not dead. An attempt was made on my life during my campaign for the New Liberty party presidential nomination. I was not killed, but, rather, imprisoned, interrogated, and tortured. I escaped imprisonment with the assistance of the Confederation of American Patriots.

"We have been trying to put out the word of our organization for years now, but members of the National Media Council, and their various affiliates, have quashed us time and again. Recently we have attempted, in ways similar to tonight's afforts, to command airtime by force, but have been unsuccessful. Tonight, however, I am here to tell you our story.

"We CAPs are not terrorists, as you have been told. While we have attacked numerous federal government installations and targets, we have never attacked innocent civilians. Also, contrary to what's been reported to you, we have never killed an innocent peace officer. Regrettably, we have wounded many, some seriously, and for this we are eternally sorry. We are also prepared to make reparations to those we have injured. But for self-preservation, it has been necessary.

"Now, while I don't have time this evening to refute every single case, I will, instead, present to you our general position on the many lies and deceptions undertaken and enforced by the New Liberty government. I would like to begin with the energy supply of our country. When America converted to a nearly exclusive electric society, we were told that the oil fields abroad were running dry, and to protect ourselves we would have to convert to electricity. At the same time, our nuclear industry was expanded dramatically, in a program that first necessitated the seventy-five-percent flat tax. I would like to show you a recording of a statement made recently on Visireal equipment. As you know, with CNA being the leader in news coverage around the world, they are one of the few networks, and this headquarters building one of the few facilities, with the proper equipment to broadcast Visireal data."

The image of Roy Horace appeared as Arthur accessed the Visireal chip. Horace was seated in a chair in a nondescript room. His interviewer is not seen.

VOICE: Your name, please?

HORACE: My name is Roy Horace.

VOICE: What is your latest residence?

HORACE: For the past two years, I had been incarcerated at the Chase Federal Maximum Security Penitentiary at Dallas, Pennsylvania.

VOICE: And what was your offense?

HORACE: I guess I just knew too much.

Voice: About what?

Horace: About the fact that the government has lied to the American people about our nuclear energy industry.

Voice: How so?

Horace: Back in 2004, I created the first highly productive cold nuclear fusion cell. I discovered that the use of lunium electrodes provided the catalyst for highly reactive nuclear fusion in deuterium molecules. The government initially put me in charge of the transition from fossil fuels to nuclear energy for power, but, within the past two years, they removed me.

Voice: Why?

Horace: Because I threatened to reveal the secret that the nuclear energy was being produced through cold fusion rather than nuclear fission.

Voice: And can you explain the difference that makes?

Horace: The difference is that we were fueling the country with seawater, basically. After the plants were built, it was costing almost nothing to power the country. And yet the government still imposed the seventy-five-percent flat tax rate on individual income.

Voice: What can you say, then, is the greatest impact of the cold fusion reactors?

Horace: The greatest impact is that, as part of the agreement to trade compliance with the Universal Employment Act for the repeal of the Sherman and Clayton Antitrust Acts, the government agreed to provide energy to the various industry coalitions at the actual cost, which is virtually nothing. The individual home owner and power consumer has been paying rates that would reflect fission-generated electricity. In return for free energy, the National Industrial Council was formed, and the New Liberty government simply kept the huge windfall from the enormous taxes they had levied.

Voice: And how did you come by this information?

Horace: I was advising President Kersey at the time.

Voice: And this plundering of the American taxpayer, what do you estimate its cost over the years?

Horace: (shrugging his shoulders) Conservatively, tens of trillions of dollars.

Voice: Thank you, Mr. Horace.

* * *

Henry Kersey screamed in the president's box at the Super Bowl in the Louisiana Superdome. "Get me out of here! Now! And get Special Services on the line. I want them shut down now!"

Owen Thomas continued. "Ladies and gentlemen, that is only the first piece of information we wish to share with you. Other information that has been withheld from you is the fact the New Liberty government is selling advanced weaponry to the People's Republic of China, the country with which we were at war just seven years ago, to fight our current ally, Russia. In return, China has been shipping to America massive amounts of the narcotic *xin ji*, known on the streets as jazz. This is the drug that is responsible for tens of thousands of drug-related deaths every year, in addition to the deaths of hundreds of police officers. The New Liberty government is using jazz to inflame the emergency zones, and to use that as an excuse for the release of violent criminals into these so-called E.Z.s And why is this? Because our prisons are bursting at the seams with political prisoners and substance abusers, legacies of the failures of this administration's social policies."

Next on the monitor appeared the recording of the prisoners during their rescue from Manassas. Priests, journalists, politicians, others, one after another, gave their names and their crimes: expressing themselves contrary to the dictates of the Social Sufficiency Amendment and the New Liberty party.

Air Force Captain Fletcher Kerr managed to pry his eyes away from the incredible information unfolding on CNA to watch the unmarked F-25 Short Takeoff and Vertical Landing Strike Fighters (SSFs) hopping off the runway at Andrews Air Force Base. The squat, brutish, and dark aircraft were laden with ordnance. The big joke on the base was that the aircraft belonged to a private contractor, but it was universally, unofficially well known that they belonged to Internal Intelligence. This was a most unusual time for these aircraft to be leaving base.

Kerr stood, half watching the SSFs and half listening to the monitor. He walked over to the ready-room door that led to the shelter where his F-22 remained on fifteen-minute alert was parked. Strong winds were blowing a fine mist into the shelter from the rain beating on the ramp macadam. Kerr trotted to the plane, folded out the ingress ladder, and climbed to the cockpit. He pressed the canopy release, and the windscreen slid forward into the nose housing. He hopped into the cockpit, and with a flick of a toggle switch, the aircraft's main mission computer began to power up and perform its built-in test routines. He pressed the command button for the radio and set it into a frequency hopping mode until he connected with the channel on which the SSFs were operating. The secure communications algorithms were identical in the F-22 and the F-25, and Fletcher guessed that since the aircraft were apparently rolled out in haste, the pilots would not have had time to coordinate alternate or wartime communication channels.

"Digger, this is control, do you copy?"

"Copy control, over."

"Raven, do you copy?"

"Copy control, over."

"Digger, the man says all bogeys over New Columbia go down. Air to ground target is at L and 20th streets."

"Murray!" Fletcher shouted for his crew chief.

"There is much more. So much more. But I can hear gunfire and explosions on the first floor of this building now, so I know that Special Services and Internal Intelligence troops are attempting to storm this building. But members of the CAP, as of tonight, will no longer keep their identities secret. We will be talking with as many Americans who will listen, sharing our evidence, hard evidence, of the deadly deceit that this government has perpetrated on all of us. Now, you may be saying to yourself, well, this government was legally elected. Let me then show you this data download, also captured on a Visireal chip."

A data screen appeared, and it scrolled downward slowly.

"These are the actual popular votes and electoral college votes in the presidential elections of 2012 and 2016. As you can see with very basic math, the independent candidates in those elections, Kurt Bradlee and Mitchell Tartan, respectively, garnered more electoral college and popular votes than Kersey. But the reporting of the vote by election officials was fictitious. And the reporting by the electronic and online media was also fabricated. And, of course, why not? This is the government of their choosing. And let me stress that if you are asking yourself how these elected officials and media were able to become so incorrigibly corrupt, one need look no further than the local, state, or federal prison, where all the honest politicians and journalists have ended up.

"Therefore, in conclusion, ladies and gentlemen, as of tonight, we members of the Confederation of American Patriots are declaring the past two presidential elections null and void, and we find the officials of New Liberty party to be committing treason against the government. The government of the *United* States of America. We are declaring the country to be in rebellion.

"It is extremely important that we appeal to the members of the military command structure abroad, and those in the strategic weapons commands in the United States, to keep their posts, not abandon their duty, and not to intervene in this struggle. For those police officers who are not members of Special Services, we appeal to you to maintain your patrols of America's streets, to keep our citizens safe. We ask that you, too, not intervene. For those members of the military in the continental *United* States, you will soon be called on to fight, to oppose us. You will have to make a personal choice. While you have sworn your allegiance to your country, you certainly have not sworn your allegiance to the illegal government that has taken control of it. I ask that, if nothing else, you at least refuse to fire on CAP troops. We intend to install a provisional government so that peaceful, legitimate elections can be held among candidates from all parties, to fill those positions so nefariously obtained. We will also be releasing all political prisoners and substance addicts from the various prisons. Finally, I appeal to all American citizens, that we cannot succeed without your help. Our effort will not be easy and will not be without sacrifice. But we have allowed ourselves to be divided, pacified, and conquered. We need to come together, not as Europeans or Asians or Africans, but as Americans. Now, with the sound of gunfire drawing nearer, I must return you to your regularly scheduled programming."

Owen moved from behind the desk. Bryan Carruthers lay his head to the desk, in tears. Matt had aligned his squad in the hallway and they watched the broadcast on hall-mounted monitors. Arthur inserted a last cartridge into the control board and pressed play as the rest of Passarella's half-squad departed the control room.

On monitors across the country, and in the hallways at CNA, an old American flag, the Stars and Stripes, appeared, flapping in the breeze. As Matt looked up, his Thompson pointed at the elevator doors, "The Star-Spangled Banner" began to play.

Captain Kerr picked up the pair of SSFs on his all-weather radar as soon as he was in the air. The two stubby, composite and titanium strike fighters could do nearly Mach 2, but the newer planes would be no match for his older but more capable fighter. He armed four of his fourteen AIM-X short-range heat-seeking missiles.

Jimmy White Horse staggered through the stairwell door on the fourth floor. He was shot through both legs.

"White Horse!" shouted Sheridan. He was the last one on the floor. His squad was hustling Owen and themselves back to the roof, where the VTOLs were shortly to pick them up.

Tears were streaming from White Horse's eyes. "They're all down. Every fucking man is down."

"What happened?" Matt asked, rushing to support White Horse.

"They drove a Schwarzkopf into the lobby. They have, like, two hundred men. Had two hundred men. We took out as many as we could. We blew the elevators, and we fought 'em floor by floor. They're right below us."

"All right, let's get outta here. Everyone else is up on the roof."

"Take off, Sheridan. They've got guys right fuckin' below us. They'll be up the steps in a few seconds."

Without asking, Matt threw White Horse's arm across his back and lifted him to his shoulder. He held the Thompson out by the pistol grip and entered the stairwell.

The I.I. flight leader locked onto the first CAP VTOL at five miles. His wingman attempted to lock onto the second, but since the VTOLs were flying in close trail formation, he could not be sure the lock signal he got was actually the second craft. The VTOLs were closing on downtown from the west, flying very low, but were still easy marks for the look down/shoot down capability of the AIM-150 Over-the-Horizon radar-guided missile. At an altitude of two thousand feet, the flight leader shouted, "Fox One," and released his missile. One second later his wingman shouted "Fox One," and fired as well.

Moore and Crocker dove for the deck when they got the locked-on signals on their radar warning receivers. Unable to evade maintaining close formation, they broke left and right at the last second. They both cringed when their radar warning receivers picked up the missiles' homing signals.

Fletcher Kerr cursed when he heard the two men shout, "Fox One," and picked up the launch on his radar. From five thousand feet, he saw a bright orange fireball as a target exploded. There was another flash as the second missile detonated on the wreckage of the first aircraft. A second target then appeared where the first target had just been shot down.

"Digger, we did not acquire second target."
"Copy Raven. Second weapon selected. Acquiring second target."

Sue Crocker bit the inside of her mouth to keep from crying out as she continued to race for the CNA building, bringing her closer to the deadly SSFs. If she did not make it to the rooftop, all the troops would be lost. *If they could shoot me down at five miles, why not at two miles. If I could get down, in between the buildings . . .* she thought.

Fletcher Kerr had dropped to two thousand feet. "F-25 at radial 031, identify. Identify, F-25. What are your intentions, over?" he shouted over the emergency frequency.
Digger, the flight leader, responded. "F-22, this is a national security matter, and we are acting on executive orders. Break off."
"Negative, F-25. My IFF tells me you just shot down an unarmed federal commuter aircraft, and you've got another one locked, over."

"Fuck you, F-22!" shouted Raven, firing his second AIM-150 at the VTOL.

Captain Kerr squeezed off two AIM-Xs.

Crocker got the launch warning just as she crossed over the Potomac again. As the missile separated from the SSF, she dove to fifty feet, headed for the narrow streets and tall buildings of Foggy Bottom, New Columbia.

The first AIM-X plowed into the engine exhaust of Raven's SSF. The pilot was still dumping flares when his plane erupted into a huge fireball over the downtown office buildings, shattering windows for a two-mile radius.

Digger was also dumping flares furiously, and as the AIM-X approached, he pulled back hard on the stick, propelling himself into the half-loop of a crushing Immelman turn. The AIM-X flew past, detonating in K Street at 21st.

As Crocker flew perilously among the building on I Street, between 22nd and 21st, the missile intended for her became confused and deactivated itself, dropping inert into the parking lot of the George Washington University Hospital.

Fletcher was right behind the SSF, grunting as he absorbed seven Gs in the Immelman turn. Still upside down after the half-loop, he acquired the F-25 again and fired another of the fourteen remaining AIM-X missiles slung beneath his fuselage.

Digger had just rotated, righting the aircraft, when the AIM-X exploded in his left engine. The left engine then exploded, and flying metal and fan blades destroyed the right engine as well. As the plane headed for the old Russian embassy, just blocks from the White House, Digger ejected from the craft. The plane crashed directly into the nineteenth-century mansion, exploding.

Fletcher was wheeling around toward the remaining bogey. By now the air was full of incoming traffic, minutes away.

"What are your intentions, federal commuter?" he asked over the emergency channel.

"I am evacuating friendly troops from the CNA building roof," said Crocker in a quaking voice.

"Consider yourself escorted," said Fletcher.

The men on the roof, bracing against the rain, heard and saw the vicious explosions erupting around the city. Soon, a VTOL appeared and set down on the roof. The cabin door opened. The men broke for the plane at a run. Special Services forces on the street were now firing up at the building, and all the CAPs ran in a crouch. Four pressed themselves around Owen Thomas and led him to the plane. Incoming rounds soon were striking randomly on the roof.

Matt opened fire as he saw a helmet appear on the stairs below him. Fire burst from the Thompson's muzzle, and a man shrieked. The roar of the weapon in the stairwell was deafening. Soon, four or five weapons, American Arms 265s, opened up from the steps below.

Matt climbed the steps with difficulty, hauling Jimmy White Horse along. When he reached the fifth floor, he let the Thompson hang from his arm on its sling and plucked a concussion grenade from his web belt. The shots from below were singing through the stairs, and he felt two rounds graze his helmet. "Cover your ears, Jimmy!" he shouted as he pulled the pin of the grenade with his teeth and dropped it down the stairs. He leapt for the stairs upward.

Matt was knocked to one knee by the explosion, and he could feel a trickle of blood from his right ear. He patted White Horse's leg, and White Horse patted back. Many men now screamed from below on the stairs, and for a moment the shooting had stopped.

Matt was almost breathless as he reached the sixth floor and exited the stairwell. His legs burned with fire as he headed for the roof access. Above, outside the building, he could hear massive explosions ripping through the city.

Matt was panting when he emerged on the roof, into the gale-force wind and icy rain. The VTOL was on the roof, and it looked like the rest of the team was aboard. He guessed that the other VTOL had already departed.

He ran now, oblivious to the weight on his shoulders. As he reached the craft, he threw White Horse in unceremoniously, then jumped in himself.

The hatch closed quickly, and the aircraft shuddered as it lifted up into the night. The first Special Services troops were then emerging onto the roof, but they did not seem eager anymore to raise their guns.

Once a few feet clear of the roof, Crocker opened the throttles and roared away to the west. Thunder shook the aircraft.

Then Matt heard the crying. Only one or two, or maybe three men, weeping softly. He could see it was not White Horse, who, though seriously wounded, was biting down on his combat knife.

Matt looked up at the men who were strapped into their seats. Tears poured from Arthur's eyes, and Dominic Passarella bit his right index finger as he, too, wept.

Owen Thomas was slumped on the floor just opposite their seats. He had a single bullet wound through his heart.

Epilogue

Matt's eyelids drooped, and he shook his head in an attempt to clear it. He had been awake almost forty-eight hours now, and the lack of sleep was taking its toll. He bit the inside of his mouth to keep himself awake and the steering wheel straight. They were so close now, he had to stay awake.

He looked across at Janey Hazera, who dozed in the front passenger seat of the minivan. She had been awake almost as long as Matt, helping coordinate the headquarters evacuation. Matt glanced at his watch. By now, Special Services would have reduced the old house to toothpicks. Matt shuddered, realizing how close Special Services came to getting them before the raid.

Taking his eyes off the road for just a moment, he ventured a glance to the rear passenger compartment. Rick West was sprawled across the first bench seat, head back, a thin line of drool running from the corner of his mouth. He held an IV pouch loosely in his hand on the back of the seat. A line ran from the IV pouch to the left arm of Jimmy White Horse, who had been asleep under sedation for most of the trip. Since Janey doubled as emergency medical technician as well as organizational guru, she spent hours the day before working to bring White Horse's fever down. Their van was actually the last to leave the headquarters, as White Horse's condition had been unstable. Based on the shortwave reports, they were no more than thirty minutes ahead of the first Special Services personnel to arrive.

They were now on the Wright Memorial Bridge, on their way across Currituck Sound to North Carolina's Outer Banks. The location was selected for its relative isolation, and the fact that it would be largely deserted in February. It would give them time and space to regroup.

Across the sound, Matt turned off Route 158 for Route 12, and headed for Kitty Hawk. A beach-front house was arranged for them to spend a few days. After that they would receive word of their next permanent location. Communications, on shortwave and online, had been sporadic, because the CAP operations compromised as a result of the raid had been quickly reduced to shambles. The risk of further exposure was too great.

Matt found the house shortly and pulled into the sand-swept driveway. The house was the standard, faded cedar and pine structure on stilts, with a cheery pink trim. As Matt pulled in, an elderly woman with a kind face appeared on the front porch. She waved to Matt. He stopped the car and exited slowly. The cold sea air was a welcome blast to his system, and Matt felt revived. Nonchalantly, he reached under his overcoat to confirm his .45 was in its resting place. It was.

As he climbed the steps to the front door, the woman disappeared inside. He entered the house and said, "Hello," to the woman. She began to chit-chat with Matt, but he did not listen or remember what he said to her. He checked out each of the four bedrooms on the lower level, then walked up the stairs to the kitchen. Beyond, he could see the open living room and dining room areas were empty.

He brushed past the old woman and returned to the van. The other passengers were now awake, including White Horse. Janey and Father West collected some gear and headed in. White Horse groggily pulled himself up to a seated position. Sheridan perched his left foot on the minivan's running board.

"How do you feel today?" Matt asked.

White Horse rubbed his face, cautious of his IV line. "I've been much, much better."

He looked down at his legs, which were heavily bandaged and splinted. "Looks like they did a number on me," he said in a throaty, sleepy voice.

Matt nodded. "Janey says it looks like there's no major bone damage. You were lucky."

"Guess so," said White Horse.

Without a word, Matt stepped into the van and bent over White Horse in his seat. Cautiously, he placed his left hand under White Horse's legs, then slid his right arm under White Horse's left arm.

"I'll try to do this as carefully as possible," said Sheridan. Slowly, he lifted Jimmy.

White Horse gritted his teeth and grunted, and Matt had to take short, jerky steps to get out of the van. Once outside, White Horse relaxed.

"That wasn't too bad," said White Horse.

"I'm getting better," said Matt. He walked toward the front steps.

"Hey, Sheridan . . . thanks," said White Horse.

Sheridan shrugged. "No problem."

"No, I mean, back in New Columbia. You saved my ass," said White Horse.

"You would have done it for me," said Sheridan.

White Horse looked up at Sheridan. A look of shame passed over White Horse's face. He couldn't respond. But just then White Horse saw a flash, a fire in Sheridan's eyes that he had never noticed before. Sheridan was a believer.

"Besides," said Matt, climbing the first set of stairs. "This organization can't succeed without you. I'd venture to say that you're the most valuable asset right now."

"Please," muttered White Horse, closing his eyes. Each slight jar or shift in the distribution of weight on his legs sent shooting pains all the way up his spine.

"We've taken a lot of casualties," said White Horse.

"Yeah, but the message is out. The people are finally hearing and seeing the truth," said Sheridan.

"They've really kicked our ass though," said White Horse.

Sheridan grinned, turning sideways to enter the house. "Take 'em tomorrow," he said.

Karen Russell stared into Henry Kersey's bloodshot eyes on the monitor. Though separated from him by several miles and the telecom system, she imagined the smell of brandy on his breath. She could no longer see the other men and women assembled behind him in the White House War Room.

". . . So Sheridan was your plan? He knows about you and Reilly?" asked the President.

Karen nodded, the weight of exhaustion slumping her shoulders. She had been explaining for hours now.

Kersey rubbed his cheeks with one hand. "All right. You're going back to I. I. headquarters. Overt position. You *will* get us to their national command. Try to make some good out of this Sheridan fiasco."

"Sheridan is mine, Mr. President," Karen said grimly. "Sheridan is mine."

They had emerged from their houses slowly, one and two at a time. They tromped in the knee-deep snow wordlessly that Sunday night. The people of Dunning, New Hampshire, population 203, walked slowly, laboriously, to the town hall. Soon, almost fifty of them had gathered, and old Barney Gibbs, the watchman, had quietly left his post for the night.

Silently, they lowered the flag with two red stripes, one white stripe, and a blue star, which had flown proudly in a spotlight from the building. An old, tattered flag was passed forward, and it was raised. It had seven red stripes, six white stripes, and in its upper left hand corner, against a blue background, fifty shining stars.

Beneath it, they raised the old New Hampshire state flag, which bore the motto, Live Free or Die.